A DESTINY FULFILLED

"Kiss me, Susan," he said, his voice gone all husky in the space of a moment. "Kiss me mindless."

His mouth was a fraction of an inch from hers. She needed no further prompting.

Standing on tiptoes with her hands around his neck, she drew him down to meet her parted lips. She kissed him deeply, her tongue mating with his. She was swamped with desire, its depth and swiftness shocking her.

She had no idea how much she wanted him until that moment, when the world was reduced to his lips . . . his tongue . . . his wandering hands . . .

D1506784

Black-Eyed Susan

Deborah Camp

AVON BOOKS NEW YORK

BLACK-EYED SUSAN is an original publication of Avon Books. This work has never before appeared in book form. This work is a novel. Any similarity to actual persons or events is purely coincidental.

AVON BOOKS
A division of
The Hearst Corporation
105 Madison Avenue
New York, New York 10016

Copyright © 1990 by Deborah E. Camp
Inside cover author photograph by Robert Eilers
Published by arrangement with the author
Library of Congress Catalog Card Number: 89-91537
ISBN: 0-380-75742-7

First Avon Books Printing: May 1990

AVON TRADEMARK REG. U.S. PAT. OFF. AND IN OTHER COUNTRIES, MARCA REGISTRADA, HECHO EN U.S.A.

Printed in the U.S.A.

RA 10 9 8 7 6 5 4 3 2 1

A man don't have thoughts about women
'til he's thirty. Afore then, all he's got is feelin's.
—COWBOY SAYING

Chapter 1

"He'll let me stay . . . he'll send me packing . . . he'll let me stay . . . he'll send me packing . . . he'll let me stay." Susan Armitage plucked the last petal off the wildflower and released a long sigh. Closing her eyes, she sent up a fervent wish. "Oh, please! Let me stay, Logan. Let me stay."

Brushing the petals from her dark green skirt, Susan tossed aside the rest of the flower and sat straight and proper in the wicker rocker on the big front porch of Mrs. Ledbetter's apartment house—the "finest and cleanest in St. Louis," according to its proprietress. The proud landlady has boasted that the three-story structure had been built fifty years ago in 1847 by a brickmason who'd learned his trade in England, where he'd built privies and stables for royalty. There'd been more about the building and its previous owners, but Susan had been too preoccupied to listen. She'd excused herself and taken refuge on the quiet front porch where she could bolster her courage. Training her eyes on the path that ran in front of the big house, she attempted to calm her nerves by recalling her brother-in-law's good points.

Of course, her parents said he had none, but Susan had recognized honesty, integrity, and compassion in his mossy-green eyes. His unabashed smile was what made some folks think he was a devil-may-care cad with no redeeming characteristics, for Logan Vance had a wide, womanizing, wholly sensuous mouth that struck fear in the hearts of fathers and tantalized those of their daughters.

1

Even at the innocent age of eleven, Susan remembered she had slipped under his spell. Although it had been her oldest sister, Catherine, who had become his missus, he had, nonetheless, been the source of Susan's first brush with unrequited love.

Susan laughed to herself, remembering the private pain she'd endured when Catherine had caught Logan's eye. Oh, he had been a prize! No matter what her parents thought of him, Logan Vance had been coveted by every girl in Pemiscot County, Missouri, and it wasn't just because he was the new boy in town, the stranger drifting through on his way to St. Louis. No, it was more than that. It was that infernal grin of his and the way he used it.

Gathering up the rest of the black-eyed Susans she'd picked near the train station, Susan admired their deep gold color and black centers against her white blouse. Logan had once likened her to the flowers because her eyes were so dark brown they appeared black at times. But he hadn't been so affable three months ago when her family had traveled to St. Louis for Catherine's funeral. He'd been grieving, yes, but his dour mood had been the result of more than that.

"Papa," Susan whispered, recalling how her father and Logan rubbed each other the wrong way. "Oh, Papa. Why do you insist on seeing only bad in him?"

Her father's attitude had kept Catherine from visiting after the wedding. Only once had her sister's family ventured back to Pemiscot County for a Christmas gathering. Once had been enough. Susan winced, remembering the loud arguments, the accusations, the explosive atmosphere.

Glancing up from the flowers, Susan tensed as she recognized the swaggering gait of the man approaching on the footpath. Logan. Pleasure fluttered in the pit of her stomach, a sensation she always attributed to Logan since it never happened unless he was around. Secretly, she called it the Logan tingle. Secretly, because she'd never admit such a thing to anyone. He was Catherine's husband, after all, and . . . No. She shook her head, mentally correcting herself. Catherine's *widower*. Logan belonged to Catherine no more.

At an even six feet, he was seven inches taller than Susan, and his weight was well distributed, mostly bone and muscle. Head down and hands thrust into the side pockets of his black pants, he seemed totally absorbed in his thoughts as he neared the apartment house. The short-brimmed cap he wore was tweed with a brass button at the top. Susan smiled, having never before seen a cap like it. City clothes, she thought, and hoped to update her wardrobe while in St. Louis. Her papa had given her a little money, and if she was careful with it . . .

Logan looked up as he neared the steps, but he didn't see her. Sunlight speared his sandy-blond hair before he took the six steps two at a time into the porch's shadows. Sensing that he was going to stride right past her, Susan cleared her throat noisily. He skidded to a halt and swung around.

"H'lo, Logan." Susan took a deep breath, hardly recognizing her own voice. Had nerves made it so husky? "I bet you're surprised to see me, huh?"

Rocking back on his heels, Logan pushed his cap off his forehead and stared at her. His mouth went dry, and for a few moments he couldn't think of a blessed thing to say. After the initial confusion, he was hit by a bolt of anger, but then Susan sat forward and gave him a glimpse of her heart-shaped face and lustrous eyes, and his ire subsided.

"Well, well, well." He raked the cap off his head and grinned. "What have we here?" He noticed the bouquet she held. The petals trembled, put in motion by her nerves. "Little black-eyed Susan. You lost, or have you run away?"

"Neither. I—that is—well, you see—"

"Your father sent you," he said, saving her the trouble. He was still grinning, but he was far from amused. Leave it to Abraham Armitage to ruin a man's good mood, Logan thought. The man was a bulldog who wouldn't let go. "Your daddy just can't take no for an answer, can he?"

"He means well." Susan stood up and clutched the stems of the flowers until their juices dampened her palms. "We all mean well. We worry so about you and the children. It can't be easy with Catherine gone and you working at the newspaper, with no family to watch over little Etta and Jacob."

"Mrs. Ledbetter watches them."

"Yes, but she's not family.'

"She's a good woman. The children like her." He leaned one shoulder against the door frame and regarded her flushed face and midnight eyes. "So your family sent you here to watch over me and the children, and you obeyed dutifully. No protests. No regrets."

"I wanted to come."

"You're a fine-looking lady." He let his gaze drift down her body, sensing her uneasiness and using it to gain an advantage. Maybe if he shook her up enough she'd hightail it back to the farm. "I bet you left some suitors in your wake. You should be dancing under the moon with some lovesick gent instead of taking care of us." He stuck his cap into his back pocket and tucked his hands high up under his arms. "Especially since we don't *need* taking care of, as I've told your pappy time and time again."

Susan stared at the flowers again, flustered by the way his eyes had moved over her and how they'd darkened to a shade matching her polished cotton skirt. That tingle erupted again, and her breathing shortened. She swept off her black-ribboned straw traveling hat and fanned herself with it.

"Why are you out here? Mrs. Ledbetter would have let you inside. She most surely remembers you."

"Yes, she does, but she was busy cooking and the children are napping, so I came out here to wait for you." She took a step closer to him. The smell of boiled cabbage wafted through the screen door, and she could hear Mrs. Ledbetter's distant humming. "Are you going to let me stay or not?"

His gaze wandered again, over her high breasts, girlish

waist, and slim hips. She wasn't as filled out as Catherine had been at her age. Catherine had matured early, possessing a womanly shape by the time she was sixteen. But Susan, just shy of twenty, was still evolving. A late bloomer, he thought. He imagined she'd glow at thirty, ripen at forty, and put her contemporaries in the shade at fifty.

Blinking, he realized she wanted an answer from him. Logan chuckled and straightened from his lounging pose. He opened the screen door and gestured for her to enter.

"Let's go upstairs to my apartment and discuss this."

"Are you sending me back?"

He lifted his brows at her impatience. "Probably, but I'm willing to hear you out first."

She hitched her chin higher and preceded him into the dark hallway. Logan followed her, tickled by her haughtiness. She'd always been a spitfire, he recalled. The only daughter known to stand up to the old man from time to time. Even Catherine, as stubborn as a mule and Abraham's favorite, had caved in around him.

A staircase ran up one wall and a corridor stretched out beside it, ending in the kitchen where Susan had found Mrs. Ledbetter earlier. The landlady's husky alto sounded from that direction. The children, she'd been told, were asleep in Mrs. Ledbetter's apartment, the only one on the first floor. Logan motioned her to go on without him as he headed for the kitchen. Susan started upstairs, but lent an ear to the conversation below.

"I'm back, Mrs. Ledbetter."

"Oh, so you are! Did you find your guest?"

"Yes, ma'am."

"The children are asleep just now. I'll bring them up to you when they rouse from their naps."

"Thank you."

"She's your sister-in-law, isn't she?"

"That's right."

"It's good she's here. You could use a woman's touch. It's too much for you to handle the little ones and see to the rest of it. With what you've got planned, you'll need an extra pair of hands to—"

"Yes, well, thanks again, Mrs. Ledbetter."

"Sure, sure. You see to your guest."

Hearing his approaching footsteps, Susan ran up the stairs and hurried along the hallway to the last apartment. She stood outside the door, trying to regulate her breathing as Logan advanced and opened it for her.

The apartment was just as it had been the last time she'd seen it. She recalled the teary farewell exchanged between her parents and her nephew and niece. The last thing her father had said to Logan was "Let us take them. You can't raise them proper," to which Logan had replied, none too gently, "Get out."

"It wasn't very pleasant the last time I was here." She turned to him, trying on a friendly smile. "I hope you don't harbor ill will toward me."

He grinned at her phrasing. "Ill will? No. But I thought I'd made it perfectly clear to you and your folks that I don't need your help. As you can see . . ." He extended a hand, indicating the neat, homey living area. "Everything's fine. Just fine."

Susan laid her bruised bouquet, purse, and hat on a pie-crust table and sighed. "I don't see it that way, Logan. You're leaving the children with your landlady while you go off to work at the newspaper office."

"I can't very well take them with me."

"No, but why would you prefer leaving them with Mrs. Ledbetter instead of with me? After all, *I'm* family."

He tossed his cap into a chair and chuckled. "Do you do everything your pappy tells you to?"

"No." She gritted her teeth, irritated that he thought she was under her father's thumb. "I'm here because I think it's right. You're my family, too, and you need me."

"And what about you? What do you need?" He stepped closer, forcing her to tip back her head and meet his gaze. "You're a young woman with better things to do than play nursemaid to your sister's children. Doesn't your father see that? Frankly, I'm amazed he didn't tell you how dangerous I am, how irresponsible, how untrustworthy." He inched his face closer, and his voice dipped to a growly whisper. "Didn't he tell you I'm a spoiler of decent young women like you?"

She turned aside, shaken by his intuition. He knew her father well. As a matter of fact, she'd had to wage quite a campaign to get her father to agree to this venture.

I've taken care of children all my life, she'd told her father. *I'm full-grown, and my head isn't easily turned. I've never been one to chase boys. I'm levelheaded, Papa. You can depend on me.*

But she knew the true purpose behind her father's sending her to St. Louis, and it didn't have much to do with family helping family in a time of need. Abraham Armitage knew that Susan and Logan had always gotten along, and if any Armitage could convince Logan to release Catherine's children into their care, it would be Susan.

Glancing at Logan, she shrugged off his questions. "This is an adventure for me. How many girls my age are given the opportunity to leave the family farm for the big city of St. Louis?"

"You're what . . . nineteen?"

"Yes, I'll be twenty next month."

"Then you're no girl. You're a woman, and therefore you should be ruling your own life instead of letting your pappy do it for you."

"I am!" She delivered a stern glare that glanced off his smirk. "I've told you. I'm here of my own free will. I *wanted* to come, and I *want* to stay."

"Did you come with luggage?"

"Yes, of course. Mrs. Ledbetter stowed it in her place."

"I'll go fetch it."

"Then I can stay?"

"We'll see."

"Logan!" She reached out, grabbing his shirtsleeve before he could walk out. "I won't be a hindrance. I swear I won't."

"It's not you I object to. It's your motive that makes my blood boil. You're here to talk me into turning my children over to your parents." His look was hard and piercing as he shook off her hand. "And I won't do that, Susan. You can talk until you're blue in the face, and it won't make one bit of difference. They're mine and they're staying with me.''

"They're Catherine's children, too," Susan reminded him.

He smiled coldly. "Not anymore."

A knock on the door startled them both. Logan recovered first and opened the door. Mrs. Ledbetter stood outside in the hall, her arms full of a sleepy-eyed ragamuffin named Henryetta Susan. A serious seven-year-old, Jacob Jeremiah, stood beside Mrs. Ledbetter and regarded Susan with green eyes he'd inherited from his father.

"Etta!" Susan reached out for her niece, and Mrs. Ledbetter handed her over. "Do you remember me, pumpkin?"

"Aunt Susan," Etta said, then gave Susan a hug.

At four years old, Etta was a charmer, Susan thought as she smoothed her niece's mop of blond curls. Her big blue eyes sparkled with good cheer and dewy innocence. Susan dropped a kiss onto Etta's button nose, and the child giggled. Chubby-cheeked and rosy-mouthed, she overflowed with smiles and shrieks of delight. She looked so much like Catherine that Susan wanted to cry.

Jacob, on the other hand, was a mirror image of his father, having the same green eyes and generous mouth. A towhead—as Logan had probably been at his age—Jacob also favored his father in temperament, being self-contained and self-sufficient. Susan had noticed this on her previous visit, observing how the boy had dressed himself, amused himself, and watched over his sister with little supervision or instruction.

"It's good to see you again, Jacob," Susan said, running a hand over his cornsilk hair.

Jacob's smile was barely intact as he turned his gaze to his father. "Are Grandma and Grandpa here, too?"

"No. Just Aunt Susan." Logan gave a jaunty salute, acknowledging his landlady. "Much obliged."

"They're never any trouble," Mrs. Ledetter assured him. "Best children I've ever watched, and I've sat with many of them. See you later, loves." The landlady smiled at each child before she hurried away.

Jacob stepped almost cautiously inside the apartment, and Logan closed the door.

"Well!" Logan clapped his hands, getting everyone's attention. "Your aunt has come for a surprise visit, isn't that nice? How about if we russle up something for supper? Y'all hungry?"

"Yes!" Etta shouted, bobbing up and down in Susan's arms.

"I'll help." Jacob went toward the tiny kitchen area, head down, an intent expression on his young face.

Susan looked from Jacob to Logan, who was watching his son with the same gravity. When he felt Susan's interest, he glanced at her and shrugged off whatever troubled him.

"How does bacon and rice sound?" he asked.

"Fine. May I help?"

"No room. Two's a crowd in our kitchen, and three is out of the question." He grinned and chucked Etta under the chin. "You're glad Susan is here, aren't you?"

"Yes." To prove her point, Etta planted a wet kiss on Susan's cheek. "I *looove* Aunt Susan."

Logan studied his daughter's happy smile for a few moments, then heaved a short sigh as his gaze wandered to Susan. "Well, you have one Vance on your side."

Susan went to sit in a rocker with Etta while Logan and Jacob prepared supper. With Etta draped in her lap, Susan relaxed, content to let Etta point out objects in her favorite picture book. It was nice to be away from the farm, Susan thought, nodding absently at Etta's questions and exclamations about the "bossy moo-cow" and "quackity-quack ducky." About time I was on my own, she told herself. No future for me back there.

She thought of Calvin Pointer, the gangly, gentle-hearted young farmer her father had handpicked for her. As usual, such thoughts brought a scowl to her face and a heaviness to her heart. Calvin was a dear man, but he didn't make her moony-eyed or weak-kneed, and wasn't that how a girl was supposed to feel? In her heart, she felt it was, but there wasn't anyone to talk to about it. Her mother would have fainted if she'd asked such things, and bringing up the subject in front of her father would be nothing short of catastrophic! As for her younger sisters, their knowledge of romance would fit into a thimble.

Thank heaven for books, she thought with a smile, remembering snatches she'd read about women in love and how their beaus made them feel. Dizzy-headed, lighthearted, swooning with the sheer joy of it all! And Susan Armitage had *never* felt such things around Calvin Pointer. Furthermore, she'd ceased to hold out any hope of it. After all, she'd known him for years. A widower, he was looking for another wife and had let Susan know right off that she'd do, but Susan had other ideas. Although her parents had arranged for her and Calvin to be together often—he was invited *every* Sunday to dinner, and once or twice a month he invited the Armitage family to his place for a taffy pull or corn popping—Susan's attitude toward Cal hadn't changed. He was a friend, and that was that.

So it was good to be away from the constant urging of her father to "give Cal a chance before you opt for spinsterhood, Susie!" Hugging Etta closer, Susan prayed her time in St. Louis would last more than a night. She didn't want to go back. She liked being her own woman.

"Smell, Aunt Susan." Etta took a deep breath. "Bacon frying!"

"Is it making your mouth water, pumpkin?" Susan kissed Etta's forehead, thinking she was the prettiest little girl she'd ever seen. "How have you been, honey? Still missing your mommy?"

Etta nodded, suddenly grave. "Mama is gone to heaven." She pointed at the ceiling. "Up there . . . and she's playing a harp and singing with angels."

"That's right." Susan hugged her again, touched by the child's recitation. Had Mrs. Ledbetter or Logan painted this picture of death for her? It was so sweet, so dreamily romantic.

"At night we can see her."

Susan studied the child for a few moments. "You . . . you can? How? In your prayers?"

"We *talk* to her that way, but we *see* her in the sky,"

Etta explained patiently. "She's the first star in the Big Dipper's handle."

Susan smiled, bemused. "Who told you that, pumpkin?"

"Papa."

"Supper's on," Jacob said, motioning them out of the rocker. "Come on before it gets cold."

Susan followed her niece and nephew to the table and chairs set behind a screen divider. Logan set a big bowl of rice in the middle of the table. A platter of fried bacon and a pitcher of milk were already there.

"The milk's lukewarm," he said, helping Etta into her chair. "The iceman's coming around tomorrow."

"It looks delicious." Susan sat at one end of the table while Logan took the other. "This is the first time I've had my supper cooked by men." She grinned at Jacob, and he blushed. "I'm truly honored."

"Men cooking the meals around here is nothing new, is it, son? I've been the pot warmer and pot scrubber in this family for years."

"You have?" Susan asked, puzzled. Catherine hadn't been ill for years, only weeks before she had died of consumption.

"Did you see Uncle Coonie today, Papa?" Etta asked.

"Yes, sugar, I did, and he said he wishes you'd set a wedding date 'cause he's hankering for a missus."

Etta giggled, covering her mouth with a dimpled hand. Susan looked from the child to Logan, watching the two share the moment.

"I didn't know you had a brother," Susan said, serving herself a helping of fluffy rice. When Logan sent her a befuddled glance, she added, "Etta called the man her uncle, didn't she?"

"Coonie's my best friend. He's like family to me, and both Jacob and Etta dote on him. It didn't seem right for them to call him Mr. French."

"You work with him?"

"Yes, we're business partners."

Susan chewed thoughtfully on a bite of cured bacon. "Business partner. You mean at the newspaper?"

"No." He swallowed and dabbed at his mouth with a napkin as he glanced at his children and tried to keep from grinning. Finally, he looked at her straight on. "I don't work at the newspaper anymore. I quit last week."

"Quit? With two children to feed?"

"That's right. Coonie and I are starting up our own newspaper—"

"How enterprising of you!" Susan said, excited by the idea.

"—in Indian Territory."

"You must be mad!" She stared at him, dumbfounded.

His smile went frigid. "Spoken like a true Armitage."

Susan tried to keep her voice level as she selected her words carefully. "Logan, you can't be thinking of taking these children to that godforsaken place."

"Where I go, they go."

"I can't allow it." She placed her hands on either side of her plate and squared her shoulders, as she'd seen her father do in his most formidable mood. "I simply shall *not* allow it!"

Logan mirrored her posture, but his shoulders were much more impressive than hers. "I didn't ask for your permission, Susan, and I think the sooner you head back to your mama and papa, the better."

"But I—" Susan stopped herself, refusing to argue in front of the children. "We'll discuss this later."

Logan shrugged. "As far as I'm concerned, there's nothing to discuss.'

She glared at him and he glared back, pitting iron will against iron will. He blinked first.

Chapter 2

With the children tucked into their beds and the apartment as quiet as midnight, Susan settled in the big rocker across from Logan, who sprawled on the camelback sofa. He ran a hand down his face in a weary motion, then looked toward the open window where a breeze danced with the lace panels. Although he wasn't smiling, Susan could find the places in his lean cheeks where his dimples were buried. Stubble darkened his cheeks, chin, and upper lip. He's a good father, she thought, then wondered what kind of husband he'd been. Catherine hadn't complained, but she hadn't seemed entirely happy either.

Susan stirred from her thoughts when Logan glanced her way, as if sensing her curiosity about him. "The children seem well," she commented, seeking safe ground.

"Why shouldn't they be?"

"They've suffered a great loss," Susan said. "It would be natural if they were still reeling from it. Jacob seems a bit withdrawn."

"He's a loner. It's his nature, and it takes him longer to warm up to people. You have to earn his affection while his sister gives it freely."

"Are you sure he isn't hiding his feelings? I don't remember ever seeing Jacob cry. Even at his mother's funeral."

"He hasn't, but then neither have I."

"Yes, but you're a grown man. A boy losing his mother . . . well, one would expect—"

"I know what you're getting at, but Jacob is handling

13

his grief. Maybe not as you'd expect him to, but he's handling it. We've talked about his mother and death. He understands. He's accepted the situation."

"Why does he resent my being here?"

"Did he say that?"

"No." Susan followed Logan's gaze, watching the panels lift and fall to give glimpses of a starry night. He was withdrawing from her, loath to look at her, but why? What had she done to make him back so far away from her? Like father, like son. "Jacob wasn't happy to see me. That was quite obvious."

"He's a smart boy. He's lost his mother and he doesn't want to lose his father."

"What does my coming here have to do with that?" Susan asked, then stiffened when Logan chuckled as if she'd made a joke. "I'm not here to take your children, Logan, and I don't appreciate you filling their heads with such nonsense!"

"I haven't, but Jacob's no fool. He knows why you've come without being told."

"Rubbish." She set her jaw, incensed by his uncanny ability to see through any ruse. And Jacob was just like him! She looked at him again, wanting to create a camaraderie. While she didn't think he was right to take the children off to uncharted territory, she didn't think he was the irresponsible cad her father would have her believe, either. Still, there was so much she didn't know about him. So much that remained a mystery, a closed door, a lock with no key. "Where were you today if not at work?"

He swung his gaze slowly around to her. "Coonie and I were preparing for the trip. There's a lot to do, you know. It takes careful planning."

She shook her head, laughing under her breath. "I can't believe you're actually thinking of taking those children on such a treacherous journey. Haven't they been through enough?"

He flung his arms along the back of the sofa and cocked a brow at her. "What is it with you Armitages that you think you're the only ones capable of making sound decisions? Weren't y'all pestering me to raise the children somewhere besides the big city?''

"Yes, but we meant—"

"I *know* what you meant." His slouched posture belied the intensity of emotion emanating from him. "You meant your pappy's farm. You want me to hit the road without the children, never to darken your doorstep again."

"No, Logan." Susan sat on the edge of the rocker, anxious to put herself in his corner. "I just want a good life for Jacob and Etta . . . a *safe* life."

He smiled ruefully, then pushed up from the couch and, to her surprise, unbuttoned his shirt. Standing at the open window, he breathed deeply as the cool air bathed his exposed skin and set his shirttails fluttering. Susan couldn't tear her gaze from his muscled torso. His flesh looked supple but firm.

"You're so young," he said on a sigh, and Susan laughed.

"You say that as if you're as old as Moses yourself."

"I *do* have a few years on you," he noted. "Six years and many more experiences than you can claim. Life isn't safe, Susan, and often it isn't good. If it were, Catherine would still be here." Sadness radiated from him, squeezing Susan's heart.

"But why Indian Territory? If you must move, why not go somewhere civilized?"

He shrugged. "It's a place where a man with little money but a lot of ambition can make a good life for himself."

"But there are heathens and savages there."

"There are heathens and savages here. They're just not as easy to spot. At least in the Territory you'll know them. They're the ones wearing the feathers and loincloths." He grinned, and Susan glanced aside before she was completely taken in. "This isn't a whim of mine. Coonie and I have been talking about it since before Catherine took ill."

"*Catherine* agreed to this?" Susan asked, unable to believe it of her pampered, prima donna sister.

"No-o-o," Logan said. He grinned and massaged the

back of his neck. "But I was working up the nerve to tell her before she got sick."

"She would never have gone along with it."

"Oh, I don't know about that." He ran a hand down his coppery-colored chest, arresting Susan's gaze and taking it along for the ride to his navel. "I can be mighty persuasive when I put my mind to it."

Realizing she was staring in abject fascination, Susan left the rocker to pick up Etta's rag doll and place it in the crate being used as a toy bin. He's dangerous, she told herself. More dangerous than anything she might encounter in the Territory. Was he so convinced she was a child that he thought nothing of almost disrobing in front of her? It stung that he would treat her with such casual disregard, and it annoyed her to realize she had minimal control over her own urges. Her heart raced, and the tingle in her stomach increased as Logan came to stand behind her.

"It would be best if you boarded the train tomorrow for home."

She spun around, her irritation flaring into anger. "You're not getting rid of me that easily, Logan Vance!" Poking a finger in the center of his chest, where a nest of fine hair grew, Susan narrowed her eyes to smoking slits. But the tip of her finger stung as if she'd tangled with a bee. "I didn't come all this way to be ordered around by yet another man! *If* I decide to leave, it will be *my* decision, not yours."

He raised his brows at her outburst. "Yet another man . . ." His eyes sparkled with understanding. "You don't cotton much to jumping when your papa yells rabbit, do you?" He gripped her shoulders and locked gazes with her. "Why are you here, Susan? And don't give me any talk about family helping family. If you hadn't wanted to come, you would have found a way out of it."

His gaze boring into her, Susan found she couldn't lie to him. His hands lessened their grip but remained steadfastly at her shoulders, keeping her in place. She felt like a fly held by a pin.

"A change of scenery," she said with a sigh. "Simple

as that. There's nothing much for me back home. Just Calvin Pointer, and I don't want him.''

"Cal Pointer? I thought he was married."

"Not anymore. Like you, he's a widower." And there the similarity ends, she thought, sensing the strength in his hands, the tenderness in his eyes and—what *really* separated him from Cal—the latent sensuality bubbling under the surface of his bronze skin. She lowered her gaze, partly ashamed of her wanton thoughts. How could she be so unmoved around other men and so completely undone around Logan Vance? It had always been so. No wonder Catherine hadn't been able to resist his advances and had put the cart before the horse. She'd been three months pregnant with Jacob when she and Logan had married.

"So Cal's been courting you, has he?"

"Well, he's been trying."

Logan laughed, and his hands slipped down her arms to catch her fingers. His thumbs nestled in the damp centers of her palms. "And what's here for you, black-eyed Susan?"

Everything I've ever wanted, she thought, gazing into his lime-green eyes. Before she was tempted to tell the truth, Susan pulled away and crossed to the window. The air felt good on her overheated skin.

"Maybe you should give Calvin a chance, Susan. As I recall, he's a good old boy."

She looked over her shoulder at him, wishing he wasn't so quick to send her into another man's arms. "Watch out. You sound just like my father."

He winced. "Ouch." Coming closer, he pushed back the curtain panel for an unobstructed view of the night sky. "You're not thinking of staying in St. Louis by yourself, are you?"

"No."

"Then you're thinking about coming with us to Indian Territory?"

She shivered. "I'm trying not to think about that."

"Why?"

"It scares me. I've heard awful things about that place. It's called no man's land."

"Only part of it. I've heard wonderful things about the Territory. It's a land of opportunity. I came to St. Louis to get newspaper experience. Well, I've gotten it. It's time to move on. Time to leave my footprints somewhere for my son or daughter to follow."

Susan relaxed, soothed by his gentle voice and pioneer's vision. The Territory didn't seem so bad when Logan talked about it.

"We've already got a building waiting for us in a place called Tulsa—Tulsey Town. It's brand-new, just settled. Coonie and I have bought ourselves a printing press, and we're going to take it overland with us. We'll be the first newspaper in those parts. We'll make a difference, don't you see? Nothing civilizes a place more quickly than the press. Before you know it, Tulsey will be an honest-to-goodness town, and my newspaper will be an important part of it. What I write will make a difference, Susan. My opinions will *matter*." He drew a deep breath, and his voice sank to a whisper. "My words will help shape the land and its people. It's what every reporter wants, but few have the courage to make it so. Do you know what I've been covering lately? Groundbreakings for a new mortuary, a bank, the Good Samaritan Lodge. Oh, and the biggest story I've had of late, the Riverboat Ball!" His upper lip curled in disgust. "Not exactly the stuff of a newsman's dreams, eh?" When his gaze captured hers, Susan felt the fire within him. "The press can civilize, socialize, and dramatize. I want it all, not just part of it."

"Are you sure you can never have it all in St. Louis?"

"Yes. Reporters define. Editors refine. Publishers opine." He smiled just for a second. "That's an old newspaper saying."

"And you'll be all three in Tulsa?"

"That's right."

"What about Coonie?"

"He'll be the printer, the pressman. That's Coonie's arena. He's not a writer."

"Do you have a house there?"

"In back of the newspaper office there are four rooms we'll use."

"Well, it seems you're determined to do this thing."

"Yes." He looked at the dim lights in the street below, but Susan knew he was looking inside himself. After a minute, he shook his head and chuckled under his breath. "You still think I'm being selfish? Believe me, Susan, the children and I have talked and talked and talked about this. They *want* to go."

"They want to go because you can be mighty persuasive," she said, laughing with him. Other thoughts made her serious. "But the journey can't be easy, Logan. What if they're taken ill along the way? What if you're attacked by Indians? People *die* on these wagon trains."

"People *die* here, too. In fact, one died in this apartment." He lay down on the sofa, flinging one arm across his eyes. "Death is something the children and I have come to understand, Susan. It's not something we fear."

Susan pulled her lower lip between her teeth and struggled with indecision. He sounded so sad, so forlorn. But what could she do for him?

"Besides, I'm quite capable of taking care of my own children, as I've told your parents over and over again. Yes, I think you should board the train tomorrow and—"

"No!"

He peeked at her from beneath his shielding forearm. "You don't want to go, but you don't want to stay. What *do* you want?"

"I want to stay . . . here with you. This is a lovely place, Logan. You can get your old job back, and I'll take care of the—"

His hollow laughter interrupted her, and he swung his feet to the floor to face her. "Play house, you mean? Is that what you'd like to do? Pretend you're the mama and I'm the papa going off to work and bringing my pay home to you?"

"You're making fun of me," she said, hurt by his cruel jesting. She folded her arms and shifted sideways, preferring to stare out the window than at his unpleasant sneer.

"I'm sorry my life isn't going along according to your plan, Susan. Besides, I want more from a woman than just a clean house and well-fed children."

That pierced her single-mindedness like an arrow. Susan turned slowly toward him, feeling justly shamed and more aware of him as a man and not simply as a means to an end.

"I'm the one who's sorry," she said. "I suppose I'm the one being selfish. It's just that I've been planning this, you see. Once Papa said I should come here, I've been thinking of how my life would be in St. Louis. I thought about how grateful you'd be to have me around—once you got over the initial irritation, of course. But I didn't take into account how you'd feel or what you'd planned for yourself and the children. You've been through so much. I loved Catherine, yes, but we'd grown apart. After she married I saw her only once, but you . . . you and your children have lost a wife and a mother, and here I am wanting you to do what's best for me instead of what you think is best for your family." She stared at her clasped hands and pictured herself sitting in a wagon on a wide-open prairie with two frightened children. "But, Logan, have you really thought this through? It will be a long journey, and the children—"

"Will be fine. Families travel overland all the time."

"And some never make it to their destination. I've heard that graves mark the way to the frontier."

"We'll all get there in one piece."

"And once you're there, then what? What kind of town could this Tulsey be? Any schools, churches, other children? How many decent families are already there?"

He ran a hand through his hair in a gesture of aggravation. "They're my children and I'll make a good life for them." His glance was biting. "I'm not sending them back with you, so you can put that notion to bed. Speaking of which, I'm tired and—"

"Logan, my folks aren't trying to steal your children. They just want what's best for their only grandchildren."

"And they want them away from me," he added, casting a searing glance her way.

"No," she stated emphatically, but an inner voice called her a liar.

"No?" His stare was a blatant challenge. "You swear, Susan? Swear on a Bible?"

She lowered her gaze to her hands again, cornered. "I think you're a good father to your children."

"I always thought you liked me. Was I right?"

"Yes." She still didn't look at him, but she felt his gaze burning into the top of her head as he left the sofa and came toward her on cat feet.

"That's probably why your papa sent you. Figured you'd be the one who could convince me I'd be better off without my son and daughter."

"I wasn't sent to convince you of that." Susan raised her gaze to his. "I was sent to help you. It's a tradition among country people, you know. We believe in doing unto others as we'd have them do unto us."

"So where's the helping hand? All I've seen so far is the back of yours."

"That's not true! Can I help it if I think you're being rash?"

He shrugged and headed for the bedrooms. "I'll let you have my bed tonight, and I'll get you a train ticket tomorrow morning."

"Logan!" Susan bolted forward and grabbed his shirtsleeve. "Please, I—" She dropped her hand and her gaze when his began to warm her blood. "Would you like me to go along?"

He looked at her curiously, smiling faintly at the note of desperation in her voice. "You don't want to go back to the farm, do you?"

"N-not if I can be of service to—"

"Stop it." He gripped her shoulders and shook her. "I'm tired of your Saint Susan act. If you want to go along, then be honest about it. Don't hide behind your family's code of honor or any other such rot. I know why you left and why you don't want to go back."

She was struck by the wisdom in his eyes. "Why? Why do you think?"

"Same reason your sister latched on to me."

Susan flinched. "She loved you."

"Yes, but she also wanted to squirm out from under

Abraham's thumb. You're squirming, too, Susan.'' He dipped his head, his brows lowering to shadow his eyes. "Tell you what . . . if you want to go along with us, you're welcome to, but I'm not making the decision for you. You want to be treated like a woman? Act like one.'' He inched closer, his breath fanning her face. "So what will it be, black-eyed Susan?''

Having him so near sent a wave of unexpected longing through her. She swayed, glad to have him support her as lethargy seeped into her bones. His challenge fluttered like a flag in her mind and she knew she should feel insulted, but she didn't. He was right. Oh, so right. She didn't want to go back to her father's home where she was expected to do his bidding. It was high time she had a place of her choosing and a chance to succeed or fail on her own merit.

"When were you planning on leaving?''

He smiled, and she basked in the glow of it. "Next week, actually.''

"So soon?''

"The sooner the better.'' He loosened his grip on her shoulders and backed up a step. "Susan, what will it be? Now, don't come along if you're just following your father's orders.''

"Believe you me, Papa would *not* want me to travel overland to some savage place nobody's heard of!'' She laid a hand to her forehead and closed her eyes. "I don't know what I should do . . . I'm so tired and confused . . .''

The knock on the door startled both of them. Logan removed his hands from her as if he'd been burned, then strode to the door and opened it.

"Coonie. For the love of God, what are you doing here at this time of night?''

"I'm a sorry substitute for a woman, but I figured you might enjoy a gutsy drink and somebody to talk to, seeing as how you was so dag-blamed lonely today.''

A chubby man with apple cheeks and a shock of white hair entered the apartment, floppy hat in hand and a bottle of spirits in the other. When his merry blue eyes happened on Susan, his skin turned bright pink and his mouth worked, but nothing came out.

"Coonie French, this is my former sister-in-law Miss Susan Armitage. Coonie, mind your manners and quit staring at her like she's the last female on earth."

"Oh, begging your pardon, miss." He transferred the bottle to his other hand. "Pleased to meet you. Logan's mentioned you to me before."

"Hello, Mr. French." She let him take her hand for a brief grasp. "And Logan has mentioned you to me."

"Well, now that we know I make mention of the people I know, why don't we all sit down? Let me have that bottle, Coonie, and I'll fetch some glasses."

"No, that's okay. I'll be going—"

"Please don't leave on my account," Susan said, extending a detaining hand. "Won't you stay awhile? I'm sure Logan would appreciate the company."

"Well . . ." Coonie shrugged and handed the bottle to Logan. "So, you just visiting?" he asked Susan as he ambled to the sofa.

"She's talking about going with us," Logan said before Susan could answer Coonie herself.

Coonie fell back onto the sofa as if he'd been socked in the gut. He stared first at Logan, then at Susan. "You gotta be pulling my leg. You ain't really thinking of tagging along, are you, Miss Armitage?"

"No, I'm not thinking of *tagging along*. I'm considering joining you so I can see after my nephew and niece!" She knew her tone was sharp, but she didn't care. If this Coonie French thought she was a worthless, do-nothing female, then she wanted to dissuade him of that notion immediately!

Logan laughed at them and took the bottle into the kitchen nook. "Come on, Coonie. Let's sit at the table like gentlemen while we make these spirits disappear. Susan, I imagine it's past your bedtime, so don't let us keep you. You'll find fresh linens in the bottom drawer of the chest beside my bed. If you need anything else, just give a shout."

Coonie pushed up from the sofa and went to the kitchen table where Logan had placed the whiskey bottle and two glasses. Susan's hackles quivered as she watched the two men sit down and commence with their business, both acting as if she'd already left the room. How dare Logan send her off to bed as if she were another one of his children!

Marching forward, Susan ignored the two men's looks of surprise as she took a glass from the cupboard and planted herself in one of the chairs. Glaring sternly at Logan, she tapped the glass against the tabletop.

"If you please, Logan?" she said, lifting one eyebrow in a haughty inflection.

"What?" He looked from the glass to her serious expression. "You want a drink of whiskey?"

"Yes, that's correct."

He chuckled and ran a hand over his mouth to erase his smirk. "Susan, I don't think you should be—"

"You'll not be doing my thinking for me, Logan Vance." She tapped the glass again. "A measure of whiskey, please, unless you two have something against drinking in mixed company."

Coonie swallowed hard, making a gulping noise, and his skin color deepened to beet-red. "I got nothing against it, but this here whiskey is mighty strong, ma'am, and it might just put you on your a— uh, backside."

"I doubt it." She moved her glass closer to Logan. "I've had whiskey before."

"Oh, really?" Logan's tone reflected his disbelief. "When, Susan? With the family? Or maybe with old Cal Pointer?"

She flashed him a scathing glare. "At a barn dance last year," she said, not bothering to tell him it had been a drop or two of whiskey mixed with a cup of apple cider. "And it didn't knock me over, I can assure you."

"All right then." Logan shrugged and poured two fingers into the glass. "I guess you know what you're doing."

"Mr. French," she said, directing her attention to the newcomer, "Logan tells me you're a printer."

"Yes'm. I know more about printing presses than any

other man in these parts, I'd wager.'' Coonie lifted a hand to stop Logan from pouring more than three fingers of whiskey into his glass. "That'll do for now, partner.''

Logan gave himself a generous amount of the caramel-colored liquor, then set the bottle in easy reach. He lifted his glass, his eyes sparkling with humor. "Here's to Tulsey Town.''

"Tulsey Town!'' Coonie saluted, touching his glass to Logan's. "God love 'er!''

Susan nodded, and her glass connected with Coonie's and Logan's. Both men waited for her to drink first, their gazes trained on her as if she were about to perform a circus trick. After a deep breath, she raised the glass to her lips. The potent fumes slammed into her head, making her stomach lurch, but she carried through and took a big drink of the nasty tasting spirits. It was like fire, blackening her insides. She coughed, gagged, and was sure she was near death, but then she sensed Logan's mockery and decided she could endure anything but that!

Beating down her need to bring the vile substance up and out of her, she swallowed over and over again until she was sure the whiskey was well on its way to her stomach. Then she did what she'd seen men do behind the barn on dance nights. She raked her mouth with the back of her hand and let out a long, breathy ahhh! Coonie stared at her in openmouthed awe, but Logan didn't seem the least bit impressed.

"Susan, honey,'' Logan said, patting her hand in a placating way, "don't you think you've bitten off a little more than you can chew? Me and Coonie will understand perfectly if you leave the rest of this brew to us and get yourself off to bed so you'll be clearheaded when the train comes for you.''

She snatched her hand away from him. Men! Always in control. Always barking orders, telling instead of asking, pandering instead of explaining. Oh, if she were a man, she'd . . . she'd . . .

"I'm going with you to Tulsey Town.'' She blinked, realizing she'd spoken aloud after the fact.

"What?'' Logan asked, finally astonished. "You don't

mean it. Why, you won't be happy in the Territory away from your mama and papa. You'll be homesick within a week and crying to be taken—''

''I'm going!'' To show him she meant business, she tossed the rest of the whiskey to the back of her throat. It singed what was left of her innards and made her see double.

Logan stared at her for long moments, then sighed and shrugged. Coonie grabbed for the bottle and let out a low moan.

''What's wrong?'' Logan asked, one side of his mouth lifting in a half grin.

''I could use another drink. Hell, if she's going, I'd better go buy me a few gallons of the stuff, 'cause I'll sure be needing it.''

Logan threw back his head and laughed, but Susan didn't think Coonie French was the least bit funny.

After a minute, Logan's chuckles died. He eyed Susan speculatively, then smiled to himself.

''What are you grinning about?'' Susan demanded, feeling light-headed and all aglow inside.

''Oh, I was just thinking about your pappy.'' He sat back in the chair, his attitude one of pure arrogance. ''Wonder what he'll do once he finds out that another one of his angels has gone and run off with the devil.''

Chapter 3

"Why do they call it a prairie schooner?" Susan asked as she made a slow trip around the wagon.

"Because when the canvas is up and she's rolling along flat land she looks just like a sailing ship," Logan said, then grunted as he tightened ropes across trunks and crates inside it. "They're pretty from a distance, but not so from the driver's seat. How long has it been since you've handled a team?"

"Last spring, but I can assure you I haven't forgotten how it's done. Will we use mules, oxen, or horses?"

"Oxen for the wagon hauling the press and draft horses for this one." He grunted again, then knotted another rope. "Got to tie everything down good or it'll get shook to pieces. These covered wagons are practical, but a devil to ride in." He jumped down and peeled off his rawhide gloves. "You're jostled this way and that. Sometimes you'd swear the thing is going to topple to one side and smash into bits."

"Sometimes they do," she said, examining how he'd arranged the barrels and crates she'd helped him pack early that morning. "Are you trying to scare me and make me back out of this trip?"

"No, but I do think you should know what's ahead of you. Did you bring sturdy clothing and sensible bonnets?"

"Yes. What other kind would I have, living on a farm?" She made a chiding face at him. "I get the feeling you think I'm a delicate rose. Well, I'm not."

27

"Oh, no?" He touched the back of his hand to her warm cheek. "Not even a wild rose with plenty of thorns?"

An inner voice told her to move away from him, but a stronger force kept her in place as his knuckles smoothed up and down her cheek.

"If you're a wild rose," he said, his tone dipping to a raspy whisper, "then I guess that makes me a honeybee, buzzing around you, looking for a way inside, searching out your sweetness." His mouth hovered a fraction from hers. She could smell him; musky, spicy, male. She sensed his uncertainty, grappled with her own, then rested a hand on his chest, more to feel his racing heart than to keep him from her. A moment sizzled between them. She knew the decision had been made when his sandy lashes floated down. He was going to kiss her.

"Papa, make Etta share!" Jacob's voice broke them apart.

Susan jerked away from his touch, and Logan swallowed with difficulty. He cleared his throat, and regret shadowed his green eyes.

"What's wrong now?" he asked, striding past Susan to where his children squabbled.

"She won't give me a turn with the jacks," Jacob complained. "She's so spoiled."

"Etta, share with your brother," Logan said, his tone brooking no argument from his daughter. "That's a good girl."

The children had found a vacant stall and were playing jacks. The aroma of hay and manure was strong in the stables where Logan and Coonie kept the two wagons that would carry them to Indian Territory. Logan went back to the wagon, hardly giving Susan a glance as he passed by. Had the near kiss alarmed him, repulsed him, or merely annoyed him? she wondered.

"How long will it take to get to Tulsa?" Susan asked. His glance was furtive, somewhat shy. It didn't fit with her image of him. Could it be that he wasn't supreme ruler of his emotions, as she'd thought?

"We won't be in any great hurry. Two weeks, give or take a few days here and there."

"Two weeks." She shook her head. Might as well be a month, she thought. It'll seem that long.

"There's still time for you to change your mind. You were woozy last night, so I sure wouldn't hold it against you—"

"I was *not* woozy." She tipped up her chin at his insinuation that she'd been intoxicated. "Just because I had a slight headache this morning does *not* mean I was drunk."

"Whatever you say," he muttered, turning away from her as he pulled on his gloves again. He stooped and lifted a barrel stuffed with household goods onto the wagon. "I'm just wondering why you decided to go after you were so dead set against it."

"I'm wondering that myself," she murmured, walking over to the children. Their game was progressing smoothly. She thought of the times she'd played with her own siblings, and homesickness pricked her heart. "Logan, on the way back to your home, I'd like to stop at the telegraph office."

"What for?"

"To send a wire to my family and let them know I'm leaving St. Louis."

"That ought to send Abraham here in a jiffy."

Bent at the waist to observe the jacks game, Susan straightened slowly as the image of her father storming into St. Louis blasted into her mind. It would be better if he received the wire after the fact. No use courting disaster. Glancing Logan's way, Susan wondered why he was allowing her to tag along. Yes, she'd be an asset during the journey, but he could manage without her. Ever since last night she'd had a sneaking suspicion his motive was retribution. He wants to aggravate Papa, send him into a rage, she thought. And news that she'd gone with Logan to unknown territory would definitely do it.

Oh, he'll be furious! she thought, picturing her father's reaction. She'd have to word the telegram carefully to reassure him, make him think it was best for all concerned and she could keep an eye on Logan, which was her father's main objective. He didn't trust Logan and was certain he wouldn't take proper care of Jacob and Etta.

Susan sighed wearily. Once he realized she was headed for Indian Territory with Logan, he'd not read any further. He'd explode like a jar of peaches stored too close to the hearth. Susan glanced at Logan again, only to find him regarding her with a curious smile.

"Getting cold feet?" he asked, using that scratchy tone of voice that made her uncomfortable.

"No, of course not." She propped her hands on her hips, adopting a stubborn pose. "What's wrong? Do you *want* me to back out? Is that why you keep pestering me?"

"Pestering you? Me?" His smile lapsed into a smirk. He ran a handkerchief over his sweaty face, then plucked at the front of his shirt where it stuck to him. "I'm leaving the door ajar is all. The way you looked just now made me think you were in the market for a train ticket."

"You have read me wrong, as usual."

"As usual? I think I read you pretty well. I figured out you were anxious to stay away from the farm, didn't I?"

"I'm also going with you because of Jacob and Etta. If you'll recall, it was for them I came here in the first place."

"Nobody asked you."

She let out an exaggerated sigh. "Yes, Logan, you've made it perfectly clear you don't need me, want me, or believe me."

His flicking gaze was too brief to decipher, but she sensed exasperation in his jerky movements as he repositioned a few barrels strapped to the outside of the wagon.

"I believe I'll wait and wire my family next week."

"Right before we head for the Territory," he tacked on with a rakish grin. "Chicken." Without preamble, he sat on the tailgate and unbuttoned his shirt. He peeled it off, draped it across the wagon wheel, and hopped to his feet. He grabbed a trunk and hoisted it up into the wagon.

Susan told herself not to stare, but her eyes remained fixed. His coppery skin glistened with sweat, and several drops raced each other down the indentation of his spine.

Living in a household of sisters, she'd never seen a man with his shirt off before because her father would never dream of removing his in front of a lady. But Logan operated under no such moral code. He went about his business, bare to the waist, as if it were nothing untoward . . . as if there was no hungry-eyed young woman nearby.

Forcing herself to stare at *anything* besides Logan, Susan went around to the side of the wagon to examine the footholds leading up to the seat, which was no more than a wide plank of sanded wood. Bed pillows would make the ride more comfortable, and she'd need a sturdy pair of work gloves if she was expected to handle the reins.

"Logan, will you drive the team or will I?"

"Both of us, most likely."

"Then I'll need gloves and a whip." Another worry entered her mind. "And we should pack a bottle of cod-liver oil."

"Ugh!" Jacob made a face and shook his head. "We won't need none of that."

"Good idea," Logan said from inside the wagon where he was tying the rocker to iron bedsteads. "My own ma used to give me a spoonful of that stuff every morning. She said it would keep the doctor away from the door, and damned if she wasn't right."

Susan pulled herself up to the wagon seat and twisted around to look at him. "Is your mother still alive?"

"No, she died when I was ten."

"What about your father?"

"Never knew him." He put a shoulder to the dismantled cookstove and shoved it flush against the side of the wagon. "He died before I was born."

"Who took care of you after your mother died?"

"My Uncle Zeb and Aunt Dee in Kansas City. Uncle Zeb was a newspaperman."

Susan smiled. "So that's where you got your interest in the work."

"That's right." He sat back against the stacked barrels and crates and ran a gloved hand down his face. His chest rose and fell, the muscles writhing beneath his smooth skin. "Uncle Zeb and Aunt Dee were the best thing that ever happened to me. I owe a lot to them."

"They're still alive?"

"Aunt Dee is. Uncle Zeb passed on a couple of years back."

"You have no brothers or sisters?"

"Nope." His green eyes fastened on her. "Jacob and Etta are my only family."

"Don't forget me," Susan said softly.

He looked down at his grimy gloves and then planted them on his knees as his gaze swung around to her again. "I hope you don't take this wrong, but I don't think of you as family."

She felt the beginnings of rejection sting her and started to climb down from the wagon.

"Susan."

"Yes?"

"I think of you more like a friend," he explained. "Not like a sister or anything like that."

"Oh." She mulled this over, liking it after a few moments. "I think I understand."

"You don't see me as a brother, do you?"

"A brother?" She didn't dare meet his gaze because his question alone frayed her nerves. "No, but I feel close to you."

"How can you feel close to me? We hardly know each other."

"But you've been in the family for years," she said, knowing that wasn't an answer. "Don't you feel an attachment to me?"

He narrowed his eyes and regarded her with a nakedness that made her shiver. As if realizing he might be exposing too much of himself, he turned his back to rearrange a stack of boxes.

"Got to get this wagon packed," he muttered, gruffly. "Sure won't pack itself."

Susan lowered herself to the ground, shaken to the core. No man had ever looked at her with such frank sexuality. Recalling last night when she'd found it difficult to sleep in his bed, Susan hugged herself and tried to control her own raging emotions. What was happening between them? Was it the beginnings of love, or were they being drawn together by pure animal lust?

Preacher Tom had spoken to the congregation last month about lust and how it came from the devil. He'd cautioned the young men and women of Pemiscot County not to surrender to it, but to wait for chaste, matrimonial devotion. Susan shook off the sense of guilt, angry at herself for putting a tail and horns on everything she didn't understand.

Logan was a handsome man, and she was a woman of marrying age, she reasoned. There was nothing sinful about them noticing those things about each other, absolutely nothing wrong with her thinking of Logan, imagining how it might feel to be kissed by him or how lovely it would be to dance with him in the moonlight. Nothing whatsoever wrong with any of it!

Except that such thoughts occurred far too often, and he'd been her sister's husband a few scant months ago.

"Aunt Susan?" Etta tugged on Susan's hands, demanding her attention.

"Yes, honey?"

"How come your face is all red?"

"Is it?" Susan placed her hands against her cheeks, feeling the flame beneath her skin. "I . . . I . . ." She looked toward Logan and found him smiling at her discomfort.

"You sick?" Etta asked.

"Aunt Susan's hot and bothered," Logan said, jumping down from the wagon for a better look.

Susan sent him a barbed glare. "You're the one who's sweating," she snapped, making Logan laugh.

"Glad you noticed."

"A gentleman wouldn't remove his shirt in front of a lady." She raked his body with what she hoped was a disparaging glance.

"And a lady wouldn't stare, either," he countered smoothly.

Bested, Susan gave him her back and received his snickering chuckle in return.

* * *

Logan sat on the wagon seat, reins in hand, cap pulled low on his forehead. He glanced at the telegraph office where Susan was sending a wire to her father and imagined Abraham's reaction. He'd bust a gut, Logan thought with a wicked grin. Oh, if only he could be a fly on the wall . . .

"When will we see Indians, Papa?" Etta asked from inside the covered wagon.

"Not for a long while if we're lucky," Jacob answered for Logan. "We want to stay away from Indians, silly."

"I like Indians. I think they're pretty."

"Gee-golly-gosh, you're plumb nutty."

"That's enough," Logan growled back at them. "I'm not going to listen to that kind of talk all the way to Tulsey."

Dipping his head a fraction, he could see Susan beneath the fancy gold lettering on the window of the telegraph office. He'd want the same for his newspaper office window, he decided, thinking how grand it would look.

Susan was taking her sweet time composing her missive. What would she send? Dear Papa, Am heading for Indian Territory with Logan (stop) Don't worry (stop) Logan will take care of me (stop) Can't stop me now (can't stop, can't stop, can't stop). Logan chuckled to himself. Old Abe would wish he'd never hatched this plan. He wouldn't have a decent night's sleep once he received the wire because Abraham would have visions of yet another daughter ruined by Logan Vance.

Abraham had made a craft out of hating Logan. He'd never forgive Logan for catching Catherine's eye, or Catherine for disobeying his order to "stay away from that rolling stone." Abraham had taken one look at Logan and decided he wasn't fit company for any self-respecting girl, and that had made Logan even more determined to woo Catherine Armitage—to woo her and win her.

"Papa, why can't we just go off and leave her?" Jacob asked, rising up behind Logan and shattering his memories.

"What? Who?"

"Aunt Susan," Jacob whispered past a cupped hand. "We don't need her hanging around. Me and you can take care of Etta."

Logan twisted to see his son's serious expression. "Why don't you like Aunt Susan? Has she mistreated you somehow? Has she said ugly things to you?"

"No." Jacob pressed his chin against his chest. "I just don't want her around is all."

"Well, I'm sure not leaving her stranded in the middle of St. Louis. She won't be any trouble. No more than you, I imagine."

"She's not Mama."

Logan looked sideways at him, noting Jacob's trembling lower lip. "That's right, she's not. And what's more, she doesn't want to be. Your aunt is just helping out. Mama was her sister, remember? She's lost somebody, too."

"You're going to marry her."

"What?" Logan inched back to give him an incredulous glare. "Where in the world did you get that idea?"

"She's old enough for a husband, ain't she?"

"She is, and don't say ain't."

"But she *is* our *ain't*, ain't she?" Etta asked, popping up beside her brother.

Both Logan and Jacob burst into laughter, and Logan planted a smacking kiss on his daughter's cheek.

"Yes, honey-bunch, she is. Now hush. Here she comes. No more talk about me and her marrying, you hear me, Jacob?"

"Yes, sir."

"Good." He half stood to give Susan a hand up onto the seat beside him. "Everything taken care of now?"

"Yes." She tied her bonnet's bow beneath her chin and cast a worried glance at the telegraph office. "I'm just wondering how he's going to take it."

"You know that already, Susan," Logan said, flicking the reins to set the draft horses in motion. A hundred rattles and squeaks sounded from every part of the wagon as it rolled out onto the city street. "Your pappy's gonna blow like a whale." He chuckled to himself, getting a mental image. "Steam will come out of his ears, and his eyes will roll like dice." He swung his gaze around to Susan, surprised to hear her laugh softly. She sobered with some effort.

"Poor Pa." She shrugged. "I guess every parent hates to see the children grow up."

"And run off with scoundrels," Logan added, making Susan heave a sigh of boredom.

"How far ahead of us is Coonie?" Susan asked, peering past the swaying rumps and bobbing heads of the mighty steeds.

"Oh, at least two days, but we'll catch up to him. He'll be moving slower with the oxen and heavy printing press. Probably join up with him just about in time to see Tulsa together."

"Has Coonie ever traveled overland?"

"Nope."

"So this is a first for everyone."

"Sure is." He grinned mischievously and elbowed her. "Ain't it excitin'?"

She scowled at his deliberate bad grammar.

"Is Susan your *ain't* too, Papa?" Etta asked, making Logan tip back his head and release a bark of laughter.

"Come up here, you." Susan pulled Etta into her lap and hugged her tightly. "I'm your aunt," she said, pronouncing the word correctly. "And ain't is not a word young ladies like yourself should be using. Your papa even knows better."

"That's right," Logan said, nodding. "I know better. I was only teasing." His green eyes sparkled like jewels. "I get a kick out of teasing your Aunt Susan. She blushes so pretty, doesn't she?"

"Blushes?" Etta examined Susan carefully. "I thought you was hot again."

"No, and the correct way to say that is 'I thought you *were* hot.' Not was." She gave Etta another affectionate squeeze. "Sounds as if you've picked up some bad habits from your father."

"We like him, habits and all," Jacob said, his tone angry and his mouth forming a straight line. "We don't need anybody else telling us how to talk, either! Papa is a writer. He knows all about words.''

"Hey, hey. That'll be enough from you, young man," Logan cautioned in the lower, cracking tone he used when scolding the children. "Your aunt doesn't need any lectures from a cowlicked, freckle-faced boy either, so shut your trap.''

Surprised by the outburst, Susan examined Jacob's mutinous expression and her heart ached. She started to touch Jacob's cheek, but he swayed back out of reach, making Susan gasp in dismay.

"Jacob," she said, softly, "what's wrong? What have I done? I didn't mean to criticize your father. I think he's a fine man, and you're absolutely right to admire him, habits and all. We were only poking fun at each other.''

"He knows that," Logan said. "He's got a bur under his blanket this morning.''

Jacob sat on a trunk, arms folded, eyes trained straight ahead on a mound of boxes, quilts, and bedding. He refused to look at Susan. Disturbed by his resentment, Susan turned to face front again, telling herself she would speak privately with Jacob the first chance she got. She'd felt his displeasure at having her along, but this display alarmed her. Why did she threaten him so? What harm did he think she could bring to him and his family?

"Don't fret about him," Logan whispered. "He'll come around.''

"But why doesn't he want me along?''

Logan shrugged. "He's at an awkward age.''

Susan shook her head, but decided to drop the subject. Awkward age or not, her nephew had built a wall around himself just to keep Susan out. Etta scrambled from Susan's lap and went back to sit with her brother. Logan gave a little shake of his head when he caught Susan's eye, silently telling her not to pay attention to the two.

"Well, *chillens!*" Logan looked over his shoulder at saucer-sized eyes. "Off we go. Say your good-byes to St. Louis. We won't see the likes of her for some time to come.''

The children moved to the far end of the wagon to peer

out the back opening. Susan took note of the many businesses they passed and the noise of a city awakening to another workday. It was only an hour or so after dawn, but St. Louis was stretching, flexing, yawning, beginning to stir.

Homesickness stabbed Susan unexpectedly. She thought of her mother standing before the hearth, poking the embers into life and preparing to roll out biscuit dough. She could recall the sleepy-eyed expressions of her sisters, the loving grumpiness of her father, and the cooing of her mother as she herded everyone to the table for breakfast. She could even smell the aroma of freshly baked bread, fried potatoes and onions, and hot maple syrup. Susan shivered against the morning chill, and the homey picture collapsed in her mind. She reached behind her for her shawl and draped it about her shoulders to melt the rime around her heart, brought on by yet another departure in a little more than a week.

"Susan?" Logan's soft summons penetrated her icy solitude. "If you're having second thoughts, there's still time to head back home."

"No." She shifted to one hip, angling away from him. "Sorry to disappoint you, but I have no intention of backing out."

"I'm not disappointed. Glad to have your company."

"You are?" She gaped at him, dumbstruck by his admission.

"Sure." The devil's lights were in his eyes again. "Gives me one more gal to tease."

Despite herself, Susan smiled. "And you dearly love teasing and baiting and making a general nuisance of yourself, don't you?"

"Sure do." He hunched his shoulders and aimed his gaze at the horse's ears. "Can't think of anything I'd rather do than make a pretty girl blush and stutter. Well . . . I can think of *one* other thing more fun than that, but I can't talk about it in front of the children." His grin said the rest.

Susan shook off his efforts to appall her, but she couldn't

as easily shake thoughts of that other thing he liked better than teasing, and it galled her that he had sowed such seeds in her imagination. They found mighty fertile soil there.

Chapter 4

Straining backward on the reins, Susan brought the team to a halt as Logan jumped from the wagon and scouted the area. After a thorough survey, he nodded, then pointed to a stand of trees.

"Drive them over there," he instructed. "We'll camp under those pines."

Susan slackened the reins and clucked to the team. They set off, minding her voice and hand commands. After a week on the trail, the team recognized her and Logan. Logan swore they worked better when she cooed to them, but she figured Logan only wanted her to take the reins more often so he could nap, play with the children, or merely walk a ways and stretch out the kinks in his long legs. She didn't mind driving the team, since it broke the monotony of the journey.

Until this evening, she had looked forward to twilight when they alighted from the wagon for solid ground, a filling meal, and deep sleep. They'd been fortunate each evening, finding themselves guests of country people who invited them to supper and let them sleep in their barns or, sometimes, in their homes. Often, Coonie had been a guest before them.

But their travels on this day had brought them to a lonely stretch of land with no homesteads in sight. It would be their first night under the stars. Unerringly, Susan's hand went to her throat where a gold cross hung from a delicate chain. Her mother had given it to her, and touching it brought the love of home and family nearer when it seemed so distant and removed.

Sensing someone's attention, she jerked her gaze toward Logan. His watchful eyes had caught every nuance of her expression.

"Feeling homesick?"

"No, of course not." She tossed off the lie as if she were born to deceit. "Well, maybe a little," she amended to save her soul. "It's lonely looking out here."

"It'll look better once we get a fire going," Logan said.

Reminding herself that she certainly wasn't alone or without kin, Susan climbed down from the wagon and helped Etta from it. Jacob needed no help, leaping like a jubilant frog from the back opening and rolling in the long grass in boyish abandon.

"Where's the house?" Etta asked, a frown puckering her brow.

"We're sleeping under the wagon tonight, pumpkin," Susan said, injecting excitement into her voice.

"No house? No barn?"

"No house. No barn." Susan squatted to eye level with Etta. "Won't that be fun?"

"I dunno . . ." Etta looked toward her father, who was unhitching the team. "Papa, will sleeping outside be fun?"

"Sure," Logan called over his shoulder. "You and Jacob can sleep under the wagon with Aunt Susan."

"Where will you sleep?"

"Under the stars."

"Close by?"

"So close you'll be able to hear me snoring," he promised, then looked to Susan. "Best rustle up something for supper while there's still some light. I'll get the fire going momentarily."

Susan nodded, realizing it would be her first turn as campfire cook. Rummaging through the supplies, she selected a hunk of cured sowbelly and a few potatoes and turnips for the boiling pot. True to his word, Logan built a fire after he had unhitched and staked the team beneath the trees. While Susan cooked supper, he and the children readied the wagon for the night, dropping the canvas along the sides and placing the bedrolls underneath. The canvas gave privacy to the sleepers and discouraged nightcrawlers, but just in case, Logan sprinkled salt all around the bedrolls to keep the slimy pests away.

The smells of supper drew the others to the campfire. Susan filled the tin plates and passed them around. She and Logan partook of strong coffee while Etta and Jacob drank spring water from the big barrels strapped to the sides of the wagon.

Logan ate like a man possessed, hardly saying a word as was his custom, Susan had learned. He and the children attacked their food, saving any conversation for after their plates had been cleared. Usually, Logan told a story or related some wild tale from his youth to the delight of his children. Susan enjoyed them as well and wondered if his stories were more fiction than fact. Doubtless, he'd lived a more adventurous life than she, but she found it hard to believe he'd been involved in so many hair-raising escapades.

"Did I ever tell y'all about the time I learned to swim?" he asked when the children had finished their meal.

"No, tell us, Papa." Jacob sat cross-legged, eyes bright with interest. Etta sat beside him, mirroring her brother's expression. "I want to swim, too. Will you teach me?"

"Sure. Every man, woman, and child should know how to save his own neck." Logan plucked a long blade of grass and chewed on it thoughtfully. "If every dumb beast made by God can swim, then it only makes sense mankind should learn. Soon as we're settled, I'll see to it that you both swim like fish." He winked, sealing his promise, then his gaze slipped to Susan. "What about you, black-eyed Susan? Can you swim?"

"I have a treat for dessert," Susan said, changing the subject obtrusively.

"What?" Etta asked.

"Mrs. Bumgartner . . . you remember the lady we stayed with three nights ago?"

"The one with the funny way of talking?" Jacob asked.

"Yes," Susan said. "She was from across the big ocean, from a place called Germany."

"Did she swim across the ocean?" Logan teased.

"I doubt it very seriously, don't you?" Susan retorted, unamused. "She gave me a can of peaches, and I'm going to open them right now for a sweet treat."

"Peaches!" Etta clapped and her eyes grew large. "Um-um. My favorite."

"Aw, everything's your favorite," Jacob complained. "She coulda said she was opening up a can of skunk tails and you woulda said they was your favorite."

Logan chuckled and ruffled his son's cottony hair.

"Nuh-uh," Etta said, shaking her head and making her blond curls dance. "Wouldn'ta done that."

Logan laughed again. "Let's eat the peaches and cease the fussing." He held out his plate to Susan. "Me first."

"Nuh-uh, Papa," Etta said, shoving her plate before his. "Me first, Aunt Susan. Ladies before gentlemen," she said, tipping up her chin. "Ain't that right?"

"*Isn't* that right, and yes, Etta, you should be served first." Susan spooned a peach half onto Etta's plate, then one onto Jacob's, and two onto Logan's. The gesture made him lift one brow and give a negligible nod.

"Much obliged," he murmured.

"You're welcome." Susan slipped a peach half from the jar and onto her own plate. A deep, rich golden color, the fruit glistened with its own sugary juices. She tasted the treat and rolled her eyes in satisfaction. Along the trail, she'd learned one thing about herself; she had a sweet tooth. A powerful one! Oh, how she missed her mama's cookies and cakes and fruit pies. When the generous Mrs. Bumgartner had insisted she take along a jar of her put-up peaches, Susan hadn't argued.

"These sure are good," Logan said, smacking his lips, then he looked off in the direction they'd take come sunrise. "We're gaining on Coonie."

"How can you tell?"

"By the ruts of the wagon. The grass is still pressed down in some places, meaning he's no more than a few hours ahead of us. We might meet up with him in a day or so unless we have some problems."

"Like what?"

A smile inched up one side of his face. "Nothing as terrible as you're imagining."

"And what do you presume I'm imagining?"

"My, my. Where'd you learn such high-sounding words? You're just like Catherine. She loved to show off her vocabulary, too. She was fond of pointing out that I wasn't the only wordsmith in the family. Of course, she couldn't write worth a damn. She was all talk."

"Must you curse in front of the children?" Susan scolded. "And kindly refrain from criticizing their mother and my sister. Allow her to rest in peace."

Logan regarded her with an expression bordering on stormy, but then clearing. Finally, he shifted his gaze to his children. "Ready to visit the sandman, baby?" He reached out a hand and touched Etta's dewy cheek.

"Not until you tell us the swimming story," Jacob reminded him.

"Yes, Papa, please." Etta snuggled against his side and raised cornflower-blue eyes to his face. "Tell, tell."

"All right," he said, sighing but pleased to be the center of attention. "I was just a whippersnapper, not much older than Jacob. My best friend in those days was a red-headed, buck-toothed boy named Arnie, and Arnie could swim. We'd go fishing, and Arnie would leap into the stream and show off. Me, I was scared if the water lapped higher than my knees, and that tickled Arnie no end. He called me all kinds of names."

"Did you punch him, Papa?" Jacob interrupted.

"Once in a while, but you can't go punching friends just because they're telling the truth. Truth was, I couldn't swim and he could. Finally, I asked him how he'd learned, and he told me a strange story about a preacher and a revival meeting."

Susan leaned closer to the fire, drawn by the warmth and by the twist Logan's story had taken. Firelight glimmered in his eyes like distant stars reflected in mossy water.

"Seems that Arnie's folks took him to a revival on the riverbank. A preacher—man called Brother Sal, short for Salvation—got all fired up during his sermon and pointed to Arnie and said, 'The power of the Lord is on this child. This child shall be saved and then this child shall float like a leaf upon the water.' " He paused to glance at each rapt listener before he continued. "Arnie's folks spoke up and said, 'Brother Sal, our boy here can't swim, and we love him and would hate it awfully if he was to drown, 'specially seeing as how he plays the banjo so pretty and helps around the farm if'n we threaten to apply the strap to him.' "

Susan rested her chin in one hand and covered her smile with her fingers. Logan looked at her, shared a moment of amusement, then moved Etta to one side so he could lay flat on his back and cradle his head in his palms. Etta curled next to him like a kitten, and Jacob inched closer so as to catch every raspy word.

"Brother Sal said not to worry. The hand of the Lord was on Arnie, and nothing harmful could touch him. A miracle was coming, and Arnie's parents would just have to back off and let it take its course."

"Did they?"

"Sure did. Arnie said you just didn't argue with Brother Sal and his miracles. The preacher man marched Arnie into the river, put one long, bony hand at the back of Arnie's head and the heel of the other on Arnie's forehead, and pitched him back into the river, baptizing him right and proper after he asked the right questions and Arnie gave the right answers. Then he told Arnie to close his eyes and think of the Lord. Arnie did." Logan let silence float down and settle before he went on. "He laid Arnie out flat on the water as if it wasn't water at all, but a hard surface. Arnie said he just lay there, pretty as you please, and floated like a water lily."

"He didn't sink to the bottom?" Jacob asked.

"Nope, he floated. Then Brother Sal flipped him over onto his stomach and he bobbed on the surface that way, too." Logan lowered his voice to a whisper and sought out his son's gaze. "It was a miracle. Arnie never sank after that and he was never afraid of water. He said he could do the same for me."

"And you let him?" Jacob asked.

"Well, not at first, but then I decided I'd give it a whirl. So Arnie took me out into the stream until we were waist-high in the water. He put one hand at the back of my head and one against my forehead, and back I went into the stream."

"And you floated," Jacob said, rising to his knees as he sensed the climax of the story.

"Not exactly," Logan said, chuckling as he propped his head up on one hand. "I purt near drowned and almost took Arnie with me. I flailed in that stream, treading water up to my waist, and Arnie got so scared he pushed me off him and scrambled to shore. There I was, suddenly in deep water, and taking it in like a leaky hull."

"Then what happened?" Jacob asked.

"It was right strange," Logan said, growing introspective. "I was scared stiff, and then it all kind of clicked in my head. A calmness came over me, a kind of peace . . . and I started breathing normal and just stretched out into a slow crawl across the water."

"Crawl?" Jacob interrupted.

"Yes, son. I began swimming like I'd done it my whole life. I swam to shore, and Arnie stood there with his mouth hanging open. Arnie said, 'You told me you couldn't swim,' and I told him I didn't think I could. Arnie proclaimed it another miracle."

"Was it a miracle?"

Logan blinked, coming back to the present. "Well, son, it's sure as shooting a miracle I didn't drown. Ever since that day I've been a natural-born swimmer."

"Papa, you're not going to dump me in the river like that, are you?"

"No, Jacob. We'll take it one step at a time, and before you know it you'll be swimming. Don't fret." He patted Jacob's shoulder, then looked at Susan. "We'll teach Aunt Susan while we're at it . . . and Etta, too."

"I didn't say I couldn't—" Susan bit off the rest, following Logan's pointing finger. Etta, still curled in a ball, was fast asleep.

"Time to hit the hay," Logan said, lifting Etta into his arms. "I'll tuck y'all in. Come on, Jacob."

Watching him put his two children to bed, Susan shook her head slightly in wonder. Never had she seen a man so gentle and openly loving with his offspring. Her own father didn't display his affection, but she was certain of his love all the same. Susan couldn't recall being hugged by her father, and she could count on one hand the number of cool kisses he'd bestowed over the years. Conversely, she couldn't count the times Logan had kissed Etta and Jacob in her presence. The gestures warmed her heart and made his attraction more deep-seated in her heart. Brushing off her thoughts, she gathered the soiled tin plates and readied to wash them.

By the time she'd finished, Logan had fed and watered the stock. He checked their ties, making sure they were securely staked out, then, with his back to her, he removed his shirt. Wadding it up, he ran it over his chest and shoulders, and around his neck. He reached up for the stars, stretching and groaning faintly as joints popped and corded muscles lengthened in his back.

Captured by the sight of his flexible spine arching and moving beneath his skin, Susan never thought to look away for modesty's sake. Pale light from the evening sky spilled over him. Shadows collected beneath his shoulder blades and in the small of his back. He flung his head back and closed his eyes. The snuffling of the team broke the quiet, followed by the hoot of an owl. Logan turned slowly, his gaze tracking the mottled sky, then dipping to come to rest on Susan. Inquiry floated in his eyes.

"Can I do something for you?"

She shook her head even as her thoughts answered him. *Yes, you can let me run my hands down your back to see if your skin is soft or rough or something in between.*

"Sleep well. I'm turning in."

"Logan . . ."

"Yes?" He looked sideways at her, pausing in half stride.

"Did you love my sister?" Where had that come from? she wondered, surprised by her question.

"I'm not allowed to speak her name, remember?"

She frowned at being caught in her own trap. "I asked you not to criticize."

"Why ask such a question. We were married, weren't we?"

"Yes, but sometimes people get married for reasons other than love."

"And you think I married Catherine for some other reason?"

"I'm asking."

"Why is it important?"

"Why won't you answer me?"

He hesitated. "My feelings for Catherine have nothing to do with you."

"She was my sister."

"And so?" He flung out a hand. "Go to sleep, Susan. Sticking your pert little nose into a wasps' nest is a bad idea."

"Wasps' nest? Your marriage was that?"

His gaze sliced through the gathering shadows. "My marriage is finished and so is this conversation. Good night." His fingers closed around his buckle and flipped the belt's tongue from its fastener. He gave a yank and the belt hung loose. His eyes glinted. His grin taunted. His fingers freed a button, then another.

Susan narrowed her eyes, resenting his ploy. "I suppose you think I'm a quivering little bird . . . that I'll fly into a fluttering ball of nerves every time you flaunt your masculinity." Folding her arms at her waist, she stood her ground. "Well, I won't be bullied by you, Logan Vance. If you're such an animal that you'd strip naked in front of a lady, then go right ahead. This lady won't squeal and hide her eyes. This lady will merely think her parents were right about you, after all."

His face changed to stone. For an instant she thought she'd gotten the best of him, but then he released that last button with a quick flourish and started to push down his brown trousers. Susan saw a patch of sable-colored curling hair before she spun around.

"Fly away, little bird," he said, a sneer in his voice. "Fly away."

Indignation pumped through her. Shooting him a glance over her shoulder, she saw that he hadn't removed his trousers, but they rode low, just at his hipbones. Susan faced him again and jabbed a finger near his square jaw. "Listen, I'm not afraid of see-seeing your . . . you. But I wish you'd show some manners. I'm here to help you."

"You're here to get away from your pappy."

"I wouldn't have had to travel to Indian Territory for that. Are you going to mind your manners or am I to be humiliated at every turn? Which is it?" She stamped one booted foot. "I demand an answer."

His first thought was to laugh in her face, tell her to simmer down and fix her bedroll while he did the same, but then he noticed how moonlight painted her parted lips and how her breasts strained the buttons on her single ruffled bodice. One button was halfway out of its slit. Impulsively, he tapped it with one finger and the disc slipped out all the way. She sucked in her breath when she saw what he'd done, then her gaze bounced up to his. Her eyes were bright, questioning, wonderfully alive. Firelight flickered over her face. Her tongue peeked out and slid across her lower lip. His self-control unraveled like a rag rug.

Gripping her upper arms, he growled in defeat before bringing her up to his mouth. He felt the shock pass through her. He swept his tongue across her cool lips, and her resistance wavered. Moving his hands up, he spread them at the sides of her head. Never had lips tasted so sweet. Like those damned peaches she'd served, sweet and syrupy. He lapped her up, unmindful of the tiny sounds of protest coming from her throat. When at last he lifted his mouth from hers and opened his eyes, he saw the flush of anger on her face. He let go of her and she retreated hastily, as if he were a beast. She backhanded her mouth, and he felt as if he'd been spit on.

"You can't wipe it off," he said. "And it wasn't that bad. You liked it."

"I did *not* like being licked like some newborn calf!"

His head jerked back. "Licked?" he repeated. A smile

spread across his face. "Susan Armitage, are you telling me you've never been tongue-kissed?"

Her color heightened. "Certainly not!"

He ran a hand across his lips, not rubbing her taste off, but rubbing it in. "You're such a child."

"I'm not."

"You think tongue-kissing is filthy, right?"

"It is."

"Then the world is chockful of filth, honey. Crammed full of it."

"Maybe your world. In my world, kisses are sweet and—"

"Chaste?"

"Well . . . yes."

"No passion, is that it?"

"There's passion."

"How can a kiss be passionate and chaste at the same time?"

"I don't know." She balled her hands into fists of frustration. "Why are we discussing such things? I'm tired. I'm going to bed." She would have charged past him, but he caught her elbow and pulled her up short at his side. "Please, Logan. Be a gentleman and let me go. We'll forget this happened."

"No, we won't." He liked the roundness of her chin and the dusting of freckles across the bridge of her nose. He released her and smoothed out the wrinkles he had put in her dress sleeve. "You know, Susan, ladies and gentlemen kiss with their tongues."

"No—"

"Yes," he interrupted with a hissing sound. "I'm sorry you didn't like my kiss, but I'm not sorry I kissed you. You're a sweet-tasting woman, Susan. I might need another nibble . . . another lick."

Her intake of breath whistled in her throat. Susan gathered her skirts and marched to the wagon and around to the other side to undress in private. She darted glances at either end, half expecting Logan to invade her makeshift dressing room, but she escaped the confines of her dress safely and, clad in her chemise and leggings, she scooted beneath the wagon where the children slept. After a while she heard Logan lie down and release a long sigh.

She stared into the darkness, her heart beating wild and free like a creature released from its cage.

The moon began to descend before Logan heard the deep breathing that meant Susan finally slept. Cradling his head in the crook of his arm, he stared up at the glittering night and wondered about himself.

A man figures he knows himself pretty well, and then something happens that makes him feel like a stranger in his own skin. Like tonight when he'd kissed Susan. He closed his eyes, recalling the shock of her mouth under his and the undisputed pleasure he'd taken from it. Sweat beaded on his forehead and his loins ached. Godamighty, he moaned to himself. This was a helluva mess, getting stiff over a girl who hadn't even been properly kissed until a few hours ago.

Not your type of woman, Vance, he told himself firmly. And she's an Armitage. Don't forget that. Haven't you had your fill of the Armitage females? Wasn't Catherine enough for you, man?

Guilt nudged his conscience. Shouldn't blame Catherine for everything, he thought. You weren't any prize yourself. You were just a lad thinking with his privates instead of his brain. A grin tugged at his mouth as he remembered what a ladies' man he'd been back when Catherine was just one of the many pretties trying to catch his roving eye.

He'd won the reputation of being a rounder, and by gum, he'd earned it. Once he'd discovered the pleasure beneath a girl's skirts, he'd made it his obligation to scout new territory at every opportunity. Becoming a proud papa hadn't been part of his plan, but it sure had been part of Catherine's. She'd been quick to point the finger in his direction the moment she decided she was with child.

His gaze slithered sideways to where the canvas flap hid Catherine's sister from him. If he didn't control his urges, she'd need more than a scrap of canvas to keep him off her.

Logan shut his eyes and counted sheep to keep from thinking of Susan . . . little, black-eyed Susan . . . all grown up with round breasts and hips and a mouth so delicious he . . . *oh, hell* . . . one, two, three, four . . .

Susan could hear the river long before she could see it glimmering in the near distance. Sunlight gilded its roiling surface, made violent by recent storms. The team perked up their ears and their strides lengthened as the smell of water reached their quivering nostrils.

Susan glanced over her shoulder to where Jacob and Etta slept in the back of the wagon. Their heads lolled with the movement. Perspiration beaded their brows and upper lips. Etta's hair was a mass of damp curls. Jacob's hair was wet near his face. They looked tired and flushed. The journey no longer held excitement and adventure for them, Susan thought. Both children had been bad-tempered all day, whining at every request, restless with boredom, anxious to be home—wherever that was, they wanted to be there immediately. But nothing was immediate on the overland trail. Everything took time. Everything moved slowly. Even the sun and moon seemed to creep across the sky.

Rain had kept them off the trail for two days. They'd found shelter in a barn, but being forced inside had made everyone edgy. One night Logan had even opted to sleep outside under the wagon, although the ground was damp and cold.

Now he walked ahead of the wagon, still the loner. He turned and pointed toward the river.

"Look there!" he called.

Susan half stood to see above a rise. The printer-loaded flatbed, drawn by oxen and driven by Coonie, stood on the bank of the boiling river. She nodded and gave a sweeping wave as Logan ran the rest of the way. Giving the reins more slack, Susan let the team have their heads. The wagon swayed from side to side, jostling pots and pans and making a terrible racket.

"What is it?" Jacob asked, rising up to look across the

plank seat. He rubbed his eyes with tender fists and blinked up at Susan. "Where's Papa?"

"Up ahead. We've caught up with Uncle Coonie."

"Uncle Coonie!" Jacob scrambled up to the seat and swung an arm over his head. "Hey, Uncle Coonie! Etta, wake up. Look at this river. It's yellow and brown."

"Where?" Etta yawned noisily and clung to Susan's shoulder to steady herself. Her blue eyes widened. "What a big river. How we gonna get across it, Aunt Susan?"

Susan knitted her brows. "I'm not sure, pumpkin, but I'm certain your father and Uncle Coonie know how." Approaching the river, she reined in the team before they got too close to the mossy bank. Coonie grinned, swept off his raggedy hat, and waved it over his head.

"Hi, y'all! Where's those chillens?"

"Here!" Jacob bounded from the wagon but paused long enough to help Etta down also, then he raced toward Coonie and threw himself into the man's arms. "I'm so glad to see you."

Susan set the brake and eased herself to the ground. Her muscles ached and her hands felt raw. She peeled off her gloves and studied the calluses forming at the base of each finger.

"Come look at the river, Aunt Susan," Etta called, and Susan joined the others.

The river lapped at the bank, making high water marks. A ways down, a tree had been washed from the bank and stretched out across the water, held to the shore by its gnarled roots, buried deep in the upturned soil. Susan glanced at Logan as a knot of fear formed in her stomach.

"We aren't going to cross it right now, are we?"

"No, that would be downright stupid." He removed his hat and ran his forearm across his perspiring brow. "We'll wait until tomorrow and see if it settles down some. It should by then, don't you think, Coonie?"

"Sure. This here won't last long. It'll be more gentle by tomorrow," Coonie said, lifting Etta for a kiss. "I'm ready for some supper. How about you, missy?"

"Me, too," Etta answered, looking toward Susan.

"What if the river is still high tomorrow?" Susan asked.

"Scared you might get wet and melt, sugar?" Logan asked with a devilish grin, then he patted his flat stomach. "Let's make camp. I'm so hungry I could eat a bear."

"I could eat a horse," Jacob said, falling in line with a comeuppance. It was a game Logan played often with his children.

"I could eat a ox," Etta chimed in.

"Well, I could eat a pack of wolves," Logan said, already striding toward the wagon to unhitch the team.

"And I could eat . . ."

The voices faded, and Susan stared at the raging river. It made sucking sounds against the bank, as if it were trying to gobble up the land. Fear made her shiver until tears stung her eyes. Even the devil himself couldn't make her cross it, she thought, setting her jaw until her gums ached. She'd rather face her death on firm land than drown in that whirlpool of muddy water.

Chapter 5

"Logan?"

Logan turned from tightening the harness straps. Susan stood just behind him, her hands clasped tightly against the front of her simple dress, worry pinching her forehead and mouth. He pushed his hat off his forehead with the back of his wrist and gave her his full attention.

"Something wrong with the children?"

"No," she said, quickly. "It's just that . . . well, I'd like a word with you before . . . before this goes any further." She felt like her mother confronting her father. When Mama asked to speak to Papa privately—using that same phrase, "I'd like a word with you"—Papa knew it was serious business, for Mama hardly ever questioned him or set forth her own opinions. Susan swallowed with difficulty. The sun seemed to burn through the top of her head, and she wished she'd put on her bonnet. An anvil-pounding pain erupted behind her right eye, and her vision blurred and focused with each pinging strike.

"Before what goes any further?"

"This river crossing."

Curiosity tipped his head to one side. "I'm listening."

How to begin? she wondered. A breeze tickled her skin and teased a strand of hair across her face. She pulled it aside, out of her eyes and from the corner of her mouth. His gaze followed her every move, making her doubly nervous.

"L-Logan," she said, gulping out his name, "I don't

55

want to cross that river. I think we should wait a few more days until it's less unruly. By the end of the week it ought to be much lower, tamer.''

"The end of the week?'' he repeated. "You're joking. We're not camping here for days. We'll cross this morning.''

"We'll all die.''

"I doubt it.'' He went around the team, shaking his head, laughing under his breath. He checked the harness again.

"I can't swim.''

Logan looked at her over the backs of the team. The sun probably wasn't the only reason for her red face. She jerked her chin at him, and her gaze skittered into the near distance.

"So there,'' she muttered, then, more firmly she added, "go ahead and gloat. Unless you have a miracle up your sleeve, I'll drown in that river.''

He ran his gloved hand along the back of the bay while he judged the best way to handle her. Fresh out of miracles, he figured he'd have to bully her. It had worked with him. He'd left out one part of his story the other night. Arnie had bullied him into the water before the "miracle'' had occurred. Being called scaredy-cat and chicken liver had goaded Logan into the stream, so maybe it would work with Susan.

"I'm not surprised,'' he murmured, just loud enough for her to hear. She sent him a scathing glare. He sighed loudly. "I knew you weren't cut out for this kind of trip. I tried to tell you, but you wouldn't listen.''

"I'll remind you that I've gotten along very well.''

"Until now.''

"I'm only saying we should wait until—''

"Takes a woman of courage to make a trip like this. A real woman. Young girls pretending to be grown up only get in the way.''

She unclasped her hands and positioned them on her hips. Her cheeks flamed with fury. "Are you saying I'm a gutless little girl?''

"If the shoe fits . . .''

"It doesn't!" She threw daggers at him with her eyes. "Just because I've got more sense than to try crossing a river that's—"

"Don't apologize. Most women don't have the backbone for a hard journey such as this. I figure I can double back and drop you off at the first homestead we come to, give the folks some money for a horse, and you can make your way back to your pappy, can't you?"

"You're sending me home because I want to wait a few days to—"

"Yeah, that's what I'll do," he interrupted deliberately. "Coonie can wait here with the children while I take you to—"

"You're not taking me anywhere, you big bully," she shouted, then sank her teeth into her lower lip, appalled by her outburst.

He came around the team. When he was close enough to see the sprinkling of freckles on her nose and cheeks, he stopped and looked down into her dark eyes. Her expression changed minutely from irritation to something more compelling—something sexual. He wanted to trail his forefinger down her cheek to her collarbone and along the slope of her breast. But he didn't. He couldn't. He was the bully, not the seducer.

"Are you going to cross the river with us or tuck your tail between your pretty legs and scamper back to the farm?"

Her features hardened. "You won't listen to reason?"

"I don't have time to coddle you, Susan. Either you're with us or not. I want to get across that river before high noon." He rocked his wide-brimmed hat on his head, anchoring it firmly. "Make up your mind. Time's a-wasting."

"If I fall—"

"You won't, but if you do, the water will most likely just reach your shoulders. It's not that deep where we're crossing."

"Yes, but it's deeper on either side of that place. I heard you tell Coonie earlier that the shallow part isn't much wider than the wagons."

"Just keep a firm grip on the reins and your balance. The team will do the rest."

"What if we get stuck?"

He batted aside her question. "And what if we don't? Whatever happens, I'll handle it." He looked toward Coonie and the children. "Y'all ready? Well, let's roll!" Then he swung his gaze back to Susan. "You going to drive the wagon?"

"Yes." She ground her teeth together and hoped she wouldn't cry. Choking back tears, she spun away from him and went to the wagon. Her feet felt weighted, and her headache increased with each step. Jacob and Etta climbed into the wagon with the eagerness of innocent youth, but Susan took her time. She placed her foot in the nook at the side of the wagon, grasped the handholds, and hauled herself up inch by inch.

Settling herself onto the hard seat, she released the brake and untied the reins. Fear gripped her heart with icy fingers. Looking straight ahead at the river, Susan shivered uncontrollably. Ever since she'd spotted the river, she'd seen it as an adversary. It wasn't the first water they'd crossed and those other streams and creeks had made her nervous, but they hadn't filled her with deathly dread like this river did. Maybe it was the color—rust and yellow and muddy brown. Maybe it was the eddying currents. Maybe it was the trees leaning crazily out over it, as if they were being sucked into its whirling, swirling depths. Every bit of good sense told her to wait . . . one day, two. Not today, a voice cried in her ear. Don't cross today.

But Logan's domineering censure rang more clearly in her ears. He'd accused her of not being woman enough for this trip—in other words, not being woman enough for him—and she couldn't let that go unchallenged. He'd pressed her into a position where she had to put aside her inclinations and prove to him she could stand up to him, toe to toe.

If she crossed that river with her life, then she'd never let him question her character again.

Coonie's flatbed went first. It was slow going, but the oxen were gentle, strong, and surefooted. The water lapped at their broad shoulders, but they never hesitated, just trod on. The flatbed creaked and groaned. Coonie shouted encouragement at the oxen and fought for his seating. Logan, ahead of the oxen and holding on to a long lead rope, had found a strip of higher land underwater and just off to one side of the oxen. He walked it and the water wet him above the knees. Sometimes he lost his footing along the uneven riverbed and dropped to where the water hit him under his arms, but he'd quickly scramble back up to the higher ledge. With his and Coonie's urging, the oxen followed to the opposite shore, methodically ignoring the swirling water that sometimes splashed mere inches from their wide nostrils. Susan admired their courage.

Half an hour later the oxen lunged onto shore, fought for footholds, and hauled the heavy flatbed out of the grasping mud. Once on firm land, Coonie swept off his ragged hat and let out a joyful whoop. Laughing with relief, Logan shook Coonie's hand, then crossed the river again, using the narrow strip of land. He took the children across first, one after the other. Jacob tried not to look afraid, but Etta put on no pretense. She hugged her father's neck tightly and kept her eyes shut until Logan set her down on the opposite shore.

Susan began shaking violently as Logan forded the river once again. He snapped the long lead rope onto her team's harness and sent her a squinty-eyed glance.

"Ready?"

"Logan, I don't want to do this."

"For crying out loud, Susan," he snapped, his tone cracking like a bullwhip. "If two children can cross the river, can't you?"

Yes, if I can wrap my arms around your neck and let you carry me across, she thought, but only stared at him, wishing it was over.

"Let's go." He tugged on the rope. "Susan, let up on the reins."

She did, her fingers reacting slowly, as if they were frozen. The wagon swayed, groaned, jingled. The team hesitated at the river's edge and Susan hoped they would rear and refuse to go in, but Logan clucked softly and the fool animals waded in.

"Susan, watch me."

Jerking her gaze up from the writhing water, she locked onto Logan's shadowed face. He looked older . . . no, he looked worried. And well he should be, she thought, but it was too late now. The draft horses plodded on. The water reached their flanks and squiggled over their broad backs. It was enough to make them nervous, especially when the uneven ground rocked the wagon, putting strain on the tongue. Halfway across, Susan began to relax. Gradually, the evidence of her senses broke through her numbing fear. The shore beckoned her, encouraged her. She would make it . . . just a little farther . . . Logan looked less worried. The lines in his face softened. He nodded, silently telling her to keep the faith.

The horses slowed, almost stopping. Logan tugged the rope and whistled, but the horses ignored him.

"Give them a little whip," he called to Susan. "A sting will do."

"Are you sure?" she asked, reaching for it.

"Pop it over their ears to get their attention. If they stop now the wagon might get stuck."

Hating to move, but seeing no way around it, Susan gripped the whip and stood up. She'd become proficient with the whip. A flick of her wrist sent out the coil of leather. The tip snapped at the air above the horses' heads. They snorted and powered through the water in a surge of energy. The wagon creaked as the wheels turned faster. Susan started to sit down when the right front wheel pitched downward, throwing her off-balance. For an instant, she thought she had regained control, then the wagon lurched again as the wheel burrowed out of the hole. Susan fell. She let go of the reins, afraid she might topple under the wheels and be crushed. A heavy wave slapped her in the face, knocking her breathless.

"Logan!"

Hardly aware she'd made a sound, she gathered in a lungful of air before the next blanket of muddy water spread above her head. The river pushed her along, tumbling her like a pile of dried weeds. Instinctively, she held her breath. Once she saw the sky and hauled in new air and some water with it. She coughed. More water ran up her nose. She flailed, thrashing and crying, her skirts impeding her, pulling her down, tying her up. As more water ran up her nose and down her throat, the fight went out of her and her limbs fell useless. The water pounded fists into her stomach, her shoulders, her head, but she felt less and less. She floated . . . floated away from that menace to a place of warmth and light. No longer afraid of the ugly, raging river, she became one with it. It couldn't hurt her anymore.

Wait . . . What was that just ahead . . . The tree was alive and—ouch!

Pain radiated through her scalp and she reached up in an instinctive gesture. Her grappling hands encountered flesh and muscle. Sensations came flooding back, brought to life by the pain. Fingers wound in her hair and yanked again. She screamed. Another hand grabbed her sleeve, tore it, clutched at her shoulder, then slipped to hook under her chin. The current pulled her, but the hands kept her from skimming along like a leaf downriver.

From a distance she heard her name . . .

"Susan! Hold on to me, Susan."

Sobs ran through the voice calling out to her. She looked up and saw a face hovering in the blue sky like a misplaced moon.

"Grab me," the moon said and produced a hand, an arm.

Susan didn't think she had arms or hands anymore . . . she belonged to the river. But then the moon's face came closer and it wasn't a moon after all. It was Logan.

"Logan!" The voice came winging out of her like a bird, high and flutey. She disengaged one arm from the river's grasp and offered it to him. He grabbed her, got a better hold under her arm, and lifted, strained, groaned in agony.

Little by little, Susan felt the river surrender her to Logan. She made her choice, wanting Logan far more than the river's cold embrace. Her fingers clutched, her nails dug in. Life flowed back into her body, and she began shivering and then fighting to keep that living pulse within her. She grappled for a better hold. Cloth tore beneath her fingers, but then she found a wedge of shoulder, a column of neck. She wrapped her arms around that neck. Logan's arm circled her waist, and the river relinquished its prize.

"Logan, Logan," she chanted, drawing life from saying his name and feeling the warmth of his skin beneath her cold lips.

"Easy, darlin'." His voice acted like warm honey on her, soothing and enveloping. "Hold on, sugar."

"Never let go," she murmured. "Never, ever let go."

"Watch out. Let me . . . that's right, watch that tree limb."

Limb . . . where? Everything was black. Susan realized her eyes were tightly shut. When she pried them open she saw green. Splashes of green with bars of brown. The world focused, tilted upright again, and she realized she was on a fallen tree and holding on to Logan for dear life as he climbed with her through the scratchy branches. She glanced toward the river, seeing how the tree slanted out over it, held ashore by roots as thick as a man's forearm. Logan had climbed out on its limbs and grabbed her as she went sailing past.

Her scalp tingled, triggering another realization. He'd caught her by the hair of her head! That could only mean she'd been an inch away from oblivion . . . from death.

She cleaved to him, shaking until her teeth chattered. He grunted, shifted her, and then she felt solid ground touch the soles of her feet. Where had her boots gone? Someone caught her before she could crumple to the bed of grass. She heard Coonie's voice, then Etta's hysterical crying in the distance.

"Etta . . . something's wrong with her," Susan mumbled.

"She's just scared for you," Coonie told her.

"She's hurt . . ." A burning raced up her throat, and her whole chest and stomach constricted and heaved up the river's residue. She fell forward, expelling the vile poison. Someone stretched her out so that she lay on her stomach, then pressed her cheek into the cool clover. Warm liquid spilled from her mouth and tickled her lips. Gentle fingers wiped aside the rest and patted her clammy cheek.

"Better?"

She nodded, responding to the voice, grateful to hear it again. Logan. Logan.

"Jacob, see to your sister. Coonie, you hold the lead rope and I'll drive the wagon. We've got to get it out of that damned river."

"Close call, sure 'nuf," Coonie said as he spooned beans into a bowl and handed it to Logan. "Should we wake her up for these vittles?"

"No, let her sleep." Logan set the bowl aside and started to tug off his rawhide gloves. That's when he saw the tenacious, curling strands of hair clinging to the base of his middle finger.

"I'm turning in, if you don't mind."

"What?" Logan blinked up at Coonie, standing over him. "Oh, sure. Go ahead. I'll eat a bit and then I'll be resting my head, too."

"You did a good thing today, boy," Coonie said, giving a wink. "Your fast thinking saved that gal's life."

"I was the one who put her life in danger in the first place."

"Oh, hell. Could have happened to me, too. Any time you ford a river, you risk your neck. See you on the morrow."

Logan nodded, his attention captured again by those stubborn strands of Susan's hair. A shade lighter than his gloves, the strands had stayed put all this time—through his rescue of Susan, his driving the wagon and spooked horses the rest of the way out of the river, the unhitching, the preparation for camp—through all this they'd stayed put.

He carefully pulled them from around his finger and examined them in the firelight. Gingery brown. So slender, so frail, yet they'd stuck with him. Like her.

His gaze lifted from the strands to their owner. She slept

like a child, her hands stacked beneath her cheek, her body curled in a ball, her lashes fanning her lightly freckled skin. Was she freckled all over? he wondered, fingering the three long hairs that he'd pulled from her head.

He shuddered. God, he'd come within a hair's breadth of losing her. If he'd been a fraction of an instant late, he'd have missed her. He'd been damned lucky to get a handful of her hair as it had streamed under him where he'd stretched out on the fallen tree trunk, out over that gulping, grasping, sonofabitchin' river.

His first instinct when he'd seen her disappear underwater had been to dive in after her, but his good sense had intervened, making him see in that split second that he'd be no good to her trying to keep himself from drowning while that churning, murky water ate her up. That's when he'd raced along the shore, screaming her name, praying and cursing all at once, and then flinging himself onto the tree, scrambling out to its furthermost branches . . . plunging down one hand, stretching his fingers until he thought they'd leap from his hand. Grabbing nothing the first few times, then getting her hair.

Even then he'd tasted defeat. How could he hold on to her by the hair of the head? But miracle of miracles! He'd impeded her swift progress downriver, and her hands had shot up as she'd reacted to the pain he'd inflicted, so he'd given another yank. She'd reached up again, and he'd grabbed her with his free hand while he'd held himself on the tree branch by gripping it with his knees and thighs. He'd found her wrist, lost it . . . the other wrist, gone . . . her sleeve . . . her arm . . . hooking under her chin. That's when he knew he'd get her out of that monster river.

Glancing up at the star-pocked heavens, he murmured a prayer of gratitude. If he'd lost her . . . if he'd found her a day later washed up on the bank like debris . . . he'd have gone out of his ever-loving mind. The close call had left him with a few strands of her hair, a renewed faith in a supreme power, and an outbreak of undeniable desire for his former sister-in-law.

Before, it had been a mere attraction, a pondering of

the unknown, but not now. Not after the river. She was under his skin, festering in his mind, burning in his groin. Like a fever, he couldn't shake her, couldn't deny her existence. She'd have to run her course.

He held up the strands and let the puffing breeze sail them into the night. He needed no reminder of his river battle.

When he looked at Susan again, her eyes were open. She was staring at him. His heart kicked.

"Susan?"

"Yes," she answered with a croak.

"Hungry?"

"No." Her voice was raw. "I feel . . . limp."

"You rest. Go back to sleep."

"The children . . . Are they . . . ?"

"Safe and asleep." He glanced around and spotted Coonie's shape beneath the other wagon. "As is Coonie. I'll be turning in as soon as I get some food down me." He picked up the bowl and spooned some of the flavorful beans into his watering mouth.

"It's late, isn't it?"

"Yes. We're running behind tonight." He smiled. "Had us a busy day, didn't we?"

She didn't smile. Her eyes filled with tears. Logan set aside the bowl of beans and crossed the space between them on all fours. He sat down and pulled her into his arms.

"Don't cry, sugar. You're all right." He stroked her hair, still damp and heavy from the river. "I'm so damned sorry, Susan. I shouldn't have been so blasted bullheaded about crossing—"

"I was scared . . . I almost died. I felt it, Logan. Felt myself slipping toward the hereafter, but you pulled me out of it."

"Damned right." He gripped her shoulders and pushed her back until he could see her tearstained face. The fire cast an orangy glow, giving her eyes a flickering light; distant candles in a black night. "I wasn't going to let you get away from me." Tears burned the backs of his eyes. "God, Susan! To think how close I came to—" He pulled her to him again, circling her with his arms, kissing the top of her head. "I can't think about it or I'll go crazy."

She tipped back her head. The candle flames in her eyes burned brighter. "Thank you, Logan. I wasn't ready to die."

"Susan, oh, Susan." He kissed her lips lightly. They felt warm, soft, giving. He kissed her again, and she snuggled more deeply into his embrace. He wanted to taste her with his tongue, but he refrained. Her lips became pliant, her body limp. He lifted his head. She made a soft, whimpering noise.

"I'm so tired. My arms and legs feel so heavy, Logan." She rested her cheek against his shoulder.

After a minute he knew she slept soundly. When he carried her to her bedroll, she hardly moved. When he slipped her under the top cover and tucked her in, she smiled faintly and sighed. When he kissed her once more, she didn't kiss him back. She never knew. Never knew that he looked at her for a long while or that his eyes brimmed with emotion or that he ached with a delicious torture he hadn't felt in— Christ! So long ago he couldn't remember. He ran a hand down his face, suddenly hot, suddenly tight and throbbing inside his trousers.

He turned away and walked a distance from the wagons. There were times when a man needed to be alone, away from prying eyes and knowing smirks. After a spell, he returned to the wagons, limp but far from being sated.

Chapter 6

"We're stopping earlier than usual," Susan said, climbing from the back to the front of the wagon where Logan sat, reins in hand.

"Yes, but I reckon you could use the rest after your ordeal yesterday. No need to push you beyond good sense." He set the brake and wound the reins around it.

"I'm fine, Logan." She pushed her bonnet back to run a hand over the top of her head. "We can press on for another hour. It can't be much farther to the Territory."

"We're in the Territory."

"We—we are?" She made a slow perusal of the area, noting a gray-timbered shack and no sign of inhabitants.

"We should get to Tulsey Town sometime tomorrow, so we'll make camp early tonight. Besides, we might not find a better place than this." He motioned toward the crudely built house, then jumped down from the wagon. "And Coonie might catch up with us if we make camp early."

"That cabin looks deserted," Susan said, letting Logan help her down.

"Made to order," he said, smiling. He lifted Etta from the wagon to the ground, and she and Jacob took off toward the cabin. "I reckon Coonie is no more than four or five hours behind us."

"I still don't know why we can't hold back and travel together."

"Because I'm raring to go, that's why." He grinned

67

and chucked her under the chin. "I'm not one to hang back and wait for someone."

"So I've noticed, but now that we're in . . . well, Indian country, shouldn't we travel together for safety?"

"Two wagons are more noticeable than one," he pointed out.

"But not as vulnerable," Susan tacked on.

"To a raiding party, I doubt it would make much difference." He shot her a meaningful glance, then motioned toward the cabin. "Let's see to our accommodations."

She looked in the direction they'd come. "It's slow going for poor Coonie," she murmured, thinking of him and his sturdy oxen-driven wagon with its precious cargo of printing press, barrels of ink, and rolls of paper. "I worry so about him."

"I'm sure he'd be touched," Logan drawled, yanking a handkerchief from around his neck and scrubbing his face with it.

"Aunt Susan, come see the house," Etta called from the doorway, and Susan crossed the grassless yard. The porch was no more than two hands wide. The door was sturdy, a good six or eight inches thick, and a heavy beam propped just inside had been used to bar it.

Light filtered through a multitude of cracks in the walls and ceiling, illuminating the empty interior of the one-room cabin. Cots were built along the walls. The fireplace grate gaped empty and gray like the cupboards above a bare plank table.

"No spiders or bugs," Etta announced, giving the cabin her approval. "I want this bed." She patted the cot nearest the door.

"All yours, pumpkin," Susan promised, turning around to look outdoors again. Elm and cypress trees rimmed the clearing. A flowering bush grew at the corner of the cabin, its pale pink blossoms adding a touch of civilization. "I wonder who lived here?" Susan asked as Logan drew near. "It has a woman's touch."

"I'm grateful to whoever it was," he said, eyeing the sky. "Storm clouds are building. Looks like we might get rain tonight." He glanced at her from beneath knitted brows. "How are you feeling . . . honestly?"

"Honestly, I'm fine." She squared her shoulders. "A little sore here and there, but that's all. Of course, I'll never again look at a river without sending up a prayer." When he moved to lay a hand on her shoulder, she edged sideways away from him. "Don't, please."

Logan stared at his hand in mid-air and wondered when his touch had become abhorrent to her, then let it drop to his side. "Can't the man who saved your life touch you?"

Susan kept her gaze locked on the horizon, but her pulses drummed incessantly. The demons in her cried out for him, but a calmer voice reminded her of the promise she had made to herself last night after the dream . . . after seeing Catherine. "I dreamed last night of Catherine. She spoke to me."

Propping a hand high on the door facing, Logan cocked his head and peered curiously at her. "And what did Catherine have to say?"

"She shamed me for allowing you to—no, for *encouraging* your attentions. You're her husband and I—"

"I'm not her husband anymore," he interrupted. "Your sister is dead."

She shot him a quelling glare. "But her memory isn't, and I must honor it. I'm so ashamed for having let you—" She shook her head and tried a different tack. "What we're doing is wrong."

"What are we doing?"

"Don't be so pigheaded. We're dallying with each other."

His laughter brought a smoking look from her. He ran a hand down his face, wiping off his grin. "Dallying? Sorry, but I never thought of it as that. It's only natural for us to get closer." He lowered his voice to a purr as his thoughts dipped below his belt. "I'm a man, you're a woman, and we have our natural urges."

She cut him another stinging glance. "Nature is what man is meant to rise above."

"I bet your papa told you that."

She moved outside and motioned to arrest her nephew's attention. "Jacob, will you gather firewood?"

"Okay," Jacob called back, then grabbed Etta's hand, and they ran toward the edge of the woods.

"Be careful," Susan called after them. "Perhaps you should go with them, Logan."

"I think you're trying to get rid of me."

"Logan, please don't keep trying my patience."

He grimaced, hating it when she scolded him as if he were one of her charges. Someday she'd push him too far, shake a finger in his face once too often, treat him like a boy one time too many, and he'd—

"I've told you that I want this . . . this behavior between us to stop," she said in that matronly way that made his blood boil. "Catherine appeared to me last night as a caution, and it restored my good sense."

He checked an impulse to take her into his arms and teach her a lesson in good sense and human nature. Thinking she'd been through enough lately, he tamped down his baser instincts.

"I'll check on the children," he said, striding past her, teeth gritted, hands balled into fists. Damn her, she was testing him. Surely she had better sense than to talk to a grown man in that superior tone of voice. It might work with the children, but it made him want to give her a good shaking and then kiss her until she begged for mercy.

"While you're out there, why don't you— Logan!"

He whirled, her panic-laden tone chilling him. Susan pointed, and Logan saw a lone figure astride a spotted horse in the distance. The Indian was so still, he nearly blended into the woods. Only the colors of his painted face and beaded necklaces and armbands separated him from the backdrop of brown and green.

Logan motioned Susan back. "Get into the house and close the door." He glanced toward his children. Their voices floated from the dense woods. He whipped his head back toward the intruder. "Etta! Jacob! Come here right now."

"In a minute, Papa," Jacob called from the shadows.

"Right now!" Logan shouted. His heart pounded,

climbing into his throat. From the corner of his eye, he saw his children. Jacob held an armload of sticks and twigs. Etta carried bunches of wildflowers in her chubby fists. "Get into the cabin. Do as I say! Susan, let the children in with you." His knees began to shake, but he forced one foot in front of the other toward the wagon where his rifles rested under the seat. Stupid to be caught out in the open with no weapon, he cursed himself. How do you expect to protect your family with no gun or knife within easy reach?

The Indian stared at him, motionless. The Indian's pony swished its white tail, stamped its front hooves. Logan heard the cabin door open and close behind him. He breathed easier, knowing the others were no longer targets. Now if he could just get his hands on one of those rifles, he wouldn't feel like such a damned fool. But before he could reach the wagon, the Indian reined his mount around and disappeared into the shadows of the woods.

Logan's breath whistled down his throat, and a cold sweat coated him. He looked around, expecting savages to burst from the cover of the trees, but only the call of the whippoorwill disturbed the smothering calm. His eyes felt as if they were straining, bulging from their sockets. Grit grated on his tongue. He spat. His mouth was so dry, only a drop of moisture flew out. The door behind him creaked, and Logan glanced back. Susan's face appeared in the opening. Her eyes were huge, dark, glittering.

"Logan?" Her voice shook with uncertainty.

"Stay inside," he cautioned. "He's gone, but I'm not sure he won't be right back."

"Come inside with us," Susan begged.

Logan removed two rifles from under the wagon seat and propped them against a nearby tree. "After I've unhitched the team."

"Logan—"

"Do as I say, Susan," he said, glaring at her until she shut the door. Only then did he cast another worried glance around him. Where had that scout gone? he wondered, flinching at every movement. Was he gathering the rest of his raiding party, or had he decided to let this white inter-loper live to see another sunrise?

Logan unhitched the team and staked them near the cabin. He unloaded necessities from the wagon, all the while keeping an eye out for painted faces or spotted po-nies. He busied his mind with scenarios of how he would defeat the Indians should they decide to attack, but in his gut he knew he'd be a sitting duck. Maybe the settlers who had built this rickety cabin had been driven away by Indians . . . or slaughtered by them.

Standing outside the door, he took a moment to control his imagination and his niggling fear. He couldn't let Su-san or the children know how vulnerable he felt. He had to be their fortress.

"Open up," he ordered, and the door swung back as if Susan had been standing right behind it, poised to fling it ajar at the slightest sound. Looking past her, he saw his children's frightened expressions. "It's all right. He's gone. He was just curious about us, like we are about him. Here you go, Susan." He handed her a burlap sack with some potatoes and onions in it. "I'll get that fire going and you can start cooking."

"Can we go outside and play?" Jacob asked.

"No." Logan heard the sharpness in his voice and smiled to lessen it. "It'll be dark soon. Stack the wood in the fireplace, son."

Susan's glance told him she saw through his excuses. She helped him bring in the other things from the wagon; blankets, pillows, a chunk of fatback for the soup kettle, the coffeepot, plates and utensils, two canteens full of wa-ter.

The chores kept them busy enough so that they didn't have to make eye contact or conversation. Susan and Lo-gan peeled potatoes and onions while Etta and Jacob stacked the wood and arranged the bedding on the cots. Susan dumped the vegetables, meat, and water into the cooking pot to boil for trail soup. She wished for the jar of honey and hunk of bread in the wagon, but she wasn't about to send Logan out for them.

Logan spread a blanket on the floor in front of the fireplace and set the plates and spoons on it. The only sound was the bubbling of the soup pot and the crackle of the fire. Susan tried to breathe quietly, her ears tuned for any sounds outside. When Logan laid a hand on Susan's shoulder, she almost screamed.

"Isn't the soup done?" he asked, smiling at her show of nerves.

"Uh . . . yes." She dipped the soup into the deep tin plates. An owl hooted, and Etta began to cry. "Pumpkin, come here to me." Susan took the child into her arms and rocked her back and forth. "It's all right, sweetie. Nothing bad is going to happen to us."

"Then why aren't we talking?"

Susan smoothed Etta's pale hair back from her face. "We're tired. Aren't you?"

"Kinda."

"Come on, sweetie." Susan stood up with Etta in her arms and crossed the room to the cot Etta had claimed. "I'll tell you a story my mother told me when I was your age. It's about a little girl and her echo. Did you know you're never alone because your echo is always with you?"

While she told Etta the story, Logan cleared the dishes and helped Jacob undress and get into bed. He shared the cot with his son, crossing his arms over Jacob's chest, pulling him against him, thinking how fragile the boy felt. In the inconstant light cast by the bed of embers, shadows danced on the walls and ceiling. Across the room, Susan spun her tale to a droopy-eyed Etta. Logan propped his chin on top of Jacob's towhead and listened to Susan's lilting voice. The story was lost on him, but he enjoyed the expressions flitting across the narrator's face.

Susan had the most charming face, he thought drowsily, for the moment forgetting the danger that might lurk outside. Even when she was blessing him out or talking nonsense about dreams of Catherine, she charmed and beguiled. His memory of her near drowning roused him, jolted him awake. He realized he'd dozed off and had entered into a dreamlike re-creation of that river and of Susan floating past him, away from his clutching fingers.

She'd finished her story. Etta slept soundly. Jacob

snored softly. Logan looked across the room at Susan. She smiled. His groin tingled to life.

"I hope Coonie's all right," she whispered.

Coonie? He smiled to himself, finding it ironic that he was consumed with thoughts of her while she worried about another man. "He can take care of himself."

"Can we?"

"Sure," he said, placing confidence in the word.

"Don't you want to look outside and see if . . . if anyone's out there?"

"Not particularly."

She sighed and eased up from the cot, careful not to disturb Etta. "Well, I do."

"Susan, no." He extended a detaining hand and shook his head. "Don't be stupid. Leave well enough alone." He nodded toward the empty cot. "Go to sleep."

"How?" She held out her hands in appeal. "I can't sleep with savages roaming outside."

"Shhh," he cautioned, glancing at his son. "Simmer down, will you?" Grimacing, he inched away from Jacob and lifted himself from the narrow cot. "I'm going to stay outside in the wagon and keep watch."

"No!" She patted the air. "You don't have to do that. Just check outside and come back in."

"You sleep." He pointed to the cot again. "And leave the worrying to me. I'm better at it."

"Logan, you'll come back inside?"

"Yes." He grabbed one of the rifles and opened the door. "In the morning. 'Night, Susan. Sweet dreams. Tell Catherine howdy if you see her."

"You aren't in the least bit funny, Logan Vance."

He laughed in her face before slamming the door behind him. Outside, rain fell in buckets.

"Sonofabitch," Logan ground out, getting soaked to the skin before he could bound to the shelter of the wagon. He scrambled in under the oiled canvas. Shaking water from his hair, he frowned at his situation. Being the brave hero was a pain in the ass.

* * *

"Susan, wake up." Logan bent over Susan's sleeping form and shook her awake.

"What's wrong?"

"Nothing yet, but we've got to get."

"It's so dark . . ." She blinked, trying to see his face, but all she could make out was his shadow.

"We've got to be gone before it gets light. Now shake a leg, girl!" He barked the last like an officer to a greenhorn volunteer. She sat bolt upright, alert and shivering from the cool, damp night.

"The Indians—they're still out there?"

"Not far from here. I can hear their drums. I figure they're waiting for dawn to sweep in here and rid this earth of us, so help me get the children into the wagon. For Christ sake, *move!*"

He grabbed her by the arm and yanked her out of the cot. She did the rest, stumbling over to the children and lifting Etta from the tumble of bedclothes. The girl mumbled fretfully.

"Hush, pumpkin. Go back to sleep." Susan hummed a lullaby as she carried the child outside where Logan had already hitched the team to the wagon. She hesitated, realizing the ground was spongy from a soaking rain. The air smelled damp. A mist hovered around her face. She climbed up to the seat and put Etta in the back. Logan followed close behind with Jacob.

Logan went back for the bedding, having already loaded the rest. The darkness pressed in on Susan, thick and cool like winter molasses. A steady beating thrummed in the air, occasionally accompanied by a deep growl of thunder. Susan's heart tapped out its own beat, faster than the distant one. She looked toward the cabin and was relieved when Logan emerged from it, his arms full of blankets and quilts. He dumped them into the back of the wagon, then climbed up beside Susan.

He pulled a matchstick from his shirt pocket and struck it on his pant leg. A pulse throbbed just below his right ear. His lips thinned into a straight line of tension. He tossed the flame toward the cabin.

"Logan, what are you—" The rest died abruptly as the

spark touched off a winding path of black powder in the yard. The team threw up their heads and skittered sideways, but were held fast by Logan's firm grip on the reins.

Gazing past him, Susan watched the fire race through the gunpowder and scorch the earth. When it fizzled, a message stood out against the brown soil—INDIANS.

"Clever," she said, glancing at Logan. "That's for Coonie?"

"Right."

"Won't the Indians rub it out?"

"I doubt any can read it."

She nodded, glad someone was using his head, hers being stuffed with cottony fear. Logan clucked and snapped the reins, and the horses moved forward at a fast walk.

"The farther we get from here, the better I'll like it," Susan whispered.

"Reach under the seat and grab one of those rifles."

"What's wrong with that one?" she asked, elbowing the firearm propped between them.

"Nothing, but I'm going to use it. You need one of your own."

"Me?"

"You planning on sitting there and letting me take on all those Indians by myself?"

"Logan, you're scaring me."

"Good, then arm yourself and quit acting like a helpless female, which you keep saying you aren't." He delivered what he hoped was a biting glare. "If you're such an independent woman, prove it!"

Setting her jaw stubbornly, she pulled a rifle from under the seat and held it as if it were a rattlesnake.

"I thought you were familiar with firearms."

"I am."

He gave her a derisive once-over. "Oh, sure. I can see that."

Susan set the butt between her feet and wrapped one hand around the shaft, then she arched one brow at her intimidating companion. "There, Mr. Boss Man. That better? Is that more to your persnickety liking? I don't see why it's so all-fired important how I hold this old thing as long as I can shoot it.''

"That's what's got me worried. I'm wondering just how straight you can shoot. In fact, I'm thinking you don't know your ass from a hole in the ground when it comes to weaponry.''

Incensed by his goading, she braced the rifle butt against her shoulder, took a bead on a bush of white blooms, and with one squeeze of her trigger finger, scattered petals from here to kingdom come.

"Holy Moses, girl!'' Logan jerked as if he'd been the one she'd blown to bits. "What in the hell do you think you're doing?''

"Showing you I'm no liar,'' she said, calmly lowering the rifle butt to the floor between her feet again.

"Papa, what was that? Where we going?'' Jacob grumbled behind them.

"What are you shooting at?'' Etta wailed.

"Go on back to sleep, chickens,'' Susan said, turning to give the children reassuring pats. "We're heading for our new home. Everything's fine, pumpkin.'' She shifted to face the draft horses again. "I don't like having my word doubted.''

Logan regarded her for a few moments. "You know, Susan, sometimes you scare me. I mean, here we are trying to sneak off before the Indians get wind of it, and you go firing off a damned rifle. You act like you don't have a lick of sense.''

"And you act like you think I'm a cross you have to bear,'' she charged hotly. "I'm trying to do my best, and all I get from you is scorn and ungraciousness. You think it's easy for me to be out here in the wilds with the likes of you and the children? Believe me, it's not. Half the time I'm so scared I don't know which end is up, and you don't help matters by yelling and ranting and raving or messing with me like I'm a bought woman.''

"Like you're a what?'' He laughed at that, having never thought of her in those terms.

"You heard me.''

"I sure did. I'm just having trouble following you. The

problem with you is, you're so green you don't know gold dust from sawdust. If I treated you like a bought woman I would've tolerated your sassy mouth about two seconds before shutting it up.''

"How, by hitting me?" She pursed her lips in distaste. "Don't you dare lay a hand on me. You should be ashamed of yourself for making such idle threats."

That did it. She'd scolded him once too often. He tugged on the reins, tied them off around the brake lever, and twisted around to face her. She glared at him from the corner of her eye, regarding him as she would a disobedient child.

"Why are we stopping? This is no time to—"

"To hell with it. I'm going to shut you up right here and now. You've blessed me out the last time, Susan honey."

Then, before she could stiff-arm him, he pinned her arms against her sides and lowered his thirsting mouth to hers. Passion overtook him, blocking out everything else. He was hot—burning up for her. Taking no notice of her squeak of protest, he laved her lips with his tongue. She gasped and gave him the opening he sought. His tongue arrowed into her mouth, and she let out a strangled cry of alarm that only heightened his determination to master her, to make her writhe with wanting, to make her lust for him as he lusted for her.

Chiefly, he wanted to teach her a lesson. He wanted to make her understand the ways of men; that a man would rather be pistol-whipped than pussy-whipped, that he'd rather take the high road than be nagged about things that didn't amount to a hill of beans, that he wasn't something to be played with or teased or tempted to no end, that he'd rather take a beating than be mocked by a woman. She had to understand her own womanly powers and how they could be used to mold him into the man she wanted, but she couldn't force him to toe the line by throwing guilt and piousness in his face. That only made him mad. That only spurred him to dominate her, teach her who's boss, act the bully to her shrew. That kind of behavior brought out the beast in a man, not the best.

Catherine had been the queen bee at stinging retorts and blistering lectures. As much as he liked Susan, Logan knew he wouldn't—*couldn't*—put up with another woman like Catherine.

He continued his exploration of the inner walls of her mouth, so smooth and sleek, and ignored her frantic wriggling and arched back. He kissed her again and again, never giving her more than a moment to gather in a breath before he reclaimed her mouth. By the fourth or fifth kiss, her resistance ebbed. She wilted like a flower in his arms. He lifted his mouth to look into her eyes, eyes as dark and velvety as black pansies. Questions floated in their inky depths. He sensed her wonderment, her bewilderment, and the beginnings of her enlightenment. Her tongue peeked out to mop up some of the juice his kisses had left. Logan felt himself press against his fly. He shifted on the plank seat uneasily as the pressure built.

"That's better," he whispered and smoothed a tendril of hair back from her forehead. "If you and I are ever going to see eye to eye, we've got to get a few things straight—"

"Logan—"

"Don't talk. Listen."

"B—behind you . . ."

Then he noticed she wasn't looking at him at all, but just past his shoulder. Danger ran down his spine like a droplet of ice-cold water. He glanced at the rifles, then he heard the distinct double-action of a rifle being cocked. Logan rotated his head slowly, forcing himself to confront whoever had him in the cross hairs.

Chapter 7

He was the biggest Indian Logan had ever seen. Sitting astride a handsome, black stallion, the Indian was close enough that Logan could have easily reached out and patted the animal's muzzle, if he were fool enough to do such a thing.

With hair the color of gunmetal and ash-gray eyes, he was no trigger-happy young buck. Time lines wreathed his leathery face. His clothes gave testimony to clashing cultures. A beaded, multicolored chest covering was topped with a black coat any English gentleman would have been proud to wear. The coat had pearly buttons, several of which were missing. Beads and feathers stuck out here and there from his twin braids. A black derby covered the top of his head. Fancy fringe ran down the sides of his buckskin breeches, and his knee-high moccasins looked buttery soft and pretty enough for a lady to wear, with their silver studs and blue and red beading.

Brass tacks formed a cross on the butt of his Winchester saddle carbine. His aim never wavered, but a gentling around his mouth made Logan less afraid. When the Indian's gaze moved to Susan, his expression softened even more. In fact, Logan thought he saw amusement lurking in those widely spaced, eagle-sharp eyes.

Logan lifted his hands slowly to show his powerlessness. "Take it easy, old-timer," he said, knowing the Indian probably had no concept of English, but hoping his tone of voice would convey a message of peace. "We're not out to do you any harm." He could see his own rifle

80

from the corner of his eye, but he knew he'd be a dead man if he made a move for it.

"Is he going to kill us?" Susan asked, her voice little more than a wisp of sound. "He looks mean with that red paint over the lower half of his face."

"Just be still," Logan told her from the corner of his mouth. "Hey, partner," he addressed the Indian again and tried to smile. "Why don't you lower that rifle and we'll be giddy-upping." He patted the air, making a downward motion. "Put it down, pal. Down. Put . . . it . . . down. No shoot. No hurt. We go now." He frowned, perplexed to have been reduced to stilted English.

"Logan, he can't understand you."

"Maybe he'll understand we're scared shitless and aren't any threat to him. If there's no sport in killing us, he might—"

"Where you headed?"

The Indian's booming voice, like cannon fire, startled Logan and produced a squawk of alarm from Susan. Logan patted her knee, and Susan placed her hands over her mouth to trap any further outcries.

"Uh . . ." Logan swallowed hard, befuddled by the Indian's command of the language. For a confusing moment, he couldn't think of one word, then it all came flooding back to him. "Tulsa—Tulsey Town. In the Territory. It's near here. Not far from the river, I'm told and—"

"Just over that rise," the Indian said, nodding in the general direction. "Where'd you come from?"

"Uh . . ."

Susan took her hands from her mouth. "Missouri." Was she actually talking civilly to a savage? A knot of fear formed in her throat, but she forced her voice past it. "Where did *you* come from?"

Incredibly, the Indian smiled. "I live near here. You his wife?"

"No, I'm his sister-in . . . that is, I'm his *former* sister-in-law." Susan cocked her head, struck by concern. "Can you understand that?"

"You bet. I got 'em, too, but I don't kiss 'em." He grinned, showing off a fine set of teeth.

"Are you going to sh-shoot us?" Susan asked, her gaze straying to the Winchester.

"Not unless you shoot me." The Indian looked at their rifles. "Deal?"

"Deal," Logan said after sizing up the situation.

The Winchester's barrel dropped to Logan's stomach, then to the top of the wagon wheel.

"Where did you learn English?" Susan asked when the rifle ceased to be a threat.

"From someone who speaks it." He dipped his head solemnly. "I bid you good day, ma'am and mister. Welcome to my country." With that he reined the stallion around and set heels to its flanks. The horse was off like a shot, streaking toward a thicket of shrubs and trees. A few moments more, and both horse and rider were a memory.

"Good heavens." Susan laid a hand over her laboring heart. "Do you realize he could have shot us all? Thank heavens he's civilized."

"Just because he speaks English doesn't mean he's civilized," Logan noted, still looking at the spot where he'd lost sight of the Indian. "I wonder if he belongs to the same tribe we're running from."

"I hope so, because that means we can stop running." Susan sat straight, reminded of something the savage had said. "Logan, we're almost there! Didn't you hear him? He said Tulsa is right ahead of us, over that rise." She tore the reins from around the brake and flapped them. "Yaaa! Get along there!"

The team surged forward, sending Logan backward. He barely caught himself before falling back into the wagon and on top of the children. He glanced at his offspring and shook his head. They'd slept through the entire scare, and he was glad for that. They'd been through enough on this trip; blistering days, cold nights, yipping coyotes, screaming mountain cats, scrapes, bruises, drenchings, and the constant worry of what lay around each bend.

Facing front again, he gazed ahead, suddenly anxious

for the ordeal to end. He took the reins from Susan, flashed a smile, and stood up in the wagon. Giving a whoop, he goaded the team into a gallop. The wagon groaned and rattled. The children sat up, shaken awake.

Susan laughed at Logan. He looked majestic standing in the wagon, his shirtsleeves rolled up to display powerful forearms and his booted feet braced apart. Manly, Susan thought, then tingled at all that word evoked.

"What's going on?" Jacob asked, scrambling toward the seat. "We being chased?"

"No, we're almost home," Susan shouted above the din. "Home!"

"Goody!" Etta gripped the back of the wagon seat and trained her bright eyes on the double strip of bare earth that formed a trail.

As the wagon neared the crest of swollen ground, another wagon topped it, coming from the other direction. The man driving it tipped his straw hat. Logan pulled the team into a walk.

"Howdy," the man called.

"Howdy. Is Tulsey Town thataway?" Logan asked.

"Sure 'nuf is. Y'all newcomers?"

"I'm going to start up a newspaper there."

"We've been expecting you. Herd just crossed, so give them a wide berth. It'll be dusty, but it clears right quick in this open country."

"Pardon?" Logan said, shaking his head in confusion.

"Herd of cattle," the man explained. "They stampede through the heart of town every few days. Damned nuisance, but those cowboys spend a lot of money in Tulsey. When you hear them coming, just get out of the way." He chuckled and gave a curt nod. "Good luck, and welcome." Waving his hat, he sent his vehicle lumbering past them. "Name's Hall. I damn near own Main Street. In fact, I used to own your building."

"Logan Vance," Logan called to him. "Happy to meet you."

"Yours is the red one. Can't miss it."

Susan turned to watch the wagon pass them. "Is he your landlord?"

"No, he built the building we bought. He sold it to a man named Brady, and I bought it from him."

"It's red?"

"Guess so," Logan shrugged. "Brady sent a description of the place, but never said what color it was painted." He glanced sharply at her. "Does that matter?"

"No, of course not. After all, why should it concern me? It's not actually my home. It's yours."

Some of the joy went out of him and he sat down again. He started to tell her that she could think of his home as hers for as long as she wanted, that she'd earned that right, but then the team mounted the crest and Logan's heart soared up and wedged in his throat.

The main street was wider than he'd envisioned. Rutted, it stretched north and south, ending at a gentle rise of spring green. As Hall had foretold, dust hung in the air. The herd that had stirred it up could still be seen in the distance, their mooing cries riding the breeze.

Lumbered buildings and some masonry ones, all shops or businesses, stood on either side of the thoroughfare. Behind the main street sentries, houses were scattered amid squares of good farmland.

"Tulsa," Susan whispered, gazing with wide eyes. "It's bigger than I thought."

"Yeah, it is," Logan admitted. "Looks like a wide place in the road on the verge of being an honest-to-goodness township."

"It sure does. Tulsa," she said again, then smiled. "It's not half as bad as I thought it would be."

Logan laughed. "You said a mouthful there, Susan. Jacob, Etta, what do y'all think?"

"Where's the school?" Jacob asked.

Logan scanned the area and pointed to a whitewashed, peak-roofed building. "That might be it. It's got a flag outside."

"Where's our home?" Etta climbed onto the seat beside Susan.

"The red one . . . ." Logan clucked to the team, sending it onto the wide main street. "Let's find it."

Susan pointed out the J. M. Hall store and the impressive masonry building housing Lynch Hardware.

"Children, look! See that stone building?" Susan turned slightly to make sure Jacob looked in the right direction. "It has an ice cream parlor on the lower floor."

"Ice cream!" Etta clapped her hands. "I like this town."

The general and hardware stores looked grand to Susan, who had an awful itching to shop. She could barely suppress a squeal of delight when she spotted new bonnets in the window and a sign advertising Number 7 cookstoves. The livery barn, also of masonry, was large and clean. Meat markets, a drugstore, and a tannery all looked to be doing healthy trade. The only businesses that bothered Susan were the dance hall, the saloon, and a hotel that looked more like a brothel.

But every town has its warts, she told herself. Even grand places like St. Louis had sections a lady skirted. In the distance, she could see a white church, and the sight restored her faith in Tulsa.

"Red!" Jacob shouted.

"Where?" the rest chorused.

"There," Jacob said, pointing past the Tulsa Banking Company building.

And there it stood. Red. Boxy. Windows winking against the sun. No longer a dream or a vision, but lumber and nails and fresh paint. Susan realized she'd been holding her breath, and now she let it out in a long sigh of relief. She nodded, giving the building her approval. It was good-sized and the windows in front were large, allowing for adequate interior light.

"What do you think?" Susan asked Logan.

"Looks sturdy to me. Those windows ought to give good light during working hours."

"I was thinking the same thing." She dimpled, pleased they were thinking alike. Just as her mother and father did sometimes . . . She pushed aside such thoughts, finding them too intimate. Glancing back, she wondered how far Coonie was from their new home. "Oh, I do hope Coonie gets here soon. I—

"Worry about him, I know," Logan said, faking a sigh of irritation, then smiling to let Susan know he was teasing. "He'll be here directly, Miss Fret 'n' Fuss. Well, let's look inside." He pulled the wagon and team along the far side of the building and set the brake. "You children hold up and wait for us old folks," he scolded when Jacob flung himself out of the wagon and Etta scrambled over Susan's lap to climb down.

Catching the lightness in his tone, Susan glanced at Logan and saw that he was even more excited than she was. He hadn't been in such a good mood for days. Not since before the river. His green eyes glistened, and a smile lengthened his mouth. He removed his hat and ran a hand over his fair hair, mussing it attractively before replacing the hat.

"I was beginning to think this place didn't exist. And after meeting up with that rifle-toting Indian, I was wondering if it was all worth it. But now . . . well, hell, looking at this barn-red building makes me want to do a jig."

Leaping over the side, Logan held out his hands for Susan. She laughed, overcome with joy to have finally arrived, and placed her trembling hands in his. Once she was on firm footing, he wrapped his arms around her waist and swung her in a circle.

"Logan!" Susan gasped and clung to his wide shoulders. "What has possessed you?"

"Happiness. We're here, Susan. Finally, we're here! And all in one piece, thank God." He released her, and for a few moments he was content to stare into her eyes, then he motioned courteously. "After you, ma'am."

"Thank you, sir." She lifted her skirts an inch and stepped up on the boardwalk. The children stood obediently at the door, waiting for their father to open it. "Have you a key?" Susan asked Logan.

"I was told it would be open and the key would be on the mantel."

"Mantel. So there's a nice fireplace?"

"That's what I was told." Logan turned the brass knob of the future. The door swung open on oiled hinges, giving access to a smooth, wide-planked floor. The windows painted big squares of light across it. The smell of fresh paint and sanded lumber greeted them. "Well, somebody go inside," Logan said, laughing at the frozen trio.

Jacob broke rank first, quickly followed by his sister. Susan stepped over the threshold and had a fleeting sensation of a bride being carried into her new home. The front room took up half of the building. A potbellied stove squatted at the back of it. Oil lanterns hung from the beamed ceiling. The place smelled faintly of kerosene. Another door was fitted into the far wall. Jacob reached it first and flung it open to reveal the other rooms and a set of steep stairs.

"Back here is where we'll live," Logan said, taking Susan by the arm and guiding her to the second room. "There's your fireplace. We'll set up the cookstove beside it."

"Oh, it's wonderful." Susan went straight to the brick and mortar fireplace. The grate stood empty and clean, ready for a rick of wood and the strike of a match. Iron hooks hung from a crossbar, and a cast-iron pot was suspended from one. "I can already smell the good things I'll cook up here."

"I'm hungry," Etta said.

"Mention food and you get hungry," Logan teased her.

"Papa, can I go upstairs?" Jacob asked.

"Yes, go on." Logan stood at the bottom while Jacob raced up the stairs. "What's it look like up there?"

"It's small," Jacob called down. "Like Mrs. Ledbetter's attic."

Logan mounted the stairs until he could see. One window afforded meager daylight. "Bedroom," he said. "We'll let you and Etta stay up here."

"Hurray!" Jacob said, jumping up and down.

Logan descended the stairs. "There's a bedstead in the wagon for you, Susan. We'll set it up here in the downstairs bedroom."

"What about you? Will you sleep up there with the children?"

"No. I'll bunk in the office area."

"And what about Coonie?"

"Let's have a look out back. There's supposed to be some outbuildings and a mother-in-law's house. Coonie and I thought he could use it."

"What on earth is a mother-in-law's house?"

"Come and see."

A narrow door set under the stairs opened to the side of the building where Logan had left the horses and wagon. Susan followed him outside and around to the back. A privy, also painted red, sat beneath a parasol-shaped birch. A henhouse and yard were fenced with chicken wire. A hog trough, water well, lean-to shed, and two-stall stable took up the southeast corner of the acreage. Beyond it, at the property's farthest boundary, stood another building, this one of unpainted lumber with a shingled roof where a brick chimney poked through.

"There it is," Logan said, nodding toward it. "That's a mother-in-law's house. A place is called that when it's built way back from the main house." He chuckled at Susan's sound of disapproval. "I think it's a right smart idea."

"You would. I think it's mean." She sighed, softening under the warmth of his smile. "But I'm glad it's there. It will do nicely for Coonie. I think he needs his own place."

"So do I. He's a loner."

"Are you?"

He hooked one thumb in his front belt loop and narrowed his eyes to look at her with smoking intensity. A quivering erupted in the center of her chest, and she had to look away, struck by nerves. Blast his green eyes, she thought miserably. With one look, he could reduce her to a bundle of contradictions.

"Well, now, it's hard to be a loner when you've got two children, but I think I'm a bit of a maverick. I was never one to follow the herd. I like to blaze my own trail."

"So I've noticed." She cleared her throat and pretended to be engrossed in a study of a bridal wreath bush. "Somebody's planted some pretty shrubs and flowers. First thing we'll have to do is set out a vegetable garden. Won't you want to buy some hens?"

"Guess so." His green eyes took a quick inventory of the yard and buildings. "We can plant out there past the outhouse, I suppose." He walked off the property, pausing to peek in the privy and chicken house. A weeping willow drooped over a picket fence to the east. Wildflowers grew along the edges. Beyond the back fence a thicket of yellow flowers nodded their heads.

"I like it, Logan," Susan called to him over her shoulder. She held up a bunch of crepe myrtle she'd picked. "We had this back home in our yard."

Logan bobbed his head at the yellow wildflowers. "Black-eyed Susans. Should we take them as a good sign?"

She felt herself blush and knew her cheeks were the same shade of pink as the flowers she held. "I should hope so. I wouldn't want you to take it as a sign of *bad* luck." Coming to stand next to him, she bent and touched one of the buttery petals. "They're not very pretty, but they're hale and hearty."

"Not pretty, you say?" He plucked one and held it to his nose for a moment while his eyes flirted with her. "They've always appealed to me."

Night claimed Tulsa, Indian Territory, by the time Susan, Logan, and the children had unloaded the wagon. Logan stabled the horses and gave them extra rations as a reward for hauling his family across the treacherous miles of the overland trail.

Finding adventure at every turn, the children had been more than ready to bed down in their new room upstairs. After pan baths, they were put to bed by Logan, both too tired to hear a story from their father. Downstairs again, Logan helped Susan unpack necessities and make up their own beds.

Now Susan stood back to admire the iron bedstead, feather mattresses, and fresh linens.

"My, my. That *does* look luscious," she said, reaching out to press down one corner of the comfy mattress. "In fact, I never saw a bed that looked so good to me."

"Want to share it?"

She spun around. He lounged in the doorway. One crooked elbow rested at ear level against the jamb, and his hand swung loosely from his wrist. His smile was loose, too.

"I can't believe even *you* would say such a thing to me."

"I'm only funning you, Susan. Don't take things so personal."

"I'm not so sure you were joking."

"You think I'm hankering so hard for a woman that I'd fight Catherine's ghost for you? No, thanks, darlin'. My days of feuding and fussing with Catherine are over." He made a cutting motion with his hand, then ran it down the front of his sweat-stained shirt. He grinned when her gaze followed like a faithful pet.

"I see you're still making fun of my dream." She lifted her chin high and proud. "Go right ahead. I don't care if you think it's silly. It certainly cleared my mind and made me see what's real and what's not."

"Talking dead people are reality, that's for sure," he mocked with forced seriousness.

She fluffed pillows busily. "Have your laugh." Popping noises sounded in the distance, and she jumped. "What's that? Gunfire?"

"Could be." Logan straightened from the doorway and went to the front of the building. The room was empty, save for his narrow bunk set against one wall. Horsemen flashed by the windows, guns blazing. "What the hell's going on?" Logan muttered, then motioned Susan back.

Stepping outside, he drew up sharply, surprised by the number of people milling about. Looking south, he could see the tavern was doing a brisk, noisy business. North, the hotel's lights spilled into the street and shadows writhed across them. A young woman dressed in a bright green flouncy dress came striding along the boardwalk toward Logan.

"What's all the commotion?" Logan asked when she was near enough.

"The usual," she said, pushing her red hair away from her rouged cheeks. She gave him the once-over, her blue eyes sparkling with curiosity. "Hey, you the newspaperman?"

"Sure am." Logan dipped his head. "Logan Vance."

"Glad to make your acquaintance. I'm Mazie Weeks. I work down at the saloon."

"Off work already?"

"No. I've got to change clothes. One of those damned fools ripped this one. See?" She turned to show him the tear, which exposed some of her smooth back and a good part of her corset. "Oh, howdy. You the missus?"

Logan forced his gaze from Mazie and grinned mischievously at Susan. "No, this is my former sister-in-law. She's helping me get settled in. Susan, this is Mazie. She works at the saloon."

Susan took half a step back. Having never met a saloon girl, she stared at the woman, partly shocked and partly amazed. "Wh-what happened to your dress?"

"One of the boys got a little rough is all." Mazie shrugged as if it were common for her to be parading up and down Main Street in such a state of undress.

"Dearie me. That dress must be expensive," Susan said, admiring the lace crisscrossed on the bodice.

"Don't you worry. He's going to pay for another one or I'll get someone to change him from a rooster to a hen with one shot." She laughed with Logan, then threw Susan a questioning glance when she realized Susan didn't share in the joke. "Well, I'll be getting." She started off, but stopped and sent Logan a heavy-lidded glance over her shoulder. "Y'all stop by the Bloody Bucket sometime and I'll stand you for a drink."

"That's mighty neighborly of—"

"We don't partake of spirits," Susan interrupted Logan.

"Why, Susan, honey, I thought you loved communing with spirits."

She exchanged a sizzling glare with him, then he laughed.

"Well . . . the offer stands," Mazie said, making her hip-swinging way toward the boardinghouse. "See y'all."

Three more cowboys raced their horses down Main

Street whooping and hollering as if they were part of a wild west show. From the saloon came the high-pitched squeal of a woman and another volley of gunfire. Susan looked to Logan for his reaction. He rubbed the back of his neck and chuckled.

"Kind of rowdy, isn't it?"

Susan gave a sniff of contempt. "I liked it much better in daylight. Do you think it was proper of you to be ogling that dance hall girl out here in the open? She was practically naked!"

"Honey, you have a gift for overstating everything."

"Don't call me honey. Just answer me. Do you think it was proper—"

"Susan," he said through gritted teeth, "you really don't want to speak to me in that tone of voice. Do you remember what happened last time you talked to me like that?" He dropped his gaze to her mouth and left it there.

"Are you threatening me?"

"No, I'm warning you. You're not dealing with a green farm boy here." He leaned a fraction closer to test her.

She retreated into the house, her eyes wide with the memory of his kisses. Logan stuck his hands in his pants pockets and gave her his back, savoring his seniority.

"Good night, Susan," he called sweetly. "I'll see you in your dreams." Then he laughed, good and loud so she could hear him. Looking down the street, he wondered if Mazie might come sashaying back to the saloon directly. He decided to wait around awhile and see.

Chapter 8

"**U**ncle Coonie!"
     Hearing the children's shouts of jubilation, Susan clasped her hands together and looked up at the bare ceiling.

"Thank the Lord he's safe," she whispered, then wiped her dishwater hands on her apron and hurried from the living quarters and through the nearly empty front room. Bursting through the open door, she was just in time to see Coonie French hop from the wagon and gather both Jacob and Etta in his arms.

"Coonie," Susan said, reaching out to squeeze his forearm. "I can't tell you how worried I've been about you. I was just telling Logan this morning that if you didn't show up today he'd have to—"

"She was going to send me on a wild goose chase after you," Logan said, stepping from around the side of the building. His cap brim shaded his face but not his brilliant smile. He stuck out one hand. "Good to see you, partner. The Indians didn't give you any trouble, did they?"

"Naw, but I saw your sign at that cabin. Much obliged for the warning."

"There are some camped near here, and I'm told they're nothing but bad news for the townspeople."

Coonie took Logan's hand but used it to pull Logan into his arms for a bear hug. "Ain't you a sight for sore eyes? I got held up when one of these dad-gum wheels came off the wagon. Took me one whole day to mend it, grease it up again, and stick it back on. I'da been longer in getting

93

here if a couple of big old farm boys hadn't happened along and helped me get that wheel back in place. This here load is heavy, I'm here to tell you. How long y'all been here?''

"We pulled in a couple of days ago." Logan made an expansive gesture. "What do you think of your new home?''

"Looks right nice." Coonie eyed the front of the building, then looked at each child. "How do y'all like it?''

"I love it," Etta said, giving Coonie another kiss on the cheek. " 'Specially since you're here.''

"Ain't that sweet?" Coonie said, letting the children slide down his body to the boardwalk. "And I'm mighty glad to be here. We got our work cut out for us getting this press off the wagon and set up.''

Logan draped an arm around Coonie's shoulders. "All in good time, partner. Your place is out back." He leaned closer and lowered his voice. "Susan has cleaned it up for you.''

"You didn't need to do that," Coonie told Susan.

"I didn't mind a bit. It just needed a good sweeping out and some elbow grease here and there. It was nothing.''

"I think she's sweet on you, Coonie," Logan teased, his green eyes sparkling at Susan. "You always did have a way with the pretty girls.''

"Me?" Coonie barked a laugh. "You're the one who's got the women chasing after you.''

Admiring Logan's wide, dimple-bracketed smile, Susan silently agreed with Coonie.

"No, no," Logan said, shaking his head. "You've got it wrong, partner. I've never been a ladies' man like you.''

"That's not how I remember it," Susan interjected, joining in with the jesting, although what she said was no joke. "As I recall, when you came to Pemiscot County the mothers commenced to praying and the fathers loaded their shotguns.''

His expression changed, as it did so often, from teasing to tempting. Susan couldn't put her finger on how this happened, it just did. His eyelids drooped slightly and his smile took on a seductive slant. Susan's heart galloped, sending blood surging through her veins.

"Is that what you recall, little Susan?" he drawled. Even his voice had a different timbre. "I thought you were too young back then to notice such things."

"I was never as dumb as you thought," Susan retorted, then swung around in a whirl of calico skirts. "Come inside, Coonie, and take a look. I'll fix you something to tide you over 'til dinnertime."

While Logan and the children gave Coonie the grand tour, Susan removed the leftover biscuits and sausage from the warming tray and combined them into three sandwiches for Coonie. She put a jar of relish on the table and set a big glass of water beside it.

"Sit down, Coonie, and dig in," she instructed. "Why don't you children unload some of his things from the wagon after your father unhitches the oxen?"

"Yes, ma'am," Logan said, saluting her. "Hasn't she gotten downright bossy, Coonie? I swear, stretch a roof over a female's head and in no time you've got yourself an order-giver on the premises."

"It was a suggestion, not an order," Susan said, sitting at the table with Coonie. "And everyone around here knows you never do anything you don't want to do, so your complaining is wasted on us."

Winking, he gave his children's rumps playful pats, sending them ahead of him. The scrambled into the wagon and began gathering Coonie's personal articles.

"Take them around to his house," Logan said, then ran a hand along the brown hide of one ox. The other was jet-black.

Removing the yoke, he chuckled to himself over Susan and her brisk, no-nonsense attitude since arriving in Tulsa. The woman was a regular barn-burner when it came to organizing and unpacking.

Right handy to have around, he thought with admiration. So unlike her older sister in that respect as well. Catherine had spent most of her days looking for ways not to work, but Susan hustled, bustled, and accomplished more than Logan thought her able. He'd miss her when she was gone.

And she must go home, he told himself firmly, even though his heart ached a little at the thought of this place without her. No matter how industrious or appealing she might be, he knew why she'd been sent to him, and that made him want to send her back to Abraham—empty-handed. Of course, it would be a while before he had enough money to buy her a train ticket, but once he did, off she'd go. Has to be done, he thought grimly. Susan might be a sweet young beauty, but her family was a thorn in his side.

Just thinking about Abraham packing Susan off to sweet-talk him made Logan see red. Self-righteous prick, Logan thought, gritting his teeth until his jaw muscles ached. He could be a bank president—hell, he could be the President of the United States—and it wouldn't be good enough for Abraham Armitage. It was no wonder Catherine had been willing to do damned near anything to get away from her father. And it had been fine with Logan when she'd decided not to visit her folks after that one visit following their marriage. Of course, she'd corresponded with them by letter, but Catherine hadn't wanted to see her father after he'd called her a whore in front of the rest of the family.

Logan grinned, remembering how he'd packed their bags and made hasty travel arrangements. Abe hadn't tried to stop him, knowing that Logan had been itching to bust him in the mouth or worse. That visit had confirmed what Logan had suspected all along; Abraham was teetering on the edge of madness. He wondered if Susan recognized her father's instability.

No doubt there'd been a time when old Abe had been a good father, Logan thought. While his Catherine, Susan, Rebecca, and Lauralee were all growing up and adoring no other male but him, things had probably been fine. But once Catherine had reached the age of womanhood and had cast her adoration on other males, Abraham had felt himself losing control.

Logan had sensed it the moment he'd met the man. The

way Abraham had glared at him as if he were a wolf stalking Abe's lambs should have discouraged him from courting Catherine, but he'd been young and cocky enough to want to challenge Abe's contempt.

Should have left well enough alone, Logan thought as he finished unhitching the team. After Catherine's death, when the Armitages had come to St. Louis, Logan had realized that not even Catherine's demise could signal an end to Abe's hatred. Logan had an enemy for life. Twice during those awful days in St. Louis, Abraham had spoken privately to Logan about taking the children back to the farm. Both times the men had almost come to blows.

Just because my daughter married trash doesn't mean her children have to be raised up by it, Abraham had said in that pious fashion that made Logan want to throttle him.

Trash . . . the devil's own . . . whore's fruit . . . He'd been called it all by crazy Abe. And Louella Armitage wasn't any better to be around. Like her husband, Louella thought Catherine had been doomed the moment she'd smiled at Logan. She'd cried and begged Logan to "give up the children for their sake." Maybe Abe wasn't the only crazy one in the family . . .

One nice thing about the Territory, Abraham and his bunch couldn't spy on him or pester him. How could a nice girl like Susan be spawned from a couple of long-nosed, selfish troublemakers? Of course, her other sisters didn't seem too bad. Rebecca and Lauralee were sweet, but cowed by parents who knew no tolerance. Catherine's biggest problem had been that she was spoiled. Being the eldest, she'd been petted and favored, leading her to expect the same treatment from everyone. When he'd wanted to needle her, he'd called her Queen Catherine. It had fit so perfectly. In fact, he'd always felt that Catherine liked the nickname.

Leading the oxen around to the back, Logan watched his son and daughter carry armloads of clothing into Coonie's house. Etta's blond hair shone in the sunlight. So like Catherine, he thought, smiling. As long as he had his Etta, he'd never forget Catherine's face. He only prayed Etta would be good for something besides looking beautiful and making men want her. That's all Catherine had done well. Thank heavens, her sister hadn't followed in her prima donna footsteps.

He fed the oxen, tying them near the horses. He'd sell off the oxen as soon as he could, since they were no longer needed. He hoped to trade one of the horses for a mule and some chickens. While he worked, he kept an eye on the children. Jacob seemed more outgoing, as if he already felt comfortable in his new home. Despite his disregard of Susan's fretting about Jacob, Logan was concerned. Jacob kept too much inside. His wariness of Susan bothered Logan, too. It was more than Jacob merely resenting Susan's arrival on the scene after that awful last meeting with the Armitages. Jacob sensed Logan's interest in Susan, and that was at the heart of Jacob's standoffishness toward his aunt.

Should he talk with Jacob? If so, what would he say to him? Don't worry, son, I'm not going to marry your aunt. That wouldn't do, Logan thought. Susan wasn't the threat—it was *any* woman. Jacob didn't want another mother. He didn't want another woman in the house.

Glancing upward, Logan shook his head as he pondered those invisible wounds that bled into the soul. Jacob, he knew, had one or two. What of Etta? Did her shining smile hide scars?

Rounding the front of the building again, he collided with Mazie. "Whoa, there, missy." He caught her by the shoulders and steadied her. He admired her fancy blue dress and flaming hair. "It's nice running into you, Miss Mazie. It *is* miss, isn't it?"

"You think I'd be working in a saloon if I had a husband?" She punched his shoulder. "By the way, you haven't come by for that drink, and you're on the verge of hurting my feelings over it."

"Can't have that, can we?" He realized he was still holding on to her, so he reluctantly let go. "My partner just arrived. How about if I bring him around tonight for a drink?"

"On the house," she said, all smiles and flirty eyes.

"I'll be looking for you and I'll save you—" She looked past him, and her brow puckered in a frown.

Susan, Logan thought, but when he turned around he saw Etta and Jacob. They were staring at Mazie with undisguised curiosity. "Miss Mazie, these are my children. Etta, Jacob, say hello to the lady."

"Hello, lady," Etta said, ducking behind Logan's leg. "You got red stuff on your face."

"Etta, mind your manners," Logan scolded.

"It's called rouge, honey. You'll wear it someday."

"I don't want to," Etta said with typical honesty. "I don't like it."

"That's enough, Etta," Logan said, shaking his head sternly but secretly amused by his daughter's opinion.

" 'Lo," Jacob muttered, then climbed into the flatbed wagon for another armload. "When you gonna unload the press, Papa?"

"Pretty soon, son."

"You married?" Mazie asked.

"Widowed," Logan answered.

"Oh . . . that's good." Mazie grinned, pleased with his answer. "Are these the only two children you've got?"

"Yes, these and the other ten stepchildren."

"Ten—"

"I'm only funning you," he said, laughing. "These are my only two. Do you have something against children?"

"No, not so long as they're somebody else's." She swept past him, leaving a trail of lilac perfume. "See you tonight, newspaperman. Don't disappoint me."

"I won't." He turned to admire the sway of her hips. Man, oh man, he thought, running a hand through his hair and around to the back of his neck. She was some woman. Wouldn't mind feeling her legs wrapped around him and her—

"How about us unloading the press?" Coonie asked, coming outside to interrupt Logan's longings.

"Uh . . . right." Logan glanced toward Mazie again and saw her turn inside the saloon. "Coonie, I just got an invitation I don't think either one of us will want to refuse."

* * *

"The children are already fast asleep. I wish I could—" Susan stopped on the bottom step and looked around for Logan. He'd been in the living room when she'd gone upstairs to check on his children only a few minutes ago. "Logan?" she called. "Logan?" she repeated, louder.

Susan heard a bump from the pressroom and moved toward it. Logan stepped into view. His hair clung to his head, freshly dampened and combed, and he was straightening a gray tie at his throat. Susan glanced over his clean, striped trousers and black shirt. Was he taking her out somewhere? Had he arranged for Coonie to watch the children?

"Logan, what's all this?"

"Oh, Susan." He cleared his throat and looked up. "Are the children all right?"

"Yes. Asleep. You've changed clothes."

He looked down at himself, then raised one boot and polished the toe of it on the back of his trouser leg. "Coonie wants to—no, that's not right." His head came up, his eyes locked on her, and Susan didn't like what she saw. "I invited Coonie to have a drink with me down at the saloon."

She felt as if the wind had been knocked out of her. "The saloon?" Visions of Mazie Weeks flirting with Logan branded her mind. And she'd thought he'd dressed up for her! Humiliation nearly choked her. "Let Coonie go by himself. You shouldn't be seen in that place."

"Why not?"

"Your children."

"I'm going, not them."

"But what about your reputation?"

"A drink won't damage it." He started to turn away.

"You can't go." She grabbed his shirt cuff and gave a yank.

His head swiveled around to her slowly and his eyes were veiled. "What did you say?"

Susan snatched her hand away. "Logan, it won't look right."

"For a man to have a drink with a friend?"

She shifted her weight to one foot. "And I suppose you put on fresh clothes for Coonie?"

"I'll be meeting people, and I want to make a good first impression."

"You don't have to worry, Logan. You've already made quite an impression on Miss Weeks." She frowned at his feigned puzzlement. "I saw you talking with her earlier. You'd do well not to encourage her interest if you really want to make a good impression with the townspeople."

"Watch out. Your Armitage blood is showing." He walked his fingers around his shirt collar to make sure it was turned down. "The Armitage clan is always the first to tell others who's decent and who's trash. Thankfully, I don't shun folks just because others do. I give people the benefit of the doubt. Miss Weeks has been nothing but nice to me, so why should I be so rude as to throw her offer of a drink back in her face?"

"Are you sure it's a drink you're after?"

His eyes narrowed to cagey slits. "And what if it's not? What if I want more than that? What's it to you?"

"I'm thinking of my nephew and niece."

"Why am I not convinced of that?" he mocked, coming forward, smelling faintly of fresh pine. "Why do I get the feeling you just don't want me anywhere near Mazie?"

"A family man shouldn't be sporting with a dance hall girl. It's not proper."

"Well, this family man is missing a very important part of his family—his wife."

"Can't you be satisfied with being a good father?"

"Can you be satisfied with being a good daughter and nothing else? Even *you* must yearn for a man from time to time."

"I don't like the way you said that. You make it sound as if I'm somehow different from other women."

He looked past her and nodded. "Be right there, Coonie. I'll meet you out front."

Susan spun around, embarrassed to have someone else hear their argument. Coonie ducked out the side door. Capturing her shoulders, Logan turned her back around to face him.

"You ought to kick up your heels while you can, black eyes. Once you get back to the farm, all you'll have to keep your mind occupied is Cal Pointer." Before she could dart out of his way, he planted a kiss on the tip of her nose. "Don't wait up."

"You're making a mistake going there," Susan called after him, then winced when she realized she might wake the children. She held her breath and listened, then relaxed when no sounds drifted down the stairs. Marching to the outside door, she leaned out to watch Coonie and Logan stride along the boardwalk toward the saloon. "Men," she muttered under breath. "If he comes home drunk, I'll . . . I'll . . ."

What? an inner voice taunted. He's not afraid of your ire or your tough talk. Logan Vance will do what he wants to do, and you can't stop him.

Reduced to wandering aimlessly through the living quarters, she arranged table scarves and plumped pillows. She'd worked hard the past couple of days to make the place a home for Logan. Futile work, she thought with a despondent sigh. Her efforts hadn't kept Logan by her side. He hadn't even told her he appreciated her pitching in to help. Not one word. She'd thought he'd finally opened his eyes tonight to see what she'd done for him and his children, and that he'd decided to reward her with an evening out. Ha! She flung back her head but couldn't laugh. It hurt too much to laugh at herself.

Ever since he'd met that Mazie Weeks, he'd been straining at the bit to pay her a call. That gal sure got under his skin in a hurry. How in heaven had Mazie managed it? What did Mazie and Catherine have that she lacked?

Susan went to the mirror propped against a wall, waiting to be hung in her bedroom. Stray wisps of ginger-brown hair curled at her temples, and she smoothed them with the backs of her wrists. Standing properly straight and turning this way and that, she examined herself as she never had before. She tried to see herself as a man might—or, more specifically, as Logan might.

After a few moments, she decided she wasn't a bad-

looking woman—pretty, even. Her hair was thick and lustrous and she had good eyes, set wide apart, round, and
fringed with long lashes. Cal had told her once, when he'd
been uncharacteristically talkative, that her pride in herself
was what attracted him. But did men really notice such
things, or had Cal only been telling her what he thought
she'd wanted to hear? Having trouble imagining a man
like Logan hankering after a woman's spirit, she switched
her attention to her more obvious attributes.

Firm ass, she thought, grasping her buttocks for confir-
mation. High, pointy breasts. Good figure, she decided,
sliding her hands down her waist and hips. Could use more
pronounced curves, but she decided what she had was
enough to attract most any man. Logan had been attracted
to her from time to time. On the trail she'd felt his interest
keenly, but not so much since they'd arrived in Tulsa.

Just as I'd suspected, she thought. He was chasing after
me because I was the only available female around. Now
that he has other chickens clucking around him, he's getting right choosy and he's thrown me over for a more
colorful bird.

She thanked her lucky stars for holding out and not giving in to the pulses that had clamored in her body every
time he'd been near. His kisses had drugged her, but she
had found she was made of strong stuff. Still, it smarted
that he had lost interest in her so quickly. She'd grown to
enjoy the teasing, the taunting, the double meanings of his
words. Wonder what he was saying to Mazie Weeks?

Sitting in the rocker, she picked up one of Logan's books
on newspapering and began to read. He'll be home in a
few minutes, she told herself. Doesn't take long to have
one drink.

Three-quarters of an hour later, she shut the book with
a snap and glared at the mantel clock. What was he doing,
drinking a whole bottle? Rocking more furiously, she tried
not to see the visions her imagination threw at her—
glimpses of Logan laughing and fondling the ever-ready
Mazie Weeks, of him sneaking upstairs with her to some
den of sin. Coonie was probably already home and in bed
while Logan stayed in that liquor palace.

Susan went to the back and peered outside. A light shone in Coonie's bedroom window. Had it been there before? Grabbing a shawl, she swirled it over her shoulders, checked on the sleeping children once more, then stole outside. Making her way toward the saloon, she tried to walk in shadow, not wanting anyone to recognize her. Even if Logan cared not one jot for his reputation, she certainly wanted hers left untarnished. Nearing the front of the saloon, she stopped and wondered how she could look inside without being looked at. Two drunken men came stumbling through the bat-wing doors, and Susan darted into the alley between the saloon and the pool hall.

Discordant music spilled from the place, along with the rumble of voices, the tinkle of glasses, and bursts of lazy laughter. The tossed-out men stood unsteadily and brushed dirt off their clothes. They grumbled to each other, then weaved down the street toward the hotel. Realizing the alley was dimly lit, Susan glanced up. A window was cut in the side of the saloon above her. Barrels and kegs lined the alley, and Susan rolled one beneath the window. She hiked up her skirts and scrambled up onto the barrel. It rocked, but she kept her balance by grabbing on to the window ledge. She leaned closer to the grimy glass, and her eyes adjusted slowly to the glare of lights inside. Two wagon wheels, rimmed with lanterns, swung from the ceiling.

A bearded man played a piano in one corner of the big room and two other men flailed at banjos. The trio butchered a rendition of "Bring Back My Bonnie" and received a wild round of applause. Only drunks could love that kind of music, Susan thought, remembering her own piano lessons and the enchantment of a Chopin etude well played.

Small tables filled one end of the long room. A bar ran the length of the wall opposite her. Logan stood at the counter, mug in hand, Coonie and Mazie flanking him. Susan could see their reflections in the mirror behind the bar. They were all smiling, having a grand old time. Mazie said something, and both men tipped back their heads and let loose brays of laughter that carried easily to Susan.

What could be so all-fired knee-slapping funny? Susan

wondered. They'd probably drunk enough spirits to think every utterance was hilarious. Shame on you, Logan, she thought, narrowing her eyes against her mounting anger. Sporting with a woman like that and drinking liquor while your two angels sleep down the street. For shame, for shame, for shame!

Hearing her inner scoldings, she smiled despite her disappointment in Logan. Lordy, she sounded just like her mother! Nonetheless, Logan should be home instead of parading around with a woman of ill repute.

The musicians struck up the Virginia reel, and a few patrons grabbed the saloon girls and twirled them around. To Susan's horror, Logan bowed low before Mazie, then took her hand and escorted her to the center of the room for a dance. Jealousy speared Susan. She wanted to look away, but couldn't. A memory from long ago floated to her, and she could see Logan dancing with Catherine while she, the little sister, had suffered through a bout of jealousy. Once again, Susan found herself on the outside looking in.

She'd wanted to dance with Logan back then, and she wanted to dance with him now. Mazie tipped back her head, giddy with the music and the man who whirled her like a top. Taking long steps, Logan pranced and bobbed, ducked and dipped. The couples flew in a swirl of petticoats and tapping bootheels. The sight of Logan's hand clasping one of Mazie's while his other splayed along her waist disturbed Susan. Lantern light gilded his shoulders. Mazie raised her hand and ran her fingers through the side of his blond-streaked hair. A cry of anguish pushed past Susan's heart and scalded her throat. She climbed down from the barrel, her movements jerky, her insides numbing with cold reality.

Hardly aware of where she was stepping, she charged along the alley to the boardwalk. Blinded by her own jealousy, she collided with someone who'd just come from the saloon.

"Why, Miss Susan," Coonie said, backing up and giving her room to gain her balance. "What are you doing here?"

"Nothing . . . I . . ." Susan looked guiltily down the alley where the barrel squatted beneath the window. "I was looking for you and Logan."

"Logan's inside. I'll get him."

"No!" She grabbed Coonie's arm before he could leave. "Never mind. Let him be. Are you going home?"

"Yes, ma'am."

"Then I'll walk with you."

"Fine by me." He gave her a curious glance before his gaze darted into the alley. Susan knew he'd spotted the barrel and its conspicuous positioning. "You should be careful moving about in these streets after dark, Miss Susan. All kinds of rascally types are floating around this town."

"Yes, I've already met one or two." She smiled, trying to convince Coonie of her innocence. "I just thought I'd take a little walk. I figured you and Logan would be heading home and I might run into you. I was partly right, wasn't I?"

"Logan will be along soon. No need for you to worry."

"Worry?" She laughed, too loudly and too shrilly to be believable. "I'm not worried. Logan is a grown man and can do as he wishes. It's nothing to me, I assure you."

"He just needs to kick up his heels a bit. It's natural for a man."

"It's natural for a woman, as well," Susan said, abandoning her forced good humor. "Maybe I should leave after dinner tomorrow night for a few heel kicks. Catherine always said, what's good for the gander is good for the goose."

"That's not how I heard it," Coonie said, his hand rasping over his chin whiskers.

"Well, that's Catherine's interpretation," she explained with a smile. "She was good at twisting things around to suit her."

"But women have to be careful not to soil their reputations," Coonie said, slanting a worried glance at her.

"And men don't?"

"Men can get away with more mischief."

"Well said." She shrugged, giving up her empty

threats. "I'm not going to lower myself to such despicable behavior. Just because Logan likes to lie with dogs doesn't mean I should wish for flea bites."

Coonie chuckled, ducking his head and turning raspberry-red. "Miss Weeks wouldn't like you calling her a dog."

"Did I mention her name?" She shared a smug look with Coonie, then a smile of camaraderie. "Do you think Miss Weeks is pretty?"

"In her way, I suppose." When they were almost home, Coonie heaved a heavy sigh. "You know, Miss Susan, sometimes a fella can't separate the wheat from the chaff."

Studying him, Susan shook her head. "I don't understand what you're getting at, Coonie."

"Your family," he said in a rush. "When Logan looks at you, that's what he ends up seeing, and your folks never gave that boy a fair shake. I reckon he figures you won't either."

Standing outside the newspaper office, Susan examined the front window she'd cleaned so the sign painter could write on it, in golden letters edged in black, *The Democrat Argus.*

"Coonie, before I leave here, I intend to prove him wrong."

Chapter 9

The Mission School had originally been built as a church, but it now housed Tulsa's hall of education. Standing in front of the picket fence surrounding the property, Susan ran a critical eye over her nephew and niece. She straightened Etta's hair bow and slicked down Jacob's cowlick.

"Your mother would be so proud of you," she said as a knot formed in her throat. She kissed Etta. Jacob moved away to avoid any such demonstrations from her. "You two look so grown up. I want you to be very good today in school and do exactly what your teacher tells you." For those few moments, she felt like a mother instead of an aunt, and it was a feeling sweeter than honeysuckle nectar or maple syrup freshly tapped. Oh, Catherine, she thought to her departed sister, you have such beautiful children. In them, you've left a wondrous legacy that I'm honored to share.

A stately woman came forward, a brass bell in one hand, a McGuffey Reader in the other.

"New students?" she inquired.

Susan cleared her throat and stood up straight. "Yes, ma'am. These are Jacob and Etta Vance. Their father is editor and publisher of *The Democrat Argus.*"

"Ah, the newspaper. Children, I'm your teacher, Mrs. Lindsey. You may go inside now." She placed her hands on their heads and smiled at Susan. "I'll make sure they're settled in and kept busy, so they won't have time to be homesick."

"Thank you," Susan said, relieved to see that their teacher was sympathetic. "I think I'll miss them more than they'll miss me."

"It happens that way sometimes." Mrs. Lindsey patted Jacob's and Etta's heads. "Let's go meet the other children." Then she herded them toward the school building.

"Lovely children," someone said near Susan, making her blink away her sudden tears and turn toward the speaker. "I'm Mrs. Dunlevy."

"Nice to meet you," Susan said, extending her gloved hand. "I'm—"

"Mrs. Vance," the other woman provided.

The name hit her like a fireball. "No, I'm not . . . I'm Miss Armitage."

"But I thought I heard you tell the teacher that the name was Vance."

"Yes, that's the children's name. I'm their aunt. They're my sister's children, but she died some months back."

"Oh, how unfortunate. You're taking care of them? What about their father?"

"He's their guardian, of course. I'm only helping out until they're all settled in their new home and the newspaper is running smoothly," Susan explained, then told herself not to be so defensive. It wasn't any of Mrs. Dunlevy's business!

The other woman's gaze fastened on the street where buggies pulled up to let off children. Her expression became even more shuttered. "And where are you living, Miss Armitage?"

"I'm living with . . . that is, I have a room in the house."

"The house where the children's father stays?"

"Uh . . . yes, where the family lives. Behind the newspaper office. It's quite nice and I have my own bedroom. The children sleep upstairs and Logan . . . uh, Mr. Vance sleeps in the office."

"The office?"

"On a cot." Susan glanced up, certain the sun was bigger and brighter than it had been a few moments ago. She was as hot as a stove lid. "He's—he's like a brother to me," she lied, and saw the sin was a wasted effort. The woman clearly didn't approve. "My visit is temporary."

"Yes," Mrs. Dunlevy said, drawing out the word as she issued another speculative glance.

"My parents sent me," Susan said, as if that in itself made everything aboveboard.

"Did they?"

"Yes, they did. It's a custom, you know."

"Yes, but usually the unmarried lady lives in a separate abode. Isn't there a house out back?"

"Coonie stays in it."

"Who?"

"Lo—Mr. Vance's business associate."

"I see." The woman's up-and-down glance made Susan want to squirm. "I don't mean to make you uncomfortable, but this town has wagging tongues. You should be aware of that—for the children's sake if for nothing else."

Susan saw Etta and Mrs. Lindsey waving to her from the top step, and she waved back. "Is Mrs. Lindsey an Indian?" she asked, searching for a topic other than herself. She'd noticed the teacher's dark coloring and high cheekbones.

"Yes," Mrs. Dunlevy said, glancing toward the teacher. "Part Creek, I believe. We all thought it would be best to have a teacher who could relate to both the white and the Indian children."

"Are there many Indian children in school here?"

"More all the time as they become accustomed to our ways. That's what Mrs. Lindsey does best."

"What—I don't understand," Susan said, shaking her head.

"Ease the Indian children into civilization," Mrs. Dunlevy explained, looking down her thin nose at Susan. "They must *all* learn to live our way, don't you see? We can't continue having them dress so outlandishly and practice their savage rituals."

"I see . . ." Susan shrugged, finding the other woman's views rather narrow. "Well, I must be going. Good day." Susan set off, anxious to escape Mrs. Dunlevy's gossipy company and censuring glare. It humiliated her to be looked upon as if she were . . . were . . . well, as if she were Mazie Weeks!

Taking long strides, she dodged stragglers along the boardwalk. Rounding a corner, she heard the familiar deafening rumble of hooves and looked up to find it was too late to dart across the street. The herd thundered down Main Street, their horns shining white in the sun, their hides brown and black and russet. Some of them sported horns as long as eight or nine feet from tip to tip. A person would have to be crazy to get anywhere near them, Susan thought, plastering herself against the building behind her. It was a big herd, and they were still damp from crossing the Arkansas River. In the distance, she could see the cowboys. Their voices carried to her. Shouts and yah-hahing, sounds of cracking whips and bursting pistols.

"Oh, no," Susan moaned, seeing trouble coming her way. These rowdies rode full out, which usually meant they were hellbent on destruction. Having been warned of these almost weekly events and having witnessed a couple of cow trains already, Susan knew it was foolhardy to be on the street when trail-drunk cowpokes came barreling through.

Glimpsing a break in the herd, Susan picked up her skirts and darted across the street. She streaked into the newspaper office like a bolt of greased lightning. Logan looked up from a tray of type.

"Cowboys are coming," Susan announced breathlessly, dropping her skirts. "I heard earlier when I passed the bank that it's payday."

"Hell's afire," Logan groused, moving to the window for a look. Popping gunshots split the air. "Damn it all. This cowtown needs a full-time sheriff in the worst way."

"What could one sheriff do?" Susan asked, whipping off her bright yellow bonnet so as not to be a good target for a juiced-up cowboy. "I'm just thankful I got the children safely to school before they barged in. Can't someone warn us when a herd's expected?"

"Nobody knows when they're coming." Logan cursed again under this breath and motioned for her to get out of the way. "Lie down on the floor. These boys are mostly shooting holes in the sky, but you never know when they might aim at a window."

Vexed by the uncivilized interruption, Susan lay on her stomach after carefully arranging her skirts so they wouldn't wrinkle. "Where's Coonie?"

"At the store. I sent him for some kerosene." Logan lay beside her and propped his chin in both hands to wait out the rowdies. "Did you meet the schoolteacher?"

"Yes."

He slid his gaze sideways at her. "Why did you say it like that?"

"Like what?"

"Like there's something else to it besides yes. What's wrong with her?"

"Nothing. She seems like a good teacher." She started to tell him about Mrs. Dunlevy and how she'd seemed shocked at Susan's living arrangements, but she decided not to make more of it than necessary. "I never expected Tulsa to have so many families."

"I'm told this is one of the more civilized townships in the Territory. Guthrie and Kiefer are supposed to be hell-holes." Suddenly he laughed, then laughed harder.

"What's so funny?" Susan asked, smiling.

"The craziness of this just hit me. Here we are, two adults sprawled on the floor and talking about schools and families like it was normal, this waiting for cowpunchers to ride past."

"Here it *is* normal," Susan said with a giggle.

Logan shook his head. "Damned shame, too."

"You wanted a pioneer life," she reminded him.

"Yes, but some things you just don't bargain for," he said, giving her a heart-jolting look. "Some things sneak up on you."

Shots rang out, and Susan stifled a shriek. The pounding hooves diminished, but the cowboys seemed to converge outside the newspaper office to fire their last rounds. No Fourth of July was ever as noisy. Blast after blast echoed and ricocheted. Finally, they subsided, and just when Susan thought it might be over, another volley of gunfire ripped the air. Glass shattered and showered to the floor.

"Damn it all!" Logan bolted to his feet.

"Logan, be careful," Susan said, grabbing his ankle. "Get down!" She looked up to see his shoulders sag in relief.

"Thank God. He only shot out the door's window." He raised a fist and shook it. "If he'd shot out that front glass I'd be strangling him this minute."

Susan rose to her knees to examine the damage for herself. Shards of glass sprinkled the floor in front of the door, but Logan's pride and joy—his fancy lettered sign on the front window—was fully intact.

"Help me up and I'll get a broom and sweep up the glass." She accepted his extended hands and rose to her feet. When she started to pull away, he tightened his hands around hers. She looked up into his eyes, and the tingling erupted in her stomach. The Logan tingle. "You can let go of me now."

"Seems me and you have been warring the past couple of days," he said, his tone slow and honeyed.

The tingle found its way into her bloodstream. "Not really."

"Ever since I had a drink down at the Bloody Bucket."

She wrinkled her nose at the awful name of the saloon. "I'm not at war with anybody." She averted her gaze, not wanting to continue the line of conversation or encourage any further contact. She'd had that dream again—the one with Catherine scolding her for flirting with Logan. "I should clean up that glass before—"

"Nothing happened."

Susan swung her gaze to his again. "When?"

"With Mazie that night."

She tried to free her hands. He forced them around to the small of her back and held them there, bowing her body into his.

"We had a friendly drink, danced a little jig, and I came right home like a good little boy. That's what you want, isn't it? A good little boy? At least, that's what you *think* you want. Personally, I think you need yourself a full-grown man. In fact, I think you need one bad. I *know* I need a good woman bad.''

''Logan, please let's not talk like this to each other. It makes me uncomfortable.''

''Don't be, sugar. I don't mean to tease you. I just . . . well, my intentions always start off good and end up naughty.'' His gaze slipped to the pulse visible at the base of her throat. ''Being good around you is a tall task. Holding myself back is like holding back the dawn. Can't be done. No matter how hard I try . . .''

His voice trailed off as he touched his lips to that fluttering skin. The patch was warm, the pulse strong. His own pulses burst to life. Releasing her hands, he traced the curve of her waist to the swell of her breasts, then his lips located hers and the world tipped sideways. He felt the ground leave his feet, and his heart floated up in his chest. He closed his eyes and opened his mouth to take her in. She moaned, and the sound filled him. He moaned back, and she melted against him. He broke the kiss, apprehensive to go further, afraid he wouldn't be able to stop.

''Logan,'' she breathed, resting her forehead against his chin. ''What do you want of me? Sometimes I think you hate me and other times I think you might even I—''

''Oh, 'scuse me.'' Coonie's boots ground the glass to bits as he tried to back out of the office. He looked down, then swung around to the door. ''Did them rowdies do this?''

''No, Coonie. Susan did, and I'm punishing her for it,'' Logan drawled, chuckling as Susan's face flamed to match Coonie's ruddy complexion, made more so by his inopportune intrusion.

''No need for you to be so mouthy,'' Coonie grumbled, ducking his head. ''We should clean this up.''

''That's what I'm going to do this second,'' Susan assured him, already sprinting for the living quarters with Logan's laughter acting like a whip on her.

Jacob sat at the kitchen table, head bent over an open book. He pulled absently at his white-blond hair as he worked on his spelling words. Susan tiptoed closer and was almost on him when his head jerked up and his green eyes narrowed suspiciously. He looked around for someone to save him from being alone with her.

"Where's Etta?"

"I just put her in bed."

"Where's Papa?"

"Out back with Coonie. They're playing checkers."

"I'll go upstairs, too," he said, closing the book.

"No, wait." Susan sat in the chair nearest him and clamped a hand on his forearm, forcing him to obey. "I'd like to talk with you, Jacob."

"I'm sleepy."

"I won't keep you long. Jacob," she said more sternly when he tried to pull away. "Sit still, please."

He became like stone, staring ahead with dread, his breathing almost ceasing.

"Jacob, why do you hate me?"

No response.

"I asked you a question. Must I call your father in here to remind you of your manners, young man?"

His gaze flicked sideways to her, then away. "No, ma'am."

"Good. Then please answer me. Why do you hate me?"

He pressed his lips together for a few moments before letting the words fly in her face. "Because you want to take me and Etta away from Papa, that's why!"

"What rubbish. Did your father tell you that?"

"What if he did? It don't matter who said it. You're gonna try it, but I won't let you. I'll fight you!" He stood up, fists raised.

Susan stared at him, refusing to let him see how upset he'd made her. Angling her chin closer to one of his fists, she offered it up. "Go ahead. Hit me. Punch me. It won't solve a thing between us, but if that's what you want, if that will break down the wall between us, take a swing."

The fist wavered, tightened, then dropped. Hatred burned in Jacob's apple-green eyes.

"Are you through wanting to hit me now?" Susan asked as calmly as she could. "Then please be seated and let's talk about this as if we both have some sense." She leaned around him and patted the chair seat. "Jacob, at ease."

That brought a hint of a smile to his lips, and he backed up and slid onto the seat.

"I loved your mother, Jacob. She was my oldest sister. You're a part of her, which means I love you, too. Maybe your father thinks I showed up to wrestle you from him, but it's not true. I came here to be with you and Etta, to help in any way I could since your mother can't help you anymore."

"She never did help."

"Wh-what?" Susan swallowed hard. "Jacob, that's an ugly thing to say. I know you don't mean it. You're only angry because your mother left you. She didn't want to leave, sweetie. The Lord took her. You understand that, don't you?"

"Yeah, yeah," he said, using his most bored tone. "I bet you think Grandpa wants us to stay with Papa, too," he said, indulging in sarcasm.

"I don't want to talk about Grandpa," she said, side-stepping that subject. "I want to talk about me—and about you. I think your father is a fine man."

"You want him to marry you."

"I do not!" She took a deep breath and told herself not to yell. "Whatever made you think such a thing?" Had Logan said this as well? Did he actually think she was running after him, hoping to rope and tie him to the altar? "I don't want to take you away from your father and I don't want to marry him. Is that clear?"

Jacob glanced at her. "Yeah, yeah."

"And don't use that tone of voice with me," she warned. "I love you, but that won't stop me from applying the switch to your backside if you sass me."

"You're not my mother," Jacob said slowly, pushing his face up closer to hers.

Susan held her ground. "No, but I'm your elder and I always will be, and you're going to respect me, you little upstart. I've paddled bigger children than you, believe you me."

He retreated.

"I've been nothing but good to you," she reminded him. "And all I've gotten from you is mean looks and a meaner mouth. That all stops right here and now. Whether you believe what I've told you makes no difference to me. What *will* be different is your behavior toward me. Either it improves or I'll improve it for you." She vied for his stubbornly averted gaze by ducking into his eyeline and finally pinned it down. "Do we understand each other, little mister?"

"Yes."

"Yes, what?"

"Yes, ma'am," he said between clenched teeth.

"Good. Now skedaddle upstairs."

He was off like a shot, leaving Susan to stack his schoolbooks and worry that she'd handled him all wrong.

Trying to recall how her mother made bread pudding, Susan closed her eyes for a moment to search out the number of eggs needed and the amount of milk her mother poured over the whole thing. Should have spent more time in the kitchen and less in the fields, she thought. Homesickness blasted through her and she fingered the gold cross necklace for comfort.

It'll all seem like home to you soon, she consoled herself, then frowned at the flip side of that coin. I'll probably be sent away just about the time I'm settled, she thought morosely. My garden will come in, this house will feel like home, and Logan will hand me a train ticket.

In a way she wanted to go back to the Armitage farm, but in a way she didn't. Mostly it depended on the day.

Some days she yearned for the familiar. She ached to see her father's face, her mother's kind eyes, her sisters' gay smiles. On those days she smelled the rich Missouri soil, the fields of wildflowers, and the tempting aroma of her mother's cooking floating across the farmland, more effective than any clanging dinner bell. The farm was safe, peaceful, constant. No roaring pistols or rampaging rowdies. No lying on the floor while bullets whizzed overhead, no streets so muddy that ladies couldn't cross except in two places—at Hall's General Store and the Mission

School—where planks had been laid. No new sounds or smells or people; sometimes that seemed oh-so-heavenly.

Then there were other days when the newness of Tulsa acted like locoweed on her. On those days everything was worthwhile and laughter was her companion. She loved watching Etta and Jacob, listening to their wide-eyed stories of what happened at school and what the Indian children were like. Their names tickled them—Becky Bacon Rind, Homer Knot Nose and Stay-put Buffalo Eyes. The town was a constant source of wonderment, and Susan never knew what to expect next. A peaceful morning could erupt in a flurry of misadventures. She could never predict her day's chores any more than she could predict when the next herd of cattle would stream down Main Street.

Sometimes she had days when she didn't know what she wanted. She didn't want to go back to the farm, but she couldn't remain in Tulsa under the same roof as Logan. Some days the strain drove them both to distraction. On those occasional days, she and Logan had little to say to each other and went off to their beds early so they wouldn't have to talk. Those days made Susan feel as if she were balancing on a thread, with what she should do on one side of her and what she wanted to do on the other.

Today was one of those indecisive days, but she knew that tomorrow she'd want to be home with her family. Tomorrow would be a hard day to get through . . .

Opening her eyes, Susan looked down into the mixing bowl. Sighing away her dilemma, she decided four eggs should be plenty. Whirling around to head for the egg basket, she nearly collided with an Indian standing there. Her heart lodged in her throat and she had to swallow hard before she could release a high-pitched squeak that brought a blink of surprise from the Indian. It was only after she screamed that she recognized him as the one they'd run into just outside of town. This time he didn't have his Winchester.

"You . . ." She pressed her fingers around her aching throat. "You scared me. What are you doing? You can't just walk in here as if you own the place. This is my home!"

"You're a skittish woman."

"Only when strange men trespass on my property." And he was certainly strange, she thought. "Now what do you want?"

"Nothing. Brought these for you." He held up two freshly killed prairie hens. "Ought to be good eating."

"I—I can't accept—"

"You got to, lady." He put them on the table. "Bad manners to turn down a welcoming gift."

"What's your name?"

"Manygoats." He touched the brim of his derby hat. "Tom Manygoats."

"I'm Susan Armitage." She wiped her hands on her apron, telling herself that if Jacob and Etta could attend school with Indians she could at least learn to be friendly with one. "It's very kind of you to bring us this gift."

His pewter eyes swept the area. "You made nice home for your brother-in-law."

"Thank you."

"Better watch out." His eyes swung to her and glittered, deep-socketed and mysterious. "He'll be wanting to hitch his team to your wagon—for better or for worse. That's what you white-eyes say, isn't it?"

Susan smiled through her nerves. "Mr. Vance is up front. Did you see him when you came in?"

"No, I came through that side door." He pointed it out. "Had no business with the mister."

Her nerves erased her smile altogether. No one knew that this Indian was in her kitchen, so no one would think to keep a careful eye on her. Susan swallowed, making a gulping sound, and told herself not to give in to her growing panic. "You should be going, shouldn't you, Mr. Manygoats?"

His expression was a study in placidity. "Maybe so, Miss Sister-in-law." Mischief teased the corners of his stern mouth. "Those hens are young, so their meat shouldn't be too tough." He touched his derby again, and Susan noticed that he had stuck three gray and white feathers in the hatband. "I go in peace and with God."

His parting words took her breath. Tom Manygoats

didn't fit her image of a savage. In fact, the rowdies herding cattle fit that image more than the civilized Manygoats.

"Another Tulsa surprise," she muttered to herself.

"Did I hear you call for me?" Logan asked, sticking his head around the pressroom door.

"You heard me scream." Susan picked up the hens by their scrawny necks and shook them at him. "That Indian we met on the trail brought these by—unannounced and certainly uninvited."

"He what?" Logan came into the kitchen, green eyes searching for any sign of the invasion. "So where is he?"

"Long gone, I hope." Susan took the birds out to the chopping block near the back door, and Logan followed her. "His name is Tom Manygoats. I think he's a Creek."

"He came to the back door?"

"No, the side door. I learned that after."

"After what?"

"After I turned around and saw him standing in my kitchen."

"Why, that cheeky bastard!"

"Logan—" She reached out and grabbed the back of his shirt before he could storm off. "It scared me at first, but he was really nice. He gave us these birds as a welcoming gift."

Logan lost some of his ire. "Nice of him, but we can't have Indians parading in and out of this house." He gave a swift shrug. "Well, before you start chopping and plucking, come up front. I want to show you something." Taking one of her hands, he led her to the pressroom.

Coonie and Logan had set the Washington handpress squarely in the center of the room where the light was best. Case racks stood on either side of it like wings. They held the type cases. Rolls of newsprint around Logan's bed served as a room divider.

Susan had gathered a smattering of knowledge about the press and movable type. She'd gotten used to hearing its hiss, clang, and clatter, and she hardly noticed the smell of ink anymore. In fact, the press fascinated her, and she could hardly wait to see the first newspaper it would produce. It had become such a part of their lives that Coonie had named the press Clarabelle, and it had stuck.

Clarabelle was quiet now, and Coonie was nowhere in sight. Logan led Susan to a slanted table that held a page-sized case.

"Take a look," he instructed, nodding at the case and stepping back to let her get closer.

She examined the type, all backward, but she'd gotten used to reading it that way. The banner across the top told her what it was, and she spun around to bask in Logan's smile.

"The front page!" Susan exclaimed, clasping her hands beneath her chin. "Is the first edition ready to print?"

"We'll roll it off tonight and deliver at daybreak," he said, hooking his thumbs under his suspenders and giving them a prideful pull. "By dawn, we'll be official."

"Oh, Logan, that's wonderful." She put her hands on his shoulders and rose up to kiss his cheek. The spontaneous gesture brought a blush of pleasure to his face and neck. "What sort of news is in it?" She turned back to the inky, raised type and read a bit of the top story, then one near the bottom of the page. "Logan . . . what's this about locals wanting to drive the Creeks off their land?"

"You can read all about it tomorrow." He laid a hand on her shoulder and pulled her around to face him again. "I know tomorrow's your birthday."

"Y-you do?" She wondered if he could guess how much it meant to her that he remembered.

"It's going to be a special day for both of us, so I thought you and I could . . . well . . ."

"Celebrate?"

"Yes," he agreed.

"Of course we will. Jacob and Etta and Coonie—"

"No, just you and me. Tomorrow night."

"But what about the children?" she asked, thinking how Jacob would take to seeing his father escort her for an evening out.

"Coonie will watch them. I already asked him. We'll all celebrate tomorrow when the children get home, but then I thought I'd take you out for your birthday. We'll go to that ice cream parlor you've been talking about and we'll try the food at the Tulsa Hotel.''

"Oh, my. You don't have to—"

He pressed his forefinger to her lips to silence her. ''And I'll waltz you under the moon.''

Susan stared at his full lips, transfixed by the way they puckered to say *moon*. A slow grin spread across them, deepening the dimples in his lean cheeks. If he had moved to kiss her, she would have suffered gladly. But he retreated.

"So wear your best dress and put on your dancin' shoes, y'hear?''

She nodded, starry-eyed, but he didn't see. He'd already turned back to his racks of type.

Chapter 10

"**Y**ou're taking her out alone and leaving us here?" Jacob asked with an incredulous air.

Logan angled a glance down at his son, checked out the derision in his eyes, then refocused his attention on his own wavy reflection in the mirror. He adjusted his new tie—a brown and cream printed one—and stuck his only tie pin in it. It had been too damned long since he'd spruced himself up for a female friend. He missed the effort, especially since he'd once been so good at it.

Recalling his sporting days brought the lopsided smirk that nearly always accompanied such memories. Undoubtedly, those years had been the best of his life. Before Catherine he'd been blissfully happy. His future had been assured, or so it seemed. He'd comb the country in search of journalism experience and he'd eventually be editor of a major newspaper. Along the way he'd find a special gal, someone who believed in him, supported his dream, and wanted to bear his children, and who thought he was a stallion in bed and a lamb out of it.

Hell, it had been so many years since he'd launched a flirting campaign he wasn't sure he could remember all the steps. Tonight would be a good time to sharpen his dulled spirit. Fine material to sharpen it on, too. His off-center grin straightened and curved into an arc of sensuality.

Yes, *ma'am,* Miss Susan, he thought with a gush of anticipation. You and me are going to indulge in a little pull and tug tonight to see who gets yanked off-balance first.

123

"Why can't you take me and Etta?" Jacob insisted, reminding Logan of the years that had passed since his last serious flirtation.

"Because I don't want to," he answered a tad too sharply. "It's Susan's birthday, and it'll be good for her to get out with another adult. She's with you children all the time."

"Good for her or good for you?"

He slanted another glance downward. "What's your worry, Jacob Jeremiah?"

"You're gonna marry her."

Logan laughed, but kept the sound trapped in his chest. "Not tonight. I'm only going to dance with her." He picked up his hairbrush. "You and Etta will be in bed soon. That's why I'm not taking you with us. Besides, you wouldn't have any fun. We're going to do silly things like talk and walk and—"

"Kiss."

He used a few drops of tonic to keep his hair back off his forehead, but as he looked down at his son again he felt a lock or two slip forward. "What do you think would happen if we did kiss?"

"You'd marry her."

"Son, I haven't married every gal I've kissed."

"But you would her."

"Why?"

" 'Cause she makes you think of Mama."

Logan squatted and grasped his son's shoulders. "No, Jacob."

"And then she'll take us back to Grandpa's."

"No, Jacob."

"And we'll never be family again."

"No, Jacob." Logan shook him gently. "You're working up a lather over nothing. I've told you a hundred times—I'll never give you up. Never."

"What about Etta?"

"Goes for both of you." He brought his son to his chest and hugged him. "I love y'all. You're my life."

"You won't let her talk you into it?"

"No, of course not. As soon as I have the money, I'm

buying her a train ticket and she'll go back to Grandpa and Grandma.'' He winced as a knife twisted in his heart.

"And she won't take us with her."

"No. She'll go alone." That twisting knife again . . . deep, hurting, so unexpected. He looked squarely into Jacob's eyes. "And even if I steal a kiss or two tonight from her, it won't change my mind." He touched a fingertip to Jacob's freckled nose. "By the way, she doesn't remind me of your mama one bit."

"Then why do you look at her like that?"

"Like what?" Could Jacob see what even he couldn't admit to feeling?

"Like . . . well, like you used to look at Mama before she started staying away so much."

Ah, yes, Logan thought with a bittersweet smile. He'd forgotten the tenderness he'd once known for his wife. Seemed so long ago . . . a whole lifetime ago.

"Papa?" Jacob probed, and Logan shook off the hazy memory.

"I look at her that way because she's pretty. I look at all pretty girls, not just your aunt." He caught Jacob's chin in one hand and gave it a wiggle. "We're all squared now, aren't we?"

"Yeah." Jacob stuck out his bottom lip. "If you say so."

"I say so." He stood up as Coonie unlocked the front door and stepped inside. "Right on time, Coonie."

"Don't you look like a traveling preacher," Coonie observed, running his gaze over Logan's suit—a brown tweedy one. He held up a battered book. "Brought my storybook, Jacob. There's one in here about three billy-goats I think you and Etta are going to like."

Jacob grabbed Coonie's hand. "Let's go. Etta's upstairs already."

"Can you get into bed in say . . . a quarter of an hour?" Coonie challenged.

"You betcha."

"Then git!" Coonie gave Jacob's rump a pat, sending him racing into the other room. "That boy. He's growing like a weed, Logan."

"Sure is. Those long pants will be short pants next year." Logan ran his hands down his jacket. "So tell me. Do I look respectable?"

Coonie gave him a critical once-over and shook his head. "Respectable? That's too tall an order for you, pard. But you look clean and fashionable. Will that do ya?"

"Guess it'll have to," Logan said, giving a wink. "Thanks for watching my little scamps."

"I'm not doing it for you, you ugly cuss. I'm doing it for that sweet lady in there. She deserves a night out, even if she has to settle for you as an escort."

Logan whirled around for a final check in the mirror. "Maybe you should have asked her out, Coonie. She likes you better than she likes me."

"Not hardly, pard." Coonie slapped him on the back. "Better be careful. She might be dragging a loop, and it would be just like you to step in it and get roped and branded."

"Not me."

"It's happened before," Coonie said softly, jerking Logan's gaze his way.

"I learn from my mistakes," Logan said just as softly.

"Let's hope so." Coonie ducked his head and ambled from the shop and into the living room, but he stopped short just over the threshold. "Holy smokes!"

"What?" Logan asked, right behind him, then he saw what had cracked Coonie's voice.

How had he ever thought of her as merely pretty? he wondered, for as his hungry eyes took in the purity of her face and the budding of her figure only one word came to mind—beautiful.

His breath caught in his chest and pushed beneath his heart. He pressed one hand over that telltale organ. It pounded through muscle, skin, and fabric. Can she hear the *thud-thudding* of my heart? he wondered, and the thumping seemed to fill the silent room.

"Glory be, child. You're all grown up," Coonie said, stepping aside so Logan could get an unobstructed view. He glanced around at Logan, chuckled, and went toward the staircase. "I'll go on upstairs. You two have a fine time, y'hear?"

"Thank you," Susan said. "Good night, Coonie."

Logan knew he should say something, but he couldn't make his voice work. He continued to stare, content to visually feast on her. Such a sweet face! Flushed cheeks, black eyes, freckled nose. She had a small head with a long neck, left exposed now by her dress's scooped neckline that stopped just above the promising fullness of her breasts. Her hair, in its crowning glory, spilled to her shoulders in loose ringlets, but had been brought up at the sides and held at the top of her head by invisible pins. The style brought more depth to her eyes and a sharper definition to her cheekbones.

Her dress was well suited to her lithe figure, hugging her long, narrow waist, and the puffed sleeves left her slender arms bare. A modest bustle and apron-style front accented the simple lines of the dark gold fabric. Black lace edged the apron front, the neckline, the layered bustle. She was an exquisite flower of womanhood. His black-eyed Susan.

On her head she placed a pert black lace and tulle hat with velvet ribbons and a small plume on the left side. After slipping a velvet purse into a hidden pocket in the folds of her skirt, she held her arms out from her sides and directed a nervous smile his way.

"All ready? You look handsome, Logan. *Extremely* handsome."

The compliment rattled him enough that he rediscovered his voice. "And you . . ."

"Yes?" she asked when he didn't finish. She glanced down at the dress she had packed so carefully in her trunk, hoping she might wear it to some social function in St. Louis. "Does something disagree with you? Granted, this dress isn't the latest from Paris, but it's not too outdated. Not for Tulsa."

He crossed the room with giant strides and was in time to press a finger against her lips before she could say another word. Her delightfully dark brown eyes widened, and her head jerked at his swift gesture to contain her jumbled excuses.

"And you," he repeated, his finger still stifling her voice, "make me feel eighteen again." Then he replaced his finger with his lips. Just a touch. Her lips felt like rose petals, set atremble by a sudden breeze. "Shall we dine first?"

"First, yes. Then what have you planned?"

"Why, dessert, of course." He gave her breathing room. "Ice cream."

"Ah, yes. And then?"

"Then we'll find something to occupy us. That's a promise, my beauty." He let his eyes say the rest and enjoyed the blooming roses in her cheeks.

"It's delicious, isn't it?" Susan asked, then spooned another dollop of vanilla ice cream into her mouth.

"Ummm-hmmm," Logan grunted, more concerned with the sensual disappearance of Susan's spoon into her mouth than the taste of the ice cream. The spoon slipped back out. Logan's tongue tingled, wanting to be that spoon. Inside and out, in and out, in and out. Lucky, lucky spoon. The tingle raced down his chest and exploded in his groin, spreading to the tip of his member. He shifted uncomfortably as it pressed against his buttoned fly.

"Aren't you going to eat yours?" Susan asked.

"No, you can have it." He pushed the small bowl across the table to her. "I ate too much dinner."

"That pork loin was wonderful," she agreed. "But I saved room for dessert. I suppose this ice cream is terribly expensive."

"Not so much." He twisted around so he could cross his legs. At the mention of loins, his had started to twitch. Was she entirely removed from any sexual lusting? he wondered. It was infuriatingly lonely to be savaged by wanting while she swooned over dessert, oblivious to his pining.

"Seems like we've been here a long time, doesn't it?"

she mused, almost to herself. "I suppose I'm feeling better about this place."

He nodded, enjoying the sound of her voice. Light and cool like the ice cream.

"You must feel awfully wonderful tonight."

"Why?" he asked, swiveling his head around to her again.

"Because you published your first newspaper today," she reminded him with a curious smile. "Have you already forgotten that momentous occasion?"

"For a minute, yes." He shook his head, amazed that his manly needs could circumvent his ambition. "It has been quite a day. Quite a day." An image of his front page floated behind his eyes and pride filled his chest. "Folks seemed right surprised that we got an issue out. Guess they didn't have much faith in me."

"That's because they don't know you. I never doubted that you'd publish your newspaper." She met his gaze with confidence and a smile that turned his heart to butter.

For a few seconds he was so full of gratitude he was speechless, then he cleared his throat and reached across the table for her hand. "Susan, I want you to know how thankful I am to you for all the work you've done."

"Oh, I haven't—"

"You've made that rather cold house a warm home for me and my children," he said, cutting short her modest argument. "I confess I never imagined you to be so resourceful."

"Oh?" she asked, laughing, eyes dancing.

He looked at the hand he held. Her fingers were slim, soft, fragile-boned but powerful in womanly ways. He had no doubt they could render a man helpless with one caress. "I make the mistake too often of thinking you're cut from the same cloth as Catherine. I don't want you to take this as an insult against your sister, but she was never much interested in housekeeping." He chanced a look at her through his lashes and was glad to see her slight nod of agreement. "So I expected much the same from you. But I was pleasantly surprised."

"Thank you, Logan. I've so wanted to hear you say

those things to me.'' She bowed her head, suddenly shy. "I know a charitable soul shouldn't look for compliments, but I'd hoped to please you, and since you never said much, I thought I'd failed somehow.''

"No, just the opposite. You far exceeded my expectations.''

"I've carried my own weight . . . haven't been a burden?''

"You've been a blessing, Susan,'' he rasped and he knew she'd never guess what those words had cost him for he could never again pretend he didn't care, didn't notice her every movement, didn't respond to each smile or frown.

He shifted his attention from her to outside the window where night had drawn shades of dark blue and purple. His ears picked up the strumming of a guitar, joined by the plucking of a banjo. A harmonica jumped in to form a trio. He judged from the sound that the musicians were sitting in front of Hall's General Store, just down the street from the ice cream parlor. Susan had finished her second bowl. Keeping her hand in his, he pulled her up from the fancy metal chair and escorted her outside where the street was relatively tame for a change.

"Where are we going? Home?''

"Not yet.'' He wasted no words. It was as if he were full—so full of emotion he choked on the commonplace things like idle talk.

"Oh, listen!'' She squeezed his hand and the pressure shot up his arm to his heart. "Someone's playing.''

He nodded. "Across the street. Over at Hall's.''

She had to trot to keep up with his long, purposeful strides. Logan heard her rapid breath, but strode on. He had one objective, to get her in his arms. Dancing would do the trick.

"Evening, boys. Sounds mighty pretty,'' Logan saluted as he and his trailing lady drew near. "I'm Logan Vance and this is Miss Susan Armitage.''

"Mr. Vance is editor and publisher of *The Democrat Argus*,'' she added with obvious pride that made Logan want to give her a smacking kiss.

"What's that?" the harmonica player asked as he shook spit from his instrument.

"The newspaper. Didn't you receive one today?" Susan asked, peeved by their ignorance, endearing her even more to Logan.

"Oh, yeah." The guitar player nodded. "We read that this morning, remember, Pete?"

"Yeah, slipped my mind." Pete shrugged, completely unimpressed.

"Do you know the Missouri waltz?" Logan asked, deciding to spare him and Susan any further humiliation.

"Why, sure," the banjo picker said, then strummed an intro. "Y'all gonna dance or just stand about listening?"

"We're going to dance."

"We are?" Susan asked, falling back a step. "Right out here in the middle of the street?"

"Why not?"

"We'll get run over, that's why!"

"Not over here, we won't." He pulled her up to the boardwalk in front of Hall's store. Logan gave a nod and the trio struck up the Missouri waltz.

"Logan . . . I don't think this is quite—"

"Hush, Susan," he said, taking one of her hands in his and slipping the other around to her back. "I told you once you should be waltzed under the moon, didn't I? Well, I'm going to do it. I'm not going to let a little thing like no proper dance hall stop me, either."

She darted worried looks from side to side, but fell into step, flowing with him to the familiar tune. The music worked a spell and tension left her body, making it easier for him to mold her to his. She sent him a confused glance when he held her too close for a waltz, but he disarmed her with a smile. When she smiled back, he knew his worries were over.

"You're a fine dancer," she said, looking up so that the moon was reflected in her dark eyes.

"So are you. You must have had plenty of practice."

"Not really. Mostly I've practiced with my sisters." She laughed at his stricken expression but never missed a step. In fact, she felt as if she were floating in his arms.

"It's true! Papa and Mama are strict about our behavior at barn dances and the like. We aren't allowed to dance with every eager young buck who asks, you know."

"Only if they're good enough for an Armitage to be seen with. I remember."

"Oh, Logan." Her face puckered into a frown. "Let's not talk at cross purposes tonight. It's my birthday and—"

"You're right. Twenty is a milestone. Everything should be perfect on your first day as a twenty-year-old woman."

Her smile returned. "I thought today would be so lonesome for me, being away from my family and all. But it's been glorious! The best birthday I can remember for—oh, so long! Thank you for making it special, Logan. Thanks ever so much."

"I have a birthday gift for you." He knew his voice had grown scratchy, but he couldn't help it. The burning ache had returned full-force. More than anything, he wanted her. He didn't ask himself why or if it was she he wanted or simply a woman. When a man ached as he ached, such questions were pure folly.

"You didn't have to buy me anything else. The dinner and dessert were quite enough."

"I didn't buy this." God, his chest was tight! Like a vise squeezing him while a weight sat atop his head. "I'm only giving it to you."

She tipped her head to one side at a curious angle, and her expressive, delicate brows drew together. She stilled altogether as the last note of the waltz hung like a memory in the night air. "Oh, and what is it?"

He was going to explode into a million pieces, just burst through the seams of his clothing. "This," he ground out, then he circled her waist with his arms and drew her tightly against him until her feet all but left the ground. Bending over her, he claimed her mouth with a shocking fierceness that surprised them both, stunned them into passivity. As the next minute unraveled, they entertained not one sane thought, but let their emotional selves command them.

Thrusting his tongue deep into her mouth, Logan drank

her in. Her lips and the inside of her mouth were cool from the frozen dessert. She tasted faintly of vanilla—pure and sweet. He urged her to respond to him with his hands, mouth, and tongue. Still, she held back. Taking, but not giving. He clamped his hands on either side of her head and angled back to look into her eyes. Hers were blank, dazed.

"Kiss me, Susan," he commanded in a hoarse whisper.

"I am."

"No," he said, gritting his teeth and driving his fingers through her thick, soft hair. Her hat tilted, slipped. "Kiss me as a twenty-year-old knows how to kiss." He narrowed his eyes, sending her a brief, hard challenge.

"I can't." She raised a hand to pull the hat free.

"Lap me up like you did that ice cream."

"Logan!"

He pulled her mouth up to his. Tracing the seam of her lips with his tongue, he melted her resistance. Instead of arrowing his tongue inside her mouth, he held back and waited for her to answer his silent request. She trembled. He nudged her lips with his. She whimpered. He ground his mouth against hers. She relented.

The tip of her tongue danced upon his lips, testing him. He curved one arm around her back and prayed she'd continue. Finally, her curious tongue darted in and out like a busy bumblebee. The small gesture sent a ball of fire through his stomach.

"Again," he begged.

Emboldened by his pleading, she entered again and was met by his tongue, rough and brash in contrast to her timidity. But she didn't back away or whimper when he caressed her and sucked gently. Her breasts flattened against his chest, and he swore he could feel her nipples tighten into buds of desire. He raised one hand and found one of those small, soft mounds. His thumb moved unerringly over the center. Yes, it was hard, peaked, flushed. He knew the feeling. His whole body throbbed, drummed, pulsed.

"Susan, Susan . . ." He poured moist kisses over her upturned face and panted her name. "I want you."

"Logan . . . please . . . I can't—"

"Yes. Say yes, Susan. I'll love you to the moon and back again." He stared into the dark, glittering pools of her eyes. "I'll show you heaven right here on earth, sugar. All you have to say is one little word, and I'll hand it all over to you on a star-studded platter."

She passed the tip of her tongue over her lips and her answer hovered there. Logan held his breath, hoping, praying . . .

"Mr. Vance . . . *Miss* Armitage . . . ?"

They burst apart as if dynamited. Logan whirled to confront the three women, all matronly, all scowling. The tallest kept her gaze firmly on Susan's red face.

"It's a pity *decent* women can't walk the streets of this town without having to witness depravity at every turn," the prune-faced interloper announced for all to hear.

The musicians gathered up their belongings and headed toward the Bloody Bucket, where such chastisement was about as welcome as a scared skunk.

"I . . . we were . . . Did you see Logan's newspaper?" Deftly, Susan pinned her hat into place again.

The three old crows crossed their arms against their heaving chests and glared.

"We were celebrating . . . his newspaper and I . . . it's my birthday. I'm twenty." She said the last after dropping her head in shame. Logan wanted to roar with anger and blast the old biddies off the boardwalk.

"Then you're old enough to know how a *lady* conducts herself on public streets," the short, plump one intoned. "And you, sir, living with an unmarried woman under the same roof as your own children! How can you hope to—"

"I don't know who you are and I don't care," Logan interrupted, stepping up to the trio. "But you're poking your noses in business that doesn't concern you."

"You've offended us," the tall one snapped. "Such demonstrations on a public street! It's scandalous!"

"Then don't look." Logan made a shooing motion. "Get on with you." He grabbed Susan by the elbow and made off with her, tugging her into a fast walk to leave the three mettlesome women in their dust. "Silly old bitches."

"Logan, they're right," Susan said, breathlessly. "What we were doing—oh, I can't believe I stooped to such a level."

"Bullshit."

"Logan!"

They reached the newspaper office, and Logan wasted no time in unlocking the front door. Grasping her hand, he whipped her inside ahead of him. He locked the door again and closed the shutters, throwing the room into darkness. There was just enough light to see it pinpointed in her luminous eyes.

"So we got carried away," he said. "What does that tell you?"

"That I've allowed this wild and woolly town to seep into me. *I* must change it," she said, beating a fist against her chest. "And not allow *it* to change *me.*"

"What happened should tell you that you want me as much as I do you," he told her patiently.

"I'm not as strong as I thought. I'm weak in so many ways, but I must resist," she went on as if he hadn't spoken. She began to pace fretfully.

"Susan, you're letting those biddies dictate your feelings. Why listen to a flock of old birds?"

"Logan, one of those old birds is a merchant's wife, one of them is a preacher's wife, and the other is a banker's wife. What they think counts in this town, and they think we're living in sin. They think we're having a terrible influence on your children."

"I'm sick of worrying about what other people think. How I raise my children is my damned business. Nobody else's!" It was a sore spot, newly opened by the confrontation. Anger and frustration churned in his gut. "My children are fine. But about you and me—"

"Logan, listen to me." She stood before him and gathered his lapels into her fists. "This has opened my eyes."

"Thank God."

"I must find other lodging."

"You *what?*" He fell back a step.

"I can't continue living here with you."

"But isn't that the point? You came along to help make a home for me and the children."

"Yes, but not having my family close by . . . well, things are different. What started out as a good idea—"

"On your part. I still think Abraham sent you to soften me up so I'd let you take the children back to the farm."

"Listen to me!" She shook him by the lapels. "If you're to be an important influence on this community, then you must be respected. Those women—no matter what you think of them—are the social conscience of this town. Their husbands will listen to them even if you don't, and if we don't suffer, the children most certainly will."

The churning ceased, and her words penetrated his armor of indignation. "Okay, I'm beginning to see what you mean."

"I can find a room somewhere."

"That's stupid. We don't sleep in the same room. Can't people understand that?"

"They don't. They can't know what's going on behind these closed doors. Being human makes them think the worst."

"Naturally," he drawled with disgust.

"Especially after what they saw tonight." Her cheeks grew pink, and she released him and placed her hands over them. "I can't believe I let you . . ." She closed her eyes and shuddered.

"Let me what?" He rested his hands on her shoulders and caressed her neck with his thumbs. "Susan, it's time you admitted to yourself that you're a woman with the same needs as any other woman. God knows I have the needs of any normal man."

She turned dark eyes up to him. "All the more reason for me to find lodging elsewhere."

He frowned as that invisible knife sliced his heart again. "I don't want that."

"What are you saying?" she whispered. "What shall we do?"

The thought came winging from some uncharted region

of his heart; or, perhaps, he saw it in her eyes, in the way she looked at him, so trusting, so willing.

"We'll get married." For an instant he wasn't sure it had been he who had spoken.

"M-married?" she stuttered.

"Yes." He shrugged, striving for indifference even while his heart beat like a wild thing. "Why not? It seems the most logical solution to this problem. If a marriage license will silence those pesky old biddies, then by God we'll give them one."

Chapter 11

Must be out of my ever-lovin' mind, Logan thought as he lay on his cot in the pressroom. Moonlight peeked between the shutters, giving a haziness to the room and outlining the bulky press and rolls of paper.

Logan's cot was at the back against the wall, near the potbellied stove. Rolls of paper shielded it and him from snooping eyes, but he could see between the rolls and make out most of the room. However, at the moment he wasn't interested in anything except the mess he'd fallen in.

"I asked her to marry me," he whispered, still finding it hard to believe. "I just blurted it out like I had good sense!"

He ran a hand down his face then back up again to shield his eyes for a minute. He needed time to think—all night, probably, and he'd still face morning with a perplexed scowl. After he'd told her they'd marry, she muttered something like "Very well" and had taken herself to bed, leaving him to his own dawning disbelief.

Jacob had told him that he'd kiss her and marry her. His own son—a lad of seven—knew more about his own ways of thinking than he did himself! Lordy, Jacob would be fit to be tied when he heard the news that, just as he'd uncannily predicted, Logan was to marry yet another Armitage female.

She tricked me into it, he thought, propping himself up on his elbows to better wrestle with the problem. Got him to feeling all contrite and down in the mouth about those

138

clucking hens and their vicious gossip, that's what she'd done! She'd worked him like a cowboy works a dumb cow, giving him a direction, then goosing him enough to make him run right into her corral, thinking he'd made the decision himself.

What had happened wasn't his fault, and there was no reason why he should be forced into a marriage he didn't want. Oh, she was a smart one. Coming on like a guileless virgin while she hornswoggled him into a proposal! She was better equipped than her sister had been! Catherine had been forced to use pregnancy as a means to a marriage, but Susan hadn't even had to get him in bed! A few kisses and—bang!—he was a dead man.

There had to be a way out of this . . . even if he had to hurt her feelings. Of course, a train ticket would solve most of his problems. Yeah, yeah. He smiled, feeling a little relief. That's the answer! Only thing, he'd miss her. He ran a hand through his hair and swung his legs over the side of the cot. Damned if he did, damned if he didn't. Sweet misery, he wailed to himself. Sweet, sweet misery.

This wasn't the way it was supposed to have happened, Susan thought as she lay stiffly in bed and stared morosely at the ceiling. Tears burned the backs of her eyes, but she kept herself from crying. If she started, she knew she'd bring down the house with her sobs.

In her dreams, she'd imagined several ways Logan would ask her to be his wife, but not once had she thought he'd suggest marriage just to shut up some town tongue-waggers. And *never* had she supposed she'd shrug nonchalantly and reply, "Very well, if you wish" to his pitiful proposal.

Susan sat up in bed, horrified at what she'd agreed to—a marriage of convenience, a loveless union. Placing her hands over her face, she shook her head in abject misery, and her thoughts circled to make her more miserable as she recalled Logan's carnal kisses, the stroking of his hands, the rough magic in his voice. Of course she'd agreed to his hasty proposal; she'd been seduced!

But she was thinking clearly now and knew she wouldn't

get a wink's sleep if she didn't put an end to this deplorable situation. Reaching for her robe, she stuck her arms in it and headed for the pressroom. She was halfway there when she realized her robe's belt had fallen away, probably in her bedroom, but she didn't go back to get it. She forged ahead, holding the robe together with one hand at her waist.

The room's light was milky, misty. Susan tiptoed around the rolls of paper and came around the end of them to find Logan sitting on the edge of his cot. His head bounced up, and his eyes narrowed suspiciously when he saw her.

"What are you doing creeping around in the middle of the night?"

"I'm not creeping," she defended herself, then thought how little he sounded like an ardent suitor. "I must speak to you."

"Here?" he asked, spreading out his hands to indicate his sleeping quarters. "Now? It's past midnight."

"I know, but this can't wait."

He propped his hands on either side of his muscled thighs and hunched his shoulders. "Okay, out with it. What's so damned important it can't wait until morning?"

Susan started to speak, but her heart caught in her throat. Looking at him was like gazing at a vision or at a work of art by a great master. Moonglow dusted the tops of his shoulders and tipped the hair on his chest with gold. In profile, his face was heart-stoppingly handsome with its wide, full lips and straight-bridged nose, high forehead, slightly wavy, brushed-back sandy-blond hair. His eyebrows arched not at the center, but just past, and his eyes, droopy-lidded, mossy-green, deeply set, were mirrors to a most complex soul.

What actually captured her attention, if she were brutally honest with herself, was the sight of his mostly unclothed body. His skin looked warm and textured—like hot silk. She curled her fingers against the urge to caress his shoulders then trace the delineation of muscle in his bulging biceps and corded forearms.

Crisp, curling hair covered his arms, thinned out, and disappeared as it climbed toward his shoulders. Veins ran along the backs of his hands and up his wrists. Some large ones pushed at the skin in his biceps. She glanced at her own hands, unveined except for a bluish tint on the undersides of her wrists.

"Well?" he barked, making her jump.

"You're angry."

"What if I am?"

"Don't be." She came into the cordoned-off section and sat on the edge of the cot beside him. "Not at me. Logan . . ." She covered one of his flexing biceps with her hand. She'd been right. Hot silk. His gaze slid to that contact, then up to her wide eyes.

"What are you doing, Susan?"

"Touching you. Comforting you."

"Who said I needed comforting? You're the one wandering around in the middle of the night."

"Yes, but this concerns both of us. Logan, I think—"

"Susan, I think you should pick your scantily clad self up off my cot and take yourself back to your room."

He wore nothing but his thick cotton underpants that buttoned in front and reached his knees. It was all she could do not to stare at his chest, at the way the muscle created a shelf, at the flatness of his nipples, at the brown skin around them.

"But, Logan, I want to talk—"

"I don't. Go."

"Logan." She clutched his arm with both hands, knowing full well she was flirting with the devil and not giving a damn.

Something wild and spirited commanded her, something she'd never felt before but was stronger than any morals she'd nurtured over the years. For the first time in her life she wanted to be bad—to do precisely what she'd been taught never to do before marriage. She wanted a man to touch her all over, to kiss every forbidden place, to answer all the puzzling questions her body had been asking her since she began her monthly cycles.

She knew that what she was doing was wicked, that sitting on a man's bed in the middle of the night was dangerous, but nothing could make her leave his side. His very nearness intoxicated her.

Through the haze of her need she noticed he wasn't looking at her face, but lower. Her robe had fallen open. Beneath it she wore a thin nightdress of creamy white, and beneath that her breasts were clearly outlined, the nipples poking at the inadequate fabric.

"Do you know what I'm thinking?" he asked.

Looking up into his eyes, she shook her head. "I'm not sure."

"Do you know what I'm feeling?"

Laughing breathlessly, she shook her head again. "I'm not sure."

"No? Then here. This should tell you." He grabbed her wrist and brought her hand to the bulge between his legs.

Susan yelped and tried to yank her hand away, but Logan held it firmly against him. He felt enormous, hard, hot.

"Now do you know what I'm thinking and feeling, Susan? Now will you go back to your own bed?"

In the dark recesses of her mind, a tiny voice reminded her that she'd sought him on this misty night to tell him she didn't want to marry him, that his proposal and her halfhearted acceptance had been a mistake. But the clamor of her heart all but squelched that pitiful voice. Impossibly, she felt her head shake once in a firm, stubborn refusal.

His green eyes glittered with hard lights, and the corners of his mouth dipped. "Susan, I'm warning you—"

She didn't want to hear more. Words weren't what her body cried out for. Warnings were the last thing on her mind. Swaying forward, her mouth homed in on his instinctively. His hands caught her shoulders, and his fingers dug into her pliant flesh as his lips parted to invite the sweet invasion of her tongue.

He drove his fingers through the sides of her hair. She'd braided it for bed, and it fell down her back, long and thick and autumn-brown. Tilting her head to one side, he repositioned his mouth and took her lower lip between his for a gentle suckling that set off that delicious tingle in the pit of her stomach. It was a kiss to end all kisses—hot, seeking, beyond anything she could have imagined, and she was breathless when he ended it.

"Susan. *Susan.*" His sharp, hoarse voice startled her eyes open. "This minute, I'll let you go. In the next minute, I won't." His eyes held a question, demanded an answer.

That he was giving her a choice made her love him more and made her decision easier. She scooted behind him until she could stretch out full-length on his cot. The bedclothes smelled of him. She turned her head to press her nose in the goose-down pillow.

"I'm staying," she whispered. "Don't you want me to stay?"

In the semidarkness, she saw the roll of his eyes. "Christ, do you have to ask?" he bit out, then he lay on his side against her, one hand splayed across her stomach and the other clutching her chin to angle her head for another devastating kiss.

He bent one knee and slanted his leg across hers, pinning her in place. Not that she needed to be secured. She had no intention of going anywhere he wasn't. The pressure of his body on hers was exquisite torture. The angles, the muscles, the tautness of bone and skin thrilled her, made her press her flesh against his, flatten her softness against his hardness.

"What should I do?" she asked in a tremulous voice. She so wanted to please him.

"Just lie there," he whispered back, then lifted his head to look at her. "And don't hate me when it's over."

The seriousness in his expression sobered her. "I won't. I couldn't."

His smile was just this side of unpleasant. "You'd be surprised." Then he shook off whatever demon taunted him. "This is your first time, I take it?"

"Of course!"

"Just checking," he said, amused. "A man likes to know for sure before he goes very far."

"You're my first." *My only.*

"Susan . . . I don't know—"

"Logan, I do." *I do.* Hadn't she been trying to avoid those words? Isn't that why she'd crept into his lair, to tell him she couldn't speak those words to him? Was this a mistake, a foolhardy . . . "Oh, Logan!" All sane thought fled as his flaming mouth covered one of her breasts. Through the fabric his tongue stroked, moistened, flicked her throbbing nipple.

Her eyes opened wide to see his bent head over her breasts. The sight enthralled her almost as much as the suction of his mouth. He switched to the other breast, giving it equal attention.

"Let's remove this," he murmured, brushing the robe off her shoulders and then catching the hem of her gown. In one quick motion, the gown came up and over her head. In another second, it and the robe pooled on the floor. Then before she could comprehend his next movement, he'd stripped her of her pantalettes.

In that instant, any blame she'd ever placed on Catherine for allowing Logan a husband's rights before he was a husband fell away. The man was a magician, she thought dazedly, lying before him without a stitch on and only slightly aware of how it had happened. Clothes were certainly no obstacle for the deft Logan Vance!

Trembling under his minute scrutiny, she shrank into herself, and he sensed it. Taking one of her hands, he brought it to his lips and kissed each of her fingers before placing her hand over his heart. She smiled, feeling its rapid pace.

"Did I do that?"

He nodded. "And this." He took her other hand and guided it between their bodies to that place that was so powerfully masculine, so wantonly forbidden. He seemed to grow against her palm as he pressed her hand more completely against him. He groaned and closed his eyes. His head dropped forward.

"Logan?"

"Touch me." It was a hoarse, pleading whisper.

She fashioned a gentle caress that made him quake. That she had such power amazed her. She chanced another, bolder caress, and he moved against her palm as if that part of him had a life all its own.

"Oh, God," he moaned, pulling her hand away and fastening his mouth on her breast again, this time with no fabric to shield it.

The intimate contact resulted in an instinctive bowing of her body and parting of her thighs. To her increasing amazement, Susan realized she knew more than she thought about lovemaking. It was as if her mind held knowledge she had never had to use before. Called upon, it came bursting forth, giving instruction to her body, her hands, her mouth. Curling one hand behind his neck, she urged him up so that she could kiss his wondrous mouth.

He loosed her braid with tender fingers until her hair fell in a curtain about her shoulders and curled at her breasts. Kissing her soft breasts again, he stroked the sides of her hips, her concave stomach, the tops of her thighs. She, in turn, combed her fingers through his tawny hair and traced the sensual fullness of his lips.

How long had she loved him? It seemed forever. She couldn't remember a time when Logan hadn't been her dream lover. But he was a dream no longer. As his lips coaxed hers to part and his tongue explored her mouth, she cherished each sensation he aroused.

"It's been so long . . ." he whispered hotly in her ear even as he unbuttoned his cotton underdrawers. He raised up on one elbow, and she realized she could now see what he'd freed.

Sheathed in silky skin, its tip peeked out as round and flush as a ripe cherry. Fascination gripped her. She reached out hesitantly, then drew back her hand.

"Touch me," Logan urged, and in his eyes she found the courage.

"So hot," she said, her hand closing gently around him. "So hard, so alive." She smiled. "So unlike anything I've ever felt." Her gaze flew up to his, and she saw he was laughing silently. "What's so funny?"

"You. You're precious." He bent forward for a kiss, then drew in a sharp breath as her fingers moved up and down upon him. "Susan, oh, Susan, I want you."

"And I want you," she said, speaking from the most tender region of her heart. She kissed him, her lips lingering against his as the tip of her tongue darted out to touch the tip of his. "I shouldn't . . . we shouldn't, but—"

"Shhh," he insisted, nibbling under her chin. "None of that." Then his thigh parted hers and he slid over her.

His body was slick with perspiration, and his body hair was pleasantly abrasive against her virginal skin. With feverish kisses driving her to distraction, she gave little thought to his careful positioning. He curved one hand behind her left knee and lifted it. The tip of his member inched inside her, and she realized how close she was to being truly his. Her eyes widened as she looked into his, jade-green in the milky moonlight.

"Open your legs, sugar," he commanded gently, and then he fit between them neatly as if he belonged there. His eyes caught fire as he moved deeper into her, but he stopped when she made a sound of protest. "Easy, easy," he murmured, pressing his face to the side of her neck. He kissed her, nipped her earlobe playfully, gave her time to adapt to his invasion.

Having him in her wasn't uncomfortable—just different. She wanted to wiggle her hips, tighten her thighs, bow her spine, but she was afraid to move for fear it was the wrong thing to do at such a time. Suddenly his fingers dipped into her private folds and she stiffened, certain this wasn't proper. She was about to protest when he touched a place that released a spasm in her so divine she thought she might die.

She moved, uncaring of protocol or propriety. Her feet came up and her heels settled at the backs of his powerful thighs. She felt muscles bunching and flexing while inside her the same happened in places where she didn't know she had muscles. The contractions continued as wave upon wave of mindless pleasure washed over her. She clutched Logan's shoulders as he continued his magical manipulations, and her breathing was ragged, almost panting. Arching into him, she whispered his name as she would a chant, over and over again.

With a grunt and a surge he buried himself in her, tearing past the final barrier to stake his claim. The modicum of pain was vanquished by the ripples of pleasure his thrusting movements created. Susan clung to him, dazed by the fulfillment of it all. Never had she felt so connected to another person, so soulfully secured. And she was glad it was Logan.

"Logan." She breathed out his name, finding new enchantment in it. "My Logan." Even as she said it, tears filled her eyes at the sweet sound.

He lifted his head enough for her to make out his expression in the moonlight, and her breath caught in her throat at the ecstasy she saw there. His smile was unlike any she'd seen before—beatific, prideful, gloriously self-indulgent. Lifting her hands to his face, she traced each feature with trembling fingers. He stirred her within and without, each tiny movement redoubling, every tightening of muscle triggering avalanches of sensation. After a minute, he dipped his head and forehead to forehead, he shared his climax with her. His body shuddered, hers quaked in response, and then she felt his release, the lightning flashes of it zigzagging through her.

Sensitive to his every nuance, she felt him grow soft within her and mourned his leaving when he slipped from her nesting place. He pressed warm kisses between her breasts and lifted his eyes to hers. A smile, lazy and fat with satisfaction, spread over his lips like sunshine.

"In my dreams it was never this wonderful," he said, his voice hoarse from passion spent.

"You've dreamed of me?"

He narrowed his eyes playfully. "Maybe I shouldn't have told you that."

"Why? Isn't it true?"

"Oh, it's true all right, but some things a man should keep to himself. Tell a woman you've been having dreams about her and waking up wrapped in a misery sweat, you'll give her the idea she's got you roped and tied."

"I've no intention of roping or tying you," she said, brushing his hair off his forehead. "But, may I remind you, you've already proposed to me."

"Yes . . ." His gaze fell away. "Yes, so I have."

The fleeting discomfort wasn't lost on her. "And you wish you hadn't, is that it?" Then before he could fashion a passable lie, she added, "Please, don't feel beholden. I only accepted because of the children. Isn't that why you proposed—for their sake?"

"Yes, and yours."

"Mine?"

"Well, you *have* been compromised." He leaned away, his back against the wall. "Especially now."

"Is that what you call it? Compromised." She bit her lip to keep from sobbing and managed to maintain a tight rein on her disappointment. "I thought we'd made love. Silly me."

"Now don't do that, Susan."

"What?"

"Get all bothered over nothing."

"Nothing? It was *nothing* to you?"

"And quit twisting my words around!" Irritation darkened his eyes, made them flat and hard.

"Am I? You said—"

"I know what I said," he cut in. "I meant that what we've done—"

"Which you can't bring yourself to name," she pointed out, turning her head from him.

"This coupling . . . our lovemaking. I can say the words, Susan. It's the consequences I'm concerned with now."

"Don't be concerned. I'm quite capable of handling them."

"Susan . . ."

"And quit saying my name like that!" Her gaze rounded on him.

"Like what?"

"Like I'm a recalcitrant child. I am not!"

His eyes, those dangerous, limpid green eyes, scanned her bare body. "You're telling me?"

"Stop." She crossed her arms over her breasts and moved to sit up, but Logan clamped a hand on her shoulder and held her in place. "I should go to my own bed. If one of the children should—"

"Soon, not now. I won't let you leave me in your current state of mind."

"You can read my mind?" she asked, making fun of such a notion.

"I can see you're upset—with me—and I don't want you to be, not after what we've just shared . . . what we made each other feel." Keeping his eyes open and locked on hers, he leaned over her for a brief kiss. "Contrary to what your family might have said about me, I'm not a heartless cad."

"Logan, do you think less of me for surrendering to you?" she asked in a small, frightened voice.

His brows formed a deep vee. "Of course not. There was no surrender. We're both victors." He touched his smile to her lips, leaving its impression there. "Maybe it would be best if we married." He traced circles around her navel. "I know one person who will hit the ceiling if that comes to pass."

"Jacob?"

His hand jerked. "How did you know that?"

"What?"

"That Jacob is against my marrying you."

"Jacob and I have talked. He's made it clear that he will be immensely relieved when I board a train and wave farewell." She sighed, feeling a paining in her heart. "No matter what I do or say, he remains steadfastly against me. You haven't encouraged that in any way, have you? That is, I know he adores you and he might pick up on whatever ill feeling you hold against—"

"Of course I haven't encouraged him not to trust you," Logan snapped, clearly vexed. "How could you think such a thing of me? Sometimes I'm truly amazed that you can stand to be around me, given what a lowly, despicable piece of work you think I am."

"That's not true!" She laid a hand alongside his cheek, and her thumb fit neatly into the deep dimple there. "I don't think you're any of those things. I never have. But

I worry about Jacob. I worry that he'll never love me, and I can't tell you how much that hurts.''

He turned his head and left a kiss in her palm. ''Sweet lady,'' he murmured, then kissed her wrist, her thumb. ''Jacob will come around. I'll work on him.''

''You said . . . Logan, you've already spoken to Jacob about marrying me?''

''No.''

''That's what you said.''

''I meant . . . well, Jacob has been afraid I'd pop the question.'' He was struck again by the uncanny ability his son had shown in predicting his actions where Susan was concerned. ''He's afraid I'll let you take him and Etta away from me should we marry.''

''But why?''

''Because of your father, that's why. Abraham never hid his intentions from me or the children. He has said in front of them that I'm not fit to raise them and that he means to take them away from me.''

Susan shook her head. ''He was speaking from a wounded heart. Losing Catherine . . . it hit us all hard, Logan.''

''Pardon me, Susan, but grief is a damned poor excuse for threatening kidnapping.''

''They'd never—!''

''No, but they'd send you to do it for them, wouldn't they?''

Enraged, she sat up, but he sat up with her and grabbed her forearm. ''Let go. I'm not listening to any more—''

''Okay, so we won't talk about your family.''

''I'm going to my own room.''

''Not yet.'' He cupped one of her breasts in his free hand and ran his thumb across her nipple. It perked up, betraying her.

''We should think about this marriage,'' she whispered, forcing herself not to melt at his slightest touch. ''If Jacob will hit the ceiling and—''

''Actually, he wasn't the one I was thinking of when I said that.''

''Then who?''

He was gazing at her milky-white breasts with feverish delight, and he bent ever so slowly toward one as he answered, "Your father. He'll bust a gut when he gets the news."

Susan leaned back, out of range. "Logan, would you marry me just to anger my father?"

He smiled at that, a smile that alarmed Susan, then he shook his head as if clearing it of revenging thoughts and forced a serious expression on his face. "What? No, no. I wouldn't do that."

"Are you sure?"

"Yes, of course."

Somehow, she wasn't convinced. "Well . . . we should give careful thought to our choices. I certainly don't want to marry and be used as a pawn in some game of—"

"Susan?"

"Yes?"

"Let's discuss this when we're fully clothed, shall we?"

She looked down at herself and at him. Even as she watched, he thickened and lifted. Amazing thing, this man's appendage. He nibbled at her lips, his tongue flicking in and around the corners of her mouth.

"Maybe you're right," Susan agreed, all thought of revenge and proper conduct slipping away as his mouth warmed the side of her neck and slipped lower, lower. "Oh, yes, Logan, you're right. Oh, so right . . . right there . . . oh, yes, yes, right there . . ."

Chapter 12

Obviously, there'd been talk.

All through the Sunday church service, Susan felt eyes on her—eyes of censure and speculation. Sitting beside Logan with the children on his other side and Coonie wedged at the far end of the pew, Susan felt oddly conspicuous. She'd been careful to dress demurely in a high-necked dress with little adornment and a plain hat. Inside, she felt different, but she didn't want it to show on the outside. But maybe it did. Despite all her minute preparations—the severe styling of her hair, the lack of flounces and jewelry—after all that, perhaps the people around her could tell she was no longer a chaste maiden. Susan glanced down at her bodice, half expecting to see a big red letter there.

The sermon didn't help her disposition. The minister had chosen to explore the nurturing of the next generation. Setting a sterling example, the preacher shouted, was the only time-tested way to raise up good citizens. No amount of whippings or firm talking-to's would ever make as big an impact on a youngster as simply living day by day by the Good Book's rules. If you break those rules, how can you expect those following in your footsteps to do otherwise?

Ridden with guilt, Susan had chosen that moment to glance at Logan. His attention was on his children, and his expression was one of parental worry. The sermon had hit him where he lived, too.

Coming out of the church into the bright sunlight made

Susan wince, for she felt as if she were more forcibly exposed than she had been in the cool, dimly lit interior. Neighbors shook hands, farmers with bankers, merchants with customers, saloonkeepers with beer-drinkers. Standing at the bottom of the steps, Susan pasted on a vacant smile as people milled around her, shaking hands with Coonie and tweaking Etta's and Jacob's cheeks. Her memory replayed bits and pieces of last night when she'd bloomed as a woman. She'd slipped from Logan's bed at dawn and had stolen back to her own. It had been there that the import of her actions had struck her full-force.

She'd have to marry him now, she concluded as daybreak had painted her Spartan bedroom with shades of coral. To salvage the tatters of her honor, she'd have to marry Logan Vance. What other man of any merit would want an unwed woman with no virtue intact? She and Logan had entered into their act with clear minds and now they must right the wrongs they'd committed.

"Poor dears," a feminine voice cooed, drawing Susan's attention. The banker's wife, Mrs. Dunlevy, bent close to Jacob and Etta. "I feel so sorry for you."

"Why?" Jacob asked, inching away from the woman's stroking hands.

Mrs. Dunlevy's cold eyes met Susan's. "It's not you children's fault. Nobody blames you little angels."

Susan stepped behind her nephew and niece and draped an arm over each of them, pulling them against her thighs. "Good morning, Mrs. Dunlevy. Is there something you'd like to say to me?"

"No." The plump woman tipped up her double chins. "I have nothing to say to *you.*" Contempt filled her voice.

"And I have nothing to say to you either," Susan returned, then guided the children away from the gossipy woman. Another woman, shorter and rounder, blocked their path. Susan started to sidestep her, but the woman's cheerful smile arrested her.

"Hello, dearie," the woman said, sharing her smile with the children. "Don't you lambs look handsome in your Sunday best," she said, getting a giggle from Etta. "We haven't met. I'm Mrs. Brewster." Her blue eyes sparkled.

"Carrie Brewster, local seamstress. I live out past the edge of town, so I don't come in except on Sundays and once a month for supplies."

"I'm Susan Armitage, and this is my niece, Etta, and my nephew, Jacob. Their father is Logan Vance. He's—"

"The newspaper publisher, I know." Mrs. Brewster patted the white hair that waved under her bonnet. "My son brought me one of those papers. I sure enjoyed reading it. My son and daughter live on my place," she explained. "I gave them the big house when my man died, and I took the smaller one down the road from them. It's all I need," she added with a shrug of her rounded shoulders. Locking her dancing blue eyes on Etta, she bent toward her. "Do you have a dolly, child?"

"Yes, ma'am," Etta answered.

"Good. Then you could use this, I reckon." Mrs. Brewster pulled a doll's quilt from beneath her short cape and extended it toward Etta. "Take it, child. I've no use for it. All my dolls live with my grandchildren now and have enough quilts and blankets to keep them cozy warm."

"How lovely," Susan said, fingering the edge of the quilt. "Did you make it?"

"Yes. I like to keep my hands busy. You'll let her accept it, won't you?"

Susan nodded, giving the okay to an eager Etta. With a squeak of delight, Etta took possession of the quilt, bringing it to her cheek for a rub and a sniff.

"Ain't it pretty?" Etta asked.

"*Isn't* it pretty," Susan corrected patiently. "And it most certainly is. What does a polite girl say when she's given a gift, Henryetta Susan?"

Etta turned her big blues on her benefactress. "Thank you, ma'am."

Mrs. Brewster released a laugh that sounded like the tinkle of tiny bells. "You're welcome, little lamb. Quite welcome." Looking at Jacob, she sighed in distress. "I'm afraid I have nothing for a fine young man."

"That's okay," Jacob said, shrugging, solemn as always.

"Oh, except this maybe . . ." She fished in her skirt pocket and pulled out a black tie. "A young man of your age should have a grown-up tie, don't you think?" She wiggled it when Jacob made no move to take it. "Go on, child. I want you to have this."

Reluctantly, Jacob accepted it and mumbled a lackluster thanks before ducking his head and wandering toward Coonie. Susan watched him go, feeling a familiar helplessness where her nephew was concerned.

"There goes a child with a burden," Mrs. Brewster said softly.

"He took his mother's death hard," Susan said automatically, although she no longer believed that was the root of Jacob's problems. It went much deeper than that.

"And this one didn't?" Mrs. Brewster asked, placing a pudgy hand on the top of Etta's blond head.

"Well, yes, but—"

"He'll come around," Mrs. Brewster said, seeing more in a few moments, Susan realized, than most saw in a few months. "I'd like it if y'all would visit me sometime. I get lonely out there by myself with only my son and daughter-in-law for company. They're newly wed, you see, and don't want an old woman hanging around much. My other son and his family live in Guthrie and I've got a daughter living in Lawton. I've got me seven grandchildren off them." She laughed again, the sound full of good cheer and innocence. "Guess they like their mates just a little, huh?"

Susan laughed with her, feeling the warm blush of friendship. "Thank you for the invitation. And when you're in town, you must stop by and visit us."

"Please visit," Etta begged, grabbing Mrs. Brewster's hand. "I like you."

"I shall, child. I shall." Mrs. Brewster glanced over her shoulder and waved. "Dear me, my son is an impatient soul. He's that gangly beanstalk waving his arm like he's signaling a train. I must be off or he'll work up a steam." Turning toward Susan again, she placed a hand on her arm and gave a squeeze. "Don't let a bunch of loose tongues bother you, dear. They've never vexed me, though they've tried. I believe Tom Manygoats is right; you're a lady of noble soul.''

"Tom Manygoats? You know him?''

"I do. He lives near me.''

"And he spoke of me?''

"He has.''

A plaintive "Mother, I'm waiting!'' galvanized Carrie Brewster, and with a roll of her blue eyes and a pursing of her lips, she spun around and trudged toward her exasperated son. He helped her up into the buggy, withstanding her gentle scolding with a droll expression. Mrs. Brewster waved happily as her son drove the buggy past Susan and Etta.

"She laughs pretty, don't she?'' Etta asked.

"Yes.'' Susan smiled after Mrs. Brewster. "I like her. She's kind.''

"We'll visit her, won't we?''

"Yes, if you want.''

"I do!'' Etta jumped up and down, then she caught sight of Logan and went running to him to show off her doll's quilt. "Look what that lady gave me, Papa! Ain't . . . isn't is nice?''

"What lady?'' Logan asked, directing the question to Susan.

"Carrie Brewster. We just made her acquaintance. She thinks your paper is grand.''

"Does she?'' Logan asked, grinning. "A woman of taste, is she?''

"She gave Jacob a tie . . .'' Susan looked around and saw that Coonie and Jacob were walking home.

"That was right fine of her,'' Logan said, cupping Susan's elbow in one hand and taking Etta's chubby hand in the other. "So, you've made a woman friend, have you? That's good.''

"Yes, especially since the other women treat me as if I'm . . . well, fit only for a saloon.''

Logan checked his stride. "Someone insulted you again?''

"Don't tell me you didn't feel the disapproval all around us,'' she chided.

"You're imagining things."

"You're fooling yourself," she countered, inching her elbow from his grasp. "Anyway, Carrie Brewster was kind and I told her we'd visit her someday soon."

"Go on, Etta." He let go of Etta's hand and let her scamper ahead to catch up with her brother and Coonie, who were already entering the newspaper office. "Susan, about that marriage proposal."

"Having second thoughts?" she teased. "I thought as much."

"The offer remains," he said, taking the wind from her sails. "In fact, I think marriage would solve most of our problems."

"Which are?" she asked, shortening her stride as the conversation took a serious bent. "What problems, exactly?"

"You're right about us needing respectability in this community. If I'm to succeed as a publisher, I have to earn the esteem of my readership. And then I must consider the children . . . I don't want them to hear any gossip about me and you." He stopped to glance through the bank's window at the grandfather clock. "What about four or five o'clock?"

"What about it?"

"To marry," he said, as if he were suggesting a dinner engagement instead of a lifelong commitment. "I imagine the preacher could marry us then . . . right after dinner and before evening service."

"Think he could squeeze us in?" She didn't wait for a reply to her sarcastic question. Whirling from him, she lifted her skirts for a longer stride and made fast tracks away from him. The cad! she fumed. Scheduling a marriage as he would a press run! She knew he was right behind her, so she was shocked when she turned on the threshold of the newspaper office only to find herself alone.

Halfway between the newspaper office and the Bloody Bucket, Logan had been waylaid by Mazie Weeks. As Susan watched with growing jealousy, Mazie laughed at something Logan said. Seemingly enchanted by her, Logan leaned closer, placed a hand on the woman's shoulder, and whispered something in her ear. Mazie slapped playfully at his shoulder, then trailed the fingers of one hand down his sleeve. The look they exchanged smoldered, and Susan was amazed not to see a plume of smoke rising between them.

"Animals," she hissed, then bit her lower lip. How could she call that woman an animal after what she'd done last night with Logan? More importantly, how could he stand on the street and openly flirt with that woman after he'd just proposed to another? "Beast. Filthy beast! I'd rather marry Cal Pointer than a spotted jackal like you," she called to him, uncaring of any spectators.

Thunder sounded, and Susan looked up at a cloudless sky. In that split second, she knew it wasn't that kind of thunder, but the kind made by pounding hooves. Darting a look in the other direction, she was in time to see six horsemen round the corner and come barreling down Main Street, guns held aloft, belching smoke and fire. They wore bandanas across their faces, and money bags slapped against the sides of the two front horses.

"Bandits," Susan murmured to herself, automatically grabbing the doorknob and giving it a twist.

From the other direction came shouts, and the lead horsemen reined in their mounts, making them rear and paw the air right in front of where Susan stood, statue-still and momentarily dazed by the unfolding drama. Looking the other way, she spotted the three men in the middle of the street, all armed with shotguns.

Bullets ripped the air as the bandits and the rifle-toting citizens faced off in front of the newspaper office.

Oh, my God, Susan thought, opening the door. The children! "Etta, Jacob! Get down!" She couldn't see them, but she could only pray they would blindly obey her if they were within hearing distance. Stray bullets could easily find unsuspecting—

Something slammed into her from behind, burning a trail across her shoulder. Glass shattered, shouts rang out, and Susan stumbled, then crumpled to her knees. The burning became a blaze. Susan looked at the place on top of her shoulder and saw that her dress had been torn away. Blood oozed, and she smelled her own charred flesh.

"I've been shot," she whispered, trying to comprehend the pain, the deep ache, the cold chills taking hold of her. "I . . . I've been shot!" In an unconscious seeking of comfort, she lifted a hand to grip the gold cross at her throat. Her muscles gave out and the chain snapped. Her last bit of comprehension was the knowledge that she'd broken the necklace given to her by her parents. The edges of the cross bit into her palm, bloodied by the leaking wound.

Before a black curtain fell over her, she thought she heard someone scream her name.

Logan saw her go limp as if all the bones in her body had suddenly melted, and wild panic punctured his brain. Shoving Mazie into the alley and down behind a thick post, he ordered her to stay there before sprinting toward the fallen woman in front of his newspaper office.

The gunfight in the middle of the street held absolutely no interest for him. All he could see was Susan's inert figure. Reaching her, he dropped to his knees. She lay on one side, her legs folded beneath her. Logan cradled her in his arms, removing her hat with shaking fingers and smoothing back her hair. That's when he noticed the blood.

"Oh, God, no!" Trembling fingers located the wound and tore aside the jagged edges of the dress sleeve. Blood pulsated from the wound, scaring the life out of him. He pressed the heel of his hand against the hole in her, trying to dam the blood, and surged to his feet with her held securely in his arms. Kicking the door open wider, he strode inside, instinct ruling him.

"Lord God, what's all the commotion?" Coonie asked as he bustled into the pressroom.

"Susan's been hurt," Logan replied crisply, shouldering Coonie aside and taking Susan to her bedroom, where he laid her carefully on the feather mattress. "Go find the doctor, Coonie. Hurry."

"Papa . . ."

Logan glanced around at Etta's troubled expression. Her

blue eyes floated in tears. "Honey-bunch, you stay in the other room with your brother. Don't go wandering anywhere else. Hear me?"

"Yes, Papa."

"Jacob, watch your sister for me."

"Yes, sir." Jacob took Etta by the hand. "She gonna die?"

"No." Logan sent Jacob a quelling glare, not missing the unmistakable note of hope in his son's voice. "We must *all* pray that she'll be fine."

"Yes, sir," Jacob mumbled, leaving the room with Etta in tow.

Logan undressed Susan down to her chemise and petticoats. She never stirred awake, as he'd hoped she would. He fetched a shallow pan of water and a cloth and washed the blood from her hands, arm, and shoulder. One hand was tightly clenched, and he had to pry her fingers open. Gold glinted in her palm. Logan extracted it. The cross, he thought, recognizing the jewelry she always wore around her neck. Her cross from home. The broken chain dangled limply from it. He put it in the drawer of her nightstand, making a mental promise to have it repaired for her. She'd gripped the crucifix so tightly it had bruised her palm, leaving angry red marks.

Gazing down into her still, white face, Logan felt tears gather in his hot eyes. Guilt nearly choked him as he recalled how he'd flirted with Mazie just to rile Susan. If he hadn't . . . if she'd gone on in instead of standing in the open to watch the show he and Mazie were putting on for her benefit, then she wouldn't be lying here bleeding. He pressed the stained cloth to the wound that still seeped.

"Damn it, where's the doctor?" he asked the empty room. "She'll bleed to death waiting for the bastard."

At that moment he heard the bell above the press door tinkle and recognized Coonie's heavy tread and another's. Thank God, the doctor. Logan stood up from the bedside to greet the physician, but the man he expected didn't materialize. Instead, Coonie stepped back to allow a plump little woman whom Logan recognized from church to come into the room.

"Who's this?" Logan demanded roughly. "Where's the damned doctor?"

Coonie shook his head, looking dazed, rattled, frightened. "He's seeing to a couple of men wounded in that gun battle, but Mrs. Brewster here offered to come help. She worked for a doctor for years and years."

"A nurse?" Logan asked, and the woman nodded. "Thank you, ma'am. You can help Susan?"

"I believe so. Is the bullet still in her?"

"I don't know, ma'am. I . . . I . . ." His tongue stopped working and stuck to the roof of his mouth.

"Sit down before you fall down, dear boy," the woman said, smiling. Then she devoted her full attention to the patient. "Let's see here . . . no bullet. It's a surface wound, but it took a chunk out of her. I'll need a few things."

"What?" both Coonie and Logan asked.

"Another pan of clean, warm water," she ordered, handing the shallow pan of pink water to Logan. "Soap, a few rags or bandages, if you have them. Kerosene will do or coal oil . . . whatever you're using. Got any medicine cream?"

"Susan might have some in the kitchen cupboard," Logan said, realizing that he'd left the family's health completely in Susan's hands, for he hadn't the slightest notion what kind of medicines, if any, they had.

"Find it if you can," Mrs. Brewster said, perching on the edge of the bed and lighting the lamp as the men hustled out to do her bidding.

Logan sent Coonie for the water, soap, and rags while he foraged for medical supplies.

"Children, does Aunt Susan keep any medicine around?" Logan asked, opening cupboards and drawers in a frenzy.

"On top of the stove in the coffee tin," Jacob answered in a bored tone.

Sure enough, Logan found cotton bandages, several tubes of gel, and a bottle of foul-smelling liquid inside the coffee tin. Logan sniffed again and made a *phew* sound.

"Cough medicine," Etta explained with a giggle. "And for runny noses."

"We won't need it then," Logan said, stuffing it back into the coffee tin. "Now, y'all sit at the table here out of the way. Be good children."

His arms full of tubes and trailing bandages, he hurried back into the bedroom. Carrie Brewster had removed the rest of Susan's clothes and tucked the sheet up under her arms.

"What do we have here?" she mused, taking the tubes from Logan. "Oh, very good!"

"It's what you need?"

"Yes, this antiseptic is just what I need." Her bright blue eyes found Coonie. "Put that water on the nightstand, and then you two can take yourselves out of here and let me alone to nurse this poor unfortunate. That's right," she said when they stood staring at her like two dolts. "Off with you. I don't need four eyes watching every move I make."

Dutifully obeying, they left the room, and Logan closed the door behind them.

"I hope she knows what she's doing," Logan said, chewing fretfully on his inner cheek.

"Seems to," Coonie said, dropping into a chair, then pulling Etta into his lap. "I was asking for the doctor and was told he was seeing to a couple of gents that were bad off from that gunfight. Then some folks pointed Mrs. Brewster out to me and told me she knew medicine. We're lucky she came back. She said her and her family were on their way out of town when they heard the gunfire and she made her son turn the buggy around and come back. She said she had a feeling she'd be needed." Coonie looked at Etta and kissed her puckered brow. "She was darntootin' right, wasn't she, honeybee?"

"Uh-huh." Etta snuggled against Coonie's chest. "Uncle Coonie, I should get out of my Sunday dress and take my nap. Aunt Susan wouldn't want me to wrinkle my pretty clothes."

Coonie exchanged a sympathetic smile with Logan, then gathered Etta up in his arms as he stood. "Right you are.

I'll take you upstairs and you can get ready for your nap. You, too, Jacob.''

"I don't need a nap.''

"Jacob, do as Uncle Coonie says,'' Logan corrected. "When you wake up you can see Aunt Susan.''

"She'll be all right, Papa?'' Etta asked, sleepily rubbing one eye with her fist.

"Yes, baby.'' Logan kissed his daughter's cheek, then bent to leave a kiss on top of his son's head. "Sweet dreams.''

"I'm hungry,'' Jacob muttered. "If she hadn't gone and got shot we'd have dinner by now.''

"Jacob, get to bed,'' Logan snapped, losing his patience. "I'll fix dinner after you wake up.'' He shot Jacob another hard glance, then nodded toward the stairs. "Get.''

The rough order sent Jacob scurrying away. Coonie followed with a droopy-eyed Etta. Alone, Logan paced. He kept seeing Susan fall into a heap and the blood soak her Sunday dress. Entering the pressroom, he examined the glass littering the foot. The same pane he'd replaced only days ago was shattered again. Damn this town and its collection of no-gooders! How could decent citizens make homes with bandits commanding the streets even on Sundays?

A shadow fell across the floor, and Logan looked up to see Mazie standing there. He opened the door but she backed away, making him come outside to her.

"How is she?''

Logan shut the door behind him. "Carrie Brewster is seeing to her. Looks like a flesh wound.''

"Good. Carrie knows about such things. She delivers most babies around here and sees to all the sick children. The doctor mainly caters to folks with money—the banker, the merchants, some of the big ranchers in the area.''

Noticing that her lacy hat was askew, Logan righted it. "I'm sorry I ran off from you like that, but I saw Susan take that bullet and I reacted from the gut.''

"You sure it was from the gut?'' Mazie asked, angling a glance at him from under the brim of her hat. "From the way you cried out her name, sounded to me like you were heartsick.''

He shoved his hands in his pockets and decided not to reply to that comment. ''Who all were injured?''

''Sam Boatright and one of those robbers.''

''Is Sam okay?''

''Don't know. He was bleeding bad.'' Mazie leaned back against the hitching post. Every pose seemed gauged for seduction. With her hands tucked in the curve of her spine to support her, her breasts jutted out for his inspection. ''The doctor's working on him now down at the saloon.''

''The saloon?''

''Yeah, they laid him out on the bar.'' She shrugged. ''It's as good a place as any to get stitched up. Plenty of liquor around to dull the pain, don't ya know.''

''What was robbed?''

''They hit Hall's General Store and then Hattie Crawford's.''

''Hattie Crawford's . . . why?''

''It's a bawdy house, you know, and she keeps all her money in her room in jars. Guess one of those old boys found out and talked the others into robbing her. Only trouble was they gave Hall enough time to get up some guns while they hit Hattie's place. So when they started to ride out of town, they were greeted by a party of men with rifles and bullets.'' She laughed, throwing back her head. ''That's one thing about this town, it's damned hard to tell the good men from the bad ones. They all pretty much look and act alike.''

Logan looked up and down the mostly deserted street. Blood soaked into the dirt, drawing flies. ''It's a wild place, for sure. Makes me wonder if I was crazy to bring my family here.'' At his feet, another stain made him tremble. Susan's blood.

''Men like you are needed to civilize it,'' Mazie said, reaching out to lay a slender hand on his forearm. ''Don't you go giving up so fast. That gal in there is going to mend. She wouldn't want you to pack your bags on account of her losing some skin and blood.''

"Think so, huh?" he asked around a grin.

"I know so."

"You don't know her at all."

"She's female, isn't she? I probably know her better than you do." She looked at her hand resting on his arm. "I know one thing for sure."

"And what's that?" Logan asked, covering her hand with his.

"She don't think much of me, and you're using that to take advantage of her." Her lapis-colored eyes pinned him. "Ain't that right, newspaperman?"

Shame flowed through him, but he fought not to let Mazie see it. "She doesn't approve of the way you make a living. I think you're a good-looking, fun-loving girl. Susan is—well, I owe her a lot."

She eyed him suspiciously. "I guess you're trying to be honest and that's good. Otherwise, you'd have two mad, mean women on your hands."

His ability to charm rose to the challenge. "I bet you're pretty when you're mad."

Mazie leaned closer. "Honey, I'm pretty when I'm *not* mad. You better agree with me if you know what's good for you."

"I agree. Wholeheartedly."

She dimpled, then pushed back from him. "Carrie's in there looking for you," she whispered, snatching her hand from under his. "Tell your Susan that I said I hope she mends quick and I'm sorry for what happened to her."

Logan turned in time to catch Carrie Brewster's eye through the hole in the door's glass. "Out here," he called, then whirled to speak to Mazie again, but she was already down at the corner. Logan went back inside.

"How is she?" he asked.

Mrs. Brewster flicked down her dress sleeves and buttoned the cuffs. "I've stopped the bleeding and bandaged the wound." Her smile made Logan relax. "She's awake and asking for you."

Chapter 13

Her face was so wan that his heart constricted painfully. Logan closed the bedroom door and crossed the room to Susan's bedside. She lifted a limp hand, and he captured it and brought it to his lips.

"Susan . . ." He shook his head and swallowed the knot of emotion in his throat. "How are you feeling?"

"Dazed . . . dizzy." She knitted her brows. "The children, Logan. They weren't hurt?"

"No, of course not. They were inside with Coonie—all safe. But you—God, Susan, I feel terrible about you getting hurt."

"Why? It wasn't your fault."

"Wasn't it?" He let go of her hand, placing it on the coverlet and giving it a parting pat. "I was showing off for you or you would have gone on inside and not been such a pretty target."

Her frown deepened. "Oh, yes, I remember now."

"You mean you'd forgotten?" He laughed bitterly. "And I had to go and remind you. I guess I'll learn someday to keep my big mouth shut."

"You and Mazie . . ."

"Susan, it was nothing. I was blowing off steam and—"

"Flirting with her after you'd asked me to marry you," Susan finished, her eyes darkening with renewed pain.

"Liar, liar, liar!"

Both Susan and Logan jumped, startled by the shrill voice. Logan whirled around. The door he'd closed was

166

now open, and Etta and Jacob stood on the threshold. Etta, mouth hanging open, gazed at her brother, stunned by his reddened face and ugly expression. It had been Jacob who had screamed the one, damning word. He glared at his father, his green eyes gleaming with unshed tears.

"You said you wouldn't marry her," he said, his voice quivering with sobs as he pointed a finger at Logan. "You're a liar! I h-hate b-both of you! Liars! Dirty, rotten liars!"

"Jacob!" Logan towered, his hands fisted at his sides, his eyes narrowed to dangerous slits. "That's enough. Go to your room and wait for me. You, too, Etta." He strode toward them, and the children turned and ran for the staircase. Logan closed the door again and faced Susan. "I'll speak to him. Of course, there's no excuse for his behavior."

"Tell him he has nothing to worry about. I'm not marrying you." She turned her cheek into the pillow in a futile effort to hide her tears from him.

"Susan, forgive me, but don't be so hasty to deny me."

"You should go to your children. They need you."

"Not until we settle this between us. You're important to me, too, you know."

"Am I?" Still, she refused to look at him. "I'm not used to bounders. I thought you were sincere last night, but you're only interested in the woman in easy reach."

"You don't believe that."

"You propose marriage to me and then flirt openly with a saloon girl, and you think I'll continue any sort of relationship with you? All I want is to go home. As soon as I've recovered I'll expect a train ticket from you, sir, and that's all."

He stamped one boot in total frustration. "For God sake—"

"And please keep your blasphemy to yourself!"

"Damn it to hell, Susan, you're being—"

"Papa!" The door popped open, slamming into his shoulder. Already so mad he could see red, he glared down at Etta. "Henryetta, get to your room or I'll tan your hide!"

"Don't yell at her," Susan commanded, shaming him. "Can't you see she's upset? What is it, pumpkin?" Susan held out one hand and Etta raced to her, jumped up on the bed, and pressed her wet cheek against Susan's. "Tell me, sweetie. What's wrong?"

"He's g-gone."

"Who . . . Jacob?" Susan asked, examining her tear-stained face.

Etta nodded. "He—he's run away," she sobbed.

"Logan . . ." Susan swung her gaze to him. "Oh, Logan . . ."

"Where'd he go, Etta?" Logan demanded.

"Don't know, Papa. He went out the back way."

"Damn it all," Logan muttered, then marched out of the house through the back door.

Glancing around the property first, he then headed toward the train tracks, knowing how they drew youngsters like magnets draw metal shavings. Passing the livery, he called into the stableboy, asking if he'd seen Jacob.

"Yes, sir. He went thataway," the buck-toothed boy said, pointing.

"Thanks, son." Logan lengthened his strides while sweeping the area with his gaze, searching for a towhead about thigh-high. Shame dogged each footstep. What the hell was wrong with him that he'd resorted to screaming at Jacob and Etta as if they were mongrel pups? He just wasn't himself. Lately, he'd been doing things that made him cringe even as he did them! Like making eyes at Mazie just to get Susan's dander up. What a stunt. If he was eighteen, he'd forgive himself, but he was a full-grown man!

Ahead of him the Bloody Bucket was closed up tight, wooden sheets drawn across the bat-wing doors that flapped every day of the week except on the Sabbath— Tulsa's concession to civilized living. Logan stepped off the boardwalk and across the alley between the buildings. Bellowed breathing and soft grunts drew him up short. He peered into the alley, and what he saw froze his heart.

Zeke Calhoun, the town's hired gun, held Jacob aloft by his collar. Jacob's legs churned and his small body wriggled as he huffed and puffed and tried to get away from the whipcord-tough man. Calhoun, whom Tulsey folks preferred to call a regulator, grinned wickedly as he watched the boy's desperate attempts at escape.

"You're not going anywhere," Calhoun said, laughing. "I found you and I'm gonna keep you. I'll tie you up in my woodshed and make you lick my boots and anything else I want licked."

Jacob whimpered pitifully. Logan's heart melted, then turned to stone as he brought his gaze to bear on Zeke Calhoun's ugly mug.

"Let him go," Logan rasped in a tone so deadly that both captor and captive fell motionless.

"Papa!" Jacob's voice broke and he reached out, his fingers clutching air. "Papa . . ."

Calhoun released the crumpled collar and Jacob bolted down the alley and flung himself behind his father, his fingers closing around Logan's belt as he held on for dear life. Logan could feel his son trembling, and in that instant he wanted to kill Zeke Calhoun.

"Your little runt there was nosing around in this alley where he's got no business," Calhoun said, hooking his thumbs in his gunbelt. "Ought to keep him penned up if you don't want him roughed up."

"When I want an animal's suggestions on how to raise my son, I'll jerk his chain," Logan said in the same deathly tone. Jacob pressed even closer, but his trembling slackened.

Zeke Calhoun hacked up some phlegm and aimed. The ball of spittle landed just shy of Logan's left boot. "Tough talk for a pencil pusher."

"Tough enough," Logan assured him. "If I ever see or hear of you laying a hand on either one of my children, I'll beat the livin' hell out of you." He gave a sharp nod. "You got that, Calhoun?"

Calhoun grinned, showing off brown teeth. "I'm shakin' in my boots, Vance." His pockmarked face gleamed with oil, matching his slick black hair. He had a thin body, corded with muscle, and his black eyes lacked any sign of warmth, humor, or compassion. It was said around town that he enjoyed his job of scouting for undesirables and keeping the Indians in their place. He enjoyed it too much. He laughed and spun on the balls of his feet, giving Logan his back. "Shoooeee! I'm so scared I won't sleep for a week." His laughter faded as he swaggered away.

Logan swooped Jacob up into his arms and started home. Jacob wound his arms around his neck and shuddered.

"I'm sorry, Papa. You still love me?"

"Yes, Jacob. Of course I love you. Nothing could ever change that. I'm disappointed in you for running away instead of facing me. I hope you won't do that again."

"You're gonna marry her."

"I might," Logan agreed, wrapping his arms under Jacob's rump to make a seat for him. "That won't change my mind about me and you and Etta sticking together."

"You told me you wouldn't marry her."

"I changed my mind."

"You could change it about us staying together, too."

Logan sighed wearily. "Jacob, quit fretting about that, will you? I wish to heaven I'd never told you about your grandfather wanting to get control of you and Etta."

"I would've known anyway. Grandpa never hid it."

"No, he didn't." Logan shrugged. "Don't you worry anymore about me sending you away." He stopped outside the back door and leaned his forehead against his son's. "You're stuck with me, partner. You can't run and you can't hide—not from me. I'll always come looking for you and bring you back where you belong. And there's not a woman alive who can come between me and my children. Believe me?"

Jacob nodded gravely. "I believe you. Papa, would you really beat up that Calhoun man if he touched me again?"

Logan mirrored his son's serious expression. "Jacob, I'd fight the devil himself for you." Then he kissed Jacob's freckled nose and let him slip down his body to stand. "I want you to go apologize to Aunt Susan, Jacob."

"But I—"

"I want you to do this for me, son," Logan interrupted. "And because it's the right thing to do. You know she means none of us any harm and it was wrong of you to make her feel bad when she already feels so poorly. Jacob, do you know what she asked about when she came to after being shot?''

Jacob shook his head and stuck out his lower lip in a pout.

"She asked if you and Etta were safe." Logan waited for Jacob's gaze to swing up to his. "That's right. She was worried about you two before she gave even one thought to herself or anyone else." He was pleased to see regret flit across Jacob's face. "So you're going to apologize, aren't you?''

"Yes, sir.''

"Good boy." Logan placed his hands on Jacob's narrow shoulders and marched him into the house. Coonie was at the stove stirring a pot of something that smelled delicious. Logan gave an appreciative sniff.

"White beans and ham hock?" he asked, and Coonie twisted around, his eyes growing wide with relief.

"Heavenly days, you found him." Coonie shook a scolding finger. "Shame on you for running off like a wild piglet and leaving this house in an uproar. Your little sis is crying her eyes out.''

Jacob's gaze bounced upward.

"No, she's not upstairs. She's in with your aunt.''

"You can apologize to both of them at the same time," Logan said, pushing Jacob ahead of him. "Then we'll all wash up for dinner.''

Jacob stumbled over the threshold and into Susan's bedroom. Etta let out a cry of joy and Susan placed a hand over her heart and glanced up in a moment's prayer of gratitude.

"You found him. Thank God," Susan said, then slumped lower into the bed, obviously wrung out by the adventures of the past few hours.

Etta scrambled off the bed and hugged her brother's neck. "You okay?''

"Yeah," Jacob said, pulling his sister's arms from around his neck in a seizure of embarrassment. "Quit hanging on me.''

"Jacob . . ." Logan made his tone a warning.

"Where'd you find him?" Susan asked.

"Down the street in the clutches of an unsavory fellow. Jacob, you have something to say?"

"Unsavory?" Susan repeated, but Logan made a sign of dismissal.

"Aunt Susan . . . Etta . . ."

"Yes, Jacob?" Susan asked when Jacob's voice dwindled.

"I . . . I'm sorry for making you cry and worry." He shuffled his feet and gave a big sniff, as if he were close to tears. "And I'm sorry you got shot and all."

"Sweetie, that wasn't your doing," Susan said, then held out a hand to him. "Jacob, come here, won't you?"

He made no move toward her, so Logan gave him a not-too-gentle push that made Jacob stumble closer, but not close enough for Susan to touch him. She shook her head when Logan began to give him another shove.

"No, that's okay." Her hand fell limply to the mattress. "I'm glad you're home, Jacob."

"Can I wash for dinner now?" Jacob asked, turning toward his father.

"Yes, go on." He ruffled Jacob's hair, then gave Etta's backside a playful slap as she ran past him. After the children's footsteps grew faint, Logan turned to Susan. "I don't know how to make him trust you, Susan. I've tried, but he's scared you'll try to take him back to his Grandpa and Grandma."

"And he thinks that would be awful, does he?"

"They want to stay with me."

"Of course they do." She pulled the covers up higher. "I would never try to take them from you." Tipping her head to one side, she studied him as if he were a puzzle. "Do you believe me, Logan?"

He crossed his arms, feeling decidedly uncomfortable under her scrutiny. "I want to believe you, Susan. Mostly, I do."

"Mostly?"

"I know your pappy's got a strong hold on his brood. Catherine never did break clean away from him. She always worried about what he was thinking of her. Every time we got any word from him, Catherine acted like a turpentined cat—hissing and getting her back up over every little thing. While we were courting, she swore she was her own woman, but all Abe had to do was give her his famous blood-chilling glare and Catherine's nerve turned to dust. The only way she could follow her own will was by running far away from him.''

"I'm not Catherine."

Clear-eyed, he looked at her, and that strange, sweet feeling squeezed his heart. That old feeling he thought had gone the way of his youth was back tenfold as he drank in her enchanting features—her tangle of caramel-colored hair, dark eyes, pert nose, bowed mouth. He remembered her kisses, the butterfly touch of her hands on his body, the mysteries of her womanly charm.

"You're not Catherine," he agreed. "That's why I'm asking you again to marry me."

"Why?"

"Because I don't want to be out the price of a railroad ticket,'' he teased, getting a lopsided grin from her. He closed the bedroom door softly and came to sit on the edge of the bed. "Susan, do you really want to go back to your family home?" Glancing at the top of the bandage showing above the sheet, he winced. "Maybe this is a bad time to ask that question. I don't imagine you'd get hit by a stray bullet on the farm. But you wouldn't be mistress of your own house there, either. And you wouldn't have three ornery males and one precocious female to rule. We all need your firm and gentle hand, Susan."

"Can I sleep on it?" Susan asked, her lids drooping. "I'm all tuckered out and I can't think straight." She snuggled more deeply under the covers. "A woman should be clear of heart and head when answering such an important question."

Logan leaned forward and dropped a kiss on the tip of her nose. "Sleep, Susan." Straightening, he lingered another few moments to admire how her thick lashes made crescents on the tops of her freckled cheeks. He put a kiss on his forefinger and then transferred it to her soft, plush lips. At the soft knocking on the door behind him, he crossed the room and opened it. Etta motioned for him to come with her.

"Time to sup," she whispered, glancing past him to where her aunt slumbered. "Is Aunt Susan going to eat with us?"

"No, honey." Logan shut the door, then picked up Etta in his arms and carried her to the kitchen table. "She's going to take a nap and eat later."

"She'll be okay, won't she? She won't go live with the angels like Mama?"

Logan had to swallow quickly, his daughter's question catching him off-guard and stirring up emotions he thought long since buried. "She's not going to die, honeybee." He hugged his daughter tightly. "Don't you waste any more worries on that."

When Logan 's hand came to rest lightly on top of her shoulder, Susan flinched automatically.

"Sorry. Your shoulder . . . it still hurts?" Logan asked, snatching his hand away.

Susan shook her head as she turned from the stove. "No, that was habit." She rolled her shoulder, showing him she was much improved. "It's only a trifle stiff today." It had been three days since she'd been shot. Shot! Never had she imagined she'd be shot. Never in her life. Of course, many a curious thing had happened to her since she'd left the family farm.

Logan shoved his hands in his trouser pockets and rocked back on his heels. He seemed to be struggling with something, but Susan couldn't imagine what.

"Is Clarabelle acting up?" she asked, looking toward the pressroom and hearing no sound from the giant machine.

"No, we're still setting type." He studied the toes of his boots. "Have you thought any more about marriage?"'

"Yes," Susan answered truthfully. "Have you?"

"Yes. It's become obvious we can't go on like we have

been. You're right about the people in town looking down their noses at us."

"And we can't blame them, can we?" She wiped her hands on her apron. "After all, we're sinners."

He winced. "Don't go putting ugly labels on what happened between us, Susan. I won't have it sullied."

Delight lifted some of the weight from her heart. Did he love her? Was it possible?

"Making love is natural between the sexes," he said, squaring his shoulders. "I've never felt there was anything sinful about it."

"Society dictates—"

"I know all about that," he snapped. "But I'm not going to live my life by other peoples' rules—especially when I think they're bullshit."

"You think being faithful is bull—that?"

"Faithful?"

"To your spouse."

He shook his head as if rattled. "When did we start talking about husbands and wives? I thought we were talking about lovers."

"L-lovers." The word stuck for a moment in her mouth. "That's what you see us as—lovers?"

He gave her a measured look, then went to stand behind one of the kitchen chairs, gripping the back of it while he met her wide eyes again. "We seem to be talking in circles here, Susan. Let me say what needs to be said. I asked you to marry me and you said you'd let me know. Well, I've given you ample time to mull it over. What's your answer?"

"What's your reason for marrying me?"

He blinked as if her question had knocked him silly. "Have you been out of town for the past few days? You know the reason as well as I do."

"Remind me," she urged, wondering if she were the one being silly for thinking he might confess tender feelings for her.

"To appease the gossips in town. You pointed out, quite rightly, that if I'm to be a leader in this community I must be respected, and I can't be if I'm living with an unmarried woman. The children will suffer, too, if we don't correct this situation." He spread out his hands. "All clear now?"

The weight plopped onto her heart again. "That's it," she said. "That's the whole of it?"

"Yes, yes. So, what's it to be—a train ticket or a wedding band?"

"I admit I have some qualms."

"About me?"

"Yes. I don't know what my sister allowed of you, but I won't put up with your flirting around with Mazie Weeks—or with any other woman, for that matter. If you're so concerned about your reputation, then you should stay away from her."

"Susan, until you marry me, you don't have any right to tell me who I can see and who I can't," he told her levelly, but she noted that his grip had tightened even more on the chair, and she marveled that the wood didn't splinter in his hands.

"I have a right because I'm thinking of the children's welfare. Their own father making cow eyes at a saloon lightskirt is deplorable!"

"If you haven't noticed, unmarried women are rare in these parts. A man must have his needs met." His eyes narrowed and sent messages that made her temperature soar. "Will they be met by Mazie or you? It's all up to you, Susan, but I am *not* going without, I assure you. As for the children, I'll be as discreet as possible should it become necessary for me to visit Miss Weeks. Of course, it would be better for them if I were a respectable married man with no need to slip about in search of fulfillment." He let go of the chair and crossed his arms to wait her out. A lift of his left brow urged her to make her choice known.

Even if she went back to the farm, the images of Logan making love to Mazie would haunt her and spoil any happiness or peace she might find. She loved him, had loved him for longer than she cared to remember. He'd backed her into a corner, forced her hand, transformed a marriage proposal into a cold contract, but still that tingle erupted in her stomach as a winsome smile floated across his full lips and deepened his dimples. Damn his hide! Why did he have to possess so many weapons against her? It was an unfair fight.

"I'll marry you."

His chest jerked as if his heart had kicked him.

"You're surprised? Did you think I'd beg for a ticket home?"

"No . . . I just didn't think it would be this easy to get you to agree."

"Easy?" She made a sound of contempt as she turned back to the stove. "Saying those three words to you was *not* easy, Logan Vance." She fought back a wave of bittersweet emotion. "After all, yours wasn't the sort of proposal a girl dreams of." She rolled her shoulder, testing the healing wound in an unconscious gesture. "Not by a long shot."

Chapter 14

The minister was more than happy to perform the ceremony, especially when Logan offered him a half-page advertisement to call worshippers to his next Sunday service.

The wedding took place on an overcast Friday afternoon in June. Thunder accompanied the piano player, giving an ominous shading to the traditional wedding march. The guests were few—Coonie, Mrs. Brewster, and the children. One other guest was present, although no one noticed him until they left the church. Tom Manygoats stood beneath a towering oak in the church yard and tipped his feathered, derby hat at the newly wedded couple when they emerged from the stately white church.

During the ceremony, Etta and Mrs. Brewster beamed, Coonie swallowed convulsively, and Jacob stared moodily at his recently polished shoes. It was an odd collection of witnesses, Susan thought. Some happy, some melancholy, some sad. For Susan's part, she was numbed by nerves. The minister's words barely registered in her foggy brain and she answered the questions posed to her by rote. Her occasional glances at Logan confirmed that he was the most relaxed of the group. One corner of his mouth tipped up as if he were constantly on the verge of a grin, although Susan found nothing humorous in the ceremony. Logan's eyes danced. His hand, holding hers, was dry and warm; hers was damp and hot. He answered the minister's questions in a firm, sure tone; Susan's voice quavered with uncertainty.

178

In the dim reaches of her mind she knew she was marrying a man she loved, but who had never professed to love her, and that he was a man despised by her parents. She imagined their dismay when the news of her marriage reached them, for she must certainly send them a letter detailing what had led up to such a preposterous decision on her part. How could she explain it when she herself wasn't quite sure of her motives? Was any explanation necessary, since none would suffice? Her parents would never understand her reasoning, even if she unearthed some.

When the vows had been taken and the ring placed on her finger—a gold band, but wider than Catherine's had been and with a faint etching of roses circling it—the minister intoned, "You may kiss your bride, sir."

The Logan tingle bedeviled her as its namesake exchanged a brief kiss with her. Looking up into his gold-dusted green eyes, she was struck by what had transpired. Logan Vance was her husband.

Her husband! The tingle spread to her extremities and chased the fog from her brain. This man who had teased her senses, made her aware of her femininity, and escorted her from maidenhood to womanhood, gazed upon her now with gentle humor. This man belonged to her. The object of her first brush with puppy love and first erotic dreams, the man who'd married her sister and fathered her sister's children, was now beginning anew with her. Surely, life was the most cunning joker of all.

As they walked from the church to the red building, Susan felt as if she were on display. Was the whole town watching this wide-eyed young woman, dressed demurely in creamy lace and oyster linen, step lightly over the pot-holed street with her new husband in tow? Logan patted her hand, as if sensing her fluttering doubt, and her gaze flew to him. The late afternoon sun slanted across him, highlighting his fair hair with gold and sprinkling sparkles through his eyes. Susan caught her breath.

So handsome, she thought, admiring the cut of his dark blue striped suit, white shirt, and midnight-blue necktie, fashioned by Mrs. Brewster. He smiled and her heart soared. Parentheses curved at the corners of his mouth, and his dimples burrowed more deeply into his tanned cheeks. In a mad moment of rapture, she wanted desperately to let her mouth melt over his and feel the lazy sensuality of him blaze into passion as she knew it could. Hastily, she tamped down such wanton urges, reminding herself that he had married her as a convenience, a bone thrown to society's hounds, and not for anything so high-minded as love.

"Shall we slice up that pie?" Logan asked when they were inside their living quarters. He indicated the cherry pie in the center of the kitchen table. Mrs. Brewster had baked it and left it for them earlier. "Cherry pie and a glass of milk would go down good right now."

"Seeing as how we don't have a proper wedding cake, I guess it'll do," Coonie noted, rummaging through the kitchen drawer for a knife to slice it with. "Jacob, do you think you could race to the ice cream parlor, buy a carton of the stuff, and get back here before it melts?"

"Probably," Jacob said, unenthused by the challenge, but he took the money Coonie handed him.

"Go to it, boy," Coonie said, waving him off. "And be careful you don't drop it before you can get it here."

Etta sat on her knees in one of the chairs. "Mmm-mmm. Ice cream and pie." Her blue eyes grew huge with anticipation. "Can I have my milk now, Uncle Coonie?"

Coonie poured her a glass. "Good and cold, it is. That new icebox sure does a fine job. Nothing will spoil in it, I reckon."

"As long as the iceman keeps to his schedule," Logan added, then held out a chair for his new bride. "Mrs. Vance?"

If Logan had fired off a gun, it wouldn't have startled them any more than calling her that name did. Coonie spilled milk and uttered a mild curse. Etta choked on her first swallow of milk and gave in to a fit of coughing. Susan twitched as if she'd been stung and her knees gave way, letting her fall heavily in the chair Logan held out for her. Immediately, she thought of Catherine, and looking up into Logan's face, she knew that he was thinking of her, too.

Logan cleared his throat and sat beside Susan. "Coonie, slice me up a big piece, will you? Getting married always makes me hungry." He sent a teasing grin Etta's way, and she giggled and wiped the tears from her eyes, brought on by her coughing. "You okay, sweetpea?"

Etta nodded and took another drink of milk. "Is she still my Aunt Susan?"

Logan and Susan stared at each other, both at a loss.

"Papa?" Etta insisted. "Is she?"

"Yes, of course," Logan said, then shook his head. "But she's more than that now. She's your new mother."

"She'll never be my mother," Jacob said, entering the kitchen with a square carton tucked under one arm. His chest heaved from his race back home. He set the soggy carton on the table and glared belligerently at Susan. "My mother is dead."

"We're all quite aware of that, Jacob," Logan said evenly, checking his temper. "And you've made it clear you didn't want me to marry your aunt. But I don't take orders from you. *You,*" Logan said between gritted teeth as he poked Jacob's chest with his forefinger, "take orders from *me.* Sit down and mind your mouth, young man. I've had about all I intend to take of your back talk."

Jacob sat at the table and stared mutinously at the milk pitcher. Susan's heart ached for him.

"Do we call her Aunt Susan still?" Etta asked.

"Uh . . . I don't know . . . should they?" Logan asked, throwing the decision to Susan.

It was a simple inquiry—what to be called—but she could find no simple answer. Finally she shrugged and sighed. "Aunt Susan is fine. I wouldn't feel right being called anything else." Susan noted the slight relaxation of Jacob's stiff shoulders, and she knew she'd relieved him of some of his anger toward her.

"But I can leave off the *aunt,* can't I?" Logan teased, getting another giggle from his daughter and the shadow of a smile from his son. Coonie guffawed, breaking the tension in the air.

"Thanks, Coonie," Susan said, taking the dish of pie and melting ice cream from him. She wondered exactly what Coonie thought of the strange marriage. Did he think it was a love match or did he know better? Did he approve or think she and Logan were great fools? She couldn't be sure, but she thought the latter. Coonie seemed to be resigned to the marriage, but wary all the same.

The odd, makeshift family seated around the table made appropriate comments about the delicious pie, the novelty of the ice cream, and the freshness of the milk. Susan scooped up a spoonful of the ice cream, thinking that the last time she'd eaten it she'd been an untried, unmarried virgin. It seemed months ago instead of days.

Etta and Jacob were excused to change from their finery into play clothes. They raced each other upstairs while Coonie cleared the table. Susan excused herself and went to her bedroom to remove her dress—one she'd always favored and seldom wore. Funny, she'd never thought it would someday be her wedding gown.

Holding it up to her face, she let a single tear slide down her cheek. She hadn't been married in pure white but in a cream-colored dress. Of course, she could have donned the white dress she owned, but her innate honor and honesty forbade such a prevarication. She touched her throat, then chided herself, knowing the gold cross wasn't there. It had been broken and Logan hadn't been able to repair it, so she'd tucked it away. Someday a jeweler would happen along to fix it, she told herself.

Susan folded the dress carefully and put it with her other ones. She stepped out of her dressy undergarments and put on her everyday ones. The big event was over and life would settle into some kind of normalcy, she assured herself as she slipped on a dress of pale yellow that complemented her coloring. It was plain but attractive, with an attached apron front and filmy, long sleeves. Before opening the door, she listened to the silent house. Clarabelle slept, having been churning out newspapers since dawn. Logan and Coonie had delivered them before they went to the church. The newspaper came before weddings or births or any other event. Susan had learned that about Coonie and Logan early on. Nothing got in the way of delivering *The Democrat Argus*.

No sound of the children either, she noted as she opened the door to bump into Logan. She backed up, muttering an apology, then noticing the toiletries he juggled. Mug, shaving brush, straight razor, towels, bottles, comb, brush, toothbrush. She looked up into his eyes to confirm her inkling that her bedroom was about to be invaded.

"I thought I'd move a few things in," he said, stepping around her.

"Why?"

"Why?" he repeated, turning to face her. "Well, because I can do my morning ritual in here from now on instead of trying to see myself in that blamed mirror in the pressroom. I swear, I've nicked myself a hundred times trying to see my reflection in that piece of glass." While he talked, he arranged his things on a corner of her bureau, the one nearest the washstand. "Can you clear out a couple of drawers for me?"

"You're not thinking of making this your room, are you?"

"Yes."

"Then I'm to sleep in the pressroom from now on?" she asked, purposely being obtuse. When he frowned at her, she lost her temper. "How dare you *presume* I'd allow you to share this room with me!"

He propped his hands at his waist, looking damnably handsome, having shed his suit jacket and rolled his sleeves to just below his elbows. His tie was gone and his shirt hung unbuttoned to mid-chest. "Susan, do you recall saying *I do* earlier today?" he asked as if she were dense.

"And do you recall suggesting we marry for appearances?" she shot back. "I agreed to this for the children, certainly not for you to take privileges." She stepped to the open door. "Where are the children anyway?"

Susan gasped when Logan slammed the door in her face. He leaned back against it, indolent and sexily dangerous.

"A traveling salesman pulled up down the street and Coonie took them with him to hear the old boy's sales pitch.'' His eyes glinted. ''I told him we'd appreciate a few hours alone.''

''You wh-what?'' Her mouth went dry as cotton.

''Coonie understood and said he'd let them stay the night at his place. Right accommodating, don't you agree?''

''I think you're taking too much for granted, Logan Vance.'' She angled up her chin. ''Perhaps it's my fault. By letting you bed me, I've given you the impression I'm of low morals. I am not. My honor is tarnished, but intact.''

Her little speech drew his brows into a vee. Pushing away from the door, he stood on his own power, legs apart, chest thrust out. ''I don't think less of you for what's happened between us, Susan. I'm sorry *you* think less of *yourself.*'' Bobbing one shoulder, he pivoted, flung open the door, and strode from her room, but her sigh of relief was premature. ''Be right back,'' he said over his shoulder. ''Can you spare one drawer for me, please? Two, if possible.''

She closed the door forcefully and wished she had a key to lock it. Instead, she wedged the back of a chair under the knob and stood back as if expecting visitation from the devil himself. She didn't have long to wait. Footfalls grew louder, then stopped outside her door. The knob rattled. The chair squeaked, groaned, but held.

''Susan, don't play this game,'' he said, his tone telling her he was weary of her defenses. ''Open the door.''

Grabbing the bedpost, she held her breath.

''Susan. *Susan.*''

She winced at his sharp tone.

''Damn it to hell . . .''

She screamed as the chair skittered across the floor, propelled by the door being kicked wide. Logan's squinty-eyed, bared-teeth expression made Susan cower behind the ridiculously inadequate bedpost.

''Don't touch me,'' she warned.

He went to the bureau, yanked a drawer from it, and shook its contents to the floor, then put his folded undergarments into it. Replacing it in its rightful slot, he arrowed a glance at Susan. She dared not protest his actions. She'd never seen him so furious. His eyes fairly smoked!

"If you strike me . . ." She swallowed, afraid he would do just that.

He stared at her long and hard, and the smoke cleared from his eyes. "I swear to you, Susan, I'll never do that. I might curse you, tease you, laugh in your face, but I'll never lay a hurtful hand on you. You see?" He spread out his hands in a hapless gesture. "Even cads like me have codes of honor."

"If you do, then you'll leave me alone. You said I could have this room."

"It's yours," he assured her.

"Alone. Mine alone."

He shook his head, smiling slyly. "Not anymore."

"I won't allow you to take advantage of my doing you this favor."

"Favor? I think we did each other a favor. Susan, did you really think I'd marry you and then treat you like my sister?"

"I . . . I didn't think about it. You said we'd marry to stop people from thinking poorly of us."

"That's right," he agreed.

"You didn't say anything about entering into a real marriage."

"Look at me, Susan." He moved closer, so close she had to tip back her head to look him in the eye. "Do I strike you as the type of man who would do without a woman for the rest of my natural life?"

"It wouldn't be that . . . long . . ." Even as she said it, she knew he'd trapped her.

"How long must I wait? *Why* should I wait? How will a few days or weeks change anything, Susan? It's our wedding night. What better time to start off on the right foot, so to speak. After all, we've already drunk from the well." He skimmed a fingertip from her collarbone to a place just above her right nipple. When she shivered uncontrollably, he grinned. "I've worked up a thirst since then, black-eyed Susan. What about you?"

"Please leave." It was all she could manage. Her throat

tightened around her dislodged heart and her pulses drummed incessantly. Only he could make her knees tremble, she thought. Only he could make her back down from her lofty intentions.

"I remember when you were in pigtails," he said, completely ignoring her weak request. He spread his hands over her head until they bumped against the loose knot at her nape. His fingers slid into it, loosening it, sending pins to the floor. "Catherine said you were a wild weed, but I assured her you were a late bloomer. I was right."

"Logan, please don't . . ." She heard the pitiful whine in her voice and wished she were made of tougher stuff.

"Mrs. Vance," he murmured close to her ear.

"Don't call me that."

"Why? It's your name, isn't it?"

"I don't deserve . . . This marriage is a sham." She whirled away from him, finally finding enough strength to resist his purring tone and gentle hands. "It's all such a lark to you—a joke—an easy way to have a bed partner, but it goes down hard for me, Logan." She pressed a fist between her breasts. "My heart aches." Horrified, she felt tears build in her eyes and spill over. "This is your second marriage, but it's my first. When I think of what happened, how it happened, and why, I can't help but feel cheated."

"Susan, it's a little late to back out."

"Yes, I know. This was the simplest means to an end, but it certainly isn't a perfect plan. When I think of how Jacob looked—he hates this marriage with everything in him." She shook her head, unable to go on.

"Jacob will learn to accept our marriage," Logan said, then mocked Susan's shocked expression. "He will, believe me."

"You keep saying that—you keep saying Jacob will get over this or that, Jacob will understand, Jacob will come out of his melancholy mood. When, Logan? When will this miracle occur? Your son needs to talk, he needs to lash out, he needs to cry and rage and let some of the poison out of his system. You can't let it fester forever, Logan!"

He started to argue with her, but then he clamped his lips together and was silent for almost a full minute. When he spoke again, his tone was level, almost flat. "Ah, yes. I'd almost forgotten you were an Armitage."

The old argument brought the same old pain. Susan spun around, unable to face him, unwilling to let him see her tears. He came up behind her, and his hands warmed her upper arms.

"Susan, I'm sorry." He leaned his forehead against the back of her head and breathed in the scent of lilacs. "Let's not hurt each other. I want us to be good friends, to respect each other, to stand beside each other."

"That's what I want, too," she admitted in a small voice, allowing him to turn her around to face him. His tender smile went a long way toward healing her hurt feelings. "But you can't expect to move in here with me, Logan. It's not right."

"Not right?" He laughed incredulously. "What's more right than a husband sleeping with his wife?"

"But we're not wed in that mold. We married only—"

"People marry for all kinds of reasons," he cut in, and his hands tightened on her upper arms. "Don't play coy with me. You want me. I know you do."

She scowled, not completely ready to agree with that notion. Shaking out of his hold, she stepped around him. Moving to the window, she pulled back the heavy drape and looked out at the twilight stealing across the yard. The town was quiet. No thundering herds or roaring guns. The field stretched out behind the house, broken by patches of wild black-eyed Susans. She remembered Logan pointing them out to her and hoping they meant good luck. Well, their luck hadn't been all good, but they had survived and in some ways flourished.

Something gold and glinting swung before her eyes, and she inched back her head to focus on it. Logan had reached around her to hold a necklace before her nose.

"My necklace! You fixed it," she said, grabbing it for a better look.

"Not exactly. I couldn't get that one repaired, as I told you, so I bought this one as a substitute."

Upon careful study she saw that this cross had an etching of roses on it, matching her wedding ring. "How sweet." Emotion choked off her voice for a moment.

Logan took the necklace from her nerveless fingers and fastened it around her slim neck. She looked down at it and shook her head. The man never ceased to amaze her. Even while he suggested they bed lustfully instead of lovingly, he had this sweet gift ready for her. She became aware of his presence behind her, felt the heat of him at her back, knew he was running his gaze over her.

"Turn around and let me see," he said softly, beseechingly.

In that instant, she knew that if she turned around she'd be his companion in every sense of the word. She could walk to the door and open it, and he'd leave, or she could turn and confront him wearing her heart on her sleeve. With her last shred of courage, she moved toward the door. Her hand closed around the knob.

"I would dearly love to see you out of that dress."

Shocked, she sucked in a noisy breath as her gaze swept around to his. His crooked grin and dancing eyes sealed her fate. She felt her own lips curve into a smile, almost against her will.

"Logan, you are an outrage," she accused, unable to keep the lightness from her voice.

"Only nakedly honest," he said, winking at her. "Pardon my one-track mind." When she made a moue of distress, he conquered the space between them with two long strides. "It'll be all legal and respectable this time, Susan."

"You forgot expedient."

"Your hair looks pretty that way," he said, ignoring her statement and the sigh of frustration that his comment evoked from her. He slid his fingers through the ends of her hair, then arranged them to curl above her nipple line. "It's not just brown, is it? Here are some gold strands and dark, chocolate-brown strands. Pretty . . . so pretty." His gaze lifted to her face, settled on her parted lips. "Why didn't you wear white today?"

She blinked, startled. "I . . . I couldn't, could I?"

"No one knew except you and me."

"And God."

"Oh, yes." He glanced up. "I forgot about Him. I think He'd forgive you, if you asked."

"I have."

He shrugged one broad shoulder. "Well, then? Why should a pretty woman go about in sackcloth and ashes?"

"I wore cream, not black."

"And brought notice by doing it." He scowled, but his eyes remained steadily on her lips, making her jittery. "When I think of that night it's with reverence, not regret. I recall dancing under the moon with you, watching you eat ice cream, aching for you so bad I thought I'd explode. And then you came to me in the night like a vision—an answered prayer."

Blast his hide, he was seducing her with words so pretty and pious she could feel her weakened resistance slip away even as she cursed him for being so persuasive. In the dusky light of the bedroom, he loomed bigger than life, so manly, so muscled, so rock-solid.

"Maybe this isn't a perfect union, but we entered into it of our own free will—and, well, darlin', it's all we've got." His teasing grin made her smile. "There you go. One smile from you, Susan, is worth twenty from any other woman."

"I should hope so," she retaliated. "I *am* your wife and expect to be honored as such." She was halfway serious and could tell he knew it by the flexing of muscle in his jawline. "I, for my part, won't be making eyes at any other man, so you can rest easy."

He chuckled. "Somehow I never doubted that." He lifted one of her hands and pressed it flat against the side of his face. His skin was stubbly, lightly scratchy. "Beyond all else, you're as faithful as old Spot."

She tweaked his cheek and made him yelp. "Compare me to a dog, will you? Just for that, I'm throwing you out of this room." She made no move to follow up her threat, and his arms slipped around her.

"Kiss me, Susan," he said, his voice gone all husky in the space of a moment. "Kiss me mindless."

His mouth, a fraction of an inch from hers, looked delicious, and she needed no more prompting. Standing on tiptoes with her hands plastered at the back of his head, she drew him down to meet her parted lips. A groan worked up his throat and entered her mouth. Susan kissed him as he'd showed her how to, her tongue mating with his. Desire swamped her, its depth and swiftness shocking her. She'd no idea how much she wanted him until that moment when the world was reduced to his mouth, his tongue, his wandering hands.

Her searching tongue brought another moan from him, then he tore his mouth from hers to sprinkle moist kisses from beneath her ear to her collar. She reached behind her to unhook her dress, and her hands collided with his. Together, they completed the task. She stepped away to push the dress off her shoulders and arms, afraid his impatience might result in a tear. From the fever in his eyes, he might just rip the garment off her body, she thought.

Grabbing the sides of his shirt, he stretched out of it, balled it in his hands, and tossed it away. Passion's fire leaped in her as she ran her hands lightly over his furred chest and dropped a line of kisses across his breastbone. Her fingers teased his masculine nipples, and he muttered an unspeakable word that for some reason excited her even further. Without giving it much thought, she grappled for the buttons of his trousers and slipped them open.

"Susan, help me," Logan whispered, growing impatient with her multitude of undergarments. "I can't find you under all these damned frills." He kissed the square bandage that covered part of her shoulder. "And I don't want to hurt you."

"You won't." She made quick work of it, removing her petticoats and corset and letting them drop away so his hands could move over her. His skin was hot and satiny smooth, she discovered, sliding her palms across his shoulders and down the bulge of muscles in his upper arms. He's a beautiful man, she thought, leaning forward to tease his paps with nibbling kisses. Logan's arms tightened around her and he swung her up and about, falling with her onto the bed. He pulled away the last garments between them and rolled onto her, his kisses ardent and deep, taking her breath. She panted and writhed as his mouth crawled down her throat to her breasts. Her nipples gathered into tight, aching points, and her breasts filled with desire until they were hot and heavy. He laved her left breast and nipple until she cried out, then he moved to her right breast. Susan stroked him, running her hands up and down his sides, counting his ribs, exploring his navel and the nest of hair below it.

She parted her thighs, and one of his hands slipped between them, rubbing her with blatant familiarity. Arching into his knowing hand, she closed her eyes and let the searing, shooting flames of pleasure engulf her.

"God, Susan. You're so wet." And then he was inside her, full and thick and filling.

"Logan!" She released his name as a cresting wave smothered her. He felt wonderful, nestled inside her, moving slowly and rhythmically in time with her thudding heartbeats. She pressed her open mouth against his shoulder and shuddered, waiting for him to release himself in her.

One thrust more and he stilled, groaned, rasped her name and trembled from head to toe. She felt him jerk deeply inside her, and the wonder of it all glimmered through her like sun rays.

"Logan, oh, Logan, it's wonderful," she whispered into his ear, making him smile. She kissed him, then drew back. "Isn't it? I mean, if I'm not doing something right—"

"Such a little worrier," he scolded gently, moving to lay on his side and trace lazy circles around her puckered nipples. "Listen here, wife," he said, leaning over her with feigned anger.

"Yes, husband?" she answered as the dutiful spouse.

"You're not to test my patience with dumb questions," he said as gruffly as his smile would allow, then he took one of her hands and guided it down to him. He was moist, semi-erect. "Feel that? Doesn't that feel satisfied?"

"Yes." She smiled, knowing she should be outraged that he'd put her hand on his most private part. As little as she knew about such things, she did know that her mother would have slapped her father silly for such an outright impropriety. But she wasn't her mother's daughter when she was with Logan—she was Logan's woman, so she caressed the hot, throbbing hardness of him. He slammed his eyes shut and grimaced.

"Godamighty," he moaned, throwing back his head in a seizure of ecstasy. He righted his head and opened his eyes again. The naked longing in them made Susan catch her breath. "I want you like I've never wanted another woman in my whole life, Susan. Come here." He hooked his hand behind her knee and lifted her body, half on and half off his. In that fluid motion he surged inside her again, and she tightened around him, holding him there.

"Logan, Logan," she chanted, giving his shoulder love bites. His confession made her love him more than she thought possible—and it didn't matter to her whether he had been truthful or not. That he'd said such a thing to her was enough.

"Ah, Susan . . ." He rocked his hips forward, thrusting up into her and touching off fiery sparks. His belly rubbed hers; his chest hair tickled her sensitive nipples.

"Logan, I love you," she said, enthralled with what he was doing to her body. She was on fire. He cradled her face in his hands and tipped her head back so that she was looking at him, seeing the dark green of his eyes and the sensuous slash of his mouth.

Gazing at her and holding her thus, he sucked in a breath and then stiffened against her. His climax was the most erotic she'd known, for he let her see the effect of it in the deep pools of his eyes and in the play of tiny muscles across his face. When the shuddering shivers died, he let out his breath in a long, loving sigh. His lips touched hers sweetly.

"That's how I feel about you, Susan," he whispered. "And as God is my witness, I never felt anything like this for Catherine."

Chapter 15

Susan was awakened by the abrasive rasp of beard against her tender breasts. Moaning and then coming awake with a jolt, she opened her eyes to Logan's devilish smile.

"Morning, missus," he drawled, propping his head on one hand while the other flipped the sheet back to expose more of her body to his inspection. "You sure are warm-feeling and good-smelling in the morning. I think I'm going to like waking up with you."

She snatched at the cover, bringing it up to her chin. Logan scowled at her.

"It's too late to be prudish, sweetpea," he scolded. "We made love—several times already—remember?" He pointed a finger, pistol-style, at her. "And I warn you, you'd better remember."

"I remember," she said in a voice that sounded like a child's. She felt exposed, vulnerable. Chancing a glance at him, she saw in that instant the lanky length of arm and leg, the furry expanse of chest, the tight bunching of muscle under a white-skinned backside. He was shamelessly naked, lying on top of the covers. "Logan, the children could come in here any moment."

He shook his head. "Not my children. They've been trained better than that. Besides, they're not here. I peeked out the window earlier and saw them with Coonie. They're outside helping him fix up the henhouse. It's a beautiful day, so they'll stay outside most of it." He leaned forward

193

to kiss a patch of skin just above her left nipple. "And we can stay inside most of it."

"Not me." Gathering the sheet to her, she scooted off the bed. "I'm taking a bath, so if you please . . ." She arched a brow and glanced toward the door.

Logan followed her gaze with his own, then looked back to her. "Go right ahead."

With a huffy breath, she marched to the bureau and tore undergarments from it, then ripped a day dress from the line stretched in one corner of the room and curtained off. Spinning around, she was miffed to find that Logan hadn't moved a muscle—no, he'd moved one. The most manly one of all. She looked away, embarrassed, then aflame when he laughed at her.

"See something you wish you hadn't? Sorry, but I can't do a thing with it. Seems to have a mind all its own." Then, when she would have hurried out, he added, "Want me to wash your back?"

"No!"

"Your front?"

"No!" She slammed the door on his laughter, muffling it. "Rapscallion," she muttered darkly as she hitched the sheet higher and went to pump water into the big iron kettle.

In the process of filling the tub, she leaned over, and the gold cross Logan had given her dangled and caught the light. Susan straightened slowly, one hand moving up to caress the etchings upon it. It suddenly occurred to her that she'd never touch this necklace when she needed to feel close to her parents again. From now on, touching it would bring thoughts of Logan.

Had he planned that all along? she wondered, casting a glance at the bedroom door. Was he more devious than she believed him to be? Her father had always said it of him. Spawned from the devil, Abraham Armitage had often said of Logan Vance.

Well, he certainly made love with devilish delight, she acknowledged, feeling heat rise in her cheeks. But it was a delicious heat, and she savored it. By the time she locked all doors leading to the outside, so as not to be surprised by Coonie or the children, and was dipping slowly into the tepid water, Susan was drenched in memories of love-making. Sighing, she closed her eyes and lounged in the gentle lapping water. She ran the washrag over her breasts, down her stomach, over her thighs, playfully tracing the tracks Logan's lips and teeth had left on her skin. Loving him was so easy, she thought. Catherine must have— She squeezed her eyes more tightly shut, recalling his comment about how he'd never felt for Catherine what he felt for her. What *had* his relationship with her sister been like? Had it been unhappy? Catherine had never let on, although she'd never acted blissfully happy either. Susan had assumed Catherine's lack of enthusiasm had been for their parents' sakes, since everyone knew they despised her husband.

Even Jacob had suggested that his mother hadn't been around enough to suit him. Now that she was more deeply embedded in the Vance family, Susan decided it was time to learn of her sister's impact on her new husband's life. If nothing else, she meant to find out what kind of marriage it had been—happy, sad, unpleasant, unmoving, heavenly. Somehow, she seriously doubted the last.

A squeak that sent a shudder through the tub brought a similar sound grating up her throat. Susan's eyes popped open and she started to sit up, but the sight of Logan standing at her feet froze her. He gripped the sides of the tub and lifted one bare foot, clearly signaling his intention of climbing in.

"Logan, no!" She held out a hand, palm out, but her attention was divided between her instinct to keep him out of the tub and what the sight of his erection did to her insides. Suddenly, the water was no longer tepid, and she was perspiring. "Logan, we shouldn't . . . Logan?" She moaned when his other foot landed in the tub, then he was on his knees and his mouth was closing in fast. "Logan! Mmm, Logan." She could have fought him, could have squeaked and screamed and squirmed, but none of that occurred to her. Her arms came up, lassoing his neck, and her thighs parted willingly.

"I want you, Susan," he whispered hotly in her ear, then his tongue whorled in the shell of it.

She quivered and bent her knees. "Love me, Logan." And he did.

By the end of the next week, the novelty of the marriage had begun to wane and routine had begun to set in again. Although Jacob retained his icy manner toward Susan, Etta loved Susan almost enough for both of them. Coonie gently teased Susan, saying she wore the pants in the family, although she and Coonie both knew very well that Logan ruled the roost.

After many more weeks, Susan felt more comfortable than she had since their wagon had rolled into Tulsa. During the day, nothing much changed. School let out for the year and Susan assigned chores to the children and made sure they did them daily, no matter how they whined and complained. They helped her work in the house and yard, assisted when they could with cooking, washing, and tidying the house. Jacob was especially appreciated since he already knew how to perform most household tasks. When she complimented him, he told her grumpily that he'd been doing house chores since he was little. She'd smiled, touched that he no longer thought of himself as a child.

With Jacob and Etta helping her, Susan found enough free time to assist Coonie and Logan with the newspaper. She delighted in learning the skills of proofreading, typesetting, and headline writing. Secretly, she itched to write one of the stories for the newspaper, but she dared not tell Logan. He'd surely laugh at her. Besides, she had enough to keep her occupied during the day, although sometimes she lapsed into fits of boredom.

She couldn't say the same for her nighttime activities. Night changed her from a housewife to a lover, and she was an apt, avid student. Logan, for his part, was a tireless teacher.

Only one thing nagged at her about their nightly explorations; Logan had stopped releasing within her. Just at the crucial moment, he withdrew himself and deposited his seed into a handkerchief he kept at hand. Susan had never asked him why. She knew. He didn't want to have children with her.

She might be his preference in bed, but he and Catherine had made children together. Therefore, his earnest admission on their wedding night about never feeling anything with Catherine that he did with her paled and held little importance. Men had children with the women they loved. It was as simple as that.

Rain blew in the second week of August, and the air turned cool and damp for a few days. That's most likely when Coonie caught his chest cold. By Thursday he was feverish and had developed a hacking cough. Logan sent him home at mid-morning with instructions to stay in bed until his fever broke. Susan checked in on him, making him swallow a spoonful of medicine and seeing that he had a pitcher of water beside his bed, then she went to the pressroom where Logan was frantically trying to get the paper ready to be printed that evening.

She'd no sooner started to help when he announced he had to leave.

"I've got to go to a meeting," he said, and hung up his printer's apron, the front splotched with ink. "I'll be back in a couple of hours. Will you read these pages for any spelling or punctuation errors?" He had motioned to the racks of lead type marching up and down in neat columns in the page frames.

"I can do that," Susan had assured him, sending him off with a quick kiss on his cheek. "What kind of meeting?"

"Oh, just a town meeting. Nothing important. See you in a little bit," he'd called, then the bell sang out as Logan fanned the door.

It had taken nearly two hours to read the columns of type, finding a couple dozen errors that Logan would have to correct before printing the newspaper. Finishing, she'd sat at his desk in the corner of the room near the front windows. She touched the items there—inkwell, ink pen, pencils, blotter made of rawhide and sandpaper, a framed photograph of Etta and Jacob taken in St. Louis. She opened the top drawer where she knew she'd find sheets of writing paper and withdrew one, then dipped the pen in the inkwell.

She'd put it off long enough. It was time to write her parents and tell them of her marriage.

"Dear Papa and Mama," she said as she wrote the salutation at the top of the letter, then moved to the far right of the page and put the date, August 21, 1897. She sighed and sat back, wondering how in the world to tell the poor souls about what she'd gone and done. After thinking another minute, she sat forward again and poised the dipped pen. "This letter, I'm sure, will distress you, but I hope, given time, you'll understand that what I've done is for the best." Susan bit her lower lip, then wrote in a rush, "I married Logan in June in church before a minister and family and friends." She closed her eyes, seeing her parents' reaction to that sentence and hurting for them. Now what? she wondered, opening her eyes again to stare at the letter. Should she tell them she'd married to make an honest woman of herself, or should she let them think this was a love match?

Love on my side, she thought, feeling a tad melancholy, since she still couldn't say the same for Logan with any certainty. They didn't talk about important things like their feelings for each other, his expectations of the marriage or hers. They talked of safe things such as the weather, the children, the growth of the town and the people in it. Nothing that might lead to a discussion of anything which might bare their souls, even a little bit.

In her heart, Susan knew it wasn't right to sleep with a man and not be able to talk to him about anything, everything. Having always thought the most intimacy to be shared with a man would be the physical union, she was baffled that honest conversation had turned out to be the wall neither she nor Logan could break through. She yearned to ask him about his marriage to her sister, but her tongue tied in knots when she tried to voice her curiosity. She ached to ask him if he loved her, but she couldn't force the question out.

Maybe she didn't really want any answers. Perhaps her

cowardice had conquered her altogether and she was simply content to be deaf, dumb, and blind to reality where Logan was concerned. Had she been reduced to that?

Returning to the letter, she soaked the pen's tip again and wrote, "You sent me here to look after Logan and the children, and I've found I'm quite content to do just that. I pray this finds you all well and that you'll come to understand this arrangement is for the best. The children are thriving and, believe it or not, Logan is a wonderful father to them." She looked at the last of that sentence, remembering the dire picture her father had painted of Logan's paternal shortcomings. Oh, well, she thought with a shrug. Papa is a different father than Logan is, but neither is right or wrong, best or better. While her father was a strict, nononsense man, Logan was firm but loving with his children. Actually, she would have liked it if her father had been a little more like Logan. Children needed to be hugged and kissed, and the Armitage children had received none of that kind of contact from their father.

Voices drifted to her from down the street, and Susan cocked an ear, noting the voices were male. The meeting had probably broken up, she thought, looking out the window and seeing shadows pass. Bootheels drew closer, tapping importantly on the boardwalk outside.

"It's them or us, I'm telling you," one of the passersby said.

"Yes, but an uprising? I don't think they'll go on the warpath against us," another said.

"I don't want to alarm you, but my brother thought the same thing. He lives between here and Lawton. He came home one day to find his wife and three children scalped, their throats slit. Indians are Indians, and they can't be trusted. We either force them out or we . . ."

The voices died away. Susan realized she was standing, shaking her head, balling her hands into fists. She went to the type trays and found the article she'd read earlier about town officials growing concerned about the Indians camped outside Tulsa. So the town meeting was about forcing the Indians out of their homes, she thought, gritting her teeth. She had been around few Indians since she'd arrived, but the ones she'd met had been pleasant and polite. Sure, they were different, but they weren't doing any more damage to Tulsa than the weekly herds of cattle stirring up choking clouds of dust or the rowdy cowboys using Main Street for target practice! If the townspeople wanted to destroy something, she thought hatefully, let them burn the Bloody Bucket!

The tinkling of the bell brought her around to face Logan. He strode in, cap in hand, hair attractively windtossed. Did he have to be so devastatingly handsome?

"How was the meeting?"

"Fine. Find any mistakes?" he asked, hanging his cap on the tree near the door and looking toward the page racks.

"Quite a few."

He groaned. "Well, I'd better get at them or I'll be working through the night." Rolling up his sleeves, he glanced toward his desk and saw the letter. "What's this?"

She picked it up before he could. "I was writing my parents to tell them of our marriage." His wicked chuckle incensed her. "It's not funny."

"To them it won't be, but I think it's a side-splitter." He leaned over the front page, locating the places she'd marked.

"You think our marriage is a joke?"

He frowned. "That's not what I meant, and you know it."

The little things that had been nagging her ever since their wedding seemed to gather into a tight ball of nerves in the pit of her stomach. She pressed a hand there, feeling her eyes burn with anger. "Logan, what was that meeting about tonight?"

"Just town business."

"Logan." Her level, prickly tone brought his head up and around. "Were you reporting or contributing?"

His eyes narrowed and he straightened. "What's got you so riled up?"

She placed her right hand to her left shoulder where the skin was puckered but had healed. Realizing it was a sign of defensiveness, she snatched her hand away. "I heard some men outside talking about forcing out the Indians. That's what the meeting was about, wasn't it?''

''What if it was? It's my job to report on any meetings, no matter what's discussed or whether I approve.'' He shrugged and turned back to the racks. ''You know that.''

''Yes, but what I don't know is your feelings on this matter. I read the editorial. You made some vague references to 'dangerous outside influences' and how they should be dealt with so Tulsa can grow in the 'right' direction. Reading between the lines, I figured you were writing about the Indian camp outside town.''

''They are a nuisance, you have to agree.''

''No, I don't.'' She didn't allow herself even to flinch when his flinty stare created sparks. ''When I married you, Logan, I didn't take on your thoughts, ideals, and personality.''

''More's the pity,'' he grumbled, fiddling with the type again. ''How did you break the news to your folks?''

''As forthrightly as possible.''

The accusation in her tone didn't go unnoticed. His sweeping glance was at once insulting and maddening. ''Okay, I wouldn't cry bitter tears if those whiskey-guzzling savages were drummed out of town. Happy now? Can we talk about something else, or better yet, will you get the hell out of here and let me work?''

That made her flinch. He hadn't spoken to her in such a surly, hurtful tone since their marriage. She started to depart, then thought better of it. Why let him bully you? a voice taunted. Stand up for yourself! You're not his slave.

''Just one question,'' she said, waiting for him to look at her. When he didn't, she posed it anyway. ''You call the Creeks savages, but savage or no, they lived on this land before this town was founded. Why shouldn't *we* be the ones to leave?''

''Look, from the dawn of civilization the conquering army stays and the defeated either go someplace else or adapt to the new society. Most of the Creeks aren't doing either. They're camped out there, causing havoc with their dances and rituals, and scaring the bejesus out of every man, woman, and child traveling along the river road into town. It wouldn't be so bad if they'd play by our rules—''

"Why should they? What's wrong with *their* rules?"

"For Christ sake, Susan, you aren't listening to a word I'm saying," he yelled, tossing aside an inkstained rag in a fit of fury. "Just go on to bed."

"You can't send me to bed as you do Jacob and Etta," she returned coolly. "Can we please discuss this without you swearing at me?"

"I doubt it."

"Logan, what makes the Indians less human than we are?"

"I never said they were."

"Yet you endorse this plan to force them out—run them off their land."

"It's not theirs."

"It is," she insisted. "Just as much as this place is ours."

"Susan, I need to put the paper to bed if you don't mind and—"

"I do mind. It alarms me that you're so narrow-minded. Mrs. Brewster lives next to the Indian camp and she says they're dear, sweet people. Peace-loving people."

"You have a short memory. Remember when we came to town and that Creek pointed a gun at us?"

"He meant us no harm."

"When someone points a rifle at my chest, I figure he means me harm," he said with a snarl. "And you did, too. You were so scared your teeth were chattering."

"That's because I hadn't known any Indians. Tom Manygoats wouldn't hurt a fly. He was only being cautious since white men have been known to shoot Indians first and ask questions later." She rushed on to stave off his argument. "And they're trying to adapt to our society. Look how they dress. Many are wearing white men's clothing —derby hats and vests and trousers. Their children dress just like the white children in school."

"Fine, you've made your point." His expression reflected deep concentration as he located another print error, but Susan knew it was mostly an act to discourage any further debate.

"They're doing well in school, too, and learning our language quickly, which I'm told is far different from theirs and—"

"I'm not talking about them. The ones going to school and living in houses in and around here are doing what they should be doing—learning to live in a civilized township. It's the others who bother me. Those defiant ones outside of town still living in their teepees and doing their war dances are the problem." He shook his head in a brooding, scolding way, and Susan had the distinct impression he was repeating something he'd just heard in his meeting with the other self-appointed rulers. "They can't expect us to put up with that for much longer. They're just begging for trouble."

"Why, because they aren't obeying the white men in town?" Susan asked with a harsh laugh. "Why should they? We don't own them. They aren't our slaves, you know."

"I guess Abe will load his rifle and swear revenge once he gets your letter. Hell, he might even ride up one day and try to fill me full of buckshot."

She frowned at his rude interruption, but the new topic was telling. "The thought of my father being overcome with anger and grief makes you smile from ear to ear," she observed, feeling that twinge of suspicion near her heart.

"Why shouldn't it? He's never done anything to me that wasn't low-down and dirty."

"He let you marry his eldest daughter."

"He let me?" Logan repeated, finally whirling to face her. "If you believe that, you've been fed a line of bull, honey."

She swatted away his side of the story, having tired of it long ago when her father had repeated the painful incidents that had led up to Catherine's marriage to Logan. Her father's warnings, Logan's refusal to respect his wishes, Catherine's sneaking off in the night to let Logan bed her . . . it was all burned into Susan like a brand.

"Sometimes I believe you married me only to spite my father."

"Your father doesn't have that kind of hold over me, sweetness. Only his daughters and wife jump sky-high when he yells rabbit. That little banty rooster has never ruffled my feathers, I can assure you."

Her mouth had gone dry suddenly, and her heart beat dully in her chest. "You hate my father, don't you?"

"With a passion," he admitted, so swiftly and succinctly it stunned Susan into a few moments of silence. "That shouldn't surprise you. I've made no pretense of it."

She tried to find a drop of moisture in her mouth but couldn't, so her voice came out as whispery as a desert breeze. "Did you marry me just to anger my father, Logan?"

His eyes rolled up into his head and he spun back to the racks on the balls of his feet. "Oh, for Christ sake, Susan," he said with a tinge of aggravation. The silence stretching from her to him finally got the best of him, and he stole a glance to find her waiting him out, her face pinched with something akin to despair. "What the hell difference does it make?" he asked, throwing out his hands. "The marriage was a good idea. I'm satisfied with it and you're completely fulfilled, so let's not go looking for more fodder for bad feelings." He gave a decisive jerk of his head, as if adding a period to the subject, then bent over the racks again.

Humiliation rose up in Susan like a fist. He hadn't denied her accusation, and that was as good as admitting it. She wanted to strike back and make him as miserable as she felt. Instinctively, she knew just how to do it.

"I haven't been completely fulfilled," she said in a deceptively even tone.

His eyes slid sideways to her. "Oh?" His tone was equally even, equally deceptive.

"No, I haven't." She thought of him pulling out of her, unwilling to create a future with her. Good enough to bed, but let's not make any babies to tie us together, she spoke silently for him. That's what you've been thinking, isn't it, Logan? Give yourself a way out once the novelty of having wed another one of Abraham's daughters wears off?

She was so busy imagining his thoughts that she noticed belatedly that his face had gone white and his lips had thinned into a straight, uncompromising line. He wiped his inky hands on a rag slowly, thoughtfully, painstakingly. Realizing she might have hurt him more than she'd intended, she stepped toward him, but he backed away, his head swinging up, his eyes glinting dangerously like an animal's.

"I'm glad you gave it to me straight," he said, his voice toneless.

"Logan, I—"

"Because I've had better in bed, too. It's best we admit the truth and not lie to each other."

If he had slapped her hard across the face, it wouldn't have hurt any worse. In fact, she stumbled as if he had backhanded her. Tears pricked her eyes, and pain squeezed her chest like a vise.

"If you're not satisfied in my bed, why not leave it?" she asked.

His lids drooped to hood his dark green eyes from her. "I guess I should. The cot will do me as it has in the past." He shrugged indifferently. "No use forcing my attentions on you."

"You haven't forced—" She snapped her teeth together. Why ease his pain when he refused to ease hers? Giving her skirts a twitch and a swish, she went to the writing desk and retrieved her letter. Tucking it into her skirt pocket, she moved past Logan with as much dignity as she could muster. "Good night, then."

" 'Night," he said, using the most bored tone he could fashion, then laughed because he was so close to tears. He sensed her hesitating in the doorway and turned to look at her silhouetted there. "Yes?"

"Why did you laugh just now? What's funny?"

"Oh, I was just thinking . . ." He shook his head and put a shield up to his heart. No, no. Don't give her the satisfaction of knowing how deeply she's stabbed you, he cautioned himself.

"Thinking?" she urged.

"Of Catherine," he blurted out, wondering where that had come from, but going with it nonetheless. "She turned into a cold fish, too, once she got what she wanted from me—a way out of her father's clutches." He saw the glimmer of tears in her eyes. Part of him wanted to kiss them away while another part wanted to turn them into racking sobs. The latter won out. "I guess it's in the Armitage blood to use people."

Her chin angled up, poked by pride. "If anyone in this room has been used, Logan Vance, it's me."

When she was gone, Logan threw the ink rag across the room in a burst of agony, then slumped into the desk chair, feeling as if he'd been wrung and hung out to dry. He ran a hand down his face, then pushed his fingers roughly through his hair. Casting a mean glance toward the hated cot, he wondered how in the hell he'd managed to get himself back on it.

"You stupid, callow jackass," he berated himself, then opened the bottom desk drawer and hauled out the half-empty bottle of whiskey he and Coonie kept there for those days when nothing went right. He'd just had one—one that would make a monk cuss a blue streak.

Lifting the bottle to his lips, he took a big swallow. The whiskey clawed at his throat with fire-tipped fingers and landed in his stomach with all the finesse of a closed fist. He coughed, hacked, teared up, and took another drink.

What did the woman want in bed? he wondered, and why didn't she tell him before now that he wasn't lifting her skirts high enough? Christ, he couldn't even satisfy a still-wet-behind-the-ears maiden fair! Maybe he'd blamed Catherine too quickly for casting him out of their marriage bed soon after they'd settled in St. Louis. Maybe he'd been at fault. Although he'd never gotten any complaints from females he'd bedded—until a few minutes ago— Catherine had certainly let him know she could live without his caresses and lovemaking. Of course, their marriage had never been good and the sex had lost its appeal once it had become clear that getting pregnant had been her objective all along.

But he could have sworn Susan was different. He would have bet the farm that she loved every second they'd spent in bed together. Of course, just now she might have been babbling nonsense, talking until she could find a soft spot to drive her knife into. He lifted the bottle in a mocking salute. Well, Susan, you found one.

Swallowing more of the whiskey, he focused his burning eyes on the ceiling and willed himself not to cry. He hadn't cried since the day Jacob had been born and he'd been buffeted by guilt and remorse at the pain Catherine had endured during labor and delivery. He'd sworn to her that there would be no more children, and she had agreed. Staring at the remaining whiskey in the bottle, he recalled it was this brand they had drunk that night Etta had been conceived. When he returned from work one day a month later, Catherine had greeted him with an ugly sneer and the news, "I'm going to have another one of your babies, you bastard."

He finished off the whiskey, trying to drown the memory. Tossing the empty bottle into the trash barrel, he pushed himself up from the chair and watched the room spin before his eyes. He held his head in both hands to keep it from dropping off his neck. When it was safe again, he let go and moved gingerly to the racks of type. They blurred before his liquored eyes.

"Shit," he muttered, rubbing his eyes and waiting impatiently for them to focus.

He finally had to splash cold water on his face before he felt up to putting the finishing touches on the pages. Dawn found him slumped in the office chair, sleeping the sleep of the exhausted and downhearted. By the time Susan came to get him for breakfast, he was already gone, the newspapers along with him. It was afternoon before she realized he'd stopped off at the Bloody Bucket once the newspapers had been delivered. Neither she nor the children knew when he came home that night, but it was well after midnight and he was very, very drunk when he staggered in, cursing Susan's name and swearing that he'd rather sleep alone than with Susan. He passed out before he could make himself believe it.

Chapter 16

September brought cooling breezes to hot, dusty Tulsa. The school bell rang, signaling the end of a long summer and sending the children back to their books.

Not much had changed between Susan and Logan. Days slipped by, witnessing their peculiar lovers' quarrel where no hot words were spoken and confrontations were few and seldom seen.

Not a day went by that Susan didn't tell herself she'd end the silent struggle, she'd approach Logan and tell him his distance was killing her spirit, tearing chunks from her heart, and making her hate herself and him. But then he'd trot off, night after night, to that blasted saloon, and she would retreat into her shell of feigned indifference and swear that it would be a cold day in hell before she'd apologize to a man who would rather cavort with soiled doves than take company with his wife and children.

In the deepest pocket of night, she'd tell herself that he'd break down the wall between them soon. He was a man of passion, and he'd surely snap one dark night and come to her, bent on pursuing his husbandly rights. And she'd surrender . . . willingly.

But he never came to her. Instead, he went to the Bloody Bucket most nights and came home drunk enough to sleep like the dead. The day before, she'd grabbed a calendar and counted the weeks since she and Logan had shared a marriage bed. The number had struck her a hammer's blow. Four weeks. One month. That's when she began to worry that he might not storm her defenses after all. Maybe

209

he'd already made a conquest at the Bloody Bucket and was no longer interested in her bounty.

She began to fret in earnest, going through the motions of her day's errands while her mind and heart worried over her dilemma.

After dropping Etta and Jacob off at school, Susan stopped at Hall's and left her shopping list with the merchant to fill, then headed for the tiny post and telegraph office. Mr. Finch, the postmaster, waved two envelopes at her.

"Got some letters," he told her. "And one of them is addressed to you."

"Oh?" Susan's heart bumped against her ribs. It had to be from her family, as they were the only ones who knew her whereabouts. Sure enough, the writing on the envelope was her mother's. Seeing it brought tears to her eyes. "It's from my mama and papa back in Missouri," she said, more to herself than Mr. Finch.

"The other one's for your mister."

"Yes, thank you." She glanced at the longer envelope addressed to Logan and bearing a territorial seal. "I'll be sure he gets it," Susan murmured, moving in a trance from the post office and back home, her envelope held tightly in her gloved hands. She hoped they weren't so angry at her that they didn't want to see her again. Her father was a proud man who didn't take kindly to anyone defying him. Catherine had been his favorite, or he would have disowned her when she'd gotten with child before marriage.

A pleasant breeze surrounded her, lifting her skirts slightly and fanning her face. She stretched into the coolness and sniffed. Autumn was her favorite season, especially back on the farm when the trees began to blaze with color and the animals started to put on heavier coats and plumage for the coming winter.

How it would be in Tulsa for her was anyone's guess. At least the cooler weather better matched her relations with Logan. Had he taken up with that Mazie Weeks? she wondered, then thrust the idea from her head since it made her feel ill. Shouldn't have turned him away, she told herself, then wondered if her pride would ever allow her to ask his forgiveness.

A more assertive voice rose up inside her. Why should she be the one to apologize? it asked. He'd said some stinging things to her, making her doubt every other thing he'd ever said.

"He's a smooth talker," she whispered to herself as she neared the newspaper office. "Papa always said so."

Susan opened the door, and the bell tinkled above her. A man wearing a long black coat and black hat with a hatband of connecting silver and turquoise discs had his back to her, but glanced over his shoulder as she entered. His eyes, as black as night, sparked with interest as he spun around to face her. A thin, black mustache rode above his upper lip, and his face was pockmarked. When he removed his hat and dipped his head, she saw his hair was black with too much hair tonic.

"Ma'am," he said, his voice rumbling like thunder. "I'm looking to spend some money here at the newspaper if I can find someone to take it."

"Isn't Mr. Vance around?" she asked, looking past him toward the wall of paper rolls surrounding Logan's cot.

"Doesn't seem to be."

"Well, I might be able to help you." She removed her gloves and put them and the two envelopes on Logan's desk. "You wish to subscribe or take out an advertisement?"

"I'm wanting to advertise."

"Very good." She moved toward the sheets of display ads Logan kept to show prospective advertisers. "What kind of business are you wishing to advertise, Mr.—?"

"Calhoun, ma'am. Zeke Calhoun."

"Mr. Calhoun," she said, smiling at him. "I'm Susan Armi— Vance. Mrs. Logan Vance."

"So I've heard." His glance took her in from head to toe. "Lucky man, that Vance."

She blushed and turned aside, flustered by the compliment. "And your business, sir?"

"I have some words written up," Calhoun said, pulling a folded piece of paper from his inside jacket pocket.

That's when Susan saw the menacing-looking gunbelt, fully armed with pearl-handled revolvers. "Of course, I'll be obliged if you can make it sound any better." He held out the paper for her inspection.

"What the hell are *you* doing here?" Logan asked from the doorway leading to their living quarters. He held a cup of coffee in one hand, a biscuit and bacon sandwich in the other. Susan noted this with interest, since he hadn't bothered to join them for breakfast that morning, saying he wasn't hungry. More often than not, he spent time with the children upstairs in their room and reverted to his silent self during meals, if he took them with the family. Most mornings he gulped down a cup of coffee and left Susan, Etta, and Jacob to eat without him.

"Logan, Mr. Calhoun is interested in placing an advertisement in the—"

"We don't need his business," Logan snapped, his gaze never wavering from Calhoun's oily face.

"Logan!" Susan looked from him to Calhoun, at first appalled at Logan's rudeness, then curious as to why the two men were facing each other like two mad dogs. She cleared her throat. "Logan, I'm sure you'll want to reconsider and—"

"I'll take care of this, Susan. You can leave us."

She stood her ground, hating it when he sent her off as if she were his ward instead of his wife. She shook her head stubbornly when his gaze flicked over her.

"This gentleman—" she began, only to be cut off again.

"He's no gentleman," Logan said with a snarl, setting the biscuit and cup onto a slanted artist's table.

Calhoun hooked his thumbs in his gunbelt, holding back the sides of his long coat so that everyone could see he was armed and dangerous. "You refusing my business?" he asked in his bass voice.

"You catch on real quick. I guess you're not as dumb as you look."

Susan gasped at Logan's insolence, but Calhoun grimed and shrugged. His grin was decidedly unattractive since his teeth were a dirty brown, Susan noted, looking away quickly.

"What were you wanting to advertise?" Logan asked, striding to stand beside Susan.

"Me." Calhoun ran a forefinger across his mustache and then ambled toward the front door. "But I can take my money elsewheres. Don't trouble me none not to have my name in this rag."

"Good, let's not keep in touch." Logan turned aside, picking up his cup and pointedly dismissing the prospective advertiser.

Once Calhoun was gone, Susan confronted Logan, leaning down and peering up into his face with barely controlled irritation. She placed a hand across his forehead and he jerked away.

"Stop that," he grumbled.

"You don't have a temperature, so you can't use illness as an excuse. You must be insane," she said, then pointed a finger at the door. "That man wanted to pay us some money, Logan. What's gotten into you lately that you'd turn down business?"

"Do you happen to know what his business is?"

"No, but whatever it is, you shouldn't have—"

"He's a regulator, a hired gun." Logan craned closer until the tip of his nose nearly touched hers. "He kills people for a living, so don't keep harping on me. I know what I'm doing and I sure as hell don't need instruction from you on how to run my newspaper."

She took an involuntary step backward. "Well, pardon me, Mr. Vance. I had no idea I was in the way."

He caught her arm when she would have darted past him. "Wait a minute," he said with extreme reluctance. "I didn't mean it to sound that way, but you do go on, Susan."

"I didn't know he was a hired gun," she pointed out.

"I know." He shrugged and took a bite of the biscuit sandwich. "And I shouldn't have come down on you with both feet. So we're all square."

Are we? she asked him silently. He sat on a stool and began selecting type from a tray, leaving Susan to go about her business. Remembering the letters, she retrieved them from his desk and dropped his in front of him.

"I stopped by the post office," she said, then breezed out to leave him and his surly mood to keep each other company.

Sitting at the kitchen table, Susan slipped a fingernail under the envelope's flap, then withdrew the two folded sheets of lined paper. The handwriting was her mother's, achingly familiar. Taking a deep breath and then letting it out slowly, Susan began to read:

Dear Daughter,

I am writing this for your father as well as myself. You must know how your last letter shook our souls and shriveled our high hopes of you making a good marriage for yourself. I shall never forget the look on your father's face when the news was given. As for me, I took to my bed for three days before finding enough energy to leave it.

Your father blames himself for sending you off to the devil's own son. We both should have known better. Yes, we trained you well and taught you right from wrong, but something about that womanizer makes decent girls forsake their morals and embrace sin.

We can only hope that you can save the children, especially Etta. For a girl child to be raised by such an immoral animal sends your father and me to our knees in fervent prayer.

We'll always remember you as the sweet, good girl you were before you fell into the clutches of that swine. We pray you don't meet your sister's end.

Mama and Papa

A tear splashed on the last line. Susan dropped the pages and buried her face in her hands to smother her sobs. She heard Logan's approach but couldn't cut off her crying jag.

"Susan, the editor of the— Well, what's wrong now?" he asked, totally without sympathy.

She heard the rattle of paper and tried to grab the letter from his hands, but he moved out of her reach.

"That's my letter," she said tearfully. "It's none of

your business!'' Wiping away her tears, she tried to bring her sobs under control as Logan read her letter, his back to her so that she couldn't see his expression. But she could well imagine it.

He tossed it back onto the table, turning only far enough to reveal his profile. ''Not my business, huh? I beg to differ, since the whole thing is about me.''

''I've hurt them so deeply.'' She folded the letter and tucked it back into the envelope.

''You knew they wouldn't be delighted by your news.''

''Yes, but they sound as if they've washed their hands of me entirely!'' She swallowed another sob. ''I was hoping they'd have a glimmer of understanding . . .''

''You should have known better than that. Old Abe can't tolerate anyone who doesn't obey his orders to the letter.''

''Logan, you can't blame them for not approving of you.''

''Oh, yes, I can,'' he said, whipping around to face her. He placed his fists on top of the table and leaned on them. ''Not only that, I *do* blame them. I've never done one thing to warrant the kind of treatment they've served up to me.''

''You kept seeing Catherine after they forbade it,'' she reminded him, but he shook his head.

''She kept seeing me,'' he amended. ''In fact, she threw herself at me.''

''You could have refused her advances.''

''Yes, I could have done that,'' he allowed, then his eyes darkened to olive-green. ''But it's hard to be a saint when a beautiful girl undresses down to her skin and wraps her legs and arms around you.''

Susan propelled herself from the chair and stood glaring at him, eye to eye, nose to nose. ''Catherine was a lady and wouldn't have done that. Ever!''

''You're calling me a liar?''

''Yes, that's exactly what I'm calling you!''

''You don't think very much of me, do you?''

She hesitated, feeling raw and exposed. ''I . . . no, not lately. Lately, you haven't exactly been a prince.''

''And you haven't been a little princess either, my

dear.'' He straightened and flexed his fingers, relaxing his fists. ''I might take a trip to Watonga soon.''

''Wh-why?''

''I've been corresponding with the editor there. He's got quite an operation and I'd like to meet him. He invited me.''

She lifted one shoulder in a halfhearted response. ''I'll stay here with the children, if that's what you're asking.''

''I wasn't, but thanks.''

He started to leave, but Susan reached out in a moment of truth to hook her fingers in the crook of his arm.

''Logan?''

He arched a brow at her.

''Why haven't you been taking your meals with us?''

''I've been busy.''

''No, please. Let's try to be honest with each other.''

''You think this liar might have an honest bone somewhere in his body?'' he asked, throwing her words back in her face. ''I don't know.'' He shook his head, feigning worry. ''You know what a swine I am—how I came from the devil and all.'' Placing his fists on either side of his head and sticking up his forefingers, he fashioned horns. ''Just call me Lucifer Junior.''

She didn't smile because she knew he wasn't being funny. Underlining his pantomime was a core of resentment. ''Won't you sit down a minute and let's talk like two adults? We can't go on like this—avoiding each other, being overly polite, trying not to catch each other's eye or be in the same room together for any length of time. What must the children think of our behavior?''

''They probably haven't given it much consideration. As long as they have me, they're happy, or haven't you noticed?''

She wrinkled her nose at his hatefulness, then waved him off. ''Go on, then. If you insist on being an ass, far be it from me to try and talk any sense to you.''

''I thought my behavior was exactly what you wanted. I'm staying out of your bed, out of your path. That's what you wanted, isn't it?''

''We didn't sleep together before we married—except

that one time," she added quickly when he opened his mouth to dispute her. "But we were friendly and warm with each other."

"That's right, but we weren't married to each other then." He touched the slight indentation on the underside of her chin with his forefinger. "In marriage it's either all or nothing, sweetpea. I can't be warm and friendly and not want to be just as warm and friendly in bed with you. I'm not as cold-blooded as you."

"Cold-blooded?"

"That's right. I can't change my colors as easily as you—hungry for someone one minute and then pushing him aside the next."

"I didn't do that."

"Didn't you?"

She opened her mouth, but the words wouldn't come. Had she done that? The conversation they'd had that night had been so convoluted, so unexpected, so fraught with misunderstandings, that she couldn't recall it well enough to answer.

"Right," Logan said, taking her silence as agreement. "Now, if you'll let go of my arm, I'll go back to work."

Reluctantly, her fingers slipped away.

Standing outside the Bloody Bucket, Susan wrung her hands and stood on tiptoe to see over the tops of the swinging doors. All she could see were shoulders and hats.

"Excuse us, ma'am."

Susan stumbled back, but reached out to snag one of the men's shirtsleeves. "Please—"

"Yes, ma'am." He eyed her with obvious interest. Susan recalled seeing him around town, but she didn't know his name. "Will you kindly do me a small favor?"

He ran a hand down his closely clipped white beard. "If I can."

"Do you happen to know Logan Vance?"

"I know him when I see him."

"I believe he's inside with Coonie French. Could you tell him I'm outside and need to see him immediately?"

She glanced inside the saloon. "I'd go inside myself, but I've never—"

"Say no more, ma'am. I'll deliver your message," the man assured her, touching the brim of his cowboy hat.

"Thank you. That's so kind of you."

He strode inside, leaving Susan to pace restlessly on the boardwalk.

Why had she let it go on for so long? she wondered. It was October, and she and Logan still behaved badly toward each other, staying out of each other's way, grunting when spoken to, not meeting each other's eyes. Even now, when she was beside herself with worry, she cringed at having to come to this place to find him since she'd sworn she'd never be caught dead anywhere near the Bloody Bucket. As she paced outside the noisy saloon, she blamed herself for letting the estrangement go on and on. Of course, in her heart she knew why she hadn't forced a confrontation. She was afraid Logan would tell her he wanted to end the marriage, that he'd found comfort elsewhere—at the Bloody Bucket, perhaps.

A few hours ago, she'd stubbornly resisted seeking him out at his favorite haunt, but then she'd finally let some common sense enter her foggy brain. She needed him . . . needed him desperately, and no one to her knowledge had ever actually choked to death on pride. Besides, she wouldn't be risking all that much, because she knew that Logan wouldn't turn her away . . .

Logan burst through the swinging doors with Coonie right behind him. She wasn't prepared for his anger.

"What right do you think you have to send someone in after me? I'm not some dog on a chain, sweetheart. Maybe you think marriage means you can jerk me around, embarrass me in front of my friends, but it doesn't. You hear me?"

Stunned, she stared at him, openmouthed. His skin was flushed red, but his mouth was thinned into a white line of rage. He breathed heavily, and Susan smelled whiskey. How much he'd drunk, she couldn't be sure.

"Hey, pard, ease up," Coonie advised, gripping one of

Logan's arms and pulling him back a step. "She don't mean nothing by it."

"The hell she doesn't," Logan said into Susan's face as he shook off Coonie's hand. "She thinks she can boss me around like her old man tried to do. Well, it didn't work for him and it won't work for you. Now get on home. I'm not following along behind you like a sissy. I'm going back inside, and I'll come home when I'm good and ready." With that, he swung away from her.

"Logan, wait—" She clutched his shirtsleeve. He gave a vicious jerk and the cloth tore. Susan paid it no mind. "Logan, I didn't—"

"Get away from me," he said, then muttered a foul curse.

"Logan, it's Etta!" Susan blurted out just in time to stop him from slapping open the saloon doors. When he whirled back to face her, she knew she'd finally sliced through his crust of fury. "She has the croup, and I need you to help me with her."

Coonie slumped as if the news took the wind from him, but Logan became, if anything, more alive. He grabbed Susan by the shoulders, bringing her up on her toes.

"Why didn't you say that in the first place?" he asked, then let go of her. "Hell, we're wasting time out here when my baby's sick! Come on, let's get back. You shouldn't have left her when she's sick."

"I didn't want to," Susan said, trotting beside him. "But I need an extra pair of hands. Jacob's been wonderful, but he's just a little boy, and he shouldn't get too close to Etta or he'll catch—"

"How sick is she?"

"She's terribly congested. I would have sent for the doctor, but he'd only do what I've been trying to do."

"Which is?"

"Keep the room steamy to break through the congestion. I think I can fashion some kind of tent to put over her with your help."

They reached the newspaper office, but went around to the side entrance. As soon as they were inside, they heard

Etta's hoarse, heavy coughing. Logan took the stairs two at a time, followed by Susan and Coonie.

The disarray of the room spoke of the restless, worried night Susan and the children had endured while Logan had been playing poker at his favorite haunt. Kettles and pots littered the area around Etta's narrow bed. The air was steamy and damp and smelled of illness. A canvas sheet lay crumpled on the floor, and the bedsheets were wrinkled and wet in places. Etta, her skin glistening with sweat and her hair curling tightly on her wet head, lay sprawled on the bed, her little chest lifting and falling laboriously. Wheezing sounds accompanied every breath. Her eyes were closed, but opened slowly when Logan leaned over the bed and took one of her hands in both of his.

"Honeybee? It's Papa."

When she didn't smile or acknowledge him, Logan cast a worried glance at Susan. She kicked at the canvas.

"Logan, help me string this up over her bed to make a tent of it," Susan said, lifting one corner of the canvas.

"A tent?" he asked vacantly, staring at his daughter's pasty face.

"Yes. Logan!" Susan stamped one foot to get his attention. "Help me, will you?"

He started to grab up the canvas, but Jacob chose that time to wrap his arms around Logan's legs.

"Is Etta going to be all right, Papa?"

"Yes, son." Logan stroked Jacob's white-blond hair. "Now let go. Jacob, let go of Papa."

"Coonie, will you take Jacob to your place and let him stay the rest of the night with you?" Susan asked.

"I want to stay here with Etta," Jacob said, giving a stubborn kick with one foot.

"I don't want you catching what she's got," Susan said, then glanced over her shoulder at Coonie. "Will you?"

"Sure 'nuf. Come on, rowdy." Coonie reached out and snagged one of Jacob's arms. "Now don't be a stubborn mule. Let's leave your pappy and aunt alone to nurse little Etta. We can't do nothing but get in their way, you know."

He dragged Jacob along, ignoring his sniffs and snorts of rebellion. Reaching the stairs, he pulled the boy up by the collar and gave him a gentle but firm shake. "Jacob, quit acting like a jackass and get down them stairs."

Jacob glanced once more at his sister, then climbed down the steep stairs with Coonie.

"How long has she been like this?" Logan asked as he cut a hole in one corner of the canvas with his pocket-knife.

"She came home from school feverish," Susan said, grabbing up kettles to reheat them downstairs at the stove. "By nightfall she began to cough a little. It came suddenly. After I'd put them to bed—oh, a couple of hours after that—I heard her wheezing and went up to check on her. She was soaked with sweat and shivering all over."

"Why didn't you come and get me right then?"

"Because I was busy," she said, giving him a barbed glare. "My first thought wasn't you, it was Etta. I've doctored children before, and I started by giving her a sponge bath and rubbing her chest with salve. That helped some, but then she took a turn for the worse about an hour or so ago. When I tried to fix a tent over her and couldn't, *that's* when you came to mind."

"I should have been here earlier," he groused.

"Yes, you should have."

The look they exchanged across Etta's sickbed sizzled with unspoken accusations and tremendous guilt. Logan averted his gaze first. He cut another hole in the other corner of the canvas with a sharp, violent thrust of his pocketknife. Susan took the kettles with her downstairs, wondering how many trips she'd made since putting Etta to bed. Ten . . . twenty? At least twenty-five, the calves of her legs told her. She set the kettles on top of the stove again and wrung out washrags in the dry sink. She put a drop or two of menthol oil in each of the kettles, then waited impatiently for the water to boil as she had done countless times that evening.

She could hear Logan moving around upstairs and Etta's alarming cough. Poor child, she thought, then her heart hardened as she recalled in painful detail the brunt of Logan's fury. He'd assumed she'd come to drag him home, the conceited, pompous fool! It would be a cold day in hell before she'd stoop to such behavior! He could rot in that saloon for all she cared—him and his tart, Mazie Weeks, along with him! If he wanted to spend his evening hours drooling over a painted-up hussy and losing money at a card table and trying to drink other dimwits under the table, then far be it from her to spoil his fun! She wouldn't have been outside that saloon if she could have managed the makeshift tent herself.

Weary from an evening of nonstop fretting, Susan dropped into one of the kitchen chairs and laid her head on her crossed arms. The hissing of the kettles brought her head up, and she realized she'd dozed. Grabbing them, she hurried upstairs.

Logan had set up the crude tent. He'd shoved the bedposts through the holes he'd cut out on one end, then slanted it down over Etta to her waist where he'd secured it with books and warming bricks. Taking two of the kettles from Susan, he set them on the bricks under the canvas. Steam rose up, trapped by the canvas, and Etta's breath continued to rattle in her chest. Susan slipped beneath the tent and put the other two kettles on the bricks Logan had placed on either side of Etta's head. The steam curled and settled around her, making her skin gleam with sweat. She released a tiny whine of protest.

"I'm hot," Etta murmured, her rosebud mouth barely moving.

"I know, pumpkin," Susan whispered, reaching to dip a finger in a pan of water on the floor. She slid her wet finger against Etta's dry lips. "Just lie still and breathe deep."

"What's that smell?" Logan asked, giving a big sniff. "Smells like peppermint."

"It's mint oil. It helps open up the passages and lungs."

"Shouldn't we go for the doctor?"

"You can if you want, but he can't do any more than what we're doing right now. Haven't they had croup before?"

"No, never."

"Then you've all three been mighty lucky," Susan said,

smoothing Etta's damp hair off her forehead. "I've sat with my sisters many a time while they battled croup."

"But they get past it . . . they get well, right?"

"Yes, if they're doctored." She met Logan's gaze across the sick child. "Once her fever breaks, we'll be able to breathe a sigh of relief. If she doesn't improve in the next hour, then you'll have to go for the doctor." Taking one of the washrags she'd dipped in cool water, she wiped Etta's face with it. "Maybe he'll know some new tricks."

Logan dropped to his knees, keeping under the tent, and held one of Etta's hands. The light had left his eyes, and they looked flat and cold, like chunks of green rock. His gaze followed the path of Susan's hand as she bathed Etta's cheeks, chin, forehead, neck, then back to her cheeks to repeat the whole process.

"She'll be all right," he whispered.

Etta released a string of hoarse wheezes that made both Susan and Logan wince.

"God, I wish I could breathe for her," he said, bringing Etta's dimpled hand to his lips for a kiss. "I wish I could take her pain."

"I know, so do I." Susan wet the cloth again and ran it up and down Etta's arms. "Breathe as deeply as you can, pumpkin," she said in a soft, comforting voice. "The steam will break up that old stuff in your lungs and you'll breathe easier."

Responding to Susan's gentle order, Etta's little chest rose higher.

"That's good, sweetie," Susan told her. "You're such a good little girl, and I love you so very much." She kissed her damp forehead. "Aunt Susan will make it all better, honey, and Papa is here with you now, too. We're going to make our little angel all well."

Logan blinked, then stared at the woman across from him. With the steam and hazy light surrounding her head, she looked like a comely saint complete with halo. Her voice, a spoken caress, calmed him as it did his daughter. Logan slumped to rest his head on Etta's bump of a shoulder, hiding his face from Susan. He didn't want her to see him cry.

"Logan."

He was shaken awake. Flinging back his head, he found himself staring across a narrow bed at Susan. Her eyes, alight with hope, made his gaze tumble toward his daughter. Etta was no longer wheezing, was breathing almost normally. He touched Etta's cheek and released a sigh when his skin met coolness instead of clamminess.

"Thank God, her fever's broken!"

"Yes, about half an hour ago." Susan stripped off the top sheet. "Lift her up. I'm going to change these bedclothes.

He obeyed, so grateful he was nearly limp, but he found enough strength to hold his child in his arms and drop kisses on her cherubic face.

"Etta, Etta, my baby," he whispered, and received a sleepy smile from her. "Papa loves you more than heaven and earth. Papa loves you around and around this old earth and to the moon and back again."

Susan smiled at his exuberant confession. She folded the corners of the sheets under the feather mattress and motioned for him to put Etta down on the fresh linen. Tucking the top sheet around the child's small body, she felt fatigue spread across her shoulders and down her back.

"Logan, will you look in on Jacob while I tidy up this room? She's over the hump. We can all get some sleep now."

"What time is it?"

Susan straightened, placing a hand on the small of her back where a pain stabbed her. "Dawn? Somewhere just before dawn, I think."

"Lord, I'm tired." He shuffled to the stairs. "I'll go tell Coonie and Jacob we're out of the woods." Gratitude spun him back to her. She was picking up bedding with slow, muscle-sore movements. "Susan?"

She sent him a questioning look.

He meant to tell her she was a godsend, but the words

stuck on his tongue. "Leave that and I'll pick it up in a bit."

Susan nodded, a wan smile touching the corners of her mouth. "Thank you, Logan."

Bolting down the steps, Logan felt like a heel. If anyone should have been thanked, he should have thanked her—and they both damned well knew it.

Chapter 17

Rapping smartly on Coonie's door, Logan waited a heartbeat before opening it and walking in. Coonie struggled up from the rocker, then put a finger to his lips and pointed to where Jacob slept soundly on the sofa. Logan motioned Coonie outside where their talk wouldn't disturb the exhausted boy.

"Her fever broke," Logan answered Coonie's probing expression, then laughed and shook his hand in shared relief. "She's not hacking anymore and she's sleeping like a lamb."

"Thank the Lord," Coonie said, clasping his hands for a moment in silent gratitude. "If anything had happened to that baby . . ."

"I know what you mean, but Susan has doctored children with croup before and she knew what to do." He pushed his hands into his trouser pockets and flung back his head to let his eyes gobble up the dove-gray sky. Soon it would be oyster and pink, painted by a rising sun.

"Your other one in there," Coonie said, jerking his head toward his little cottage, "is plumb tuckered out. Poor chicken was worried sick about his sis."

"Let him sleep. The good news can wait until he's awake." Logan flexed his shoulders and rolled his head to release the tension in his neck and back. "I've got to go back in and straighten Etta's room. Susan was doing it, but I sent her to bed. She looked like she was about to drop."

"No doubt she is," Coonie said, and something in his

226

voice brought Logan's gaze sharply to him. "Remember when we were worried she wouldn't pull her weight? She sure showed us, didn't she?" When Logan made no comment, Coonie continued, "Take tonight for instance. There we were having a fine old time drinking and swapping stories while she fought for your daughter's life. Then when she came around for you, why you bit off her head before she—"

"Okay, okay," Logan said, none too gently. "I feel bad enough already without you pouring salt into my open wound." He reached down to pick up a homemade stick horse dropped by one of his children, but snapped back up when Coonie mumbled something. "What did you say?"

"Nothing."

Logan propped the stick horse against the side of Coonie's house. "What did you say?" he repeated, this time making it an order instead of a request.

"I said somebody ought to kick your scrawny butt," Coonie said, enunciating each word this time. "You've been acting like a mule's beee-hind for too damned long. I thought you'd get over your sulk, but I guess you like being a sourpuss."

"When I need a lecture—"

"Well, you need one, son," Coonie interrupted. "That little gal you married is too good for you. Any other woman would have packed her bags and told you to kiss her backside long before now, but she's stuck by you and your children."

"Stuck by me? That's how much you know." Logan turned aside, knowing in his heart Coonie was right, but his pride erected a shield around him.

"I know she's been seeing to your children night after night while you pretended to be single and childless down at the Bloody Bucket."

"I haven't done anything to be ashamed of."

"Maybe you haven't bedded any of them bought woman, but that don't make you blameless. You know you should have been home with your family."

"I didn't hear you complaining before."

"I'm not a married man, Logan. I've got no wife and children waiting for me to stagger home to them." Coonie laid a hand on Logan's shoulder. "Whatever happened between you and Susan can be fixed, but it'll take both of you to do it."

"The marriage was a mistake."

"But it's done." Coonie shook his shoulder roughly. "Face it like a man and deal with it like a man."

Logan cleared his throat. "She doesn't want my . . . uh, attentions. I'm not going to go without just because she's persnickety."

Coonie's apple cheeks flamed with embarrassment. "I'm not going to discuss your personal lives, but you could at least tell her how you're beholden to her for sitting with your children. You haven't, have you?"

"Not exactly."

"Tell her, Logan. I know your people taught you manners, so use them." Coonie ran a hand over his white hair and yawned. "As for me, I'm going to bed. Hell, it's getting light and I haven't had any shut-eye to speak of. Don't expect me at the breakfast table."

"Me, neither," Logan said, waving as he walked toward the house again and let himself in the side door. He listened to the quiet house, happy that the hacking cough had been silenced. As he crossed to the kitchen, his mind was on Coonie's stern advice, and he jumped guiltily when Susan's bedroom door swung open to silhouette her. Wearing a cotton nightdress, she stood on the threshold, obviously unaware that the light behind her shone through the thin material and clearly outlined her every curve for Logan.

"I wanted a glass of milk," she said, still hovering in the doorway, one hand against the jamb, the other on the brass knob.

"I'll join you." He moved then, forcing himself to go to the icebox for the jug of milk. Filling two glasses, he set them on the table. "Bread, butter, and strawberry jam. How does that sound?"

"Perfect." She drifted to one of the chairs and slipped into it, light as a feather. She'd covered the gown with her apple-green wrapper. Logan liked it. It did wonderful things for her coloring. "I'm tired, but I must eat something so my stomach will stop making awful noises and let me sleep." She fidgeted, rocking from hip to hip to unwrap the dressing gown from around her legs. "You told Coonie and Jacob?"

"Coonie, yes. Jacob is fast asleep and I didn't want to wake him." He covered one slice of the bread Susan had baked yesterday morning with freshly churned butter and her homemade jam. Coonie's right, he thought as he handed it to her. She's done more than her share. More than I ever dreamed she would. Hell, she's even handy in the pressroom! "I'm remiss, and you have every right to box my ears, but I hope you won't."

Adjusting the broad collar of the wrapper, she sent him a quizzical glance. "I'm sorry—"

"No, *I'm* sorry," he corrected. "I'm a sorry sonofagun. And I'm grateful to you, Susan, for all you've done. You've made this place a home." He paused to reflect on that, his gaze moving slowly around the warm kitchen as he recalled the good times he'd had with his family at this table and the mornings he'd awakened to a breakfast fit for a king and prepared by a woman he'd underestimated. "You married me to ease my way into this community and provide my children with a stable home life."

"They're my family, too," she reminded him. "It's not like I was doing all of this for strangers. We're blood."

"You and the children are, but you and I share none."

"Yes, but I . . . oh, well. We're even. You gave me the opportunity to get to know my nephew and niece better and to set up a home for them. I've enjoyed it."

The phrasing sent a jolt of apprehension through him. "You're not thinking of leaving anytime soon, are you?"

"I . . . no, not unless you want me to."

"No. That is, I want you to do as you please, but the children will miss you if you go."

"They have you."

"Yes, but I haven't been a good parent lately. I imagine they've come to depend mostly on you."

"No, Logan. You're wrong. You're their whole

world.'' Her eyes, dark brown and as warm as velvet, seemed to reach into him. ''Never think anyone can replace you in their lives.''

Seeing he was doing a lousy job at making her realize how deeply he was in her debt and how rotten he felt for having treated her so callously of late, he scooted his chair closer to hers and looked her straight in the eyes.

''Susan, I'm trying to apologize for being a horse's ass, so quit making me out to be some kind of knight.''

Flustered, she looked away from him and attacked the last of her bread and butter. A droplet of the strawberry jam clung to the corner of her mouth.

Logan couldn't take his eyes off the smidgeon of berry. Suddenly, he went hot all over and wanted more than anything to capture that bit of jam with the tip of his tongue. Instead, he used his forefinger. She flinched but didn't pull away. With the jam on the tip of his finger, he brought it to his mouth and inside. She watched every move. His finger popped out, all clean. Susan swallowed hard. He couldn't be sure, but he thought he saw the material over her heart flutter.

He saw something else, too. Something that baffled him and gave the lie to everything she'd said. He saw it in her eyes as they swept up to confront his. He saw desire.

Then he, too, felt it. It hit him between the eyes, seeped down into his chest, and then shot like a bullet to the bulge behind his fly. He shifted uneasily and, conversely, anger blasted through him.

''You told me I didn't please you,'' he ground out, taking her by surprise for she blinked rapidly and reeled back in the chair.

''No, I didn't.''

''You did. You said you weren't fulfilled by me. I didn't satisfy you.''

''No, I—''

''And that was a lie because all I have to do is touch you and you're all dewy-eyed and breathless. I bet you're even wet, aren't you? I bet you're sitting there ready for me.''

''Stop that talk!'' She shot up from the chair, making it

topple backward. "Just because I married you doesn't mean I have to put up with your foul mouth."

"And it doesn't mean you can make all the rules, either, honey-bunch." He came around to her, so swiftly she didn't have time to bolt and run. Clamping his hands on either side of her head, he tilted it to the right and then slanted his mouth over hers.

Still angry that she had led him to believe she didn't want him, he ignored her whimpering and rubbed her lips mercilessly until they parted, then he took her mouth masterfully. His tongue made love to her mouth until her whimper became a moan of appreciation. When she sagged against him, he set her away and forced her to stand on her own.

Her eyes were glazed with passion and her breathing was ragged as she swayed slightly and reached out one hand to touch his forearm.

"I didn't mean that you displeased me, Logan," she said, her voice husky.

"You knew that's how I took it."

"I wanted to strike out at you."

"You lied."

"No, you misinterpreted what I said."

"Then what were you saying? Spell it out and make it good, Susan. You just proved you like what I can do for you."

"Yes, but you . . . you never finish."

"I never what? Finish? What the hell does that mean?"

"It means . . ." She sighed and put a hand to her forehead in a weary gesture. "I don't know how to say it, but—"

"Just say it."

"You remove yourself from me at the last moment. You—you know what you do!"

Her meaning slammed him in the gut. "I don't come inside of you."

"Yes." She looked down at her wringing hands.

"Susan, that's so you won't get pregnant."

"I know that, but why? Why don't you want me to have your children?"

"Look, it's not you. It's me. I don't want any more children right now. I married before because your sister was pregnant. I don't want to be roped into a situation like that again."

"But we're already married."

"True." He drew in a deep breath, searching for a way to communicate his intangible feelings about marriage and children and commitment. "But we're not yet connected." He laced his fingers and pulled to illustrate. "We're finding our way, sort of feeling around in the dark. It would be a big mistake to make a baby between us before we know where we are, who we are, what we are." He could tell by her face that he hadn't expressed himself well enough. She looked as if he'd just told her he didn't want to make a baby with her because she was ugly and stupid. "Susan, will you please try to understand? My first marriage was—"

"I'm not Catherine," she said softly but pointedly.

"But I learned lessons from her I can't discard easily."

"You don't trust me. You don't feel comfortable with me."

"I never said that. Of course I trust you. I've been leaving my children with you most every night, haven't I?" He sat at the table again, propping one elbow on the edge, his arm and wrist hanging limply. "Which I won't be doing from now on."

"No?"

"No."

"Well, thank God for that. You should spend more time with the children and less with Mazie Weeks."

He opened his mouth to tell her that Mazie didn't have a role in this melodrama, but shook aside the comment. "Susan, remember my reputation back before I married your sister?"

She nodded.

"I was thought of as a rounder, a ladies' man. You know why?"

She shook her head.

"Because I love women and I love sex."

"Shhh!" She looked toward the stairs, as if his quiet voice could carry up to sleeping Etta.

"I never made any bones about it, and that's how I got my reputation. In many respects, I haven't changed. I still love women and I still love—" He smiled at her tensed up reaction, but went right ahead and said it. "Sex."

She let out a sigh of repentance for his soul.

"And you like it, too," he murmured, standing again, drawn to her. "You love it almost as much as I do."

"I was taught that the act between a man and woman was to make children."

That stopped him. Damn her, why did she have to get all pious on him? "Not necessarily. You can have sex just for the pure fun of it." He faced her wary glare. "Damn it all, Susan, do you want to be a brood mare? Do you want to go around most of the year with a big belly?"

"Is that what childbearing is to you?" she asked, appalled. "It's a miracle, not a hardship."

"And it's irresponsible for two grown people to bring an innocent babe into a marriage that's shaky at best. Look at us!" He held out his arms from his sides. "We haven't shared a marriage bed in weeks! I've been drowning my sexual urges in whiskey and you've been pretending not to care. Some union we've got here, sweetheart. You want to birth a baby into this wobbly marriage?"

She shrugged, looking tired and listless. "I don't want to be a convenience for you, that's all. I want to share everything." With another heavy sigh, she turned and started for her bedroom. "I can't help but wonder . . ."

"What?" Logan asked, feeling beaten. He looked up to see her in the doorway again, but her wrapper covered her curves.

"Did you ever love my sister? Have you ever loved any woman?" She didn't wait for an answer, but simply closed the door and shut herself off from him.

Logan stared at the door for a long, laden minute before he answered, "Yes."

"Afternoon, ma'am."

Susan dropped the checked fabric she'd been examining

and turned toward the bass voice. For a moment, she couldn't come up with the man's name, then it came to her. "Good afternoon, Mr. Calhoun."

"That material will look right pretty on you, if I may say so, ma'am." He held his black hat in his hands, and sunlight spearing through the window of the dry goods store ricocheted off the silver and turquoise hatband.

"Oh, yes, thank you." She skimmed two fingers down the soft cotton fabric of deep gold on white. "But it's too expensive."

"Let me buy enough for you to make yourself a Sunday dress."

"No!" She retreated a couple of steps, then recovered. "That is, I couldn't allow that, sir. I'm a married woman."

"Your husband wouldn't approve?"

"No, he wouldn't, but it was kind of you to offer."

"If he can't afford such things for you, why not accept them from one who can?"

Not caring for his insistence, she moved away from him. "Thank you, but no." To her consternation, he followed her as she selected a few items from the canyonlike walls of shelving. It was dark in the aisle, and Susan hurried, making her way to the pool of sunlight at the end of it.

"I heard that you were shot not too long ago."

"Yes, but it's all healed."

"No scar?"

"A small one." She glanced over her shoulder. He was only a step behind her. "But it gives me no trouble, no pain."

"I'm glad to hear it. I've never been shot myself, although more than a few have tried to send me to my maker."

Reaching the sunlight, she stood in it and turned to look at him in the shadows. "I'm told you're a gunslinger, Mr. Calhoun."

"I prefer to be called a regulator. I keep the peace, ma'am. I even scores, rid towns of varmints, track down wanted animals." He dusted his hat against the side of his trouser leg. "Somebody's got to look after law-abiding folks."

"Sounds like six-shooter law to me. Aren't marshals and sheriffs hired to keep the peace?"

"Sometimes they have more than they can handle."

"But that can't be the case here." She was near the screen doors and she crossed to them to look out. "What we need is a trailblazer to create a different route other than Main Street for the cattle to be driven along."

He chuckled. "That's what you get for living in a cow-town."

"I don't think of Tulsa as a cowtown," she said, quick to defend the town she had once disliked but had since grown fond of. "It's a growing town, a town finding its identity."

"And that's why I'm here." He reached past her, propping one of the screen doors open. "I've been hired to make sure it grows in the right direction."

"Who hired you?"

A twist of his lips sufficed for a smile. "That's confidential, ma'am." He put on his hat as he stepped over the threshold. "It's a shame a pretty woman like you doesn't have a man who can keep her in the best dresses and the fanciest bonnets."

"It doesn't distress me in the least," she assured him.

His gaze played over her, making her round her shoulders and burrow into herself. "Still, it's a waste. Afternoon, ma'am." The door slammed behind him.

Shrugging off the encounter, Susan paid for her purchases and went outside. A chill was in the air, and Susan could smell autumn. The trees were already ablaze. She pulled her shawl more snugly around her and, with basket in hand, headed for home. Going around to the back, so as not to disturb Coonie and Logan while they worked in the newspaper office, she came to an abrupt halt when she noted the sentry at her back door.

"Tom Manygoats," she said, greeting him. "It's been a while since I've seen you." Her gaze dropped to the bushel basket at his feet. "What have you got there?"

"Carrie Brewster sends you pumpkins and squash."

"Oh, how thoughtful of her."

"For your Thanksgiving meal."

"Thanksgiving." She nodded, amazed how the time was rushing by her. "Yes, it's next week, isn't it?"

He nodded, then bent and lifted the basket. "Where do you want this?"

"Bring it and yourself inside." She opened the door for him, but he waited for her to go inside first. Doing so, she felt proud that she had come so far. A few months ago, she wouldn't have dared turn her back on an Indian, but Tom Manygoats had taught her that he and his people were more civilized than the penny novels would have one believe. "Won't you have a cup of coffee with me?"

He sniffed the air appreciatively. "That's not coffee I smell."

"No, I'm boiling a chicken to make chicken and dumplings for supper." She sighed, recalling the night she and Logan had sat up with Etta while she fought to recover from the croup. The ordeal had eliminated some of the friction between Susan and Logan. He took his meals with the family again and no longer visited the saloon, but he wasn't his carefree self around her. He never teased her as he used to, and he went out of his way not to touch her.

When she turned from the stove, Tom Manygoats was sitting at her kitchen table. Back straight, long iron pigtails streaming over his shoulders, feathered derby hat wedged on one knee, he looked incongruous enough to make Susan laugh as she set a cup of coffee in front of him.

"Cream or sugar?"

"Both, please. Lots."

"Help yourself," she said, indicating the pitcher and bowl on the table. "Before you go, I'm giving you some blackberry jam and green beans and new potatoes I put up for Mrs. Brewster. How is she doing? I haven't seen her around town in a spell."

"Arthritis has settled in her bones." He stirred the coffee, liberally laced with sugar and cream. "She has been staying in because of it."

"Is she in pain?"

"Some, I think, though she doesn't complain. How are the children?"

"Fine. Etta was sick a while back, but she's all better now. Chicken and dumplings are her favorite, so I'm spoiling her."

"Spoiling children is much fun." His face wrinkled with his smile. "I have many children, grandchildren, nephews, nieces, cousins. I spoil all of them."

"How many children?" She gasped when he held up both hands. "Ten? And grandchildren?"

He thought a moment. "Double ten, maybe more. I never counted." He tasted the coffee and nodded his approval. "You should watch out who you speak to in public."

"Why? Who . . ." She stopped, reading his expression. "Oh, you mean Mr. Calhoun?"

"He is nothing but trouble."

"I figured as much. I wasn't really talking to him. He was talking to me." She glanced around, then lowered her voice. "Can you imagine? He wanted to buy some fabric for me to make a dress from! He knows good and well I'm married."

"Knows, but doesn't care. Men like him don't honor much."

"Wonder who hired him to stay around here? And who is he after anyway?" She deciphered his hooded gaze again. "You know, don't you? Tell me, Tom."

"I hear he was hired by important men in town."

"Whatever for?"

"To chase away my people."

"Oh, dear." She fell back in the chair, shaking her head and feeling ashamed. "As if they have nothing better to do than make trouble for people who aren't doing anything but what they have been doing for years and years and years."

"You're a smart lady."

She met his gaze and exchanged a smile with him. "I'm glad you think so. Tom, I want you to know that I'm on your side. I think it's awful for the people here to want to run the Creeks off their land. If they'd only try to understand . . ."

"They're afraid. So are we."

"Of us?" She shook her head, unable to imagine Tom Manygoats being afraid of anything.

He stared into his coffee cup, and a moodiness fell over him. "Not too many years ago I hunted this land—here where we sit drinking coffee—here is where buffalo herds roamed." He planted a fingertip in the center of the table. "Now this table sits and mocks that time. When things change quickly, people stumble, reel, some fall down. Your government opened this land and changes came sweeping in like a bitter wind. No one had time to think or to plan. My people huddled together, and for a time we pretended not to see the changes. For a time we pretended the bison were still here. Then our children were dressed like white children and sent to school. Once the children hold to other customs, then their parents must, or be set apart from them."

"The changes have made you sad," Susan said, noting the gruffness in his voice. He glanced up long enough for her to see that his eyes glistened with moisture.

"We have changed enough. It's time we remember the old ways. If we get too far away from our customs, we'll lose something precious."

"Yes, you will. Well, as I said, you have my sympathies."

"And what of your husband?"

"My husband?"

"Where do his sympathies lie?"

"I . . . I'm not sure."

"His newspaper calls for us Creeks to live in houses and forget our other way of life."

Susan averted her gaze, feeling shame again. "I think he's reflecting the feelings of many of the people in town. I'll talk to him."

"Not for me. I can talk for me." Tom Manygoats stood up and placed his hat squarely on his big head. "But he puts you in bad place."

"How?" Susan asked, looking up into a face that could have been carved from polished mahogany.

"You don't like Calhoun?"

"No, I don't. But neither does Logan. In fact, Logan despises the man."

"Then why did he put in money for the man's pay?"

"What?" Susan shot up from the chair as if she had a spring beneath her. "Are you sure about this? I can't believe that Logan would do such a thing. He hates regulators, and especially Calhoun."

"This is what I heard. He went to a meeting when the regulator was hired, and it was said that every man there put money in a hat to pay for Calhoun to run us off the land."

"He was at the meeting to report on it, Tom. He wasn't there to participate."

"Hmmm." Tom shrugged. "I must go."

"Let me fill that basket for you to take back to Mrs. Brewster," she said, starting toward the larder, then she turned back, acting on a burning need to set things right. "Logan does many foolish things, Tom, but I know in my heart he wouldn't contribute to scum like Calhoun."

Tom nodded solemnly, but Susan could tell he was far from convinced.

Chapter 18

"**M**issy, that was about the best bird I ever bit into," Coonie announced when everyone had eaten their fill of the Thanksgiving supper Susan had prepared. Coonie put his hands over his bursting belly and gave it a pat. "Yessiree, the best. And that pumpkin pie? Wooo-weee! It was a pleasure to put my mouth around each and every forkful."

Etta released a bout of giggles, finding everything her Uncle Coonie said simply hilarious. Even Jacob grinned.

Logan nodded when Susan offered to pour him another cup of coffee. "I don't remember having such a good Thanksgiving meal, do y'all?" he asked, looking from Jacob to Etta.

"Before Etta came, we had one in St. Louis," Jacob said. "Mama tried to cook the turkey and burned it, so you went and got some ready-cooked at a restaurant."

Logan laughed. "Ah, yes. I'd forgotten about that. We had a good time that Thanksgiving, didn't we? But the food wasn't as good as this, as I recall."

"No, and there wasn't any pie," Jacob pointed out, casting a quick look at his aunt. "Pumpkin pie is my favorite."

Astounded by his near compliment, Susan took a moment to respond. "Why, I'm glad you like it, Jacob," she said when she'd regained her composure. "We have Mrs. Brewster to thank for it. She sent us a big old pumpkin from her patch."

"When did she visit?" Logan asked. He relaxed in his

chair, replete and lazy, one elbow propped on the edge of the table and his other hand spread high up on his thigh, drawing Susan's eyes there even as she fought against it.

"She . . . uh, she didn't," Susan said, patting the napkin against the corners of her mouth. "She's feeling under the weather, so she sent Tom Manygoats." Susan caught Logan's momentary scowl. "What do you have against Tom? He's a sweet man."

"I just don't like the idea of him being around here."

"He's my friend."

"Since when?" Logan asked.

"Since . . . well, for a while. Once I got over the scare of him being an Indian, then I—"

"He's still an Indian," Logan pointed out with a hint of malice that set Susan's teeth on edge.

"Yes, but I'm no longer a blind, narrow-minded dunce." She smiled a little when Etta giggled. "Thanks to Tom Manygoats, I've come to understand that there's no need to be scared witless by every Indian I see. In fact, I'm more afraid of some of the white men in town than I am of the Indians."

"What white men scare you?" Logan asked, drumming his fingers on the tabletop, hinting of his agitation at being lectured.

"Offhand, I'd say that Zeke Calhoun would head my list."

Jacob released his fork with a clatter. "May I be excused, please?"

Logan laid a hand on his shoulder. "Yes, son. You, too, Etta."

The children slid from their chairs and raced each other upstairs where their toys waited.

"Does Jacob know Mr. Calhoun?" Susan stared at the staircase, puzzled by Jacob's sudden need to run away.

"Why do you ask?"

"Jacob seemed upset just now."

"Oh, he had a little run-in with the man. Remember when he ran away? Well, he collided with Calhoun, and the snake scared the peewaddlin' out of him."

Susan made a *tsk-tsking* sound with her tongue. "Picking on a child, shame on that man. He didn't hurt Jacob in any way, did he?''

''No, but I think he wanted to.''

''Tom Manygoats says the town has hired Calhoun to chase the Creeks off their land.''

Coonie and Logan exchanged surprised glances.

''The town? How could the town have hired someone?'' Coonie asked.

''Well, then, some of the town leaders. You've been covering the town meetings, Logan. Have they hired Calhoun?''

''Haven't you been reading the newspaper?'' he teased, but Susan remained stoic. ''Maybe he's been paid by some of the men, but it's nothing official.''

''I'm not ashamed to say that I think we'd be a sight better off if them Creeks did pick up and leave,'' Coonie said, throwing his napkin onto his plate and struggling up from the chair. It creaked nosily as he hoisted himself up. ''They're not all peace-lovin' like that Manygoats fella.''

''No, and they're not all war-painted braves, either. There are women and children in that camp, Coonie French. Would you have them chased out of their homes, too?'' Susan asked.

''Them teepees ain't homes.''

''They are *their* homes,'' Susan insisted. ''You paid a man to drive them out of their homes.''

''Naw, he's just going to scare them a little is all.''

Susan sat back, arms folded. Her gaze slipped from Coonie's wince of chagrin to Logan's scowl of displeasure. ''So you *did* pay that man.''

''Don't look at me,'' Logan said crossly. ''I've got better ways to spend my money. If I had any to throw around, I sure as hell wouldn't throw it in the direction of that piece of filth. I'm disappointed in you, Coonie. I thought you had more sense.''

''You said yourself you wished them Creeks were long gone,'' Coonie said, all huffy.

''Yes, but I'm not going to give Zeke Calhoun money to hang around here and do my dirty work for me. He's a regulator, Coonie. You know what type of man takes a job like that.''

"Yeah, I know, but once he finishes his business, he'll leave town.''

"I, for one, think there's a better way to get rid of the Creeks.''

"What better way?'' Susan asked Logan. "And who made you the law around these parts anyway?''

"What's that mean?'' Logan demanded.

"Since when do you decide who can live here and who can't?''

"I didn't say anything about—''

"Yes, you did,'' she asserted, surging to her feet. "You said you had a better plan to get rid of the Creeks. Logan, they have more right to stay than you do.''

"Says who?''

"Says anyone whose eyes aren't blinded by bigotry.''

"If you had any idea what you were saying, I'd—''

"Hey, hey, hey!'' Coonie held up his hands, as if holding off two fighters. "It's Thanksgiving. Shouldn't we be enjoying each other's company instead of engaging in a shouting match? We've had a good meal—a family gathering, so to speak—so let's act like a loving family.'' He motioned Susan toward the living room. "Susan, you go relax. Us stubborn cusses will clean up these here dishes for you.''

"Oh, no, I can't—''

"Coonie's right,'' Logan interrupted Susan. "You prepared a good meal, and we'll show our appreciation by cleaning up the kitchen.'' He waved her away. "Go read or knit or whatever you do when you relax.''

"Very well. It's awfully sweet of you two.''

Coonie made a playful face. "Don't go hurting our feelings by calling us names.''

Laughing, Susan left the two men with the dirty dishes. Sitting beside the fireplace in the living room, she picked up her knitting and worked quietly for a few minutes, but a thumping upstairs divided her attention, and she finally put aside the knitting and went to marshal Etta and Jacob into bed.

Bending over her niece's bed, she kissed Etta's forehead and received a buss on the cheek in return. Usually, she tucked Etta in last to savor the closeness she enjoyed with her niece. It helped cushion the blow she always felt when Jacob stiffly endured her attentions. Crossing the room to his bed, she willed herself to smile and not let him see how she dreaded his cool reception.

"Let's tuck you in nice and comfy," she whispered, pushing the covers in and around his small body. "There you go. Sweet dreams, Jacob." And then she bent to press a kiss to his forehead. She was turning away when she heard him whisper her name. "Yes, Jacob?"

"Happy Thanksgiving," he mumbled, averting his gaze as shyness seized him.

"Thank you. I did have a happy one." She hesitated a moment longer, a genuine smile curving her lips, then she made herself leave him to his dreams, although a part of her wanted to rush to him and give him a big hug and a sloppy kiss.

Downstairs in the living room, she stood by the fire and savored her small achievement. Jacob had spoken civilly to her! She hadn't dragged it out of him or goaded him. He'd offered those two words like an olive branch. Was it a turning point? Oh, it had to be. Finally she was making headway. *Finally* she had chipped away a chunk of the ice surrounding the little boy's heart.

Entering the living room, Logan paused to enjoy the happy expression Susan wore and the way the firelight played across her face and hair. The golden light made her eyes sparkle and fired her hair with shimmers of ginger and cinnamon. She ran her hands down her black skirt and held them out to the hearth's warmth. There was something self-satisfied about her smile that mystified him.

"What happened?" he asked as he crossed the room to stand behind her.

"What?" She blinked rapidly as if emerging from deep thought, then laughed lightly. "Why do you think something's happened? I'm standing by the fire, warming myself as innocently as you please."

"And smiling like a cat who's just dined on a fat canary, feathers and all."

"No," she admonished. "Nothing so gruesome as that." Glancing over her shoulder and up, she smiled that smile again. "Your son wished me a happy Thanksgiving. What do you make of that, Mr. Vance?"

"Well, well," he said, clasping his hands behind his back and rocking lightly on the balls of his feet.

"I didn't have to threaten him, cajole him, scream at him, burst into tears, or even drop to my knees and beg. He just came right out and said it. And did you hear him at supper when he said that pumpkin pie was his favorite? Why, I almost swooned!"

"Hmmm." Logan scowled. "Maybe he's ill. Should we round up the doctor?"

She whirled, throwing back her head and laughing, and resting her hands against his shirtfront. "No, you scamp! He's warming up to me, don't you see?"

"I . . . see." What he saw was the glitter in her eyes and the glint of her straight, white teeth. He also saw that her lower lip was fuller than her upper, bowed one and realized that was what made her mouth appear so seductive, so kissable.

Sensing his preoccupation, she started to step away, but he captured her wrists before she could remove her hands from his chest. He liked them there.

"Don't pull away from me."

"I . . . I'm not." She cleared her throat nervously. "That is, I didn't mean—"

"I'm glad you and Jacob are growing closer," he said, saving her from further awkwardness.

"Well, we're not exactly close, but I'm heartened, nevertheless. I think perhaps he trusts me more since I helped Etta through her sickness."

"Helped?" He shook his head. "You did more than that, Susan. You pulled her through it. I don't know what I would have done without you."

"Oh, you would have managed."

"Not nearly as well."

She lifted her gaze to his. "Maybe Jacob isn't the only Vance becoming friendlier toward me."

"Have I been unfriendly?"

"Distant, I suppose, is a better word."

"Shall we bury the hatchet?" He ran his thumbs over her knuckles in a caress she found inexplicably moving. "I know I've been a horse's ass, but I—"

"I forgive you."

"That was easy." He grinned and Susan's heart somersaulted. "Here I was all ready to preach a pretty sermon to redeem my soul and you forgive me before I even get warmed up. But I'm not complaining. I was dreading the part where I fall to my knees before you and cry like a baby until you take pity on me."

"*That* I'd like to see," she teased. "Of course, I don't believe for one moment that you'd do such a thing." She sighed, feeling released from a burden. "I'm glad you're joking with me again. I must say I've missed your teasing ways."

"Have you missed anything else?"

"Uh-uh," she said, shaking her head firmly. "I'm not falling into that trap, Mr. Vance. You'll get no more confessions from me."

"Even if I drop to my knees?"

"Even then." She caught her breath when he lifted one of her hands to kiss her middle knuckle. "Logan . . ." She gently tugged her hands from his and went to sit in the rocker.

"What did I do?" He extended his arms in an appeal.

"Nothing, I just . . ." She shrugged and picked up her knitting. "We've made peace. Let's enjoy it."

"I was."

She motioned for him to sit opposite her in the other rocker. "Tell me about the newspaper."

"What about it?"

She looked up at him and pleaded with her eyes. After a few moments, with a look of disgust, he sat in the rocker. "Has the paper become a habit with people? Do they expect it . . . look forward to getting it every week?" she asked.

"I suppose." He propped his elbows on the chair arms and tented his fingers in front of his face. "I'm thinking of expanding to twice a week."

"Would advertising support that?"

"You sound like a newspaperman, Susan." His eyebrows wiggled. "I'm rubbing off on you."

"A person can't live in back of a newspaper office without learning something about it."

"I bet you could run the press."

"Clarabelle?" She scoffed. "Not on your life. I'd make a mess of it." She laid the knitting in her lap. "Tell me about printing twice a week. Won't it be expensive?"

"Yes, but I think we need to establish ourselves more firmly. You asked about how we're being accepted. Well, the folks around here read the newspaper, but I don't think they'd miss it all that much if I didn't get it printed one week. Somehow, I've got to make it a habit with them, and frequency is one way to do that. Eventually, I hope to go daily."

"That will be quite a move," she said, thinking about the work involved in printing a paper every single day. Logan would have to live in the office! "You couldn't do that by yourself, could you? Go daily, I mean. You'd have to hire more help."

"Yes, maybe one more pair of hands," he agreed, then shrugged. "That's a while off. As for printing twice a week, it'll take careful planning, and that's why I'd like to visit that fella from Watonga. He's got quite a reputation among publishers and I could learn from him."

"I remember you mentioning him before. When were you thinking of going?"

"Tomorrow. I'll be back Saturday. Of course, I'll leave Coonie here to watch over you and the children."

"You'll go by rail?"

"Yes. Is that all right with you, or would you rather go with me?"

"No, don't be silly. I'd only be in the way. I'll stay here with the children. We'll be fine."

"Sometimes I wonder what my life would be like if

you'd decided to go back to the farm instead of coming here with me.''

"More peaceful?" she asked with a saucy smile.

"Definitely," he answered, then ducked when she threw her ball of yarn at him. It went sailing, spooling out heather-gray. Logan rocked back and caught the ball before it rolled out of reach. "I suppose you had a few twinges of homesickness today, didn't you?" He began rewinding the yarn.

"No, actually I didn't." She looked at him, as surprised as he by her answer. "I guess I was too busy." Pausing, she shook her head. "No, that's not right. I've made myself a home here, so I don't miss the farm as much as I used to."

"Don't you miss your family?"

"Yes, but . . ."

"But?" He leaned forward, still winding.

"But I've gotten used to making decisions for myself and doing things without asking for permission." She issued a wistful sigh. "It would be hard minding Papa and Mama again."

"I've thought about that letter they wrote," he said, handing her the ball of yarn. "You shouldn't take it to heart, you know. They were writing from anger at me more than at you."

"Yes, but I know they're crushed."

"They'll get over it."

"Will they?"

Catherine's name floated between them, invisible and unspoken, but there like a specter. Logan's gaze met hers and held fast.

"I did love your sister, but it faded. Sometimes it's like that. It burns fast, furious, but briefly. That's what Catherine and I had. A quick, bright flame."

"Were you happy with her?"

He sat back and rocked. "Happy? I suppose we had our moments."

"Moments? That's all?"

"It wasn't a perfect marriage, Susan. Catherine and I

had our problems. After all, we weren't married under ideal circumstances. She was pregnant.''

"Yes, I remember. The shock of that swept through our whole family like a tornado. I was young, but I knew that Catherine had done something awful—something Papa and Mama could never forgive her for.''

"I remember Abraham going after her with his buggy whip.'' He noticed her involuntary wince. "Did he ever beat you?''

"Once,'' she murmured, watching the flash of her knitting needles. "That was enough for me.''

"He was going to whip Catherine when he found out she'd slept with me and got herself a baby, but I put a stop to that right quick.''

"You did?'' Her hands stilled. "How?''

He looked at her as if she were slightly dense. "I hauled off and let him have one—right in the eye. You didn't know about that? How could you not have known? He had a shiner.''

"Yes, I remember that.'' She closed her eyes for a moment, trying to recall that hazy past. "Papa said one of the mules had kicked him.''

"Ha!'' Logan held up his right fist. "This mule.''

"You hit Papa?'' She marveled that he had lived to tell about it. "No wonder he despises you.''

"He hates me, but not for that. I only added insult to injury when I punched him and took that buggy whip away from him. I know he's your father, Susan, but I can't muster up any respect for a man who whips his young ones like they're part of his livestock. My God! The man's daughter had just told him she was carrying a child!'' He shook his head as if he were rattled. "I don't understand that kind of behavior.''

"Papa's strict, but he loves us.''

"I'm strict, too, but I'd never beat my children.''

"I know, and I admire that about you.''

"Don't ask me to list the things I admire about you or we'll be sitting here until dawn.''

Pleasure lit her eyes, then her lashes swept down to

conceal them from him. "So, you'll be leaving come morning?"

"Yes."

"I'll pack you a lunch."

"I'd appreciate it."

"Leftover turkey." She smiled to herself. "We always had turkey sandwiches the day after Thanksgiving." Preoccupied with those memories, she didn't realize he'd moved until she glanced up from her knitting and saw that the rocker across from her was empty. Logan stood before the fireplace, his back to it. His indecipherable expression made her stomach muscles flutter. That old feeling of slipping under his spell made her uneasy, and she put aside her knitting. "I should be getting to bed."

"Do you ever miss not having me in it?"

Uh-oh, a voice warned in her head. She forced herself up from the chair and kept her gaze trained on safe things like her knitting basket, the floor, the rag rug under her feet. Anything but Logan. Keep your eyes off him, a voice in her head warned. One look and you'll be tempted to tell him the truth.

She tried to laugh off his question even as she attempted to slip from his reach. One stride brought him flush against her. He curled a finger beneath her chin and forced it up . . . up . . . up. His eyes were mossy-green with golden centers. His lips parted. His breath stirred the curls in front of her ears. He moved his thumb along her jawline, and then his fingers slipped into her hair and tipped her head back. He hesitated an instant, just long enough to see the anticipation in her eyes before she closed them.

His mouth felt comfortable on hers, and his tongue moved in and made itself right at home. Susan surrendered to the weakness in her, allowing him to swing her slightly off-balance so that she was cradled in his arms. She sighed contentedly as his lips skimmed down her throat and then teased the lace decorating her bodice. His fingers worked her hair free of the loose bundle at the back of her neck. She felt it fall heavily into a pool in his hand, then he brought it up to his face and buried his nose in the curls.

"Susan, say you want me."

Oh, so easy, she thought. Say the words and you can have him, but for how long? Didn't he say that love burns brightly, fiercely, briefly? She gripped his upper arms, regained her equilibrium, then slid from his embrace to stand on her own two feet again. She banded her loosed hair in one hand and held it over her shoulder.

"And if I want you, will that make everything rosy?" she asked quietly, but didn't give him a chance to answer. "The problem is, Logan, I'm not sure what I want anymore, and I'm not sure I can trust my feelings."

He started to argue, then angled his head back for a better look. "You sound like a woman who won't be moved."

"I need more time to think."

"About what?"

"About where I go from here." She shook her head. "I don't mean for that to sound as if I'm dead set on leaving. I'm not. But if I stay, I have to know *why* I'm staying. We should be clear about our feelings, don't you agree?"

"We? What makes you think I'm fuddle-brained?"

"Are you sure you haven't been visiting the Bloody Bucket the past few weeks because you *want* to be here or because you'd feel guilty if you weren't?"

He turned aside with a scowl. "Believe it or not, my visits to the Bucket weren't all social. I picked up news while I was there and met the locals. That's important in the newspaper business."

It was her turn to scowl. "That's why you spent so much time there? Funny, I thought it had something to do with saloon tarts and rotgut."

His glance was piercing. "Since you're trying to sort things out—did you resent my visits there because you felt I should be home with my children or because I should be home with you?"

"The children are always *my* first concern," she replied haughtily.

"Like hell," he said, baring his teeth.

She would have fashioned an uppity exit if he hadn't been so quick to grasp the back of her neck and haul her to him. His lips closed over hers, grinding, rubbing, burning. She squirmed against him, and his arms tightened until there was no room for her to move or even breathe.

When she feared she would pass out, he lifted his mouth from hers and his hands clasped either side of her head, holding it steady and forcing her to look up into his eyes.

"While I'm away, Susan, I want you to think hard about why you married me." His fingers curled against her scalp to wrap around the strands of her hair. "And if you tell yourself it was for the sake of the children, then you can start packing your bags."

She glared at him, not liking the way he manhandled her. "That *is* why we married," she reminded him coldly, then gasped as he set her away from him none too gently. She had to grab the back of the rocker to keep from stumbling.

"That's why we *said* we married," he told her between clenched teeth. He strode toward the newspaper office, but turned on his heel for one last parting shot. "And by the way, I happen to be quite clear on why I went to the Bucket night after night. I went there to get away from you."

She hitched up her chin. "And to be with Mazie."

His lids narrowed until she couldn't see his eyes at all. "At least she never gave me the cold shoulder, which is more than I can say for you, dear heart."

Chapter 19

Sherman and Minnie stepped lightly along the rutted road leading to Tulsa. Sitting in the wagon beside Etta and Jacob, Susan let the reins lay slack in her hands since the two mules seemed to know the way and didn't need her guidance. Logan had traded the oxen for them back in July, but Susan hadn't driven the wagon often enough for the mules to get used to her or her to them. Sherman was the larger, coal-black with a brown muzzle. Minnie, more delicately boned, had a speckled gray coat with a white blazed face. From the feel of the reins, Sherman was pulling more weight than Minnie, but didn't seem to mind.

"If we had stayed the night with Mrs. Brewster, we could have had a taffy pull," Etta said, still miffed that Susan had declined Mrs. Brewster's offer of a night's lodging.

"Yes, pumpkin, but Mrs. Brewster isn't feeling well. She doesn't need overnight guests to worry about, does she? Besides, we want to be home tomorrow morning so we can fix a big dinner for when your papa gets back from his trip."

"Why'd we go there in the first place if we're a bother to her?" Jacob groused.

"Because she's under the weather, and I didn't say we were a bother, Jacob. A get-well visit is different from an overnight stay."

"I guess she's gonna die," Jacob announced with his usual dark outlook.

"Always the pessimist," Susan said, sighing heavily,

then catching the children's exchange of confusion. "A pessimist is someone who always looks for the worst and expects bad things to happen," she explained. "For your information, Gloomy Gus, Mrs. Brewster is *not* on her deathbed. Her arthritis has flared up, that's all. Her joints are swollen, so it's hard for her to get around, but she'll be feeling better come spring. Jacob, just because someone takes ill doesn't mean you can start digging his grave."

Etta giggled, but Jacob scowled, reminding Susan of Logan. Just like his father, she thought, studying his glowering expression. Logan could make the sun rise with his smile and dive with one dark look. Take this morning, for instance, when he'd set off to catch the train. His smiles had warmed the hearts of his children and Coonie, but his solemn farewell to Susan had cast a chill. Yet there had been something else in his expression, she recalled. Regret? She certainly felt it. She'd wanted to send him on his trip with a quick kiss and a bright smile, but their quarrel last night had tainted the morning.

That glum mood had spurred her to hastily plan a visit to Mrs. Brewster's. She'd packed two big baskets of food, one for her and the children and one to leave for Mrs. Brewster, then she'd bundled Etta and Jacob into layers of clothes, pressed Coonie into helping her hitch the mules to the wagon, and set off on her get-well mission.

The weather cooperated. Cool and crisp, the air smelled of woodsmoke and musky autumn leaves. The sky had cleared by mid-morning and the sun had warmed the day enough for them to shed their winter coats and jackets. After sharing their basket of goodies with Mrs. Brewster for a mid-day meal and a few hours filled with conversation and laughter, they took their leave and headed back to Tulsa. A gracious hostess, Mrs. Brewster had asked them to stay the night, especially since Coonie had been told they might, but Susan had wanted to get back to Tulsa before dark. Soon, they'd be home.

Home. Yes, she thought of Tulsa as her home now. She'd told Mrs. Brewster about her quarrel with Logan and how her marriage had deeply wounded her parents. Mrs. Brewster had waved off both her worries.

"Men and women will be fussing 'til the end of time, child, and parents will be trying to pick their in-laws for twice that long. Don't stay up nights fretting about it," she'd counseled Susan, and it was just what Susan had needed to hear.

She'd told Mrs. Brewster of her soul-searching, and the older, wiser woman had chided her for "letting the weeds conceal the flower."

"What do you need to be clear on?" she'd asked Susan.

"What I need . . . what's important to me," Susan had tried to explain.

"Do you love Mr. Vance?"

"Yes," Susan had answered without doubt.

"And what in this world is more important to you than him and his children?"

After a moment's thought, Susan had answered, "Nothing."

"Sounds like you're clear as a bell to me," Mrs. Brewster had said with a wry smile.

"But I'm not sure how he feels," Susan had said.

"And you're not making it easy for him to tell you by keeping him on the other side of your bedroom door. Dearie, men aren't like us. They just can't naturally blurt out things close to their hearts. They usually whisper those things in the dark. Trouble is, you're never around to hear Mr. Vance when he takes a notion to talk about how he feels."

"You're right," Susan had said, feeling stupid for allowing her misery to go on as long as it had. For weeks she'd felt on the verge of tears, so unhappy that she ached through and through, and it was all her fault. It was high time she mended her marriage if she wanted to keep it. And she wanted to keep it more than anything else in the whole world.

"Aunt Susan, why is that gray horse sweating so much?" Etta asked, breaking into her thoughts.

"It's not a horse, it's a mule," Jacob said, then sat forward for a better look. "Minnie is all lathered up, Aunt Susan. How come?"

"She's tired, I suppose," Susan said, but even as the

words left her, she knew it was more than that. The black hadn't broken a sweat, but the gray was damp all over. "Hmmm, maybe we should pull up and have a look at her." Susan grabbed the reins and pitched backward, tugging the mules to a stop. She tied the reins around the brake handle, motioned for the children to stay put, then hitched up her skirts and jumped to the ground.

Minnie was not only lathered, she was breathing heavily, as if she'd been running all day. Susan stroked the mule's blazed face and felt the animal's front legs. They quivered beneath her hand.

"She's ill," Susan said, answering the children's questioning looks. "I don't think we should go on. Minnie needs a rest."

"So what do we do now?" Jacob asked, exasperated. "Go back to Mrs. Brewster's?"

"No, we'll pull off the road, unhitch the mules, and give everyone a little rest. Minnie will get her wind back, and we'll hitch her and Sherman up to the wagon again and head home." Susan brushed her hands together in an efficient gesture, but got only a sour glance from Jacob. "Jacob, pick up the reins and drive the wagon over to that stand of maples." She pointed it out, then followed along behind the wagon.

"What if Minnie doesn't get better?" Etta asked as she scrambled down to the ground.

"Then . . ." Susan looked around and tried not to sound as doubtful as she felt. "Why, then we'll spend the night right here. Like we did on the way to Tulsa, remember?"

Jacob and Etta received her idea with matching frowns.

"Well, are we going to stay here all night?" Jacob demanded, arms akimbo, legs apart, wearing a fierce expression borrowed from his father.

Susan lay on the blanket they'd spread earlier for their picnic supper. She looked at the sky, knowing full well that in another half hour it would be dark. Sighing, she sat up and looked toward the mules. Sherman slept. Minnie wheezed.

"Oh, piddle!" She crossed her arms and glared at the sick mule. "Minnie's no better, is she?"

"Worse," Jacob said.

"You're always ready with an encouraging word, aren't you?" Susan asked, sarcasm dripping. "Well, I suppose we're spending the night." She brushed grass from the back of her skirt. "So let's make some beds."

"Out of what?" Etta asked.

"Believe it or not, your aunt actually has enough sense to plan for misadventures such as this." She went to the wagon and reached under the seat for the three rolls of bedding, dumping one after the other onto the ground.

"Bedrolls!" Jacob's face lit up. "I never figured you'd—" He clamped his lips together.

Susan smiled smugly, knowing he was biting his tongue to keep from praising her. "Etta, you may unroll these and place them under the wagon while Jacob and I gather wood for a fire."

Finding plenty of sticks beneath the trees surrounding them, Susan made a pouch from the front of her skirt, and Jacob piled the twigs into it.

"What if the mule is still sick come morning?" he asked as he grabbed at dry, fallen branches and twigs.

"Then we'll all three mount old Sherman and ride him home."

"Why didn't we do that a while back, instead of waiting around until it got dark?"

"Because there was a chance Minnie would recover enough to go on. I was hoping for the best." She slanted him a meaningful glare. "I don't expect you to understand."

To Susan's surprise, Jacob smiled. Then to her shock, he tried unsuccessfully to smother a laugh. She laughed with him, swinging one hip to collide playfully with his shoulder.

"You little scamp. I do believe you enjoy getting my goat." She hitched a shoulder forward. "Come on. Let's start the fire before it gets pitch-black out here."

Etta had the bedrolls laid out under the wagon by the time they were back with the firewood. With Jacob's help,

Susan had the fire going in no time. It sent out a warm golden light, surrounding them, comforting them against the encroaching darkness. Sleepy-eyed Etta crawled under the wagon first and snuggled down to sleep. Jacob sat with Susan near the fire, watching the flames try to climb into the sky.

"You hear that?" he asked after a few minutes.

She did. Drums. Not all that far off.

"Indians, right?"

Susan nodded. "They won't bother us."

"Maybe we should kill the fire so we won't draw attention to ourselves."

"No, it's all right. The Creeks are peaceful." She felt Jacob's searching gaze upon her face and made sure her expression was one of confidence. "Tom Manygoats has told me all about them. You like Tom, don't you?"

"I guess. He dresses funny."

"Don't judge a book by its cover, Jacob. You'll miss out on a lot of good stories that way." She hunched her shoulders and crossed her arms, rubbing her hands up and down her long sleeves. The air was growing chilly. "We'll be warm enough with the fire and our thick bedrolls," she said, answering her own doubts.

Jacob picked up a stick and drew trees and dogs in the dirt. "We had steam heat in St. Louis."

"Yes. That was nice. Do you miss St. Louis?"

"Not really." He drew a stick figure, then put a long skirt on it. "You don't act much like Mama."

"I guess you really miss her, don't you?"

"Not really." He drew another figure, one with a cap and breeches. "She wasn't around much, and when she was, all she did was fight with Papa. Me and Etta got tired of hearing them yell at each other. We used to put pillows over our heads to block out the sound."

Susan brought her gaze around slowly to him. She dared not speak, realizing that Jacob was telling her things he rarely shared with anyone other than his sister.

"Papa would come home and Mama wouldn't have done anything all day. They'd start fussing." He sighed, and it was the sound of pure weariness. He swung his green eyes up to her. "She didn't cook or clean or nothing."

"Whatever did she do with herself during the day?"

"She was always at the Grand."

"The Grand?"

"Theater," he tacked on. "It was around the corner from us."

"She went to the theater every day?"

"Almost," Jacob said, nodding.

"She saw the same play every day?"

"No. She and the man who ran it were—" He wrinkled his nose. "Friends, I guess."

Susan stared into the fire as a picture of infidelity formed in her mind. If that were true, it would explain so much.

"When Mama got sick, Papa said it was a blessing because it kept her at home where she belonged. That was before the doctors said she'd never get well," he added quickly. "When they told Papa that, he was real sad. Him and Mama didn't fight after that."

"Did they fight before about your mama spending so much of her time away from home?"

"Yeah, that and about us."

"What about you?"

"About how she never did nothing with us. She didn't much like me or Etta."

"Oh, Jacob." Susan draped an arm around his shoulders. He stiffened, but she refused to withdraw her gesture of support. "I'm sure she loved you."

"Maybe."

"She bragged about you to me."

"She did?" His eyes looked so much like Logan's that Susan had to bite her upper lip to keep from telling him so.

"Yes, she did. She wrote home, and her letters were filled with news about you and your sister. She thought you were as sharp as a tack and that Etta was as pretty a little girl as had ever been brought into this world. And you know what?"

"What?"

"She had every right to be proud. If you were my little boy, I'd be crowing like a young rooster."

That garnered the hint of a grin from him, then he ducked his head and went back to his dirt drawings.

"Well, don't you think we'd better turn in?" Susan asked.

"I guess." He erased his artwork with a sweep of his hand. "I'll check the mules first."

"That's a good boy. You certainly are handy to have around." She wasn't sure, but she thought she saw him smile again.

Susan pulled the covers up closer to Etta's chin, then settled into her own bedroll. She and Jacob sandwiched Etta.

"Aunt Susan?"

Susan raised her head to see her nephew, but shadows hid his face from her. "Yes, Jacob?"

"You're handy to have around, too."

Joy spread through her like a dawning sun. She lay back down, so full of happiness she could hardly speak. After a moment she said through her smile, "Thanks. Sweet dreams, little man."

She couldn't have been asleep long because the fire hadn't died to embers yet. Susan lay quietly, except for the thudding of her heart reverberating through her body. Something had awakened her, and until she was sure of the source, she dared not move.

Hooves pranced into view from her bed under the wagon. Susan sucked in her breath and counted—four horses. She moved one hand cautiously to her neck and touched the cross Logan had given her. From it, she drew needed strength and a clear head. The horses circled the wagon as the riders whispered and laughed. She couldn't understand a word, no matter how hard she tried. Then she realized why. Indians!

Just then one gave a war whoop. Both Etta and Jacob jumped awake. Susan laid a hand on each of their heads.

"Shhh," she hissed to them. "Lie perfectly still. I'll

handle this. Now you mind me, or I'll tell your papa you misbehaved.''

Etta whimpered, but neither child moved as Susan reached for the rifle she'd hidden under her bedroll when Jacob and Etta hadn't been looking. In the flickering light, Susan caught Jacob's openmouthed moment of shock when he saw his gun-toting aunt.

The Indians whooped and hollered, making such a racket that Susan gritted her teeth to keep from screaming at them. What were they up to? What did they want? Did they just mean to scare them? Well, they'd succeeded!

Suddenly, the blanket she'd draped at the side of the wagon to block out most of the firelight was shoved aside and a face straight from the land of nightmares thrust through the opening. Streaked with war paint, the young Creek bared his teeth and shook his knife. He said something, then glared at Etta, who was bawling like a new-born calf.

"Get away from here!" Susan yelled, trying to sound fierce. "Go! Get! I swear, I'll blow a hole through you . . . you . . . you savage!" She gripped the rifle, but couldn't aim it properly because of the confined space under the wagon. Fear coated the inside of her mouth with copper and she shivered from a cold sweat. Lord, don't let us die like this, she prayed as she struggled to get the rifle untangled from the covers and pointed at the evil face still leering at them.

Then another face, this one streaked with white and red and yellow, appeared on the other side of the wagon. Surrounded by the awful masks, Etta screamed and Jacob started crying and clawing at the rifle in Susan's hands.

"Kill them! Kill them!" Jacob screamed, and Susan had to pin him back with her elbow to keep him from accidentally firing the rifle.

"Jacob, stop it! You're going to . . . Stop!" She slapped at him with her free hand, then tried to wiggle out from beneath the wagon. She had to get out so she could have room to defend herself and her wards.

Suddenly someone grasped her ankles, and Susan felt herself being pulled out from under the wagon. She tried to kick, but the hands holding her ankles were as strong as iron. Clothes tangled about her body and the ground burned her back. She could do nothing but wriggle helplessly. Etta and Jacob grabbed for her, but only managed to yank handfuls of her hair from her scalp. Clearing the wagon, Susan sat and brought up the rifle. She got off one shot before someone behind her wrenched it from her grasp. Twisting around, she saw the glint of black eyes behind a band of white paint.

The Indians were all young and liquored up. She could smell the stench of it rising from their gleaming bodies. They wore hardly anything, just flapping rectangles across their buttocks and a strip of deerhide covering their privates. Two remained on horseback, the spotted horses rearing and pawing the air.

Etta screamed for Susan, and Susan scrambled to her feet, her hands outstretched toward the Indian bent over and trying to grab the children. Sinking her fingernails into his back, she left long, bloody marks. He whirled around, howling like an animal, and the flash of a knife blade arced, just missing her cheek as Susan stumbled backward into the arms of the other Indian. He held her against him and she felt the cold kiss of steel against her throat. Common sense told her to stop struggling.

Whiskey breath fanned her face. She closed her eyes, wondering if she should die fighting or on her knees.

A shot rang out, then another. She was flung aside like a sack of flour. Susan fell to her hands and knees, and her hair curtained her face, distorting her vision for the next confusing moments as she sensed that someone new had entered this war-painted party. There seemed to be a standoff as the young braves sized up their competition. Tossing her hair from her face, Susan stared at the tall-sitting Indian dressed in buckskin breeches and shirt. His face was painted, too, but for some reason she didn't fear him. He issued another low, growling spate of Creek words, then motioned with his sawed-off Winchester for the two men on foot to mount their horses. They did, and the four painted horsemen made dust. Susan gasped, her hands flying to cover her mouth as she recognized her buckskinned savior.

"Tom Manygoats!"

He nodded, then swung one leg over his horse and dropped neatly to the ground. "You hurt?"

"I don't think so." She let him help her to her feet and brushed her hands down her dirty clothes. One sleeve of her blouse had been ripped at the shoulder and her skirt pocket had been tore away. "I'm trembling," she confessed with a shaky laugh, then whirled toward the wagon. "Jacob? Etta?" She fell to her knees and reached under the wagon, catching their hands and pulling them out so she could inspect them.

They clung to her, hugging her as if they'd never let her go. Susan stroked Etta's curls and Jacob's cornsilk hair, then tipped back their heads so she could look each in the face. Their eyes shone with tears that streaked down their cheeks. Susan kissed Etta, then Jacob. For once, Jacob didn't dodge the kiss but accepted it limply.

"Are you all right?" Susan asked. "Are you hurt . . . either of you? Just scared? Me, too. Me, too." She held them against her body, rocking back and forth on her knees.

"They will be punished," Tom Manygoats said, moving to stand beside the three. "Those young ones—they drank too much firewater and acted like animals. To save their honor, they will confess and be punished by the elders. What are you doing out here like this?"

"Visiting Mrs. Brewster," Susan said, gasping as she struggled to regain her breath. "One of the mules got sick and we had to camp here for the night. Oh, Tom." She closed her eyes, her shoulders slumping. "I've never been so glad to see anyone in my whole life. They would have ki—hurt us."

"There's much anger brewing among my people and yours," he said, regret coloring his voice as he crouched beside Susan and the children. "It spills over onto the innocent. I apologize for them. From my heart, I do." He covered a good portion of his chest with one of his large hands, then angled his head toward Etta. "Do I scare you, little one? This paint on my face makes you afraid of your old friend?'' He ran his sleeve down his face, smearing most of the paint off. ''Tom Manygoats would never harm Etta Vance or her brother Jacob Vance. Never, never,'' he repeated, shaking his head. ''I'm staying here to watch over you tonight and I'll make sure you get home safely come first light.''

''Will you, Tom?'' Susan asked. ''It would make us all feel better if you did.''

''I will.'' He gave a decisive nod.

''Good. We've been listening to the drums all evening. What's happening at the Indian camp?''

''Stomp dance,'' he said, shrugging. ''It's a custom, but some of the younger ones brought in a crate of liquor. Mix liquor with anything and it gets twisted. Those four are young and headstrong. They want to fight shadows, ideas, rumors—things that can't be chased and captured. They are full of fury and fear, but that gives them no right to bother you and yours. No right.''

''We were sleeping and they just came up on us and started yelling. They dragged me out from under the wagon.'' Susan wet the hem of her skirt with her tongue and rubbed dirt off Etta's forehead and nose. ''Stop crying, pumpkin. We're fine now. Those bad men are long gone.''

Recovered enough to resort to his usual independent self, Jacob sat away from Susan's mothering. He glared for a few moments at Tom Manygoats.

''I think it's dumb to paint your face like that,'' he said with bold belligerence.

Tom smiled. ''Maybe so.''

''Children, let's go back to our beds. Now, now.'' Susan gave Etta a quick hug when she made a mewling sound. ''The excitement is over and we can all sleep soundly with our friend here keeping watch. Jacob, will you straighten the bedding for us?'' Reaching out her hand, she waited for Tom to grasp it. She squeezed his big hand. ''Thanks, Tom. I'll never forget this.''

* * *

Morning brought peace and nearly eradicated the memories of the night.

Susan, the children, and Tom Manygoats ate biscuits and ham sandwiches for breakfast around the fire Tom had kept glowing all night. After checking on the mule, Tom pronounced it well enough to continue on. He hitched the mules to the wagon and fed the animals corn from his saddlebags.

Insisting on escorting them to town, Tom rode alongside and told stories of Tulsey Town before it was tamed into a community. Once, it had been a watering hole for buffalo and deer; a place of trees and sky and long, waving grass. No railroad tracks, no buildings, no white people for hundreds of miles. It had been Indian hunting ground, and Susan could tell from Tom's voice that he wished for those times again.

Having removed his scary paint last night and fished his derby hat from his saddlebags, he looked more like the Tom Manygoats she'd grown accustomed to. The hat sat jauntily on his iron-colored hair. Feathers sprouted from the hatband and waved in the air.

"Is your wife living?" Susan asked, wondering about this enigmatic native.

"No, she died a while back. She was older than me. We had many, many years together, though."

"And you have your children and grandchildren to keep you company," Susan said. "That's nice."

"Where is your family?"

"Back in Missouri on the family farm."

"They know you married and are no longer just a sister-in-law?"

Susan pulled her lower lip between her teeth and nodded. "Yes. They know."

"They hate us," Jacob offered cheerfully.

"No, they do not!" Susan turned on him, furious. "That's an awful lie and you know it, Jacob Vance! My family loves you and Etta—and me," she added, though she wondered if she was still as dearly loved as she once had been.

"They only hate Papa," Etta explained to her brother.

"They don't—" Susan bit off the rest, hating to lie. Leave it to children to come right out with the truth, no matter how terrible it sounded. She glanced at Tom Manygoats, saw that he had heard far too much in her unfinished denial, and shrugged. "Speaking of Logan, I certainly hope we get back before he does."

"He's gone?"

"Yes, he went to Watonga to see another newspaperman. I'm sure we'll beat him home."

"He'll be one mad white man when you tell him about last night," Tom said.

"Yes, well . . . I don't suppose we have to tell him. No need to get him all upset." She glanced at the children and knew they'd never keep quiet about the adventure.

"Better tell him," Tom advised. "Men don't like it when their women keep secrets."

"I wasn't going to keep it a secret," Susan objected, "but there's no sense in alarming him. Etta, Jacob, you let me tell your father about what happened. I don't want you scaring him for no good reason. Y'all hear me talking to you?"

"Yes, ma'am," Etta said, clearly miffed by the order.

"Jacob?"

"I hear you."

"Good." Susan released a sigh and began rehearsing a harmless-sounding account for Logan. The wagon topped the swell of land and Tulsa came into view.

Chapter 20

"**W**e got attacked by Indians!"

It was the first thing out of Etta's mouth the moment Logan stepped into the kitchen. Realizing too late that she'd let the cat out of the bag, Etta clamped her hands over her mouth and turned her big blue eyes toward Susan. "I'm sorry," she mumbled behind her hands.

"Indians?" Logan looked from Etta to Susan. "What's she talking about?"

Susan tried a trembling smile. A man shouldn't be allowed to look so delicious while he was scowling, she thought. The gray striped suit was his best one, city-tailored and grander than anything Susan had seen back on the farm. He'd pulled his wedding tie off to one side to loosen the knot. The shiny boots made him even taller. He dominated the room—*any* room.

"Su-san," he said, singsong, with a warning implied. It was meant to intimidate her, but oddly enough, it made her breathless and warm all over.

"I'll tell you later." Susan extended her arms, trying to get his mind off Indians and onto the meal displayed fetchingly on the table. "Welcome home. I've fixed your favorites—pork roast, rice, gravy, and candied yams. Oh, and those yeast rolls you're so crazy about." She sniffed the air. "Don't they smell wonderful?"

"They do," Coonie said, striding into the kitchen and slapping Logan on the back. He'd gone to the rail station to pick up Logan in the other wagon. Rolling his sleeves

267

to his elbows, he eyed the table with relish. "Sit down and tell us all about your trip, pard."

Logan tossed his cap onto the bench beside the back door. "Susan, will you tell me about this Indian attack or must I hear it from the children?"

"Indian attack?" Coonie chuckled. "What in tarnation are y'all talking about? Why, there hasn't been an Indian in twenty feet of this place while you've been gone." He chuckled again, but something in Susan's expression strangled the humor in him. He glanced at Etta's big-eyed stare and at Jacob, nervously biting his lower lip, then at Susan again. "Hey now. Did something happen to y'all when you went calling on Mrs. Brewster?"

"No, it was nothing. I'll tell you all about our little adventure after we've had our supper," Susan promised, trying her best to make light of it. She removed her apron and hung it on a hook near the stove. Had Logan even noticed her dress? she wondered. She'd made it herself and hadn't worn it until now. Peach-colored with a white collar and cuffs, it was shirtwaisted and the latest style—or so she'd been told by the woman who'd sold her the pattern. "So, come on and get around the table before this food gets cold and I get red-hot mad."

Logan swept back his suit coat, propping his hands at his waist. As he tilted his head sideways, indulgence radiated from his stance. "Susan, please?"

"Oh, piffle!" She stamped a foot, wishing she could grab up the gravy bowl and hurl it at him. "We went to visit Mrs. Brewster and on the way home one of the mules got sick, so we camped out for the night. A few rambunctious young Indians gave us a scare, but it was nothing. We weren't harmed, as you can plainly see. So will you all sit down at the table, please?"

Logan's probing gaze moved from her to each of his children. After a span of tense moments, he relaxed enough to sit at the head of the table. "Very well, we'll postpone this until after supper. Etta, Jacob, you *are* all right, yes?"

"Yes, Papa," Etta assured him, scrambling into her chair.

"Yes, Papa," Jacob intoned, but his furrowed brow said otherwise.

"Hmmm." Logan sent a stern message with his eyes down the table to Susan—a message that said she had a lot of explaining to do later. She nodded, silently promising he'd get his due. Logan leaned sideways toward Etta. "How about a kiss for your old papa?"

She obliged, giving him a hug as well. "I missed you. Tell me about Wat—Wata—"

"Watonga," Logan said. "But I can't because I never made it there."

"What happened?" Coonie asked before Susan could.

"The railhead goes to Kingfisher, so that's where I met with the other newspaperman. He traveled to Kingfisher by horse from Watonga." Logan took a big slice of the pork roast, then passed the platter to Coonie. "He has quite a setup in Watonga and he gave me a lot of good information about expanding to twice weekly. Kingfisher is a nice enough town, but I like Tulsa better."

"That's 'cause we're here," Jacob said.

"Yes, I suppose so," Logan agreed, grinning at his son. "Home is where the heart is. That's what my sweet Aunt Dee always says." His gaze moved to Susan, lingering long enough to spark the Logan tingle in her stomach.

"Did you see any buffalo?" Jacob asked. "What about the train, Papa? Did anyone try to hold it up?"

Susan ate quietly, glad the children had guided their father into a conversation about his trip. She'd wanted the welcome-home dinner to go without a hitch, and it had seemed for a minute that Etta had ruined it. When she told Logan about their misadventure, she wanted to be alone with him, without the excited, exalted interjections of the children. They'd only alarm him, she knew.

And she did so want to be alone with him. That desire, overruling all else, disturbed and intrigued her. She'd missed him, she realized with a start. Not only that, but she'd been all aflutter anticipating his homecoming. And she wanted him to herself—if only for a few minutes. She wanted his full attention. And no talk of Indians!

"I ran into a fellow on the train—a traveling salesman—and guess what he sold me?" Logan asked after dessert had been served and eaten.

"What?" Jacob asked, grabbing the bait.

"Kites. Two of them. One for each of you." He grinned when Jacob and Etta bounded from their chairs and begged him to tell them where he'd hidden the gifts. "In the pressroom right beside the front door. They're in a box," he said, laughing. "Take Uncle Coonie with you and he'll show you how to put them together." He and Coonie exchanged a speaking glance before Coonie followed the children out, then Logan's jarring gaze landed squarely on Susan. "You have an explanation for me about an Indian attack?"

"Yes," she said, sighing a little as she started stacking dishes. "Let me clear the table, then I'll—"

"Susan!"

She jumped when the flat of his hand connected with the top of the table, rattling dishes and upsetting a water glass. Gripping the edge of the table, she looked down its length at him. His skin was pale, his lips tight with irritation. She swallowed hard, realizing he had taken all he could.

"Leave the dishes," he said more quietly, but no less threateningly. "Tell me now."

Why was he so angry? she wondered. He could look for himself and see no harm had come to any of them.

"While we were camped, a few of the younger Indians came around. They had been drinking and they just wanted to scare us," she said, carefully selecting each word, but not liking the way the muscles just below his ears writhed as if he were grinding his teeth. "Tom Manygoats came along and ran them off. Tom stayed the rest of the night just to make sure no one else bothered us." She flipped a hand in a dismissive gesture. "So, you see? It was nothing."

"That was all there was to it?" he asked, rising from his chair and moving slowly toward her.

"Yes.' She smiled brightly at him. "Of course, the

children will make more of it. They were frightened, but they settled down when Tom Manygoats happened by."

"The Indians didn't try to hurt you?"

"No. I told you that—" She gasped as his hand shot out to circle her wrist and bring her arm up sharply.

"What's this then? This bruise . . . these scratches? Did you think I wouldn't notice them, Susan? Do you think I don't use my eyes for anything other than reading newspaper type?"

"I don't remember how that happened. Logan, you're hurting me!"

"Then tell me the truth." He pulled her to her feet, still gripping her wrist and making her look at the telltale signs of a struggle. "One thing I won't abide from you is lies, Susan. Did they try to rape you?"

"No!" She wrenched free. "I don't know what they . . ." Tears stung her eyes, brought there by Logan's stubborn insistence. "They pulled me out from under the wagon. I tried to shoot them and they had knives and I don't know what they would have done. Tom rode up and squeezed off some warning shots and they skedaddled. He said they were mad because of all the tension in town. I don't think they would have—" She put a hand to her forehead as she recalled against her will how terrified she'd been.

"They pulled a knife on you?" he repeated, his eyes widening until she could see white all around them.

"But they didn't c-cut me."

"Christ!"

Suddenly she was in his arms and he had buried his face in the side of her neck. His arms tightened around her waist. She slipped her arms around him, up his back, her fingers hooking over his shoulders. He felt warm and solid and oh-so-manly.

"I didn't want you to worry," she whispered.

"Worry? My God, Susan, I want to find those savages and gut them myself!"

"No, no." She caressed his face soothingly. "They were drunk and didn't know—"

"Why are you defending them? They had no right—"

"Yes, but no harm was done."

"They frightened you and my children. They dragged you out from under the wagon and held a knife to you. What do you call that if not harm? Why, I ought to—"

"Nothing." She placed her thumbs over his lips. "Let bygones be bygones." She could tell he hated that idea. "Logan, I wouldn't have let them hurt the children. I'd lay my life down for them. I swear I would."

"I know that. I never doubted it." He flung himself away from her, turning his back and running both hands through his dark blond hair. "But what about you?" He groaned, low and hurting. "Susan, since I dragged you here—"

"No one dragged me here, Logan," she cut in.

"—you've almost drowned, been shot, and now been attacked by Indians. I must be insane to have brought you to this place. You should be home, dancing with Cal, enjoying family dinners, gossiping with your sisters, being young and carefree and—"

"Do you mind if I make those decisions for myself? If I'd wanted to dance with Cal, I would be back in Missouri right this minute doing just that." She came around to face him again. "None of what's happened to me is your fault. If anyone is to blame it's me. You said I wasn't cut out for this kind of life, and maybe you're right."

"No, Susan." He trailed four fingertips down her cheek. "And I never believed that bullshit anyway. I always knew you had enough backbone for the pioneer life. I just said it to rile you." His gaze moved over her face, as if he were memorizing each feature. "While I was away . . ."

"Yes?" Suddenly her heart was pounding furiously.

"I . . . I . . ." His Adam's apple bobbed. "I thought about you and about us. I know I've been about as much fun to be around as a bee-stung grizzly."

"I haven't made your life easy lately," she admitted.

"No, that's wrong. You *do* make my life easier, and that's why I feel like such a jackass for treating you badly."

"You don't."

"I do, and I know why I do." He shrugged and his dimples showed. "I'm horny."

"L-Logan!" She retreated a step, but no farther. The mischievous light in his eyes was too attractive to withstand. Feeling herself blush, she ducked her head and said in a hushed voice, "I know. Me, too."

"Wh-what?" It was his turn to stammer. He crooked a finger beneath her chin and lifted it. "Did you say you've been horny, too, or am I dreaming?"

"You heard right." She sucked in a breath. "I guess women aren't supposed to admit such things."

"I don't know why not."

"But you're shocked by it."

"No, I'm just shocked that you've been hankering—for me, right?"

"Yes. Who else?" She furrowed her brow, wondering who in the world he had in mind beside himself.

"Cal?" he suggested around a grin.

"Oh, pooh." She batted a hand at him. "How you do go on."

"So . . ." He poked his hands in his pockets and rocked back on his heels. "Let me get this clear in my noggin. I've been keeping you up nights? You've been feeling an itch you've been wishing I'd scratch? You're all hot and bothered and—"

"That's enough," she begged, warding off further embarrassment. "You're the one who started this, so what about you? Have I been keeping you up nights?"

"*It* would be more accurate."

"It?"

He glanced down at his fly. "It. You've been keeping *it* up nights." He laughed and grabbed her by the wrist when she would have spun away from him in modest horror. One yank sent her straight into his embrace. Hooking an arm around her waist, he tipped up her chin with his other hand and made her look him right in the eyes. "And it's acting up again, if you get my meaning." He rocked his lower body against her so that there'd be no mistaking his need. Her face tinted hot pink and he grinned in delight, loving the way she could blush like a schoolgirl and look sexy as hell at the same time. "Susan, Susan, Susan," he murmured, capturing one of her delicate hands and bringing it up to his lips to kiss one finger, the next, and then the next. He took her pinky finger into his mouth, all the way, then back out. She watched and reacted with a loud gulp. When her gaze moved to rest on his lips, he mouthed, "I want you."

She parted her lips to respond, but the sounds of Coonie and the children floated in from the front of the building. She started to pull away, but Logan shook his head. Keeping a firm hold on her, he started backing toward the bedroom.

"Logan, we can't. The children—"

"Coonie will look after them."

"But they'll wonder where we are and they'll—"

"Coonie will figure out right fast where we are and what we're doing." One eyelid dropped seductively. "He'll take matters into hand."

"He won't know . . . how will he . . ." She watched, puzzled, as he let go of her to slip his suspenders off his shoulders and swiftly unbutton his shirt. He peeled it off and hung it by its collar over the bedroom doorknob.

"That's how he'll know," Logan told her with a wink. "It's an ancient signal between males of all ages. Now, come here, you." He took her by the hand and pulled her inside the bedroom with him, then shut the door so that his shirt hung like a flag on the other side for all to observe.

Logan pulled the drapes across the windows, blotting out the sunlight. Enough light bled through to give shape and form and a sense of intimacy. He tossed his tie onto the dresser. His boots were next as he stood on one foot and then the other. Standing beside the bed, one hand resting on the high bedpost, Susan watched, a smile teasing the corners of her mouth.

"Are you going to make me do all the work?" he asked. He threw aside his heavy socks and padded over to her. "Let's start with this." He drove his fingers through her hair, against her scalp and then out to the ends. Pins flew and scattered, pinging against the floorboards.

Susan flung her head from side to side, sending her hair spreading down her back and over her shoulders. "You do care about what happens to me, don't you?"

He'd been rubbing a strand of her silky hair between his thumb and forefinger, but her question stilled him. His eyes narrowed. "How can you doubt that, Susan? Do you think I feel nothing for you?"

"Sometimes I wonder."

His hand clamped her wrist and brought her open palm up against the front of his trousers where a hard ridge had formed. "Feel that and stop wondering."

She should have been shocked, but she'd grown accustomed to his frankness. He was a man who didn't waste words about things of importance. So she kept her hand there, her nimble fingers finding the three buttons and freeing them, one by one. She'd grown so accustomed to his directness, it had rubbed off. Her hand slipped inside his trousers, right up against the hardness of him. He gasped and his head fell back so that he was staring at the ceiling.

"I hurt you?" she asked, worried that she'd gone too far.

He laughed, closed his eyes, shook his head.

Spurred by his pleasure, Susan leaned forward, mouth open and thirsting, and dropped kisses randomly over his chest. He tasted better than she remembered—musky, slightly salty. He clutched her upper arms but remained tensely still as she nuzzled the nest of hair in the center of his chest. He rocked against her, his pelvis bumping hers.

"I wish there was a part of my body that could show you what I'm feeling," she whispered. "Men have bodies that speak of love and desire, but we poor women must find the words or—"

"Not so," he said, then kissed her hard on the mouth. "Your body talks. You just haven't been listening."

"That's not what I meant. I hear it talking, but there isn't anything you can see."

"Not so," he insisted. He ran a finger over the tiny buttons arrowing down the front of her dress. "Haven't I taught you anything?" he asked, sighing dramatically. "Don't you know that your body responds in many ways and in many places?'' He started unbuttoning from her neck, she from below her navel. Their hands met between her breasts. They both worked the top of her dress off her shoulders, down her arms, then past her hips until it circled her feet.

Frowning at the remaining layers hiding her from him, he inched the straps of her chemise off her shoulders. ''Once again, you're overdressed,'' he chided.

''Help me loosen the stays of my corset,'' she begged, as eager as he to remove it.

''You don't even need this thing,'' he complained. ''My hands can span your waist without it.'' He demonstrated once the corset was tossed away with her chemise and she wore only her ruffled, beribboned pantalettes. Sure enough, his thumbs and fingertips almost met, front and back of her.

''I could say I'm small-waisted,'' she said, stroking his chest and neck. ''But I think you have exceptionally large hands.''

He shook his head. ''They look big against you.'' His fingers splayed at his waist from her armpits to her hipbones. ''You're delicate, fine-boned, and budding like a rose.'' His gaze dipped. ''You want me. I can tell that by your breasts. They're blushing, and your nipples are tight. Tight, pink pebbles.''

She got only a glance before his mouth closed on her left breast and her eyes rolled back in her head in a near swoon. While his tongue swirled around the taut center, he pushed his trousers down his legs and kicked them off. They clunked against the floor, their pockets still full.

''Wait, wait.''

His mouth left her breast. Susan swayed, feeling abandoned and adrift in a sea of passion all her own. Instinctively, she reached out for him, wanting him back with her. Her breasts tingled. The one he'd tongued stung a little. Her eyes finally focused, and she saw that he was fishing something out of his trouser pocket. She smiled, thinking he looked adorable dressed only in his long underwear.

''I've got something for you.''

She caressed her necklace. "You didn't have to."

"You probably won't even want the thing, but I figured, what the hell. The photographer insisted—he was at the railroad station, drumming up business." He handed her a rectangle of stiff paper. "It's a good likeness, don't you think?"

"Logan!" She smiled as she examined the photograph of him. He was holding his cap in one hand and had one booted foot propped on a barrel. The backdrop was a patchwork quilt strung up against a wall. It *was* a good likeness—that grin, that heart-tickling grin, was firmly in place, bracketed by those deep, darling dimples she loved so. His hair had been brushed back—probably by hand— but a few strands fell sideways across his high forehead. She looked up from the photo to the real thing. "When you smile like this, I get all tingly inside." She clutched the photo to her bare breasts. "Thank you. I'm going to frame this and put it on my dresser—there, where I can see it whenever I want."

"Don't get all mushy," he said, pink coloring his cheeks, then he screwed up one eye. "Tingly, huh? Where? In your tummy or between your thighs?"

"My . . ." She pressed a hand to her midsection, "My tummy. How'd you know that?"

"Experience. Happens to my thighs." He wet his lips. "My loins." His brows moved up and down suggestively. "Kinda feels good, doesn't it?"

"Kinda." She laid the photo aside and crossed her arms over her breasts. "Never happens unless I'm with you."

"That's good." He squirmed out of his longjohns. "If it happens when you're around any other man, let me know."

"Why?"

"Because I'll want to kill the sonofabitch."

"Logan," she said, laughing, scolding, loving. Hooking a hand behind his neck, she brought him to her for a kiss. She sucked on his lower lip and then painted it with the tip of her tongue, amazed she could do such a thing. Cal Pointer would bust a gut if she'd ever kissed him this way. Why, shoot. For all she knew, Cal didn't even *have* a tongue!

"Remember when you didn't want me licking you?" he asked, amusement deepening his voice.

"I remember." She kissed the tip of his nose, thinking back to that girl she'd once been. "Where I come from, that kind of kiss is what heathens do."

"You don't think so now," he said, half asking.

"I don't think so now." To prove her point, she slipped her tongue between his full lips and sent it all the way around. He moaned into her mouth, then his tongue courted hers.

He slid his hands under the waistband of her pantalettes and inched them down her silky thighs. His palms kissed the length of her legs. She lifted one foot, then the other. With a flick of his wrist, the final garment sailed across the room. Naked, she crossed her arms at the back of his neck and molded her body against his. The coarse, crisp hair covering a good part of him created a frail barrier. His chin and cheeks were already abrasive, although he'd given himself a clean shave that morning. His cheek scraped against hers, then slipped down to the valley between her breasts. He kissed the curves, the soft undersides, the pillowy fullness above her nipples. She trembled inside and felt herself grow moist.

As if sensing this too, he cupped her femininity and his fingers parted the folds. She gasped, muttered something only her heart understood, and her back arched instinctively.

"There's another place where your body tells me what it wants and needs," he whispered near her ear. His teeth sank into her earlobe and tugged affectionately. "And then there are your eyes. They tell me everything I need to know." He caught the lower part of her face in his hand. "Right now they're as black as night and the centers are big, gobbling me up."

"I wish I could," she said, huskily. "I wish I could take all of you inside me and keep you there forever."

Her wish inflamed him. His lips moved over hers. His tongue was a thief, robbing her senseless. Reaching past and behind her, he grabbed a handful of the bedspread and jerked it off the bed and to the floor, then pressed her back onto the cool, sunshine-smelling sheets. As he lifted a knee onto the bed, Susan glimpsed him. He was full and riding high. The sight stimulated her further. She walked her fingers up his shoulders and down the other side as he stretched out on top of her, one muscular thigh nestled between hers.

Bringing his thigh up high and hard, he rubbed her. Susan sucked in her breath and released a keening sound that came from somewhere down low. Beneath her restless hands, he felt taut. His skin was satiny smooth and hot . . . and slick . . . getting slicker as his body heat increased to form a patina of perspiration over him. His mouth closed on one breast while he kneaded the other. She watched, fascinated, as a drop of glistening sweat rolled from his temple to his darkened jawline and then evaporated against her. It was as if she were drinking him in, she thought incoherently as her legs inched wider apart to give his thigh more room to work its magic.

He touched off sparks, and Susan's breathing grew rapid. Then one long-fingered, blunt-ended hand moved down her belly and into the nest of damp hair. One caress, one stroke, and the wildness of passion overtook her. She thrashed. She moaned. She hugged him with her legs, her arms, her whole body.

Squeezing her eyes shut, she thought she might die of pleasure. His tongue skimmed across her collarbone and shoulder. He placed a tender kiss on the healed wound there.

"Bastards," he muttered darkly. "Does it give you any trouble?"

"Hmmm? What?"

He laughed. "Guess not." Weaving her hair between his fingers, he angled her head sideways and slanted his open mouth over hers. His kiss seemed to tug at her soul. Her heart strained, lifted, floated in her chest.

She felt him groping and realized he was shifting for a smooth entry. Susan reached for him and closed her fingers around the base of his manhood. Then she guided him inside her. Her hand slipped away to let him drive up against her, fully buried.

Making a strange, savage sound, he rocked into her, then away. He repeated the motion until a natural rhythm commenced—her hips grinding against his, her back arching as his bowed. The coming together dominated them. She didn't want it to end, and neither did he. She could sense his careful pacing, his concentration on not giving in to the overpowering need to spill forth.

Susan gripped his buttocks, holding him firmly. His gaze met hers, and she knew then that he had realized her intent. He shook his head even as the cords in his neck strained against his sweaty skin.

"No, Susan. Let me go." His voice was rough, yearning.

She shook her head vehemently. "Leave a part of you in me, Logan."

"No, no." He ceased all movement, head flung back, every muscle in him tensed. "You don't need . . . I don't . . . Susan, please!" His hips jerked, but she held fast. Opening his eyes to slits, he glared at her, then bared his teeth. "Oh, God. Oh, damn it all." He ground out the last in a growl of defeat.

She couldn't be sure if she really felt him spilling inside of her or if it was her imagination. But it was wondrous, whatever the truth of it might have been. She felt warm inside—glowing with tiny embers. The life inside her excited her as nothing else ever had, and she trembled with her own oncoming release.

Logan's mouth swooped to hers. His tongue imitated the love act. It was more than enough to send her over the brink again. Sounds escaped her and then his name tumbled out, over and over again like a favored prayer. His lips traveled from her mouth to her breasts, circling her nipples and then painting a line straight down her stomach to her navel. His tongue dipped in and out, quick as a fox, then came back up. He kissed the undersides of her breasts, then levered himself up on stiff arms to look down into her face.

"You tricked me," he accused.

"I didn't. I just . . ." She shrugged. "I got my way, that's all."

"Let's just hope you didn't get a baby as well."

"Would that be so bad?" she asked, her heart beginning to ache in anticipation of his answer.

He shook his head sadly. "You tell me."

"I'd be a good mother, I think."

Even his smile was sad. "I never doubted that."

"But you doubt me."

"Us. It's the *us* that's doubtful."

"You married me."

"Yes, I did. I married your sister, too."

"Logan, how many times do I have to tell you—"

"I know. You're not Catherine. That's just it, Susan. I don't want us to repeat the mistakes I made with your sister. We might not have married if it hadn't been for her being pregnant with Jacob."

"But you don't regret having Jacob . . ."

"Hell, no." He frowned with irritation. "But babies aren't harnesses to keep a man and woman hitched together. I want us to be sure we want to stay together and not just be shackled by circumstances."

She turned her head slightly, thinking she'd never feel shackled to him. But his musings sent sad thoughts through her. He was still working out his feelings—or lack of them—for her sister. It wasn't fair. She shouldn't have to pay for her sister's shortcomings!

"We're still trying to find our way—get our balance with each other. I don't want to rush into it, Susan. I want us to know what we're about before we're faced with something as permanent as a child." He rested his forehead against hers in a weary gesture.

"After what we've done, you have doubts?" How could he? She'd never been so sure of anything in her life!

"Susan, there is more to a marriage than good sex."

She huffed out a sigh. "I know that."

"Trust is one thing."

"I trust you."

"Really?" He lifted her arm by the wrist and ran his thumb along a dark bruise, then touched a fingertip to an angry scratch. ''Then why didn't you want me to know about the Indians attacking you?''

''I was going to tell you—in my time and in my way.''

He scolded her with his eyes—narrowed and a deep hunter's-green.

''Did Catherine step out on you?''

He glanced sideways, then sighed. ''Probably, but she'd never admit to it. From this moment on, Susan, promise me you won't keep anything from me. Promise me that you'll trust me enough not to hold anything back.''

''I promise.'' She raised her head to seal the oath with her lips. Before she could extract the same vow from him, his mouth opened over hers and the words died on a long, luscious moan of contentment.

Chapter 21

"This meeting is adjourned, ladies," Mrs. Lindsey said, rapping her knuckles on the book in front of her. "Thank you all for coming."

Susan rose from the bench and glanced at the row of benches and desks used by the students, wondering which ones Jacob and Etta claimed. The schoolhouse smelled of chalk and newspaper and pungent ink. At the moment, those smells were being challenged by scented oils, dusting powder, and sachets. The mothers of Tulsa had gathered for one of several yearly meetings concerning the school and how their children fared in it.

Feeling beholden to do it, Susan had taken notes. Logan was influencing her in more ways than one, she thought with a secret smile. She even had an itch to write a story about the meeting for the newspaper.

It felt good to be on firm footing with Logan again. He made her feel needed and wanted again. Lately, he'd been showing her more about his business, how the press operated, how newspaper stories should be written, and how advertisements were created. In their private time, he made her body thrum with hot passion, and she sensed his feelings for her deepening into devotion.

She'd never been so happy in her life. Now if only she could convince Logan that theirs was a marriage that could withstand any blow, then he might relent about her having a—

"That Jacob is sure shooting up, isn't he?" Mrs. Dunlevy said, then offered a tentative smile when Susan

283

whirled to face her. "How do you like married life, Mrs. Vance?"

The name still surprised her—Mrs. Vance had been Catherine's name—but Susan recovered quickly and realized that Mrs. Dunlevy was trying to make amends for having been rude to her before her marriage to Logan. The bank teller's wife, Mrs. Treadmore, stood next to her, her smile just as timid.

They should be feeling poorly for having treated me like a trollop just because I'd been dancing in the streets with Logan, Susan thought. Then she recalled what else she'd been doing on that city street, and her intolerance toward the women wavered. Giving a mental shrug, she smiled back at the peace offerers.

"I like it fine," Susan said, then dimpled and let her happiness show. "I *love* being married. How are you two ladies coping? I suppose you're planning festive Christmas celebrations."

"Oh, yes," Mrs. Treadmore said in a rush, as if she were greatly relieved that Susan had shown forgiveness. "It will be your first Christmas with your new family. A special one for you.'

"Very special, yes.'

"My husband sees your husband at the men's meetings. He says Logan looks as happy as a cat," Mrs. Treadmore confided.

Susan smiled and ducked her head, pleased to know that she wasn't the only one aglow. Then her head bobbed up again. "Men's meetings?"

"Yes, you know." Mrs. Dunlevy lowered her voice and leaned closer to Susan. "Those meetings the men in town have been attending to discuss our Indian problem." The last two words were mouthed as if Mrs. Dunlevy couldn't bring herself to say them aloud.

Susan's spine stiffened in response. "Indian problem?"

"You know . . ." Mrs. Dunlevy bumped elbows with her. "We heard about the fright you received at their hands. Why, my mister said your mister was fit to be tied when he related it to the others yesterday afternoon."

"Yesterday . . . ." Susan thought back, the days melting

one into another since she and Logan had mended their fences and he'd moved back into her bedroom a week ago. Yesterday afternoon he'd left for a few hours to cover . . . what had he called it? A town meeting . . . no, a planning meeting. She'd assumed it was a meeting of the town leaders to plan Christmas festivities. "Logan told them about the Indians scaring me and the children?"

"He sure did," Mrs. Treadmore said, laying a hand on her arm. "You poor dear. Mr. Vance was shaking, he was so mad. My husband told me about it. We're lucky to have men sworn to protect us."

"To protect . . . What are they planning to do about the Indians?" Susan asked, drawing surprised looks from the other two women.

"Why, we don't know for sure, and it's none of our business," Mrs. Dunlevy said. "The men will handle those heathens."

"Heathens?" It was Mrs. Lindsey, cutting into their circle of three. "I hope you aren't calling the Creeks names. Their children attend this school and are bright, loving youngsters."

"Their children aren't the problem,," Mrs. Dunlevy said with a huffy lift of her round chin. "It's their liquored-up fathers and brothers doing the damage around here."

"I don't see any damage," Mrs. Lindsey said.

"And they were here first," Susan pointed out, getting a nod of approval from the schoolteacher. "We mustn't forget that we intruded on their lives. If they're resentful, they have every right."

"They tried to rape you," Mrs. Treadmore whispered. "They had no right!"

"They were drunk, and I don't know what they were trying to do other than release some anger in the wrong way," Susan said. "Regardless of that, we have no right to hold secret meetings about them. It can come to no good."

"I agree." Mrs. Lindsey crossed her arms and gave them an imposing look that, no doubt, silenced the most rambunctious child. "Men have a tendency to try to solve every problem with violence. Women usually show more sense.''

"Well!'' Mrs. Dunlevy poked her nose into the air. "We should be going, Lucille,'' she said to Mrs. Treadmore.

"I should say,'' Mrs. Treadmore agreed, and the two turned and marched off in unison.

Mrs. Lindsey laughed. "The town busybodies. Every community must have one or two, I suppose.''

"What do you know about the secret meetings, Mrs. Lindsey?''

"Nothing much. Just that some of the men are talking dangerously. They're blaming things on the Creeks that no one can prove. Stirring the embers can only lead to a flash fire.''

Susan nodded, agreeing. She walked with the teacher to the door. "I'm going to talk to Logan about this. I can't believe he'd actually take part in something so—''

". . . Mazie Weeks in Kingfisher.''

Susan whipped her head around, searching for the woman who'd spoken that bit of jarring news. It was Darla Beauchamp, the butcher's wife.

"Mrs. Beauchamp,'' Susan said, touching the woman's shoulder. "You said something . . .''

"Yes, Mrs. Vance?'' the short, blond woman asked.

"About Mazie Weeks?'' Susan finished, pushing the name past her numb lips.

"Yes. I was just telling Mrs. Cox here that Mazie moved to Kingfisher.''

"You're sure?''

"Why, yes.'' Mrs. Beauchamp extended a puzzled look. "Are you close to Mazie?''

"No. Are you?''

"She's my second cousin, I'm afraid.'' Mrs. Beauchamp smiled, taking the sting from her words. "She wrote me from Kingfisher several weeks ago to tell me she was settled in and doing well.''

"I . . . I see.'' Susan tried to smile but couldn't. "Excuse me.''

Somehow she made her way home, although she did so

in a daze. Mazie Weeks was in Kingfisher, and that's where Logan's travels had taken him. A coincidence? An inner voice called her a fool to think so—to hope so.

Did she know her husband, or did she only recognize the face he wanted to show her? Her parents had often said Logan was steeped in duplicity. Were they right about him, after all?

The doubts! She stopped just short of going inside the front door of the newspaper office. God, how she hated doubting the man she loved, but facts were facts. He'd been sneaking off to meetings about driving the Indians off their land. How could he be so narrow-minded, so cruel? Had she brought this on? Had that stupid, ill-timed skirmish with those drunken young braves been the match touched to a fuse? If so, she had to stop it. She had to confront Logan and ask him about the meetings. Maybe he was only covering them as a dogged reporter. There was a chance of it.

As she opened the door, she felt cowardice color her spine bright yellow. She didn't really want to hear Logan's answer, for she was afraid he would tell her he and the other men in town were planning a massacre—a short-sighted payback, spurred by her misadventure.

Clarabelle was making a racket, and only Coonie stood beside the hissing, clattering machine. He flashed a big grin when he saw her, and silenced the press.

"Hello. Meeting over, is it?"

"Yes." She closed the door and glanced around. "Where's Logan?"

"He took the tykes with him to the blacksmith."

"Oh, yes." She nodded, recalling his mentioning the trip. "New shoes for the mules."

"That's right. Should be back by now."

"They probably stopped for ice cream." She removed her hat and gloves and placed them on Logan's desk. Smoothing back wayward wisps of hair, she arched her back and stretched the tension from her backbone. "Printing the paper?"

"Yes'm."

"Looks good." She picked up the front and back page

spread, her eyes searching for any mention of the meeting Logan had attended. There was none. "Do you recall that meeting Logan attended yesterday afternoon?"

"Ummm, not really."

Her sharp eyes caught the guilt rouging Coonie's already rosy cheeks. "It was a *planning* meeting, but I see no mention of it here."

"No? Maybe nothing much happened, so Logan didn't write it up. How was your meeting?"

"Interesting. I took notes. If I write an article about it, do you think Logan would publish it?"

"Don't see why not." Coonie looked so relieved at the change of subject that Susan hated to disappoint him, but she couldn't help herself.

"About Logan's meeting, Coonie. What plans are being made? I assumed it had something to do with Christmas, but now I'm not so sure."

"I couldn't tell you."

"You've been to these planning meetings, haven't you?" She stared at Coonie, knowing he disliked the Indians even more than Logan. In fact, Susan suspected that Coonie egged on Logan's growing irritation with the Creek clan outside of town.

"Some."

"Well?"

He pretended to be absorbed with Clarabelle, bending over the printing press and squirting oil in its joints.

"Coonie?"

"Hmmm?"

"The secret meetings. What goes on there? What kind of planning takes place exactly?"

"Doesn't concern ladies."

"It concerns me." She stepped around the press, glaring across it at him. "I want to know!" She had to shout to be heard above the clamoring machine. "Tell me what Logan is doing there!"

"It's men's business. Got nothing to do with—" He snapped his jaws shut and whipped his head around.

A moment later Susan did the same, realizing they had

a newcomer. Logan closed the door slowly, eyeing them curiously.

"I'm interrupting something?" he asked, tossing his cap onto the desk beside Susan's hat.

"You want answers, go to the source," Coonie grumbled, nodding toward Logan.

"Yes, Susan," Logan said. "You have questions for me?"

"Where are Etta and Jacob?"

"Out back playing."

"Oh."

"That's what you were yelling about when I came in?"

"No, of course not." She puffed out a breath, frustrated at being caught off-balance. Flashing Coonie a scathing glare, she was glad when he muttered an excuse to stop the press and amble out of the office. Susan glanced toward Logan and yearned to ask him about Mazie. *Is that why you wanted to take a trip, Logan? Did you dally with another woman behind my back?* But the words stuck in her throat, burning, making her cough.

"What were you and Coonie yelling about when I came in?" He unbuttoned his shirtsleeves and began rolling them up. "Y'all looked like you were ready to go for each other's throats."

"No, we weren't. You read too much into it."

"So straighten me out."

She crossed her arms and rubbed her hands up and down them in a bout of nerves. "I wondered why you didn't write up anything about the planning meeting you attended."

"Oh, that." He shrugged. "Wasn't anything to write. Nothing definite was planned."

"About what?"

"How was your meeting?"

"Answer me!" She hadn't meant to snap, but she had. Logan angled his head slightly, and his brows formed a bridge over his eyes. "Answer me," she whispered. "Please."

"The meetings are centered on planning the future of this town. Why are you so steamed?"

"Because I heard at my meeting—which, by the way is not secret but aboveboard—that the men have been discussing ways to drive the Creeks off their land."

"I'm a reporter. I go to meetings not to take sides, but to report on what transpires."

"So where's your report?" she asked, glancing toward the page proofs. "I don't see it here."

"I told you. Nothing much happened."

"It's a secret—a dirty little secret. That's why you're mum about it. You're taking sides by *not* reporting what's happening right under your nose!" She made a sound in her throat, feeling as if she were choking. "It's disgusting what you and the other so-called gentlemen are doing behind our backs!"

"I told you. I'm doing my job." His tone, in contrast to her high-pitched voice, was deadly quiet. "I'm doing nothing behind your back."

"You haven't been honest with me about the meetings. You let me think—"

"I told you I was going to them."

"Planning meetings." She scoffed at that. "I thought they had something to do with Christmas.

"And that's my fault? I never mentioned Christmas."

"You never mentioned Indians either."

"Why are you so fond of those renegade Creeks out there at the edge of town? A few of them almost raped you. Remember that?" He grabbed one of her wrists and pulled back her loose cuff. "See this bruise? It's fading, but it was put there by one of your precious, pitiful Indians!"

She wrenched free. "I pray you're not instigating a massacre on my account, Logan. There are not only men in that Creek camp, but women and children. If you mean to slaughter them, do not do so in my name."

He stumbled back a step and stared at her with openmouthed amazement, then laughed hollowly. "Slaughter? You think I'm the sort of man who could murder women and children?"

"I don't . . . I . . ."

"You said you thought I might be planning a massacre."

"Not just you. The men in this town."

"I'm one of them."

"Are you?"

"What, a man? You bet your sweet ass I am."

"No," she said, gritting her teeth to keep from screaming at him again. "You intentionally twist my meaning. Are you one of the men planning murder?"

He opened his mouth, then closed it with a snap of his teeth. His eyes grew red-rimmed as he continued to glare at her with a mixture of anger and utter disbelief. He drew a shaky breath, then exhaled it just as shakily.

"Your question condemns me already," he whispered in a voice ragged with emotion. "So I'll save my breath." With that, he strode past her, brushing against her body so hard he made her lose her balance for a moment and fall against the press.

Whirling, she dogged his footsteps into the kitchen where he dipped himself some water from the sink bucket. He drank thirstily, his throat flexing as he made slurping noises. A few drops rivered down his chin and spotted his shirt. His eyes slid sideways to her, then he lowered the battered dipper. He wiped his mouth with his sleeve.

"What now? I've said all I'm going to about those goddamned meetings, so if that's what you're cocked and ready for, you can—"

"Did you sleep with Mazie?" She hadn't meant to ask, but now that she had she felt an immediate sense of relief.

He blinked once—hard. "When?"

That qualifier didn't go unnoticed. It tore a piece from her heart. "In Kingfisher."

"King—?" He scratched his jawline, his fingers rasping against his beard-stubbled skin. "Is Mazie in Kingfisher?"

"Don't treat me like an imbecile," she warned. "I heard about it at the meeting. You know good and well Mazie moved to Kingfisher! That's who you met there, isn't it? There wasn't any publisher from Watonga." She gasped as his hands fastened on her upper arms, and he brought her up so sharply that her heels lifted from the floor. He thrust his face close to hers so that his breath tattooed her face.

"I'm damned tired of proving myself to you. It seems that's all I've done since I had the misfortune of running into the Armitage family. Well, here's a news bulletin for you, sugar. Logan Vance is no saint and he never professed to be one."

"You did sleep with her!"

"I didn't know she was anywhere near Kingfisher." He smiled bitterly and pushed her away from him. "But why am I wasting my breath? You're my judge and jury, and I'm a sinner in your eyes. Your old man has told you so often about what a rotter I am, you expect me to maim and rape and cheat at every turn."

"This has nothing to do with my father."

"Bullshit!" he spat, rounding on her again, his face ruddy with fury, then his gaze slipped past her and she heard the scuffle of footsteps. "You children go on back outside and play. Now." His low command did the trick and the door slammed shut a second later. Logan's green eyes shifted to Susan again. "You came here to take them from me, so you shouldn't be so quick to accuse others of cheating and lying and sneaking."

"I did not come here to steal your children," she denied hotly.

"You're telling me that Abraham didn't give you such instructions before you left the farm?" he challenged, closing the space between them with one, long stride.

"He . . . he . . ."

"Go ahead," Logan said, his upper lip curling in a snarl. "Lie."

Susan snapped her teeth shut on the untruth, exchanging it for the truth. "That was *his* plan, not mine."

"What was *your* plan?"

"To live in St. Louis for a while. Perhaps find me a young man. Mainly, I wanted to help you and the children—" She stopped herself, incensed by his harsh laugh. "It's true! I *did* want to help you and the children in whatever way I could."

"Saint Susan rises again."

"Bastard!" Even she was surprised by the epithet. She clamped a hand over her mouth, but Logan grasped her wrist and forcibly drew her fingers away.

"Go ahead. Speak your mind." He gave a hard nod. "I *am* a bastard, and you're *not* a saint. You wanted me before Catherine died and I wanted you."

"No, never! I didn't . . . I . . ."

"Okay, maybe we didn't realize the depth of what we were feeling. I know I fooled myself by thinking I saw you as my little sis. An engaging, freckle-faced tomboy, that's what I called you aloud. But deep down I *must* have felt something sexual because the moment I saw you sitting on the front porch of Mrs. Ledbetter's, my blood pooled between my legs."

"No," she whimpered, turning her face aside, but he gripped her chin and pulled her head around so that her eyes clashed with his. "Don't say these things, Logan. We mustn't."

"We need a little truth around here. Now how about you? You never thought of me as a brother, did you?"

She swallowed hard. "No."

"And you came to St. Louis to see what would happen when you were alone with me—without Catherine or your parents hanging around."

She nodded. It was the hardest thing she'd ever done in her life. His fingers gentled and spread from her chin up to her flushed cheeks.

"You knew I wasn't a saint. You knew your sister hadn't been the only woman I'd known in the biblical sense. You knew I'd told your father on more than one occasion to go straight to hell. You knew all of that, but you still wanted me."

Again, she nodded. His fingers caressed her cheek and slid down her slim neck. His gaze moved lower still.

"And I knew I wanted you in my bed and that if you came to Tulsa with me I'd get you there sooner or later." He heaved a long sigh. "So there. We've told each other the truth."

"You . . . you didn't see Mazie in Kingfisher?"

His eyes iced over. "Didn't I just say that?"

"Yes."

"Then quit asking me. If you don't believe me, than I can answer that question a thousand times and it will only be a waste of time." Crooking his fingers around her neck, he pulled her toward his parted lips. They felt wonderfully soft and tame beneath hers. "You married a ladies' man, a rounder, a bastard. But you didn't marry a liar, Susan, and you didn't marry a wife-cheater."

"But you *have* been going to those meetings and you *do* want the Creeks to leave."

"Hell, yes!" His hands fell away and he gave her his back. "Yes, yes, yes. I'd dearly love to see them pack up and go squat someplace else. They're nothing but trouble brewing."

"The secrecy and duplicity of this town disgusts me."

"Then leave." His tone was hollow and felt like a cold wind blowing across her skin.

"Just like that," she said, wishing he'd face her again.

"If you don't like this town . . ." He shrugged. "Every town has its good and bad points, Susan. Everything can't go *your* way, you know."

"I know that," she said, angry again. "I can't control the town, but I was hoping that—" She bit back the rest, but he turned slightly to glare at her.

"Were you hoping you could control me?" He laughed, the sound of it calling her a fool.

Throwing up her hands, she surrendered to the helplessness she felt. It seemed she didn't know her own mind anymore. She'd changed so much, so quickly she didn't know who she was or what she wanted, what she should allow and when she should stand up for herself.

"I'd like to get away from all of this," she said, mostly to herself. "I want to go where the air is clean and the people are pure and simple. I hate Tulsa's shadowy, sneaking problems and two-faced people."

Logan smirked. "Where, pray tell, are the people pure and simple?"

"I want to go home." Once the words left her, it was as if a burden had been lifted from her heart and a gray veil had been swept from her eyes. Warmth spread through her. It felt like sunlight. "Yes, that's right," she said, seeing Logan's surprise. "I want to go home for Christmas, and I want to take the children with me. You can come along, too. It will be good for all of us to get away from here for a while."

He laughed at her. "Not likely."

"Logan, you can't make me stay here."

"I have no intention of doing so. You can go back to Abraham and the fold, but you're not taking my children with you, and I sure as hell don't want to visit that place. No thank you!"

"Why not? What are you afraid of?"

"Not of your old man, that's for damned sure."

"Then what?"

"Nothing. I just don't want to see Abraham again, that's all."

"You should bury the hatchet and—"

"Spare me, Saint Susan."

"Oh, you make me so mad."

"The feeling is mutual."

"Won't you please just—"

"No."

"Logan, please."

"No."

She glared at him and he glared back. The banging of the back door made them blink and jump a little.

"Papa, can we come inside now?" Etta asked in a high, breathless voice.

"Yes, sugar."

"Etta," Susan said, spinning around and dropping to her haunches in front of her niece, "would you like to visit Grandma and Grandpa's farm during Christmas?"

"Yes! Oh, yes!" Etta clapped her hands and showed off her dimples. "Will the kittens be there?"

"No, they're all grown, but there might be some new kittens by now."

"Really? And the horses and cows?"

"They'll be there, pumpkin. And all your aunts. Won't it be fun?"

"Uh-huh!"

"I'm not going and nobody can make me," Jacob said, running to his father and wrapping his arms around one of Logan's legs. He looked up into his face. "Please, Papa. Please. I won't leave."

"You won't have to." Logan rested a hand on the boy's white-blond hair. "Aunt Susan is leaving, but we're staying right here."

"But, Logan—"

"And that," he said, cutting off Susan, "is my final word." He motioned for Etta and she flew into his arms. Logan stooped and brought Jacob up on his other hip. The children held to him creating a tight trio.

"We know what you're trying to do," Jacob said, hugging Logan tightly around the neck. "You're trying to steal us and hurt Papa!"

"Jacob!" Susan gasped, then directed her horrified glare to Logan. He was actually smiling! "I see you're happy about this, Logan. Congratulations. You've turned your children against their own flesh and blood." Tears built in her eyes as she slowly shook her head. "Who are you?" she asked in a choked voice. "I swear, I don't even know you anymore. In fact, I wonder if I ever did at all." She made sure his smile had slipped downward before she marched into her bedroom and slammed the door.

Chapter 22

Sitting at the vanity, Susan pulled a brush rhythmically through her long hair. She gathered the ends in one fist and brushed them vigorously, then started to braid her hair when the bedroom door swung open to admit Logan.

"Don't braid it," he said, coming into the room and closing the door slowly, softly behind him. "Leave it loose."

She twisted on the bench to more fully take in his lounging stance against the closed door and the gentle lights in his eyes. He's apologizing, she thought. In his own roundabout way, he's saying he's sorry for being such a jackass earlier. Her lashes swept down as she averted her gaze, reluctant to let it go easily. That he'd turned the children solidly against her family was something she couldn't—shouldn't—forgive and forget with a shrug and a smile.

"I'm not going to apologize."

Her head came up, and surprise parted her lips.

"That's right," he said. "I probably should, but I'm sick of apologizing to you for despising your father when I have every right to hate that man."

"But it's not just him, don't you see?" she asked, rising from the bench. "You've made the children think badly of my entire family. What have my sisters done to you, Logan?"

"Nothing."

"Then why should Etta and Jacob hate them?"

"They don't."

"But they don't want to visit them. At least Jacob

297

doesn't. Etta, bless her loving heart, still can't manage to write all of us off so easily. And my mother—has she ever hurt you in any way?''

"She supports your father in whatever he does."

"Isn't that what a wife is supposed to do?"

He eyed her with a mixture of amusement and censure. "You tell me."

She realized her blunder too late and felt heat rise into her face. "Well, a woman should support her man most of the time . . . whenever it's possible."

"Hmmm." He pushed away from the door and yanked his shirttails loose from his trousers. "That's what I've heard. Can't say I've seen much of that kind of loyalty around here."

"That isn't true. I just can't blithely agree to secret meetings where murder is discussed."

"Murder hasn't been discussed."

"That's why that regulator came to town, right?" she asked, backing him into a verbal corner. "He has nothing to do with murder."

"I don't have anything to do with Zeke Calhoun."

"But I bet he's been to every meeting, hasn't he?"

"Yes." He hissed the word at her. "Satisfied? Look, I told you I've been covering the meetings as a reporter. That's what I do for a living—keep up with what's going on in this place."

"You said you'd like to see the Creeks leave."

"I'd like to see Calhoun leave, too, but I'm not going to run him out of town at gunpoint." He shook his head and nearly ripped the shirt off his shoulders and arms. Wadding it into a ball, he pitched it into a corner. "Are you going back to Missouri for Christmas?"

"Yes." She hadn't decided until that moment, but the word felt good on her lips and in her heart. Thinking of the holidays with her family surrounding her sounded like heaven on earth.

Besides, she needed to get away from the temptation of Logan in order to think clearly. She had to know her own heart and head, and she couldn't do that with him in easy reach. Even now, as he stood bare-chested only a few feet from her, she felt her heart kick and her stomach float against her ribs. It was an odd, thrilling sensation. When his gaze slipped to her cotton-covered breasts, she knew what he was staring at because she could feel the throbbing heat of her nipples. One look from him and they had gathered into tight buds of longing.

"I'll miss you."

She blinked, momentarily confused.

"When you go back to Missouri," he said, seeing her puzzlement. "I was looking forward to Christmas, but now . . ." His mouth twisted with regret. "I wonder if you'll ever come back here once you're on the farm."

"I'm your wife, remember? I can't just leave."

"If you want it that way, I won't stop you from divorcing me."

Pain shot through her heart, and she swayed slightly. For a moment, she was afraid she might fall, but then her knees locked. "That's mighty accommodating of you, Logan." She dropped to one knee and reached under the bed to drag her carpetbag from beneath it. "I'm going to pack. Tomorrow I'll buy a train ticket. You'll let me have the money?"

"Of course."

She began throwing clothes at the open bag, furious at him for standing there like a stump and hurt that he didn't raise a finger to stop her.

"The children sure will miss you."

"Etta will. Jacob won't. You've done such a fine job turning him against my kin that he'll probably never let himself love me."

"I didn't turn him against you."

"Didn't you hear the hatred in his voice before?" she asked, gesturing toward the bedroom door. "Do you think I'm so stupid I don't know that a young boy like Jacob has to *learn* hatred? It doesn't come naturally to children, Logan. You've taught them how to hate."

"No. Your father taught them."

"In a pig's eye!" She shoved blouses and skirts into the bag, unmindful of the sloppy job she was doing. "They haven't been around my father long enough to grow such hatred. Maybe he planted the seeds, but *you* cultivated them, Logan Vance. Why not share the blame for once?''

''I've shared the blame ever since I laid eyes on your sister, so don't preach to me.''

''That's another thing. My sister.'' She stopped cramming clothes into the bag to glare at him. ''Their mother, but you've blotted out her love for them, too.''

''I have not.''

''They don't think of her lovingly—well, maybe Etta does. But I swear, Jacob is glad she's dead. Now who is responsible for that?''

''Catherine.''

She gasped, lifting a hand to her mouth. ''That's a terrible thing to say. Catherine adored them.''

''How do you know?''

''I saw her with the children. She was patient and loving and kind and—''

''And hardly ever around. She never cared much for Jacob, but she was sweeter to Etta.''

''Logan!'' She backed away from the bed and the clothes strewn over it. ''How can you say such awful things?''

''I'm only telling the truth.''

''No!''

''She didn't want Jacob. She had to have him to get away from Abraham. Etta was different. Yes, she was an accident, but she was born of a flash of passion and not of desperation, as Jacob had been.''

''What are you saying?'' She wiped tears from her eyes. ''I won't have you talking about my sister that way.''

''If you don't want to hear the truth, then quit asking questions.'' He glanced at the bed, and his facial muscles tensed. ''So you'll be leaving in a day or so?''

''As soon as possible.'' She bore up under his steady gaze. ''I still would like to take the children.''

His smile was wicked and cruel. ''I'm sure you would.''

''Logan, I'll bring them back.''

''When? When they're in their twenties?''

''Listen to me, will you? My family adores Jacob and Etta. Why can't we all be a family? You've soured Jacob on the people who love him—his only living grandparents and aunts. You've made him distrust his flesh and blood just because you've never gotten along with his grandfather. Is that fair? Do you really mean to deprive them of all family except for you?''

"And you," he reminded her.

She shrugged. "I don't see how I can go on living here when it's clear you don't trust me. You actually believe I'd steal your children." She shook her head, knowing that her suffering showed in her frown and in her dark, shimmering eyes.

Panic flickered in the green depths of his eyes, and one corner of his mouth convulsed. He swallowed and let out a quick, quivery breath. "Susan, are you saying you aren't coming back?"

"Not to a man who doesn't trust me."

"I do trust you."

"You just accused me of trying to steal your children."

"No, it's Abraham. He'd try it."

"But they'd be in my care. I'd bring them back after the holidays. You have my word." She drew a finger diagonally over her chest twice. "Cross my heart, Logan, and hope to—"

"No!" He surged forward, his jerky movement halting her words. "Don't swear that, Susan. Even in jest, don't hope to die." He gathered in a great, chest-expanding breath. "You shouldn't kid around with hopes and wishes like that."

He was close enough for her to see the haggard expression and the deep lines between his eyes. His disheveled hair appealed to her, and she clasped her hands together to keep from running her fingers through it. She sensed his struggle, but refused to make it easy for him since he certainly hadn't made her decisions easy. He tucked his hands high up under his arms, and his breath hissed between his teeth as he looked off to one side in a moment of tense concentration.

"Aw hell." He closed his eyes for a few moments. When he opened them, she saw they were bloodshot. As she looked on, he winced. "You have me by the short hairs, don't you?"

She flinched at his coarse summation but couldn't deny it. "Come with me, Logan," she pleaded, reaching out to lay her hands lightly on his forearms.

"No," he said, firmly, sternly. "I don't care if I ever see Abraham Armitage again."

Dejected, she continued her packing, but his hands settled on her waist.

"The children may go."

A squeak of joy escaped her. "Logan, really?"

"But I want you back here *before* Christmas. They're my children, and I'm not spending Christmas alone here without them. Is that clear?"

"Of course." She framed his face between her hands and rose up on tiptoes to bestow a loud, smacking kiss to his lips. "Oh, Logan, thank you, thank you, thank you!"

He pressed her back to arm's length. "Hear me, Susan. Are you listening?"

She nodded, wondering what had darkened his eyes to leaf-green.

"You can run off, leaving your problem behind you, but if you're not back before Christmas, by God, I'll come and get the children *and* you." He gave her a little shake and gritted his teeth. "Don't think for one minute I won't. I'll drag you kicking and screaming back here, and I'll trample your father in the process if I have to. You understand?"

"Of course. You want your children home by Christmas."

"And you." His hands were gentle bonds on her upper arms. "I want you home by Christmas, too. Your *problem* will be here waiting for you."

"You're not all bad, you know." She drifted her hands up his arms to his firm shoulders. His possessiveness thrilled her. "I'll bring them home to you, Logan."

His eyes crinkled to the corners. "I do believe your will is as strong, maybe stronger than your father's. He might just have met his match in you."

"And what about you?" Her hands moved over the crisp

hairs dusting his chest. They crackled against her skin. "Have you met yours?"

His mouth took advantage of hers, drawing a response before she was consciously ready to give one. He painted her lips with his tongue over and over again until she moaned and arched into him to feel the ridge of his desire riding against her belly. Her breasts became heavy, achy. She curved her fingers along the sides of his neck.

"Logan, love me tonight," she whispered close to his ear, then her tongue slipped out to trace the intricacy of lobe and cartilage. "Give me another memory to sustain me while I'm away from you."

He had given her his trust, and she wanted to give him something in return, so she shimmied down his body to her knees. Kneeling before him, she unbuttoned the front of his trousers and parted the fabric. He was so full of wanting it took a few moments for her to free him from the confines of trousers and underwear, but then he finally sprang out.

She looked up into Logan's face and smiled at the expectancy there, then she kissed the hot, satiny skin of him. He jerked in her hands, alive and straining. Logan's fingers tangled in her hair. He locked his knees to keep from pitching forward.

"God, Susan." His voice, roughened by lust, seemed to originate below his navel. "Honey, oh, sugar.' He murmured other things as her mouth moved along the length of him, up and down and all around. He began to quiver, then quake, then tense up in preparation for an explosion he wanted to postpone for a few minutes longer. "Susan, stop. For the love of God, please."

"You don't like it?"

He bared his teeth. "I like it so much I'm about to end this before you get any pleasure."

"I've had my pleasure. I want you to have yours."

He caught her beneath her arms and lifted her up and then over to the bed. "We want the same things." With long sweeps of his arms, he pushed all her clothes and the carpetbag off the bed onto the floor. He laughed with her at the mess he made, then they both stopped laughing together as passion caught hold of them. Kicking off his shoes, he then shucked his trousers and underwear. Sliding onto his side beside her on the bed, he covered one of her breasts with his hand and grinned. "I feel your nipple tightening. I love when it does that."

"So do I."

Leaning over her, he covered the mound with his mouth and dampened the white cloth of her nightgown. Passion stirred in her belly and spread. She kneaded his shoulders and shut her eyes tightly to watch the colors of love explode against her lids—blue and purple and bright, hot red. Her legs parted just in time for his hand to slide between them and deliver feathery caresses, moving up, up, up and then pressing against her. The heel of his hand made little circles against her, creating heat and sparks.

Whispering his name, she brought his head up and his mouth to hers. With swift tongue thrusts, they imitated the love act until they were both moaning with pent-up frustration. Finally, he lifted her nightgown and drove himself into her. She locked her legs around his lean waist and allowed him everything, becoming putty in his hands. They reached the peak of fulfillment together in a wild flash of desire that left them panting for breath and limp with relief.

"Logan," she said, fondling him. "I'll miss you at night most of all—and in the mornings when I awake before you and you look like a little boy asleep."

"A little boy, hmmm?" he asked, glancing down at himself.

"Well, in the face," she amended with a laugh, then rolled on top of him and spread her hands along the sides of his head. Her thumbs dipped into his dimples. "You can't begin to know how it makes me feel that you're entrusting me with your children." She kissed his waiting mouth once, twice, then rained nibbling kisses on his nose and chin and throat. "I love you, Logan Vance. For better or worse, I do."

"Why are you crying, Aunt Susan?" Etta asked.

Susan brushed away the tears as she closed her carpetbag and dropped it beside the two smaller cases she'd packed for Etta and Jacob. "I'm being silly, pumpkin. Pay me no mind."

"Are you sad to be leaving Papa?"

"Yes, but we'll be back real soon. I want to see Grandma and Grandpa, don't you?"

"Oh, yes. And the kittens and other baby animals." Etta skipped out of the bedroom.

Susan smiled, wondering if her niece was excited about the trip because of the farm animals and really couldn't care less about seeing her relatives. Who could blame her? She was but a child and had so few memories of the Armitage clan. This trip would remedy that somewhat. It would be good for both Etta and her brother to reacquaint themselves with their other family, and she had no doubts what such a visit would do for her father and mother. It would be an answer to their prayers.

How would they treat her now that she was Mrs. Logan Vance? Would they be cool toward her? If so, they'd break her heart. She wanted them to understand and forgive, just as she had understood and forgiven them for writing such a despondent letter to her after her marriage. Time healed all wounds, Susan told herself, but she only halfway believed it. After all, time had done nothing to heal the wound between Logan and her father.

"Why the frown?" Logan asked from the doorway.

Susan shook off her anxious countenance. "Oh, I was wondering how my parents would receive me."

"After marrying me, you mean?"

"Yes."

"They'll be so happy to see that you've brought the children to them, they'll welcome you with open arms. Don't you worry about that." He came up behind her and wrapped his arms around her waist, pulling her against him. His mouth slipped down her neck to where it curved into her shoulder. The neckline of her dress stopped his progress. "Of course, they'll be hoping you'll tell them how unhappy you are with me and what a brute I am. When they ask, you be sure to describe how your nipples pucker up every time I get within two feet of you."

"Logan, stop that," she said, trying to sound irritated even as her breasts began to ache. His hands came up and covered them, giving lie to her feigned irritation. "Logan, stop that," she said again, this time in a pleading whimper.

"You're going to miss me."

"I know," she said, feeling the tears collect in her throat and burn in her nostrils.

"Especially at night.'

"I know." The tears made tracks on her cheeks.

"And, *Christ*"—it was growled between clenched teeth—"I'm going to miss you."

She pivoted in his arms and brought hers up and around his neck. Her aching breasts found some relief against the wall of his chest, and the emptiness in her belly filled a little as she rubbed it against him.

I hope I'm pregnant. The thought zinged through her head, making her gasp at her own secret wish. She found herself staring into Logan's questioning eyes. Afraid to share the secret, she closed her eyes and offered up her hungry mouth. He took it, his tongue flirting and fondling and robbing her senseless.

When they were both breathless, he put her away from him and ran both hands through his hair. His expression told her how undone he was and how he hated to be taking her to the train station. He didn't need to say the words.

Wordlessly, he picked up the cases and bags and preceded her from the bedroom, his long legs taking him to the front of the building where the hitched wagon waited.

With a numbness born of mixed emotions, Susan placed her straw hat firmly on her head and checked her appearance in the full, tilted mirror before she moved slowly through the house she'd made a home for the Vance family. Outside, the children were already in the back of the wagon and Logan was settling himself in the driver's seat. Coonie helped Susan climb up to sit beside her husband.

"Y'all have a fine visit," Coonie said, giving them a smile. "We'll be missing you back here in Tulsey Town."

"Bye-bye, Uncle Coonie," Jacob said.

"Love you, Uncle Coonie," Etta called.

"Now don't you go marrying anybody in Missouri," Coonie teased Etta as Logan set the wagon in motion. "Remember I'm your old sweetheart."

Etta giggled and waved. Jacob simply stared morosely as Coonie turned and started back into the building.

"Will we be coming back here?" Jacob asked as the train station came into view, revealing his doubts even after a long talk with Logan earlier about how nice it would be to visit his kinfolk. Obviously, his father's feigned change of heart hadn't convinced Jacob.

Susan saw the discomfort flit across Logan's face, so she twisted around to answer for him. "Yes, Jacob. We'll all be coming back here within a fortnight. I promise we'll be home for Christmas."

Logan smiled, and Susan could tell he believed her. Jacob, on the other hand, quirked his mouth into a know-it-all smirk. He believed Susan about as much as he believed cows could fly.

Chapter 23

"You can help us name the kittens," Louella Armitage told her grandchildren as she knelt beside the basket of fur balls with Etta and Jacob.

"Really, Gandma?" Etta asked.

"Yes, my angel." Louella hugged Etta tightly. "Doesn't she look just like Catherine, Abe?" she asked, glancing up to her husband, who was standing nearby.

"She does. Spitting image," Abraham agreed.

Sitting on the hay bales with her two younger sisters, Susan was glad she'd brought Etta and Jacob for a visit. Her family had welcomed them, although she'd noted that her parents weren't as loving toward her as they had been before she'd married Logan. However, bringing the children had mended some of the rips in their relationship.

In the few hours she'd been back on the farm, she'd noticed changes in her parents—especially in her father. While he'd never been a particularly affectionate man, he seemed even colder now. Even with Etta and Jacob, two children Susan could hardly keep from kissing and hugging, Abraham Armitage remained so reserved that he rarely touched them.

Thinking back, Susan could recall a time when her father had been more loving, back when she and her sisters had been much younger and knew nothing of a world outside the Armitage farm. It was easy to love us then, she thought. We accepted everything he said, obeyed his every command, and never looked at another man for love, respect, or guidance. It seemed that the moment Catherine

308

reached the age of maidenhood, Abraham began to change from a strict but good father to a grim tyrant.

He's even worse now, Susan thought as she watched his granitelike face as he stood near Etta and Jacob. He's had not one, but two, of his loyal subjects defy him, and he's having trouble living with it. Sadly, she knew he'd never love her again.

"Did you have a vegetable garden in Tulsey Town?" Rebecca asked.

"A small one, but we're going to plant a bigger one come spring," Susan answered her sister.

"Any flowers in the Territory?" Lauralee, the youngest, asked.

"Oh, yes. Lovely flowers. Wildflowers," Susan said. "There's a huge plot of black-eyed Susans in my backyard. I'm planting roses next year. My friend Mrs. Brewster is giving me a few miniature rose bushes."

"So you like it there?" Rebecca plucked at her apron and glanced toward her parents, who were helping Etta name the kittens.

"Yes, I do." Susan's thoughts moved across the miles to Logan. He'd be writing up his articles now, sitting at his desk, his brow furrowed as he composed sentence after sentence. He was a good writer, if she did say so herself. He had a knack for taking complicated matters and presenting them so that even the most simpleminded person could understand them. She touched the necklace he'd given her, then ran the pad of her thumb across the etched roses on her wedding band. She'd brought Logan's photograph with her, but looking at it only made her more lonesome for him. The time away had cleared her mind and made her trust her own heart. She loved Logan, and beside him was the only place she wanted to be.

"And do you like being married?" Rebecca asked, leaning toward Susan and lowering her voice to a whisper. Lauralee swayed closer to catch Susan's answer.

"Yes." Susan glanced toward her parents, glad to see they were still absorbed with the children. "I *love* being married. Logan is a wonderful man."

"Mama and Papa think he's a demon," Lauralee whispered.

"They say he has no morals," Rebecca added.

Susan shook her head and frowned. "Not Logan. He's a bit ornery, but he has a good heart and he's a noble man."

"Did you know that Cal got married?' Lauralee asked.

"No. Who'd he marry?"

"Donna Pitchard." Lauralee made a face. "The widow living with Bob and Mildred Samples. I believe she's Mr. Samples's second cousin."

"Oh, yes." Susan conjured up a dim picture of the widow woman. "Why, she must be ten years older than Cal."

"Twelve," Rebecca said with a raised brow. "He's scraping the bottom of the barrel, if you ask me."

"He was crushed when he heard you'd up and married somebody else," Lauralee said. "Took it hard."

Susan squelched the twinge of guilt pricking her heart. "Cal had no claim on me. I never once made him think I'd marry him."

The kittens named, Louella stood and looked toward her three daughters. "I can't tell you how happy you've made your father and me," she said to Susan. She touched Etta's curly hair. "Having them here . . ."

"Can I keep this one?" Etta asked, holding up a squirming, meowing orange kitten.

"You can keep all of them," Louella said.

"No, Mama—" Susan objected

"We can't take all them cats on the train," Jacob interrupted.

"What train?" Louella asked, looking to Abraham and laughing. "Y'all aren't going on a train again. You're staying here on the farm where you can watch these kittens grow up to be big old cats."

"That's right," Abraham concurred. "Y'all are home now."

Jacob sent a glance toward Susan that made her stand, anxious to correct the misunderstanding.

"Mama, Papa, we're only here for a visit. I told Logan

we'd be back within a fortnight. He's expecting us home by Christmas, you see.'' She heard her two sisters gasp behind her, but she kept her gaze pinned on her mother's face. Louella's faded blue eyes filled with tears as she grasped Etta to her flat bosom and turned her gaze up to her husband in a desperate plea.

Abraham stared stonily at Susan. "You mean *you're* going back to him, Susie. Not these innocent lambs." He used the tone of voice that made the Armitage females leap to do his bidding, but Susan didn't flinch, much less leap. "Isn't that correct, Susie?"

"I'm taking the children back with me, Papa. They belong with me and Logan."

"You can't protect them from him," Abraham said, almost bellowing.

"I don't have to. He'd never hurt them. Why, he can hardly bring himself to spank them when they misbehave. He leaves the punishment to me most of the time."

"I'm talking about their minds and souls, girl," Abraham said, pointing a finger at Jacob. "He'll blacken them as surely as he blackened their mother's and yours!" The finger swung like a pendulum to her. "You were a good girl until he got alone with you, and look at you now." His thin mustache twitched. "Kindling for hell's fires."

Lauralee and Rebecca gasped behind her. Susan's mother averted her face, but said nothing.

"Mama, will you take Etta and Jacob outside, please?" Susan asked, not wanting them to hear any more such rubbish. "They don't need to witness this argument."

"There will be no argument. I've spoken," Abraham intoned.

Susan released a bark of bitter laughter that sent her mother scurrying outside with Jacob and Etta in tow. Right behind them ran Susan's sisters, leaving Susan to face her father alone.

"You laughed at me, Susie?"

"Once upon a time I wouldn't have questioned your authority, Papa, but I must now because I'm responsible for Etta and Jacob, and they are going home with me when I go." She was proud of herself for not stuttering or trembling with her father staring at her as if she were a two-headed demon from hell.

Abraham's mouth dipped into a grim arc. "I can't believe you'd bring those babies here and then think I'd let you take them away."

"Papa, they aren't yours to keep!" Susan propped her hands on her hips and told herself not to back down or she'd regret it for the rest of her life. She felt Logan's courage, Logan's strength, Logan's belief in her creating a shield against her father's growing wrath. "The children belong with Logan. *He's* their father, not you." She forced herself to calm down. "Now let's not argue about this. I'm looking forward to a lovely visit. After the holidays, you and Mama might come and visit us in Tulsa. It's not such a bad place, you know. The people are strong pioneers, but as friendly as you please and—"

"You'll not take them."

She drew in a deep breath, seeing that her father was determined to win this one. "I don't need your permission, Papa." She spread out her arms. "Look at me. I'm a grown woman now. Married, with responsibilities. I have my own home, I grow my own garden, I make my own clothes *and* my own decisions. I love you, Papa, but I no longer intend to obey your every command."

"You won't defy me."

"Papa, I don't wish to, but I can't—"

"First Catherine defied me and I turned the other cheek, but now you? I can't pretend blindness, deafness. This trouble has a name—Logan Vance. I must smite him. He's the devil's messenger, and I can no longer be meek. I must smite him."

"Papa, please . . ." Susan sighed, recognizing the jargon. Her father was on the verge of a preaching frenzy. It never failed when he heard something he refused to accept. "Let's not do this. Logan is a good father. You never gave him a chance to—"

"You're his whore."

She staggered back, buffeted by the force of his hatred. "Papa!" It took a moment to regain her breath, her equilibrium. Tears collected in her throat, her eyes. "I'm his *wife*, not his whore."

"Satan takes no wife. He takes women and makes them whores."

"Logan isn't the devil. He's a man who has done his best amid adversity. He married Catherine, then lost her. You know, Catherine was no spotless angel herself."

"And now he's turned you against your own dead sister." Abraham shook his head, his eyes glinting coldly. "Has he turned you against the rest of us, too?"

"No, of course not. And I love Catherine—always will. You can love someone and still see faults. I love you, although I think you're being bullheaded about Logan."

"And I think it's time you recalled where your allegiance must lie, Susie." Without removing his gaze from her, he reached for the buggy whip hanging from a hook near him.

Staring at him, she half suspected he was bluffing. He wouldn't whip her, she told herself. Not now. She was a woman—a married woman. He wouldn't . . . couldn't . . . He was going to. The whip lifted and whistled in the air.

"Papa," Susan said, forcing the words from her dry, cottony mouth. "If I feel the kiss of that whip, then you can kiss Etta and Jacob good-bye—forever."

Time spun out on a slow spool. Abraham tapped the short whip against his pants leg. Susan saw the movement with peripheral vision, but she never moved her gaze from her father's eyes—eyes so devoid of tenderness that Susan wondered if the man could ever have loved her. She sensed his fingers tightening on the whip handle.

"I mean it, Papa. I'll fight you and I'll win. You touch me with that whip and you might as well write off me, Etta, and Jacob. You'll never see any of us again. We'll write you off, too. You'll be dead to all of us. You and Mama. Is that what you want?"

"You always were the daughter who had defiance in your heart," he said, mostly to himself. "I told your mother when you were just a tot that you'd be trouble. You asked too many questions and talked when you should have listened. And I remember how moony-eyed you got every time that Vance man came around sniffing after Catherine. I saw how he looked at you, too. Always grinning when he eyed you. I knew then, and I told your mama, that we had to get that man away from you and Catherine or the three of you would end up full of sin with no redemption. I was right, I reckon. First Catherine, now you. I bet he's braying like a jackass, knowing he's tripped up another Armitage girl and sent her spinning into hell.''

"Oh, Papa." She rolled her eyes, tired of his sermon and his narrow mind. "Listen to yourself. I was a child back then. I never was moony-eyed for him. He was Catherine's beau.''

"He would have taken you then if I hadn't stood between you."

"No. He only had eyes for Catherine."

"And every other skirt in this county."

"I believe he was a faithful husband to Catherine."

"You'd believe he was an angel with a trumpet if he told you such rot. When you lie with animals, you start acting like them." His gaze burned up and down her slim body. "And when I look at you I see nothing but a godforsaken creature.''

She tipped up her chin defiantly. "And when I look at you I wonder how I could ever have respected you. Logan would never say such things to his children, Papa. He loves them too much." Her gaze drifted to the whip he held. "Now put that away. For the sakes of Etta and Jacob, try to act like a civilized family man. I don't want them to be scared of you.''

Susan didn't wait to see if he followed her instructions. With a lift of her skirts, she moved confidently past him into the sunlight. Her heart smiled. Logan would be proud of her, she thought.

Susan tucked the edges of the quilt around Jacob's narrow shoulders, then leaned over him to press a kiss to his cheek.

"Good night, love," she whispered, knowing she'd get no endearment in return. But she didn't care. She loved Jacob and she wanted him to hear it and know it.

"Is Etta already asleep?" Jacob asked, his green eyes sliding sideways to peer at his sister's cot.

"Yes. She's dreaming of pretty horses and cuddly kittens. Close your eyes, Jacob. Sandman's coming."

"I gotta look out for her."

"Why?" Susan glanced at Etta's sleeping form. "Is she sick? Is she running a fever or—"

"No, but they might try to hide her from me."

"They who?"

"Grandpa and Grandma."

"Oh, honey. Why would they do such a thing?"

"They want to keep her."

"Jacob, hush up." She swept a lock of hair off his forehead. "That's silly talk and you know it. Grandma and Grandpa love you and Etta, and I wouldn't let them take you away from me or your papa. Please believe me."

"They don't want me. Just Etta."

Susan rolled her eyes in exasperation. "Where do you come up with such notions? They love you and Etta equally. Just as I do."

"I only came along to rescue her if they try to take her away."

"That's enough, Jacob," she said, making her tone stern. She lowered the wick in the lantern until it emitted only a dim glow. "And don't talk such silliness to your sister or I'll tan your backside, you hear me?" She kissed his cool forehead. "See you in the morning."

Shaking her head at Jacob's wild imagination, she tiptoed from the room and went toward the kitchen for a glass of fresh milk. She slept in the same room with Etta and Jacob, but she wasn't sleepy yet. Milk would do the trick. It always did. But even as she thought it, part of her laughed. She hadn't been sleeping well since leaving Tulsa—since leaving Logan. Her narrow bed felt like a coffin without Logan's rangy body beside her. More than once, she'd awakened with a gnawing sensation in her stomach and a cry burning in her throat. She'd found herself clutching one of her feather pillows. A poor substitute for Logan's muscled arms and solid torso. She longed to smell him, taste him, devour his thirsting mouth. She wanted to feel him inside her, hard and pulsing.

Standing in the hallway outside the living room, Susan pressed a hand to her flat stomach.

Is his baby growing in me?

The question made her catch her breath and hold it for a few shattering seconds. A smile curved her mouth, and she had to choke back a giggle. Wouldn't it be wonderful to have a baby in me—Logan's baby? she asked herself, and her heart swelled with love and longing.

Logan wouldn't like it, she told herself. She'd had to beg him to leave his seed in her, and he still did so with a measure of reluctance.

". . . if it weren't for that devil dog, Catherine would be alive today."

Susan crept forward, drawn by her father's voice, but she stayed in the shadows. She could see her mother's hand resting on the arm of the rocker her grandparents had brought over from England. A shadow licked the floor, cast by her pacing father.

"It's the God's truth," her mother said, her voice sadly soft.

"And now he's turned Susie against us."

"Poor baby. I thought she'd be stronger."

Susan rolled her lips between her teeth to keep from speaking aloud to object to such condemnation. That her parents could so blithely dismiss her cut to the bone. Had Catherine known this treatment from them? No wonder she'd kept her distance and had come home only once. And was it any wonder that Logan would just as soon be dragged a mile behind a horse than spend an hour in the company of Abraham and Louella Armitage?

"She'll not defy me," Abraham swore. "Revenge is mine."

"What about Jacob?" Louella asked in a small, quivering voice.

"She can take him with her. He looks and acts too much like his father."

"Yes, but Etta . . . Oh, Abraham! I look at her and my

heart aches. So much like Catherine . . . her image . . . her twin.''

"We'll keep her and that will square things. He took Catherine from us, and now we'll take Etta from him. An eye for an eye, the Bible tells us.''

"But Susan won't let us.''

"I'm not so old and feeble that I'll let a daughter of mine stand in my way, woman. Susie will do as I say or I'll make her sorry she ever sassed me.''

"We don't want trouble, Abraham. I'm afraid Logan Vance will come for Etta and—''

"Let him come. I'll have my shotgun loaded and cocked. People around here know what a hothead he is and will be glad I rid the county of such vermin. They'll thank me, they will, and we'll be free of—''

Susan listened to no more. Clamping one hand over her mouth and the other against her midsection, she moved stealthily along the hallway toward the bedroom she'd just left. She felt ill, as if her insides were raw and bleeding. But her head was clear. She knew exactly what she had to do.

"Jacob?'' she whispered, shaking him awake. "It's Aunt Susan. Listen carefully.'' She peered through the dimness at him until she was sure he was wide awake. "We're leaving this place. I want you to get up and get dressed, but don't make a sound.''

"Now? We're leaving now?'' He rubbed his eyes and looked around for any sign of daylight.

"Yes. Right this minute.''

"We're running away?''

She sighed. "In a way, yes. I don't want to stay here any longer than I have to. We're going home where we belong.''

"How? We gonna walk?''

"No, silly. I'll hitch up a buggy and we'll ride into Springfield and catch the five-oh-eight.'' She ruffled his hair, not wanting to alarm him. "Quiet as a mouse now while I wake up Etta. Okay?''

"Okay!'' he whispered back, his eyes lighting with excitement as he scrambled off the feather mattress.

"Etta, baby?" Susan pushed back the covers and lifted Etta from them, holding her close to muffle her grouchy sounds. "Shhh, honey. We're going to get dressed now and go home to Papa."

"Papa?" Etta roused at that, her sleepy blue eyes blinking in the dim light. "He's here?"

"No, we're going home to him. Help me get you dressed and keep quiet. We don't want to wake anyone else."

By the time she had them dressed and their bags packed, an hour had slipped past and the house was quiet. She'd heard her parents shuffle off to bed half an hour ago. They'd be asleep by now, she hoped. Opening the door a crack, Susan stumbled momentarily when a face peered back at her.

"It's okay," someone whispered. "It's me. Rebecca."

"Becky!" Susan grabbed her arm in relief. "You scared the living daylights out of me. We . . . uh . . . What are you doing up?"

"I know what you're doing," Becky whispered, then held a finger to her lips as her gaze slid sideways. "Lauralee and I hitched up the buggy for you. It's out back. Come on and be quiet. Papa isn't a sound sleeper, if you'll recall."

"Yes, I do." Susan swallowed a knot of emotion in her throat, put there by her sisters' actions. "Thank you. Thanks so much." Turning, she lifted Etta into her arms and motioned for Jacob to move on cat's feet ahead of her. Rebecca helped carry their bags and cases out back where a sickle moon illuminated a buggy hitched to a healthy sorrel. Lauralee stood next to it, ready to help Jacob up onto the padded seat.

"Leave the buggy at the station and one of us will pick it up later," Rebecca instructed.

"How did you know I was leaving?"

"I saw you standing outside the living room listening to Papa hatch his plan," Rebecca admitted. "I knew you'd light out."

"So you decided to help me and go against Papa?"

"Susie, Papa's been a little funny in the head ever since

Catherine got herself with child, and he's gotten much worse since she died. He blamed Logan for everything and he's kept on blaming him for every misfortune that's fallen on this family since then.'' Rebecca's lower lip trembled. ''Mama goes along with him because he's gotten so mean and we're all scared of him, but I know she doesn't take to heart all his rantings and ravings.''

Susan handed Etta over to Lauralee, then hugged Rebecca. ''Thank you, sweet sister. I hope I don't get you in too much trouble.'' She released Rebecca to throw her arms around Lauralee. ''If you two ever need a place to stay, come to my home in Tulsa.''

''Really?'' Lauralee asked, her brown eyes widening. ''Logan would let us stay?''

''Of course! He'd love it.'' Susan looked up at Etta and Jacob, their round faces beaming down at her like small moons. ''We'd best get on. If Papa wakes up, he'll come after us and drag us back.''

''He'll have a hard time of it,'' Rebecca mumbled sheepishly. She shared a sly smile with Lauralee.

''What are y'all up to?'' Susan asked.

''We let the other horses out into the east pasture,'' Lauralee confessed.

''Oh, Lord.'' Susan shook her head, laughing under her breath. ''He'll never round them up in those woods in the dead of night.''

''Won't see those nags until mid-morning when they come looking for oats and water,'' Rebecca agreed with a giggle. ''Now go on, and Godspeed.''

After another round of hugs and kisses, Susan took her place on the padded seat and grabbed the reins. She took a few moments to share long, loving looks with her sisters before clucking the horse into a slow, quiet walk. The buggy creaked and jingled, the sound as loud as fireworks in the silent night.

''I was right, wasn't I?'' Jacob asked with certainty. ''Grandpa was going to keep Etta and send me back with you.''

''Let's not talk about that,'' Susan said, hating to admit such a villainous plan aloud to innocent children. Her father must surely have gone around the bend, she thought with a twinge of regret. He'd always been a tyrant, but now he was a crazed, vengeful vindicator.

A sudden howl startled them. At first, Susan thought it was an animal, then a split second later she realized with a jolt of fear that the sound came from her father. She laid the reins across the sorrel's back and sent him into a break-neak gallop even as she rocked onto one hip and looked around the buggy's flapping canopy.

The moon's light was bright enough to reveal her father standing in the backyard, a shotgun aimed at the departing buggy. A shriek of fear stabbed Susan's throat, and she took up the buggy whip and lashed the sorrel into a fear-inspired race. He wouldn't shoot her! Not her own father!

On the heels of an explosion came a ripping noise as pellets peppered the buggy's black bonnet. Jacob pushed Etta to the floorboards and crouched over her, his sobbing louder than his sister's whimpers.

"Papa!" Susan screamed, more angry than afraid. "You bastard!" She looked over her shoulder again. Strands of hair streamed across her eyes, hindering her vision. When the wind finally rearranged the strands so she could see more clearly, she watched as her father aimed the shotgun again.

Susan cringed, making herself a smaller target, and prayed they were out of range by now. Then, through her tears, she saw her mother and sisters fall upon her father and wrench the shotgun from his hands. He struck out, sending her mother and Lauralee to the ground, but before he could slap Rebecca, she rammed the shotgun's butt into his midsection and he crumpled forward, driven to his knees.

"Ah-ha!" Susan faced front and threw back her head to release a triumphant laugh. "Take that, you old coot!"

As her words echoed, she stifled a sob of regret. Her father. Her father had shot at her, had slapped her mother and sister to the ground as if they meant nothing to him! Shame for him grew in her, and she felt the seeds of ab-horrence sprout in her heart. Those seeds had been there for some time, but tonight's horrid scene had been enough to make them burst open. Any respect she'd ever had for her father was choked out by the quickly growing animosity.

Knowing he couldn't follow them, Susan tugged the reins and brought the sorrel to a canter. Her soothing voice slowed him to a walk and made Jacob look up at her, his face tearstained and his eyes red-rimmed.

"Come on up here with me, loves," she said, smoothing a hand over Jacob's hair, then pulling her lace-trimmed hankie from her cuff to dab it under Jacob's runny nose. "Blow, sweetie."

Jacob obeyed as Etta hugged close to Susan's side and hiccupped. Susan wrapped an arm around the child and sent Jacob a comforting smile.

"All's well," she told him. "We'll be home before you know it."

"To Papa?" Etta asked, looking up at Susan with tear-washed eyes.

"Yes, honey. Home to Papa." Saying it made Susan's heart swell with love and devotion. "He'll be so glad to see us."

"Grandpa was trying to sh-shoot us!" Jacob blurted out.

"No, honey . . ." Susan stopped herself from excusing her father or making up pretty stories for his benefit. Examining the fright still evident in her charges' eyes, she nodded gravely. "He tried to shoot *me,* not you or Etta. Grandpa is touched in the head, I'm afraid. But you don't have to fret anymore. We won't be seeing him again."

"No?" Jacob asked. "Promise?"

"I promise," Susan said, reaching out to stroke his velvety cheek. "I had to try to mend the fences, Jacob. Please try to understand. Grandpa is *my* papa, and I couldn't turn my back on him without trying one more time to make him love me again. But he so hates your papa, it's impossible." She shrugged, although her heart continued to ache. "I've done my best, but it wasn't enough for Grandpa, so we'll stay out of his way from now on."

"What about Aunt Becky and Aunt Lauralee and Grandma?" Etta asked, then hiccupped again.

"Maybe we'll see them again. Maybe they'll come visit us."

"Aunt Susan?"

"Yes, Jacob?"

"You really love us, don't you? You love Etta and you love me."

Startled, she felt emotion rise up and tighten her throat as Jacob gazed at her with eyes that reminded her of Logan's. Etta's blue orbs never wavered from Susan's face, either. The two children waited for Susan's answer, which to her mind, should have been understood long ago.

"Yes, Jacob. I love you and Etta with all my heart." She cleared her throat of its thickness. "I always have and I always will." She smiled back at Etta, then confronted her nephew's solemn countenance. "Do you love me, Jacob?"

"I love you," Etta piped up, giggling when Susan placed a loud kiss on her turned-up nose.

"Jacob?" Susan asked again, then held her breath, wondering if he'd break her heart again. The Vance males had a knack for doing that.

His small chest lifted and fell and then—much to Susan's disbelief and then ultimate joy—he grinned. It was that Logan grin that never failed to warm Susan through and through.

"I love you, Aunt Susan. I love you a bunch." The special smile wilted a smidgeon. "Why are you crying?"

Susan shook her head and took a few moments to compose herself. "Because I'm a sentimental fool," she confessed, then laughed to assure her niece and nephew that all was well with her and their world. "And because being loved by you two is the most wonderful thing that's happened to me lately."

Fixing her gaze on the bobbing head of the horse, Susan knew a few moments of pure satisfaction. She felt as if she'd come to the happy end of a long, arduous journey.

Chapter 24

After arriving unannounced at the Tulsa train depot, Susan hailed Mr. Hall's delivery boy, who obligingly gave her and the children a ride home in the back of his grocery wagon. As the wagon rattled to a halt in front of the newspaper office, Susan could see Logan and Coonie inside. Clarabelle was going full tilt, but Logan must have sensed movement outside the windows because he glanced up, then down again, then back up in openmouthed surprise. Happiness split his handsome face in a grin.

"Papa!" Jacob shouted, leaping from the back of the wagon.

Susan helped Etta slide to the ground, then followed more slowly. A dull pain writhed through her stomach, but she refused to dwell on the familiar ache. She held out her arms for Logan's embrace. He caught her around the waist and whirled her in a circle, making her throw back her head and laugh up at the blue sky. Clutching his shoulders, she looked down into the face of love.

"You're back!" His comment reflected the shadow of doubt he'd been nursing. "And so soon! You've been gone only a few days." He let her slide down his solid body until her feet touched ground again. "Couldn't stay away from me, is that it?" he teased, then his gaze probed hers. His thumbs came up to gently stroke the dark circles under her eyes. "Something happened . . . what?"

"I'll tell you later." She laughed at Etta and Jacob, who were jumping around Logan, vying for his attention. "Say

323

hello to your children. They missed you something awful.''

"Are you sure you're okay?" Logan persisted.

She gathered his hands in hers and forced them from her face. "I'm just tired. I'm going to lie down for a few minutes." She shook her head at his worried expression. "Logan, *really*. I've been up since before dawn and I lost a few hours' sleep, that's all."

"Very well. Take a rest while I rassle these two young'uns to the ground and hog-tie 'em." His growling threat evoked giggles and squeals from Etta and Jacob.

Leaving the two rambunctious children in Logan's hands, Susan went inside and said hello to Coonie, then made her way through the living quarters to her bedroom. It looked dear to her as she closed the door and took a minute to appreciate it as she'd never done before. Her gaze lingered on the bed where she'd known divine pleasure, then she forced herself away from the memories and went behind the dressing screen. She removed her undergarments with a sense of dread. The small stain on her pantalettes confirmed her suspicions.

"I've got my time," she murmured, disappointment churning through her. "I'm not pregnant, after all."

A few minutes later, having changed her underclothes and added the layers of soft, absorbent cloth she used during her monthly cycle, she rinsed out the stains and lay on the bed. Stacking her hands beneath her cheek, she rested on her side and readjusted her image of herself. For days she'd fancied herself a budding mother, falling victim to her own wishful thinking.

Well, Logan would be relieved. Of course, he didn't even know of her inkling of pregnancy, and there was no reason to tell him now. She'd been worried about how he'd react should her hunch pan out. Now she could stop fretting.

A hot tear rolled from the corner of her eye and onto the pillow. Funny how she'd changed since losing her virginity. She never used to imagine herself as a mother. It had seemed so foreign, not something she wanted to experience any time soon. But then Logan had shown her the art of loving, of giving, of receiving, and from that had been born a yearning that swept through her at least once a day.

At first she hadn't known what she yearned for, only that she did. Then Logan had spilled his seed in her, and she'd given name to that yawning emptiness. More than anything she'd ever wanted in her life, she wanted Logan's child. She wanted to hold something tangible— living proof of her love for him and of her faith in a future with him. And she wanted to release the mothering instincts that had been growing inside her ever since she'd taken charge of Jacob and Etta.

She could mother them, but she'd never *be* their mother. Over the months, this had become clear in her mind and heart. Only a baby of her own would suffice. And not just any baby. Logan's baby.

The bedroom door creaked open, and Logan stuck his head around it. "Susan, are you asleep?"

"No, come in." She started to sit up, but he waved her back down.

"Are you ill?" he asked, sitting on the side of the bed.

She curled herself around his backside. "It's my time, that's all."

"Oh. You're cramping?"

"Some. I . . . I've only spotted. I suppose I'm tense and that's making my muscles ache." She trailed a hand down his rounded back. "I cut our stay short. I would have wired you, but there wasn't time."

He caught her hand and brought it to his lips. "Jacob says you ran away in the middle of the night. Abraham shot at you?"

Susan rolled onto her back with a sigh. "Those two always beat me to the punch."

"He *did* shoot at you?"

From the corner of her eyes, she noted Logan's increasing agitation and knew a storm was brewing. "He sure did, but he missed."

"Godamighty!" The storm broke. Logan surged up from the bed and rammed one fist into the other. It sounded like the crack of lightning. His eyes blazed with fury.

"That man— I'm going to— I swear I'll— You won't ever go back there. You hear me? I won't allow my children or you, for that matter, to ever again put your lives—"

"I'm not going back and neither are the children," Susan cut in, propping herself up on her elbows. "None of us wants to." She mirrored his look of surprise. "Do you think I'd be fool enough to give him another chance to blow my head off?"

The storm passed, leaving his eyes shining and clear. "Tell me what happened."

"Oh, Logan." She fell back again and stared at the ceiling as the horror gripped her again like a clammy hand. "Papa has gone round the bend. I heard him plotting to keep Etta and send me and Jacob packing. He said it was an eye for an eye or something insane like that. You know how he dearly loves to twist the Bible's words to fit his own deeds. He said you took Catherine and now he was going to take Etta." She sucked back a sob. "When I finally figured out that he was past forgiving and forgetting, I bundled up the children and lit out—with the help of Becky and Lauralee and even Mama."

"But he caught you?"

"Almost. He got a shot off before Mama and the girls could pull the rifle from his hands. Scared ten years off me." She bit her lip, wondering if that fright might also have dislodged a precious seedling taking root inside her. She closed her eyes, the notion too painful to contemplate.

"Sounds like him," Logan said, pacing. "Sounds just like the crazy bastard." He threw Susan a black look. "Sorry, but it's hard for me to be a gentleman when I talk about him."

"I know. I understand more fully now." She sat up, curling an arm around her midsection. "Logan, I don't quite understand everything. What led up to you and Catherine marrying?"

"She got pregnant." He pivoted to face the window.

"I know that part . . . but what led up to that?" She stared at his imposing back, wishing she could bore holes through it with her eyes. "And I know how women and men make babies, so don't sigh and roll your eyes like that. I want to know . . . well, if . . ."

"If I loved her madly?"

She bowed her head, ashamed of the need to ask. "Yes."

"This shouldn't come as any great surprise, but Catherine was your father's favorite."

"Yes, I know that," she said, wondering how that answered her question.

"You do?" He looked over his shoulder, examining her acceptance of it. "You do. Seems odd to me for a father to have a pick of the litter, but I guess when you grow up with a man like him you come to accept certain peculiar bents."

"Catherine, being the firstborn, always came first in everything," she said, repeating what she'd heard from the cradle on. Now, however, it sounded like a poor excuse for the inexcusable. "And she got her way with Papa more than the rest of us ever did."

"Yes, but when it came to me, he put his foot down hard. When Catherine bloomed into womanhood, she was no longer your papa's little angel," he explained, still gazing out the window. "Old Abe didn't like that one bit. He blamed me for turning her head, but if it hadn't been me it would have been some other young buck. Catherine was a looker and as hot as a branding iron." He twisted around for her to see his grin. That grin said it all, and Susan had to laugh. "What's funny?"

"I was remembering the two of you. Catherine seemed to be constantly out of breath when she was around you, and you—you with that heart-melting grin of yours." She shook her head in a gentle rebuke, and her arm fell away from her middle. The ache had subsided, and she felt whole again. Had his smile done that? "You knew that grin's power over females, and you showed them no mercy."

"You're giving me more credit than I deserve."

"No, I don't think so. I was only a girl, and I fell victim to it."

He turned to face her and rocked back on his heels as

he stretched his suspenders with his thumbs. ''That so? Was I your first case of puppy love?''

''You know you were, although at the time, I didn't realize what it was I was feeling.''

''Neither did I.''

She exchanged a sizzling glance with him that was too hot for either to handle. He looked aside a moment before she did.

''You don't think Catherine sensed anything, do you?'' Susan asked after another few moments.

''She knew I liked you a lot, but Catherine and I had too much on our plate to add a helping of you to it.'' He sat in the rocker, sliding down until he was sitting mostly on his spine. His posture was lazy, but his eyes were alert. His gaze flitted over her like a curious butterfly. ''I never loved her madly.''

Susan nodded. She'd known it already. ''Why did you . . . Why did you rush headlong into a trap from which you couldn't escape?''

''Catherine was hot on my heels, and I was a willing victim. Abe saw me as a rolling stone, and he wanted Catherine to stay far, far away from me. He decided she wouldn't be allowed around any males unless she was chaperoned. Well, that went over like a ton of bricks with your sister.''

''I remember her wailing and threatening to run away,'' Susan murmured as the voices of that time echoed through her mind.

''I didn't know about Abe's threat. Catherine sneaked around behind Abe's back to meet me at barn dances and the like. When he found out, he whipped her.''

Susan pleated the bedspread between her fingers. The voices in her head grew angrier, and she recalled how frightened she'd been back then. Frightened for Catherine . . . for her entire family.

''So Catherine seduced me, although it was an easy task, I admit.'' His mouth tipped up at the corners. ''She'd been a good girl until then. I'd tried everything to get under her skirts, but no doing. That whipping Abe gave her was the last straw. She wanted a ticket out of town, and I was it.''

He glanced up, his expression tinged with sadness. "When she told me she was pregnant and that she wanted to move to St. Louis with me and get married, I knew I'd been played for a fool, but it was too late. Catherine read me like a book, and she knew I'd do the honorable thing." His shrug was quick, telling. "I did."

"She was so desperate she surrendered her virtue," Susan murmured. "I suppose she didn't think you'd marry her if she weren't with child."

"I suppose."

Susan swallowed with difficulty, and a question burned the tip of her tongue. She wanted to ask but held back.

"I loved her," Logan spoke up, his voice rough around the edges. "But not enough to marry her. Aw, we went through the motions, you know, but our love faded early on, so it couldn't have been deep for either of us."

"How sad."

He nodded, his lips lifting from the center to form an endearing frown. "Yes, it was. We both deserved better." He braced his hands on his knees and stood up, sending the rocker in motion. "I'll let you rest." Crossing to her, he dropped a kiss on her forehead. His lips lingered, caressing her with each word. "He didn't hurt you, did he? No bruises or welts? I know Abe, and he likes to hit his women."

"He didn't touch me. I wouldn't let him."

Logan straightened, and pride glinted in his eyes. "Good for you, Susan." He gave her a wink and a nod. "I always knew you had pluck." At the door, he paused and glanced back at her. "You *did* miss me, didn't you?"

Smiling, she blew him a kiss. "Only as much as you missed me."

"Good Lord!" He rolled his eyes dramatically. "In that case, no wonder you have circles under your eyes. You poor, wretched thing!"

The pillow just missed him.

Susan awakened moments before the bedroom door flew open and Logan stumbled in, his shirttails flying, his hair a tumble across his forehead, his eyes wide with terror.

He held Etta in one arm and flung the covers off Susan with his free hand.

It took her a few moments to recognize where she was. Earlier, Logan had awakened her and suggested she dress for bed. Still tired from the trip, she'd obeyed and climbed right back into bed. But how long ago had that been? she wondered, blinking questioningly at Logan. And why was he holding Etta? The expression of panic on Logan's face swept the silly questions from her mind. Something was wrong. Something horrible had happened. His next words confirmed her sixth sense.

"Get up. Fire."

"Here?" Susan was already out of bed and reaching for her robe as she stuck her feet into carpet slippers.

"Down the street. Coming this way." He was so out of breath he could hardly talk.

"Where's Jacob?"

"With Coonie. Outside. Come on!" He grabbed her hand, preventing her from taking anything with her as he dragged her from the bedroom and through the dark rooms. A single lantern shone in the living room. Outside, the world was ablaze with pulsating light.

The air tasted dirty as Susan sucked it into her lungs and coughed it back out again. Her eyes stung and teared as she searched out Coonie's familiar, rounded form and Jacob's tiny figure standing next to it. Dropping to her knees, she hugged Jacob and thanked God that the most important people in her life were safe from the shooting flames causing havoc down the street.

The fire moved briskly, encouraged by a gusting breeze. Smoke hung below the moon in nasty clouds. Shouts and screams rose above the fire's roar. Glass shattered, tinkling like piano keys. A ragtag line of men snaked along the street, creating bucket brigades. Coonie and Logan moved to take their places among them.

"Logan, what can I do?" Susan asked, reaching to grab his shirttail.

"If the fire gets closer, we'll have to start hauling things out of our place and save what we can. Keep an eye on the children. Don't let them get anywhere near the fire."

He pointed a finger at the youngsters to get their attention. "Y'all hear me? Stay with your moth—uh, with Susan." He shook his head, looking rattled, and strode to the other the end of a line where the bucket stopped and water was tossed at the flames.

Sensing someone's intent regard, Susan tracked it to Jacob. His green eyes studied her with more than their usual intensity.

"He didn't mean it," she told him, knowing Logan's slip had disturbed Jacob. "He's thinking about the fire and—"

"It's okay." Jacob shrugged and sat on the boardwalk across the street from the newspaper office. "You're doing everything a mother does."

Susan nodded, wanting to kiss Jacob and hug him so tightly he'd beg for mercy, but the cracking of lumber and spitting of glass caught her attention. Sitting on the boardwalk between her two charges, she draped her arms around them and watched as the fire claimed one building after another in its march down Main Street.

The hotel went up so quickly that Susan could hardly believe her eyes. The dry wood turned to ashes on the first floor and the two floors above it collapsed. Sparks flew, and the men closest to the doomed building had to turn tail and run to keep from getting hit by flying lumber and brick. Susan saw Logan sprinting. He'd taken off his shirt, and his sweat-soaked skin glistened. His soot-smudged face made her think of an Indian on the warpath.

It *was* a war. And they were losing.

Finding an abandoned wagon, the horses long gone, Susan sat Jacob and Etta in it.

"Y'all stay right here. If I see you anywhere but in this wagon I'm going to wear y'all out," she said, trying to sound stern instead of scared silly, which is what she was.

"Where you going?" Etta asked, rubbing her eyes with her fists. The hem of her long nightie was black with dirt and ashes.

"To help get some of our things from the house in case the fire reaches this far."

"Get my dolly."

"I will."

"And my kite," Jacob chimed in.

"I'll try. Where is it?"

"In the corner by my bed."

"I'll look for it," she promised. "Now y'all mind me." She kissed them both before leaving them huddled together, their arms wrapped around each other. No brother or sister could be any closer, she thought. The poor things had weathered many a storm together.

Coonie was already carrying out an armload of type cases when she stepped into the printing office.

"You stay outside," he bellowed at her. "Me and the others will cart your things."

"I want to help. The children want some of their toys and—"

"Susan, get out of the way." Logan's hand clamped on her shoulder, and he shoved her roughly aside. "Stay with the children."

"I'm not a child! I'm going to help save my belongings and—"

"Listen to me." He grabbed her shoulders and dipped his head to be eye-level with her. "I don't have time to argue with you. Will you stay with the children so I can at least know my family is safe while I fight this goddamned fire? Will you do that for me, Susan?"

Releasing a sigh of surrender, she gave a grudging nod. "Yes."

"Thanks." He kissed her left eyelid in a hit-or-miss fashion, then left her to race inside.

Susan went back outside to sit in the wagon with the children, feeling totally useless while Coonie and Logan carried load after load out to the street. Gradually, others fell in to help while women gathered around the wagon and sobbed and comforted one another as Tulsa's main artery caved in around them. Other children were deposited in the wagon, making it a big safety pen.

Bucket after bucket of water was thrown at the fire— like stones thrown at a giant. But a giant had once been slain by a stone, Susan recalled, and she prayed that history would repeat itself. Closing her eyes, she lifted her face to the heavens and asked for help while cries of anguish rose up around her.

The first snowflake felt like an angel's kiss.

Susan opened her eyes to the swirling white above her.

"Aunt Susan," Etta whispered. "It's snowing."

"Will it put out the fire?" Jacob asked, standing up in the wagon.

"I don't know . . . maybe." She realized then how cold it had become since the wind had shifted from the north. A woman she'd seen in church shoved a blanket at her. Susan took it and made Etta and Jacob sit down again. She tucked the blanket around them to silence their chattering teeth.

"It's dying," one of the women shouted.

Susan looked down the street. The bank building next to the newspaper office had a crown of flames, but the flames were yellowy-orange, not white and blue with streaks of red as they had been only minutes ago. The fire's roar had diminished to hisses and gasps.

Against the backdrop of falling snow and blackened buildings stood Logan. Susan slipped off the wagon and went to where he was standing in the middle of the street like a sentinel. Their meager belongings lay scattered around him, and cases of lead letters spilled at his feet. She nestled one arm around his waist, and leaned her head on his shoulder. He said nothing, just draped one arm around her and rested his cheek against the top of her head.

The giant had been slain.

After a few minutes, Susan felt weariness spill over him like the snowflakes on his shoulders and in the damp hair on his chest. He shivered.

"We should go inside. Shouldn't we invite the others in, too? The ones who've lost their businesses and homes?"

He nodded, rubbing his cheek in her hair. "Yes. We'll make room for them all until other arrangements can be made."

"Hey! Look there!" someone shouted.

Logan turned with Susan in the direction people were pointing. On the rise where Main Street started sat four horsemen. The rising sun behind them stained their bronze skin with streaks of pink and pale yellow. Feathers stuck up from their braided hair. A thick cloud of smoke rolled across the street, obscuring them from view for a few seconds. When the smoke cleared, the Indians were gone.

"Now we know who started this fire!"

Susan whirled to see who had flung out such a quick verdict. Zeke Calhoun flashed a row of teeth that looked like a rotting picket fence. His glance made her aware that her robe had inched open to expose the thin, lacy front of her nightdress. Susan tugged the robe around her body and shivered against the man's leering regard. He turned on his heel and strode arrogantly toward the Bloody Bucket, followed by a knot of his faithful followers.

"I hate that man," Susan said, meaning every word.

"So do I, but he might be on to something."

"Logan, no! There's no proof of that! Those Creeks might have come into town to help us." She stared at him, silently begging him to side with her and not with a troublemaker like Calhoun.

He ran a hand down his face, smearing the black soot into lines of fatigue, and looked toward the wagon where his children waited dutifully. "Let's get the children in the house before they freeze to death out here."

Chapter 25

Trailing popcorn garlands behind her, Susan crossed the pressroom to the fir tree that Logan and Coonie had set up in the corner nearest the front windows. She wound the garland, situating it among the four others she'd already strung on the tree. Standing back, she ran a critical eye over the Christmas tree and decided one additional garland and a few more of her homemade paper angels should do the trick.

"And a star," she murmured. "I'll need to make some kind of star."

"Allow me," Logan said, striding into the office. "I'm good at cutting out stars. It used to be my contribution to the Christmas tree when I was growing up."

"Then by all means . . ." She extended a hand. "I've strung one more garland. I'll just go get it."

She went into the silent living quarters. It was almost ten at night and the children were fast asleep upstairs. As Christmas drew near—less than a week away—excitement was mounting. She and Logan had wrapped and hidden presents, and she'd spent most of the day planning her holiday menu. Casting a glance toward the office door to make sure Logan wasn't watching, she went to the kitchen cupboard and located the coffee tin. Prying off the lid, she wriggled her fingers through the beans until she felt the folded handkerchief, which she pulled out.

Glancing around once more to make sure she was alone, she unwrapped the handkerchief and once again appreciated the workmanship on the pocket watch she'd bought

335

for Logan. On top of the silver lid was an etching of a feather pen, and inside she'd had engraved: "The pen is mightier than the sword—To Logan, Love, Susan."

Smiling, she wrapped it again in her handkerchief and tucked it back into the coffee tin. Returning to the office, she found Logan bent over his desk with scissors and paper in hand.

"Do you think the town will decorate?"

"Doubt it," he mumbled, intent on his creation. He turned a square of paper this way and that, carving points.

"What about the other merchants? Are we the only ones putting up a tree?"

"The fire dampened the festive mood, I reckon."

"Yes . . . the fire." She went to the door and stepped out to look down the street where the aftermath of the fire was most evident.

Whole blocks of buildings had been demolished. Only chimneys and some walls stood against the night. The brisk wind carried the stench of ashes and charred wood. After the fire, they'd opened their home to those whose lives had gone up in smoke. As many as ten had stayed with them on makeshift cots and pallets. The last couple had moved out that morning.

"What do you think? Hey, Susan?"

"Yes, right here." She came back inside, closing the door against the winter wind. Her gaze lit on the paper star he held by one point. He'd cut out tiny stars in it, so that light peeked through. "That's lovely! How can we fix it to the tree?"

"Child's play," he assured her, then fastened it with paste to a couple of the wood splints he used to separate lines of lead type. Showing off his quick work, he then dragged a chair over to the tree and stood on it to reach the top. After a minute of trial and error, he nestled the star among the top branches. "How does it look?" he asked over his shoulder.

"Like Christmas," she said, thinking he resembled a boy with his hair tumbled onto his forehead and his eyes shining with humor. "I do believe this is your favorite time of year."

"You're right." He hopped down from the chair, grabbed up the last garland, and looped it around her shoulders, using it to haul her against him.

"Logan, you'll break it," she fussed.

"Only if you struggle." He bent lower to scoop a kiss from her lips. "We're so lucky, you know. It's a miracle this place didn't catch fire. That snow came in the nick of time."

"Yes, and it only fell long enough to put out the fire." She toyed with the buttons on his shirt, remembering how there had been no trace of the snowfall by noon the next day, only soggy, blackened lumber and earth. "It's about time we had a bit of luck."

"Amen." He nibbled and tickled the side of her neck, making her laugh lightly. "I'm glad everyone's gone—our guests, I mean." His hands moved to her hips, then over them, kneading gently. "Privacy is a wonderful thing between a willful man and a willing woman."

"I'm willing, am I?" She spread her hands on his chest, giving a teasing push.

"Still having your time?" he asked, his brows forming a bridge over his eyes.

"No." She unbuttoned the first button on his shirt. "Lucky you, I had a light one. Only lasted a couple of days, and then it didn't amount to much." She sensed his worry. "Because of the tension—you know, of Papa shooting at me and the fire and all."

"Well, it's been quite a week," he agreed, his chin hitting his chest as he observed her steady progress with his buttons. "Know what?"

"What?"

"This poor, burned-out town might get itself incorporated if some of the town fathers have their way."

"Incorporated? What's that mean?"

"It means Tulsa might become an honest-to-goodness, recognized city in the Territory."

She shared a smile with him, then parted his shirt and pressed her mouth to the hollow of his throat. His hands tightened on her rump and lurched against her in a suggestive way.

"There have been meetings about how to go about it, and the wheels have been turning," he whispered, his voice catching as her mouth grazed his right nipple. "Once a few of our problems are ironed out, we should get the nod from the governor himself."

"What problems?" she murmured against his rapidly warming skin.

"Oh, you know . . . the rowdies plowing through town . . . those Creeks squatting on the outskirts."

She swung her hair out of her eyes and cleared her mind. "The Creeks." Sighing, she gently disengaged herself from him and drew the popcorn garland off her shoulders. "You men just won't leave them be, will you?"

"We *men?* Sweetheart, the women in this town aren't too fond of those savages, either."

"Savages?" She turned to face him, leaving the garland hanging limply from a branch. "Will you listen to yourself, Logan? You know as well as I that they aren't savages. Their children go to school with Etta and Logan. The Perrymans and the Lindseys have Creek blood. Look at Tom Manygoats. Do you think he's a savage?"

"He's an exception. Those others live in town. They've joined our way of life. But the ones camped in their teepees and doing those dances night after night—that's not good for a growing town."

"Right. They're 'problems' you want to get rid of." She finished arranging the final garland, cautioning herself to curb her tongue. "I only hope you don't fall in with a bunch of hotheads."

"They say the Creeks started the fire."

"That's only a rumor. Nobody knows for sure how the fire started."

"But if they don't join us, if they insist on living in the past, then what are we expected to do? Anyway, nothing's been decided. We're only talking."

She faced him, slyness stealing over her along with a sense of justice. "Did you hear what you just said?"

"Yes."

"You said *we're* only talking."

"So?" He shoved his hands in his pockets and scowled at her. "What of it?"

"I thought you were attending those meetings as a spectator—as a reporter. Sounds to me like you're doing more than recording history—you're making it."

His eyes narrowed. "Ever since you and the children were attacked by those Creeks, I've found it hard to be impartial."

"We weren't—"

"Attacked," he bit out. "And quit denying it."

"They were drunk."

"Rape is rape, no matter if it's done drunk or sober."

"You don't know that's what they would have done."

His green eyes didn't miss an inch of her. "Yes, I *do* know. Any man can look at you and know what those young bucks would have done if Manygoats hadn't scared some sense into them."

She stared out the window, crossing her arms tightly to ward off her anger. "I have no respect for men who break their word of honor—whether it be to white men or Indians, it makes no difference."

"I never gave them my word."

"The government we stand for did that for us."

"Look, this Indian thing is more complicated than you know."

"Or deceptively simple."

"Susan . . ." His hands covered her shoulders, and he kissed her offered cheek. "Are we going to fuss and fume tonight? Is that what we're going to do?"

"I don't want to, but . . ." She looked him straight in the eye. "The newspaper will have to take a stand on the Indian issue. What will that be, Logan?"

His hands slipped away, and he stepped back. "Well, I can see it's going to be a long, cold night." He laughed, but without humor. "I'm going to urge the removal of the Indian camp, Susan. We can't be a civilized city with those renegades out there having their war dances and getting pickled on moonshine night after night."

"Why is their drunkenness more offensive than the white

men's? You don't blow your top about the cowboys down at the Bloody Bucket.''

"They don't menace my woman and children, either.''

"They would, given the chance,'' she returned hotly. "And you know it. A rowdy shot me, but you're not threatening any of them. Why are you picking on the Creeks? Because they're different, pure and simple.''

"They're different all right,'' he agreed, rubbing the back of his neck and shuffling his feet. "And if I ever find out who shot you, I'll beat the bejesus out of him. But that was an accident, Susan, which is more than I can say for your run-in with those Indians.''

"I don't want to lock horns with you, Logan, but this sneaking around and plotting against other families bothers me. It worries me to think what tragedies might come of it.''

"It's not as if I haven't given it some thought, Susan. I have, and I *still* think the town would be best served if the Creeks broke up camp. They can live like us or go to a reservation.''

She trailed a finger along the worktable where pages of the newspaper were created. "If you write such an editorial urging their removal, then let me write one asking for a peaceful solution.''

"My solution could be peaceful,'' he noted. "No one wants bloodshed, you know.''

"Is that why Zeke Calhoun is still in town? You know good and well he only stays where there's the scent of death in the air.''

"Okay, okay!'' He held up his hands, then swung them down to his waist. "Write your damned editorial. It won't hurt to run two opinions.''

"That's what freedom of the press is all about,'' Susan said. "You can edit my work, of course. Just as you edited that piece I did on the school meeting.''

"Why, thank you kindly, ma'am. It's generous of you to let me know what I'm allowed to do on my own newspaper.'' He sat at his desk and shuffled papers.

"Are you going to work now?''

"For a while, yes.''

"I've made you mad."

"No." His hands lay still on the desktop and he let his head drop back and closed his eyes. "No, Susan, I'm just tired of defending myself to you."

"Don't look at it like that, Logan. I'm not accusing you of . . . I don't expect you to—"

"If you're going to write an editorial, then get on it," he said, shutting her up as he bent over a news story. "I'll need it by tomorrow."

"You think it was wise to run both them editorials?" Coonie asked as he wiped printer's ink from his hands onto his smudged work apron.

Logan glanced over his shoulder at Coonie, then returned his attention to the advertisement he was piecing together. "Why not? Our newspaper is big enough for two different points of view."

"But hers don't make any sense. Women trip all over their feelings and make fools of themselves. All that bull about the Injuns having squatters' rights and how they're not hurting anybody—that's a pile of horseshit. How could she write that after they nearly scalped her and the little 'uns?"

"She has a generous heart." Logan stared into space, thinking he'd never said anything more true.

"They started that fire."

"Nobody's proved that," Logan pointed out, jolting himself with the realization that he'd changed his opinion at some point. He'd been certain the Creeks were behind the fire until— When had he changed his mind? A grim smile flitted over his mouth. Guess her point of view had more impact than I thought. Anyway, it made me think. "That's what a newspaper is supposed to do."

"What's that?" Coonie asked, coming to stand beside him.

"Hmmm?" For a few seconds, he was still lost in contemplation. "Oh, I was just thinking that one of a newspaper's functions is to present viewpoints and make people look inside themselves."

"I thought you were with us."

"With you how?"

"On the Injun problem."

"I just said there was no proof the Creeks started the fire." He leaned closer to the type he was arranging.

"We're not gonna let them Injuns ruin what we've built up."

"What do you think of this ad?" Logan asked, standing back to let Coonie have a look. "It's for that new gunsmith in town."

"Looks okay to me. I ought to invite him to the next meeting."

Logan sighed. "Pal, you've got a one-track mind." He slapped Coonie on the back. Untying his printer's apron and pulling it off over his head, Logan laughed at Coonie's consternation. He hung the apron on the hat tree with a shrug. "I'm going to see what Susan and the children are up to." He sniffed the air. "I believe I smell cookies baking."

Sure enough, as he entered the kitchen Susan was removing a flat of cookies from the oven. He admired the roundness of her hips as she bent over to reach inside the oven. She'd put on a pound or two, but it looked good on her; made her seem more mature, more womanly to his eyes. She straightened and turned, tray in hand. Her brows shot up when she spotted him.

"Right on time," she said, nodding to the treats. "You can sample one of these for me."

"One?" He shook his head. "Five or six."

"Logan, these are for Christmas."

"Three or four?"

She laughed. "Okay. Want some coffee with them?"

"Please." He turned a chair around and straddled it while he waited for her to serve him. "Where are the ragamuffins?"

"Down the street at the livery. They're fond of the blacksmith's children. He and his wife have seven, you know."

"Godamighty!" He shook his head. "Seven to raise up. That man would do well to learn some self-control."

She set a coffee cup and four cookies in front of him.

"Sometimes you make children sound like weights around a man's neck. Most people think of them as blessings."

The sharpness in her tone surprised him. "You have something to say to me, Susan?"

"No," she said flippantly.

He shrugged, figuring her courage had deserted her. "The town's talking about the editorials," he said around a mouthful of oatmeal cookie. "Coonie thinks it was dumb to run both of them."

"Mine, you mean. He thinks it was dumb to run mine."

"Well, yes." He shrugged. "He's got some old-fashioned ideas about women."

"He's not the only one."

"Is that another remark aimed at me?"

"I was only talking in general." She spooned dough onto the baking sheet.

"Good cookies."

"Thanks. My mother's recipe."

He sensed pain behind her words. "You miss her?"

"Oh, sometimes." She gave a little jerk of her head that wrenched his heart.

"I'm sorry for the trouble you had with them."

"I always thought I could go home . . . No matter what happened, I had somewhere to go."

"You still do."

"No, I don't think Papa will ever forgive me."

"I was thinking about here—with me . . . and the children." He waited, but she said nothing. "But you were thinking about when you leave here, you want somewhere to go."

"No, I was just talking . . ."

"You got plans to leave?"

"No, Logan." She sighed and shoved the baking tray into the oven, then added a few more sticks of wood to the fire. "I'm finally getting used to this contraption. Took me ages to figure out how to keep the heat even while I'm baking."

He started to tell her how her editorial had shaken some of his principles, but pride stopped the admission. Maybe if he trusted his feelings more he'd feel closer to her, he thought, watching her flutter around the kitchen like a butterfly. She'd decorated the place for Christmas with wreaths and holly and big red-velvet ribbons. The family Christmas tree stood in the living room, decked out with popcorn garlands, paper angels, and painted tin lids the children had made in school. It was more elaborate than the one up front in the office.

Home, he thought. It felt like it to him, but did it to Susan? Sometimes she seemed settled in, and other times she talked as if she might pack up and move on now that he and the children were dug in. Other times it seemed she was picking fights to keep him away from her. Like this damned Indian problem. Why should she embrace one side while he stood with the other? Did she really have such strong opinions about the Creeks, or was she just being obstinate and keeping him at arm's length? Come to think of it . . .

He rose slowly from the chair, realizing that he hadn't made love to her since she'd returned from Missouri. He came up behind her and cornered her between the dry sink and the dish cupboard. She turned, her arms folded against her breasts, her eyes questioning his motives.

"What's this?" she asked, breathless.

He nuzzled her hair. She smelled of flour and spice. "I'm testing the waters. This summer I'm going to teach you how to swim. You and the children."

"Logan . . ." She twisted and pushed at his shoulders. "I've got a lot to do. Tomorrow is Christmas Eve, and I promised the church I'd send over one of my fruitcakes, and I've got bread to bake and oh, yes, I want you or Coonie to take Mrs. Brewster a basket of food—Logan!" She angled her head away from his mouth. "Are you listening to me?"

"Not really," he admitted.

"Logan, please!" She stiffened, and her eyes told him she wasn't playing games.

"What's gotten into you lately? You've been acting like you don't want to get too close to me 'cause you might catch something."

"It's not you."

"What then?"

"It's just that . . ." She glanced around the holly-decked kitchen. "I've been blue . . . kind of melancholy, and I can't seem to shake it."

"What's this?" He pinched her chin between his finger and thumb and made her look at him. Tears shimmered in her dark eyes. "Is it this Indian thing?"

"No, not really." She sighed and closed her eyes. Tears made tracks down her cheeks. "It's several things . . . the fire and what happened back home." Her voice wavered and she looked up, eyes brimming. "I hate to think that I'll never see any of my family again."

"Then don't think it. Blood is thick, honey." He touched the end of his nose to hers. "Even when Catherine went and got herself with child and then ran off with a rolling stone like me, your folks didn't disown her. Give them time and they'll get over their anger."

"Mama might. Papa won't." She leaned her head against the wall. "You know, I thought for a while that I . . . well . . ." She wrinkled her nose. "Never mind. Stand back and let me get to work."

"That you what?" he asked, curious. "Tell me. Talk to me. It seems we haven't really talked in quite a spell."

She met his gaze. Hers was speculative, then she looked aside and heaved another sigh. "I thought I was pregnant."

He'd pushed away from her and spun on his heels before he could stop the reaction. Glancing back over his shoulder, he was ashamed when she nodded sagely.

"That's why we don't talk," she said, reaching for the batter bowl.

He chewed the inside of his cheek while he berated himself for making her think he couldn't stand the idea of having another child. It wasn't that . . . but he should be telling her. Why were the words sticking to the roof of his mouth like molasses?

"Susan, let me explain—"

"No need. You've made it clear more than once that you don't want to make a baby with me."

"It's not personal."

"Not personal?" She whirled to glare at him. "How can you say that? It's the most personal thing between a husband and wife. Of course, our marriage is none too steady, as you've pointed out, and there's no reason for us to pretend otherwise. You've always looked upon this as temporary—"

"Temporary? When did I—"

"—and so did I . . . at first," she charged on as if he hadn't spoken. "So a baby wouldn't do. I know that. You know that."

"Susan, hush a minute, will you?" He took hold of her upper arms and brought her up on tiptoe. "Good Lord! When you get wound up, you go off like a top."

"I'm sorry." She melted and he took her weight. "I'm sorry, but I was so disappointed when I wasn't pregnant. I'd been so sure. Ever since that day, I've felt unsettled."

"Like this morning," he reminded her.

"Yes. I guess I sampled too many of my own cookies and cakes yesterday," she said, reasoning away the bout of sickness she'd endured. "It passed quick enough."

He smoothed his hands over her silky hair, wanting to free it from its knot at the back of her head.

"And now the town is pointing the finger at the Creeks for every little thing," Susan explained. "Mrs. Lindsey told me she saw some rowdies hanging around the bank earlier the night of the fire. She thinks *they* might have set it."

"Why would they start a fire?"

"Because they weren't paid all they thought they were due. Their employer had cheated them out of full wages because the longhorns they'd brought in were underweight."

"Who told you this?"

"Mrs. Lindsey, the schoolteacher. She knows everything that goes on in this place."

"She's also part Creek."

"And the other part of her is white," Susan said, tipping up her chin defiantly. "Which makes her a sight more impartial than you or me."

He chuckled and passed his thumbs beneath her eyes

where the skin looked bruised. "Right you are, sweetheart." He laughed again when her eyes widened. "Surprised that I'd admit such a thing? Believe it or not, Susan, I think you've got a good head on those pretty shoulders." He kissed the slope of her neck. "Why don't you take a break from baking and stretch out on the bed—with me?"

"The cookies . . . I can't . . . They'll burn."

The back door slammed shut, sounding like cannonfire. Both Logan and Susan jumped, then turned to see Jacob, his green eyes reflecting wild alarm.

"What's wrong, partner?" Logan asked, moving toward him.

"N-nothing. Etta's still at the livery."

"Why aren't you?"

"I d-decided to come h-home." Jacob edged toward the stairs. "I wanna play with my blocks."

"Okay." Logan grabbed his son's coat collar before he could dash upstairs. "Did something happen, Jacob? You look a little rattled. You haven't been fighting, have you?"

"No, Papa."

Logan studied the boy's solemn face. "You're sure?"

"Yes, Papa."

Taking pity on him, he let go of Jacob's collar and patted his silky hair. "Go on, then." When he turned toward Susan again, she was removing the tray of cookies from the oven. A grin overtook him. "How about resting for a few minutes?"

"I'm not that tired."

"Me, either." He caught the tails of her apron sash and yanked. The bow slipped loose and the apron fell to the floor. Susan gasped, then shook a finger at him. The action didn't deter him in the least. "We'll take a grown-up's rest."

"What's that?" she asked, then laughed as he pulled her with him into the bedroom.

"That's what my aunt used to call it when she and my uncle closed the bedroom door in the middle of the day," he explained, shutting the door and dropping one eyelid in a cunning wink. "Those rests always put a smile on their faces. I could use a smile.'' He trailed his fingertips along her arms. "Couldn't you?"

Her arms stole around his neck. "If anyone can make me smile, it's you."

He started to tell her that one smile from her was worth the world's riches to him, but the sweetness of her breath wafted over his face and he bowed to his yearnings. Her lips softened under his, and her tongue, bolder with each encounter, caressed the inside of his lips and feathered the roof of his mouth.

For a moment, he thought he might keel over, then hot desire pumped through his veins and filled him with purpose. Still kissing her, he wiggled from his shirt and unfastened his trousers. The aching grew, pooling between his legs. He shoved and pushed his way out of his trousers and underwear, then helped her undress. A couple of buttons came loose and flew across the room.

"Christ, I'm sorry, Susan," he muttered, then grinned when he saw she was laughing. "Can't you for once wear a dress with fewer than fifty buttons on it?"

"You want me to tailor my clothes to suit your ways, do you?"

He gripped her by the waist and swung her up, around, and down onto the bed. She gasped with delight. He drove his fingers through her hair and plucked pins from it. She moved against him, rubbing all his sensitive places, making him hard, putting the spurs to his pulse.

Sunlight and shadow dappled her skin. He kissed a sunlit breast and then a shadowed hipbone. He traced her curves with trembling hands and realized he adored the gentle swell of her hips and the budding plumpness of her breasts. Small breasts, but he loved them. Loved the way they fit so perfectly in his palms and how the nipples felt like sun-kissed pebbles. Yes, they'd made quite an impression. For the life of him, he couldn't remember what any other breasts had looked like. And he'd fondled his share. But he couldn't remember them . . . didn't want to . . .

Wrapping strands of her hair around his fingers, he angled her head to one side so that his mouth could take every bit of hers. His tongue imitated the act his arousal strained for, riding against her soft belly. He had little control over it. That was part of the excitement.

Her dark, fathomless eyes told him she wanted him inside her and he complied, driving up and up until he was fully buried in the moist warmth of his woman. Her fingers flexed against his shoulders, kneading and caressing. Her mouth flirted with his. She rained kisses across his collarbone and neck. Her teeth sank into his earlobe. A small bite, but mighty. He felt his erection give a kick and then the sexual seizure came over him, moving his hips, grinding his pelvis, creating harsh sounds in his throat.

"Don't leave me . . . don't . . . don't . . . Stay right there," she murmured, her hands skimming down his body to clutch his buttocks.

He had no intention of leaving. Ever since that time when he'd let her overrule his good intentions, he'd gloried in the ultimate sensation of lovemaking. His release came in spurts and grunts. He wanted to murmur sweet nothings in her ear and stroke her insides with slow thrusts, but his romantic intentions were paltry in the face of his blazing passion.

Smoothing her damp hair from her temples and forehead, he kissed her gently and hoped that made up for the words he hadn't said. She sighed and curled onto her side, fitting herself against him, snuggling in his arms.

"I'm smiling," she whispered. "Are you?"

"Ear to ear." And he was. God, it felt good.

"It'll be a wonderful Christmas. I probably won't even get homesick much. Even if I do, it's expected. Mrs. Brewster said Christmas was the worst time for a woman away from her people for the first time. But with you and the children and Coonie . . . I'll be fine. Probably won't have a minute to think about Missouri."

He squeezed her shoulders and kissed the top of her head. He'd bought her a fancy bonnet for Christmas and had had a dozen Irish linen handkerchiefs embroidered with her initials and his intertwined, but now he worried the gifts weren't enough. What could he buy this woman that would be equal to the joy she'd brought to his life? Was there such a gift to be bought in the town of Tulsa?

Remembering the sadness in her face when she'd told him she had thought she was pregnant but hadn't been, his heart swelled painfully and he knew he had to make her understand that his reluctance to have another child had nothing to do with any doubts about her.

"Susan, about children . . . you've got to understand why I've been . . . well, careful." He sighed and stared at the ceiling long enough to collect his thoughts and choose his words. "I don't ever want to be in a marriage with a woman who is staying with me only because she's had children. That's what Catherine and I had, and it was hell—unfair to both of us. I want you to be sure you want to keep me for a husband before you take me as a father for your children." He waited, but she said nothing. Was she crying, smiling, rolling her eyes in exasperation? *What?* He raised his head to peer down at her face, then his head dropped back to the feather mattress.

She was sound asleep.

Chapter 26

"**H**ow will Santa get in if the doors are locked?" Etta asked, fretful lines appearing between her eyes.

Logan smoothed the lines away with his fingertips and sat on the edge of her bed. "He touches his finger to his nose and poof! He becomes as small as your thumb. That way he can slip into keyholes or under doors or down chimneys. Don't worry. He'll find a way inside."

"Hope he brings me my train engine," Jacob mumbled from under the covers.

Logan kissed Etta, then went to sit on his son's bed. Pulling the covers down so he could see Jacob's face, Logan kissed his forehead. "Train engine, huh? That's a pretty nice gift. Think you were a good enough boy to earn it?"

"I think so."

Logan grinned. "So do I."

Jacob's smile revealed missing teeth.

"Got any loose teeth in there?"

"One." Jacob touched a gentle fingertip to one of his eyeteeth. "This one is kinda loose."

"Now don't go losing those teeth. You keep them in that jar I gave you. If you drop one on the ground and a dog steps on it, you'll grow a dog's tooth. If a horse steps on it, you'll grow a horse's tooth." He barely kept from laughing when Jacob's eyes widened with horror. "That's what my folks always told me anyway."

"You ever see someone with horse teeth?"

351

Logan thought for a few moments. "Yes. My primary school teacher had a mouthful of them. I swear she did. Old Miss Anderson." He shook his head, recalling the woman's horsey face. Jacob pulled the covers back over his head. "Hey there, why are you acting like a mole here of late? You never slept with the covers pulled over your face before." Logan tugged the covers back down. He saw fear in his son's face. "Listen, partner, what I told you about your teeth—well, you shouldn't get all scared about that."

"I'm not scared . . . about that." He chewed his lower lip. "My teeth will grow back, won't they? I won't have teeth like that mean man—Calhoun?"

"Your teeth with grow back," Logan assured him. "Has Calhoun been bothering you again, Jacob?"

"Not me. He didn't see me at the stables yesterday."

"Yesterday?" Logan braced a hand on either side of Jacob's body. "What happened? You saw him?"

"Uh-huh. He was with Uncle Coonie."

"Coonie? What the hell was he doing with Coonie?"

"They're gonna pay the Indians tonight."

"Pay the Indians . . ." Logan shook his head, then it all fell into place. "Jacob, did they say pay the Indians or pay *back* the Indians?"

"Pay back, that's it."

"Oh, hell." Logan stood up and wished Coonie was around so he could kick his ass.

"Something wrong, Papa? I don't like that Calhoun man. He always stares funny at me. Why is Uncle Coonie his friend?"

"They aren't friends—I hope." He patted Jacob's cheek. "Go to sleep so Saint Nick can come around with your goodies." He tucked the covers around Jacob's shoulders. "And don't cover your head. Nothing's going to happen to you. I won't let it."

"Okay. Papa. G'night."

"Night-night." Logan dimmed the lantern but let it stay at a glow to chase shadows into the corners. "I love you. Both of you." Then he moved silently across the room and down the stairs. Susan was out caroling with some of the other women in town. He thought about leaving a note, then told himself he'd be back soon enough. Finding Coonie and boxing his ears wouldn't take long. If nothing else, he could warn the Creeks that trouble was afoot. He strapped on his gunbelt and prayed he wouldn't have to use the heavy Colt.

It took only a few minutes to saddle his horse and point it out of town. As he rode toward the river, he heard the sweet notes produced by the carolers and imagined he could pick out Susan's voice from the others.

The night was bright with stars and crisp with winter's chill. It pinched his cheeks and dried his lips as he galloped to the outskirts of town. As the horse topped the rise, Logan caught the faint smell of smoke, but he told himself it was from campfires. But soon the smoke became visible, curling among tree trunks. The horse nickered, his ears standing straight up and his nostrils flaring.

"Easy, boy," Logan crooned, trying to settle the animal. The road forked, and Logan reined his mount to the left. After another quarter of a mile, he saw flames dancing among slender trees. "Oh, Christ!" He dug his heels into the horse's sides, and the nervous gelding stretched into a bumpy run.

Too late, too late, he thought, his gut beginning to churn with anxiety. Screams rent the air. Some were chopped in half. Some died to wails. Each one tore at Logan's heart. What have they done? He leaned over the horse's neck, and its mane stroked his face.

The scene ahead was nightmarish, made more so by the bobbing torches held by running, shouting men. Guns popped. Arrows whizzed. Rifles barked death. The screaming fear of women and children fell on Logan like hailstones. Then he caught sight of a shock of white hair and apple cheeks. Coonie.

"Coonie, you damned idiot," he said, cursing a blue streak as he wrestled for control of the horse beneath him. The fire was spooking the gelding and making his eyes roll white. Reining the horse to a prancing halt, Logan sprang from the saddle and ran toward his friend. He drew the Colt from its holster in an instinctive gesture of self-defense.

"Coonie!"

The wind snatched away his voice. It whipped the fires to a frenzy, and the teepees went up in cones of flame and smoke. Shadows fled across the ground. The light was so inconstant that it was impossible to tell the shadows from the people who cast them. Logan smelled blood; he tasted fear. Mainly, he shook with rage. There had been talk of retaliation, but he'd thought the saner voices had overruled such folly. What in the hell were they thinking of, coming out here and setting fire to these teepees and shacks where women and children huddled from the cold?

A ball of flame illuminated a patch of darkness, and Logan recognized the feathered derby and flying braids of Tom Manygoats. Cupping his hands to his mouth, Logan called out to the Indian, but the other noises drowned out his voice. He started toward Manygoats, seeing that he was unarmed. Just like the crazy Creek, Logan thought, automatically moving in a crouch so as not to attract stray bullets. Where was Manygoats's Winchester now that he really needed it? Logan wondered. Manygoats, with nothing but a stern frown, stood tall and proud like an oak tree facing a forest fire. A puff of smoke wafted from the man's chest and he stumbled backward, his big hands coming up to clutch the smoking buckskin. For a few moments, Logan couldn't understand what he'd witnessed. Only when Manygoats fell to his knees and then pitched forward did Logan comprehend that the defenseless Indian had been gunned down.

"Oh, no." It was a gasping sound, a cry of remorse. Logan raced to the fallen Creek, his feet hardly touching the ground. "Tom? Tom!" He grabbed the back of his buckskin shirt and used all his strength to roll Manygoats into his lap. Gray eyes stared lifelessly at Logan. "Oh, God. No, not this man. Not this one." He thought of Susan. She'd just lost a treasured friend because of a groundless rumor. He looked around at the flaming hell and the work of devils. Shame enveloped him, and he wanted to scream at the others—scream until they stopped this massacre.

A toddler, no more than three, waddled near Logan, rubbing his sloe eyes with dimpled fists and sobbing for his mother. Logan reached out to the pitiful child.

"Here, baby. Come here." Logan let Manygoats's body slide to the cold ground and reholstered his gun. He came up on one knee, hands outstretched to grab the distraught child. If a bullet hit this poor angel, Logan knew he'd go absolutely berserk.

Several Creek women came running toward him. Logan scooped up the child and thrust him into one of the women's arms.

"Here, take this one," he said, seeing fear glitter in their eyes. "Now go this way. My horse is back there." He pointed to it. "See? Take it. Get away from here. Run!" He gave each a push, sending them in the right direction, away from the torch-waving madmen.

A young boy staggered near him, his eyes glazed with shock, his handsome face streaked with soot. Logan gripped him by the shoulders and aimed him away from the flaming village. A round-faced Indian woman grasped the boy's hand and pulled him away from Logan, but her eyes reflected that she understood Logan wasn't the enemy.

Past the boy and the woman who'd taken charge of him, in the dim distance, Logan caught a glimpse of blue metal. His sixth sense told him it was a gun and that an itchy finger was closing on its trigger.

"No!" Logan lurched to his feet and shoved the two Indians aside, into the shelter of some waist-high brush.

Zeke Calhoun stepped from the shadows, his glittering eyes and deadly gun trained on Logan.

"Injun lover," Calhoun shouted above the din. "I always knew it. I can spot a red-meat lover a mile away."

Logan flapped a hand at the posturing hired gun. "Big man," he taunted. "Shooting women and children takes such bravery."

"You protect these heathens, then you die with them," Calhoun yelled, straightening his gun arm and taking deadly aim, then pulling the trigger.

Fire blossomed in Logan's belly. He heard a familiar voice call his name. As he wilted to the ground, driven there by the flames in his gut, he saw Coonie, his face distorted with rage as he raised a rifle and squeezed off a round.

"You sonofabitch! You shot him on purpose," Coonie screamed. "I saw you, you bastard!"

"Damned right," Calhoun shouted back. "He's fighting against us, or hadn't you noticed?"

"I'm shot," Logan said in wonder as he looked down at the dark stain above his belt. He grabbed at his midsection to keep the blood from pouring out in buckets. It painted his hands, making them warm and sticky.

Calhoun raised his gun again, pointing it at Logan. "Now I'll finish what I started."

But an explosion sent Calhoun stumbling backward as Coonie's next shot slammed into his shoulder.

"Sonofabitch!" Calhoun tried to point his gun at Coonie, whose rifle still smoked. "You're as cr-crazy as Vance. I'll k-kill you, too, you dumb—"

Another bark from Coonie's rifle cut off the rest. The last thing Logan saw clearly was Zeke Calhoun reeling toward the firelight. His clothes were dotted with crimson, and he had a black hole in the middle of his forehead. Then he pitched forward, dead before he hit the ground.

After a moment, Coonie's face swam above Logan like a whiskered moon.

"Logan, I'm sorry," Coonie whispered. "I never thought Calhoun would . . . Hell, he was nuts, wasn't he? But I took care of him. Christ! You're not gonna die on me, too, are you?"

"You stupid bastard," Logan mumbled, his tongue feeling like a flap of leather in his mouth. "Blood . . . everywhere, blood. Shame on you." Coonie's tears splashed onto his face.

"Logan, I'm home!" Susan went from room to room, then upstairs to check on the children. Both were asleep, but she dropped kisses on their rosy cheeks anyway.

Downstairs again, she looked for a clue to Logan's whereabouts, but she found none. Worry set in though she tried to deny it. He was a grown man and didn't have to inform her of every move he made, she told herself. Still, it was odd that he hadn't even left a note.

The ringing of the cowbell above the front door made her sigh with relief. He was home!

"Logan, where in the world did you—" Susan skidded to a stop just inside the pressroom. Logan was slung over Coonie's shoulder like a sack of feed. Another man stood in the office, leather bag in hand—the town doctor. "What happened?" she asked, surprisingly calm as a numbness stole over her. "Is he dead?"

"No," Coonie said, shouldering past her into the living quarters. "Logan needs the doctor bad."

Relief hit her, and she slumped against the wall. "He's alive," she whispered to herself, comforting her poor, pounding heart. "He's still alive." She breathed deeply and patted her cheeks to revive herself. To keep from fainting, she forced one foot in front of the other until she found the others in the bedroom.

"Who shot him?"

"Zeke Calhoun," Coonie said, letting Logan fall onto the bed. The springs sang out as Logan bounced before settling in limp unconsciousness. "That snaggle-toothed sonofabitch."

The doctor cleared his throat and glowered at Coonie. "Watch your language, French. The lady sure doesn't need that kind of talk from you. This man's your husband?' he asked, glancing at Susan.

"Y-yes."

"Are you going to faint, young woman?"

"No." She sat in the upholstered chair, just in case. "At the Bloody Bucket? Is that where it happened? No . . . no, it's closed tonight. We passed it caroling, and it was shut up for the holidays."

The doctor tore Logan's shirt, ripping it off his body. Susan pressed her fist into her mouth to keep from crying out. She turned her face away and shut her eyes, telling herself the wound wasn't as bad as it looked, like sure death. Big, gaping, flesh curling, entrails showing red and blue and waxy white. The stench of gunpowder and burned skin vanquished the bedroom's scents of lavender and spice.

"Bullet's still in there," the doctor mumbled, then spoke more clearly to Susan. "Can you get me a pan of hot water and some wide pieces of cloth, young woman?"

"Yes. Yes, I can do that." She forced herself up from the chair. Her feet felt as if they were weighted with irons, but she was glad to do something besides swallow over and over again to keep from vomiting. When she reached the dry sink, she held on to the edge and released the contents of her stomach. Her muscles quivered and her insides felt shivery and raw. She rinsed out the sink and poured hot water from the kettle into a pan. Wide cloth . . . wide cloth . . . wide . . . She went to the linen hamper and pulled out a stack of printer aprons she'd laundered and ironed.

"Here's the water and cloth," she said, handing them to Coonie. Something in his expression bothered her. He looked embarrassed, but why should he be? Still, he couldn't seem to meet her eyes.

"Got some whiskey around here?"

"I do," Coonie said. "I'll get it."

"Bring a couple of bottles."

"Okay." Coonie hurried to fetch the whiskey, his head bowed, his gaze shifting away from Susan as he passed her.

Gradually, the shock wore off, and Susan's insides stopped churning. She crossed to the bed. Logan's face was white, and his stubbled beard looked inky-black in contrast. Black smeared his forehead, too. She wiped through it with two fingers and then examined her fingertips, rubbing them with the pad of her thumb. Soot. She sniffed the sir. The smell of smoke wafted from Logan's hair and clothing.

"Was he in a fire?"

"Guess so," the doctor said, paying her little attention

as he bathed the wound and wiped away dried, crusty blood.

"In town?"

"Here's the whiskey." Coonie uncorked one bottle and set the other on the bedside table.

"Splash some of it over this wound," the doctor ordered, and Susan retreated to the chair again.

She turned her head away, unable to watch. Logan looked so pale, so lifeless. He didn't seem to be breathing . . . He chose that moment to moan, then gave a loud, rasping gasp. Despite her queasiness, Susan whipped her head around to see what had provoked him. She was glad the doctor was blocking her view of the wound. The doctor had rolled up his shirtsleeves and his elbows poked the air as he investigated the wound with sharp, probing instruments from his black bag. Coonie pinned Logan to the bed, no small feat as Logan thrashed and tried to escape the pain.

"You're hurting him," Susan said, then realized how stupid she must sound. Have to get the bullet out, she told herself. It'll be over soon. She fastened her hands over her ears to keep from hearing Logan's grunts and groans. Unable to bear it, she stood and walked off her nerves and fears and questions. Back and forth, back and forth, she stepped off the width of the bedroom, keeping her eyes away from the struggle going on in her bed. A bed she shared with Logan—a bed where pleasure had lived. Now it was a bed of bloody pain.

Finally, the doctor chuckled and pulled a lump of metal from the bloody pool, brandishing it before dropping it into the pan. "Get me some fresh water, will you?" he asked, glancing at Susan. "And don't pass out now. The worst is over, young woman."

"Thank God." She picked up the pan and took it with her to the kitchen. Tossing out the red water, she refilled the pan and returned to the bedroom.

The doctor was preparing to suture. "Douse that hole with whiskey again and then make him take a long drink," he instructed Coonie.

"I think he's blacked out again, Doc."

"Hmmm?" The reed-thin doctor peered into his patient's face. "So he has. Well, take a drink yourself then. We'll be all done in a few minutes. I can stitch up a tear in no time a'tall." He glared at Susan from under bushy eyebrows. "Put the pan down on the table. It looks bad, but he's going to live."

Susan did as she was told but couldn't wrench her gaze from the ragged hole to the right of Logan's navel, made larger by the doctor's hunt for the slug. Ignoring the doctor's grimace of irritation, she reached out to push Logan's hair from his eyes.

"Logan?" she whispered, her heart beginning to beat normally again, sending warmth to her ice-cold extremities. "Logan, it's Susan. You're going to be fine, sweetheart. The doctor says so."

"That's right, now move aside," the doctor said gruffly, shouldering her away from the bed. "Let me at him."

Standing at the foot of the bed, Susan searched Coonie's face for an indication of what had landed Logan in such a mess. Coonie still kept his gaze stubbornly away from her. He's feeling guilty, Susan thought with a slight nod. He and Logan have been up to something underhanded.

"Coonie, where was this fire you two were in? I've been all over town tonight caroling, and I didn't see any trouble."

She might have been talking to a wall for all the response she got.

"I did notice there weren't a lot of men around tonight. The other ladies noticed, too. Husbands who were supposed to be home weren't home. It's not like Logan to leave the children without an adult in the house."

Coonie had been struck deaf.

"Doctor, do you know anything about how this happened?" Susan asked.

"Happened out of town, didn't it?" the doctor asked, directing his question to Coonie. "When you came looking for me, you said something about him getting caught in the middle of a gunfight."

"Gunfight?" Susan repeated. "Who drew on him? Was Logan carrying a—" That's when she saw the gunbelt buckled around Logan's hips. The gun had been removed. Glancing around, Susan spotted it lying on top of a trunk shoved in a corner. "Where did he go wearing that?" she asked, pointing to the weapon.

The doctor seemed interested in Coonie's answer, pausing in his sewing to await the response. Coonie frowned, shrugging his round shoulders.

"That's not an answer," Susan said.

Footsteps sounded through the house, and Susan whirled to see one of the banker's sons come charging into the bedroom. His eyes were wide like a hunted animal's as he stared past Susan to the doctor.

"Doc, you gotta come."

"I'm busy here. What's wrong, boy?"

"People are dying out there . . . some are back in town. My pa sent me. He's okay, but he says Mr. Treadmore and Mr. Beauchamp are shot and need you. They're in a buckboard outside. The others are still out there. I hear that even some of the women are hurt bad."

The doctor cut the thin, black thread and tied it expertly, finishing off the suturing. "What's been going on? Did rowdies bust into town and do all this shooting? Did some gang of outlaws do some shoot-'em-up outside of town?"

"No, sir," the boy said, rocking from one foot to the other in an anxious dance.

"Young woman, you can finish up here. Keep the wound covered. I'll be around in a few days to check on him, but if he gets a fever that lasts more than a day, come get me. Wrap one of those clean rags around him," he said, pointing to the aprons. "I'm leaving this for you to use when you dress the wound. Change the dressings every day." He tossed some medicine onto the table, then confronted the boy. "Well? What's been going on?"

"They raided the Indians," the boy announced, his blue eyes skittering to Coonie, then back to the doctor. "Paid them back for burning out some of the merchants. But lots of people got killed and hurt bad." The boy nodded to Logan. "He ain't the only one. My pa says the Creeks are bad off—most are dead, I reckon."

The doctor snapped his bag shut and grunted with disgust. "So that's what our high-minded Christians have been up to on this eve of the holiest day." He made a shooing motion, sending the boy ahead of him. "Get. Show me the way, boy. I'll take care of the ones outside first, then I'll go check on the Creeks, though I don't imagine they'll want my help." The doctor paused to knife Coonie with the sharpness of his tone. "For some reason, they're getting to hate the sight of white men."

When the last two were gone, Susan rounded on Coonie, her hands gathered into fists at her sides.

"You two couldn't rest until you'd slaughtered them, could you? Women and children! You and Logan gunned down women and children!" She brought her fists to her mouth, afraid she might vomit again as she stared in horror at the man she'd trusted with Etta and Jacob.

"That ain't true," Coonie said, his blue eyes filling with tears. "We didn't gun down no mamas and their babies. No, ma'am. That wasn't the plan. We were only gonna burn some of their teepees, but some of their hot-tempered braves come running at us with tomahawks and throwing knives, so what was we supposed to do? We had to fire on 'em."

"You didn't have to go there in the first place," Susan charged. "You don't know they had anything to do with the town fire. You're only a bunch of scared, gutless men flapping your lips about nothing!"

"Them Creeks were seen in town the night the place went up in flames. You saw them on their horses right after."

"I saw you there, too. Maybe you started the fire. Zeke Calhoun was there. Maybe he did it."

Coonie winced and glanced at Logan. "It was Zeke who shot Logan. The bastard."

Susan laid a hand across her eyes for a few moments to assimilate the information that was coming too fast, too disjointedly. "I should go out there and see if I can help. I'll find Tom Manygoats and . . . what?" She'd seen something pass over Coonie's face. Something she didn't like. When Coonie started to turn aside, she grabbed a handful of his shirt and gave a yank that tore it at the shoulder seam. "What are you hiding? Something about Tom?"

"He's dead, Susan." Coonie pulled away from Susan's touch and examined his ripped shirt. "Zeke shot him, I think. There was so much going on, and it was dark and smoky."

"Tom . . . Not Tom Manygoats."

Coonie nodded. "Some of ours got killed, too. It got way out of hand."

"Some of *ours?*" she repeated, astonished. "Speak for yourself."

"You should dress Logan's wound," he said, laying a hand just above the puckered skin. "Man, he feels hot. Must have a fever."

Christmas Eve, Susan thought, staggering back as if she were living a nightmare. It's Christmas Eve, and it's supposed to be a wonderful night full of gingerbread and Saint Nick and warm embraces, and instead we're caught in the middle of this horror. Logan and Coonie went hunting for humans on Christmas Eve!

"You gonna dress this wound?" Coonie asked, giving her a quizzical look as she continued to retreat from the room.

"Dress it yourself. You two are as thick as thieves, so you do it!" She spun away and went into the living room where the Christmas tree seemed out of place. Upstairs the children dreamed of wrapping paper and ribbons, while downstairs Susan was just beginning to grieve for a gentle friend named Manygoats.

Voices from outside drifted to her, and she walked into the office where she could see onto Main Street. The doctor squatted in the buggy, administering to other wounded. Horses and riders galloped past. Women ran along the boardwalk. Lights glowed in all the windows. The news swept through town, killing the Christmas spirit and disturbing the slumber of the innocent.

"Logan, how could you have done this?" she whispered. She wanted to go to the Creek settlement and help them if she could, but she was afraid to leave Jacob and Etta.

A strong maternal current ran through her, and in a haze of shock and grief, she managed to gather the hidden presents and place them under the tree. She and Logan had planned to do it together, but he'd had other plans he hadn't told her about, she thought with a heavy heart.

A few hours before dawn, Susan went upstairs to the children's room and slept fitfully in the rocking chair.

Chapter 27

Maybe someone had a pleasant Christmas in Tulsa, but Susan couldn't imagine it.

The day dawned cold and bleak. The excitement Jacob and Etta felt when they saw that Saint Nick had visited ended abruptly when they were told that their papa had been shot and was in bed.

The rest of the day was spent in quiet anger. Susan forced the children to sit for dinner and eat. No one had any appetite. Coonie didn't even join them for Christmas dinner, and Susan didn't beg him to change his mind. Just looking at him made her temper boil. She gave a sketchy account to the children of what had happened to Logan, leaving out the despicable parts. When she delivered the bad news about Tom Manygoats, both children sat in her lap and comforted her. The feel of Jacob's little hand patting her back and Etta's chubby arms squeezing her neck in a sympathetic hug sent sweet, aching love through her.

On the day after Christmas the town buried its dead. The Creeks began their period of mourning. Susan insisted on writing an account of the raid by the townspeople and spent two days interviewing witnesses. Coonie didn't want to publish her story, but she stubbornly went ahead and set it in type herself, then positioned it prominently on the front page. In a tense standoff, she waited in the pressroom until Coonie finally inked the front page and printed a proof of it for her to read, edit, and approve. Nothing was said between them, but Susan knew she'd made it clear to

Coonie that, with Logan laid up, she was now editor-in-chief.

Adding that title to her list of activities was a blessing because she now had no time to think, no time to dwell on the extreme disappointment she nurtured in her heart. She left Logan to Coonie, although she did check in on him once or twice and fed him three meals a day. If he noticed her cool attitude toward him, he kept it to himself. Susan suspected that Coonie had told Logan that she was furious with both of them because Logan was noticeably grateful for every little thing she did for him.

She slept in his bachelor bed in the pressroom and grieved for the end of her loving days and nights.

The newspaper issue she supervised sold out and required an additional printing, providing the only bright spot in a long week of regrets and grief.

On New Years's Eve, the town was still respectfully quiet. Susan had sent Jacob and Etta outside to clean the henhouse and horse stalls while she tidied up the front office and answered business correspondence she'd allowed to pile up. Submerged in the work, she gave a strangled cry when a hand landed on her shoulder. Whirling around in the desk chair, she was amazed to see Logan.

"What are you doing out of bed?" she demanded, standing up and grabbing him by the elbow and forearm to drag him back to the bedroom.

"Hold on," he said, gently swatting aside her hands. "I'm tired of lying there looking at the ceiling. It's time I stretched my legs." He'd pulled on his trousers and shirt, but hadn't buttoned the latter. Slipping one hand inside, he covered the bandaged area in a protective gesture. "What were you doing before I scared the life out of you?"

"Answering the mail," she answered crisply. "We received a dozen more subscriptions this week."

"A dozen, huh? That's good."

"Yes, everyone wants to read about blood and tears," she said stiffly as she faced the desk again and resumed the letter she'd been writing. "Even the governor wants last week's issue and sent money for a year of mailed newspapers. I'm writing him now, explaining the process and how the newspapers will be a week old by the time he gets them.''

"He probably already knows that."

She sighed. "Do you want to handle this now? Are you feeling up to going back to work? I certainly don't mind turning it all back over to you if that's what—''

"Whoa there." His hand grazed her cheek, but she moved out of reach. "I'm not saying you aren't doing a good job because you are. I was just commenting. No need to get all steamed." He sat on the edge of the desk. "I want to thank you for taking care of me and my newspaper."

His appreciation made her temper simmer. She wanted to tell him she hadn't done any of it for him. She'd been thinking of Etta and Jacob and her own self-interest. After all, she'd been as much a part of establishing *The Democrat Argus* as anyone else.

"By the way, I'm fit enough to be a bed partner again instead of a patient. You don't have to sleep out here again tonight." He stroked her hair with the backs of his fingers, then scowled when she jerked away. "What's wrong?"

"What's wrong?" she asked, incredulous. "How can you ask such a question? Do you think a soft touch will make me lose my memory? No. You won't shut me up with kisses this time, Logan Vance."

His deep-set eyes regarded her with a mixture of dismay and pain. "I'm not trying to shut you up. I'm trying to thank you and make amends."

"Amends," she said, scoffing at such a notion.

"That's right. Coonie says you're angry, and I don't blame you. I'm mad as hell, just like you."

"Why, because you got shot?"

"Well, yes. That and—''

She pushed back her chair and stood to face him. Her lower lip trembled, and she wished she could control her angry tears, but she couldn't. "Tom Manygoats is dead."

"I know. I saw him take a bullet in the heart. He died instantly." He bowed his head. "I'm sorry, Susan."

"You sure are," she agreed. "You're sorry and you're dishonorable and I deserve better."

"Dishon—" His teeth snapped together on the rest of the word. For a few moments he said nothing, just stared at her before looking off to one side. The muscles along his strong jawline flexed. "I know you're upset about Manygoats—"

"You're damned right. What hurts more is that you're one of the reasons he's dead."

"Me?" He stared at her as if she were the guilty one.

"Yes, you!" Leaning into his face, she itched to slap it. "Are you going to apologize for that as well? Do you think mere words can undo the wrongs you've committed? You have no shame, do you? No shame, no conscience, no honor."

He slid off the desk to stand tall and look down at her. "You Armitages always leap to think the worst of me."

"And quit talking that way about my family. I don't slur yours, do I?"

"If you're so certain my heart is as black as sin and that your family is so high-thinking, then why don't you go back to them?"

"Maybe I should!"

"Go!" Logan said, whirling to face her again and sending one hand up in a shooing motion that stung her more than a sharp slap would have. "Go and good riddance!" He winced and laid a hand over the square bandage. Griping the edge of the slanted table, he seemed to take a few moments to garner enough strength to stand on his own again. "Go back to them," he said, his voice dipping to low, rough tones. "If you think so badly of me, then get the hell out of my life." He laughed harshly, bitterly. "You know, I thought you loved me, trusted me, but it was all my imagination."

"And I thought you were a man of—"

"You've said quite enough!" he yelled, then closed his eyes slowly, deliberately, as if he were warding off a spasm of pain. "Quite enough." When he opened his eyes again, Susan was startled to see the sheen of tears. Was his wound paining him so, or could it be that he was deeply ashamed of his actions? Did he regret what he'd done??

"Logan, why did you do it? You never liked Calhoun, so why did you follow him out there with the rest of them?"

One side of his mouth twitched and his lower lip trembled slightly—so slightly that Susan wasn't sure she'd seen it. He cleared his throat and shook his head in a stubborn way that told her he was finished talking. Pushing away from the table's support, he moved from the pressroom with stiff, shortened steps.

Susan slumped into the desk chair, then dropped her face into her hands. What would she do on her own? She couldn't go back to the farm, and Logan knew it. Logan said he didn't want her, and she didn't want to be with him, either. Did she?

Lifting her face from her hands, she marveled at the tricks the heart could play. Even with the mind and soul full of pain and distrust, the heart could still love. No matter how disgusted and disappointed she was with Logan, she still loved him.

Oh, yes, she thought. The heart wore an armor of faith that resisted all logic.

Destruction was boldly stamped on the Creek ground. Remains of teepees had been gathered into a pile, but black sentinels of charred trees remained as dark witnesses to man's vengeful nature.

Walking on the blood-soaked ground, Susan mourned not only the dead, but also the living. Women with tear-heavy faces and children whose eyes were glazed with incomprehension huddled by the riverbank. An old man dressed in animal skins and full headdress raised his scrawny arms to the sky and spoke in the ancient tongue.

Hearing of this ceremony from Mrs. Lindsey, Susan had decided to accompany the schoolteacher to the Creeks' honoring of their dead. She hoped her presence would assure them that there were white people in town who shared their loss.

"We'll stand here," Mrs. Lindsey said, holding Susan back. "It's close enough for visitors."

"You're part Creek. Are you familiar with this ceremony?"

"Yes, but I've never participated in one. The oldest male leads the others in remembering and honoring those who have passed into another world. Once this ceremony ends, the dead ones' names will not be spoken again."

"That seems harsh."

Mrs. Lindsey shrugged. "It's the Creek way of putting aside things that can't be changed. The past decades have seen red people fall by the thousands."

"It's terrible that we can't all live together peacefully."

"Maybe someday we can," the schoolteacher said, curving her arm around Susan's waist and giving her a quick hug. "We must look to the next generation and teach them well."

Susan smiled, thinking of Etta and Jacob and how much she wanted to teach them, show them, share with them. Although Logan had as much as packed her bags, she hadn't allowed herself to think of leaving the children or the home she'd helped make for them. After their last angry confrontation, Susan and Logan had been civil only in front of the children. Otherwise, they didn't speak to or acknowledge each other. After three days of such behavior, Susan felt as if she might crack down the middle from the strain.

The ceremony ended, and the Creeks broke into twos and threes. Spotting Mrs. Lindsey, several women came forward to greet her.

"This is Logan Vance's wife," Mrs. Lindsey said when they eyed Susan with curiosity. "The newspaperman, remember?"

One of the women smiled, nodding. "You are friend of Tom Manygoats and Brewster woman."

"That's right," Susan said, feeling like a wolf in sheep's clothing and blaming Logan for it all. "I want to apologize for my husband," she said, knowing she must try to make amends since Logan wouldn't. "What he did . . . well, there's no way I can—"

"Tell him we send many thanks," the Creek woman said, holding out one hand to shake Susan's. "Tell him Mary Runningwolf's boy has his health."

"Was Runningwolf's boy hurt?" Mrs. Lindsey asked.

"No. Logan Vance pushed him from harm's way. He helped others get away, too. Gave them his horse so they could leave fire and go to river where it was safe."

"Logan did that?" Susan shook her head. "But he was part of the raiding party."

"No, he come after. He come to warn us, I think, but he was too late. The others were here with their fire and bullets."

Mrs. Lindsey placed arm around Susan's shoulders. "I've heard this, too."

Susan realized she was staring into space with her mouth hanging open in utter shock. She gathered her senses, shaking her head to clear it. "I've made a horrible mistake," she murmured, then the import of it sent a wave of faintness swimming into her head, and she would have crumpled to the ground if Mrs. Lindsey and the Creek women hadn't caught her.

They led her to a flat boulder and let her sit on it while she waited for the world to stop spinning. One of the Indians brought her a tin cup of water. Mrs. Lindsey wet her lacy handkerchief and, after unfastening the top three hooks on Susan's blouse, she laid the cooling cloth against the base of her throat. The simple remedy revived her.

"I don't know what's gotten into me," Susan said, laughing at her embarrassing weakness. "Just about any little shock makes my head reel. I suppose it's because I've had more than my share lately."

"It's all right, dear," Mrs. Lindsey said, sitting beside her on the cold, gray rock and putting her arm around her shoulders. "Perhaps you should see the doctor."

"Oh, no. I'll be fine."

"Yes, I know, but it's always wise to see a doctor in the first few months of pregnancy."

Susan knew her face turned as pale as the snow dotting the ground because she suddenly grew cold. She shivered and tried to laugh. "Pregnant? I'm not—" The rest stuck in her throat. Could it be? She'd spotted . . . not heavy, but enough to make her believe she'd only imagined the life budding inside her. Time had slipped by, but now she counted back and realized she's missed another cycle. Spreading her hands over her stomach, she looked down at the place where a baby might be growing after all.

"Oh, I hope you're right, Mrs. Lindsey," she whispered even as the certainty of it took hold of her. She'd been weak at odd times and had been shifting from unsatiated hunger to bouts of sickness, mostly in the mornings.

"You mean you didn't think you were pregnant?"

"I wasn't . . . No, I didn't. But I do now." She let the smile overtake her and felt color flow into her cheeks again. "Yes, I do believe I am." Tears made her vision shimmer. "It's about time something wonderful happened."

"I most heartily agree." Mrs. Lindsey hooked her dress again, then draped the shawl more artfully over Susan's shoulders. "Mustn't catch a chill, little mother."

Susan shared a smile with her. "Could we visit Mrs. Brewster before we go back? I want to tell her about my discovery."

"Mrs. Brewster isn't home. She went to visit relatives in Lawton. I don't look for her to come back for a month or more."

"Oh, I'm sorry to hear that. I didn't know she was planning a journey, but I'm glad she wasn't here to see this carnage."

"She *was* here," Mrs. Lindsey said. "That's why she left."

"Oh, dear." Susan sighed. "Poor Mrs. Brewster. It was a terrible blow when I heard about Tom Manygoats, but it must have been ten times worse for her."

"No doubt," Mrs. Linsdsey agreed, her deep-socketed eyes focused on the winding, metal-gray river. "She and Manygoats shared a blanket for nigh on five years, I guess."

"Sh-shared a blanket?" Susan repeated. "You mean, they were lovers?"

"Yes. You didn't know?"

"I thought they were friends."

"Well, they were," Mrs. Lindsey said matter-of-factly. "But they were also lovers. After Mr. Brewster died, well . . . Tom and the widow just took up together."

"I never suspected," Susan murmured, though she'd been a fool not to, she now realized.

"You don't think less of either of them because of it, do you?"

"No. Not at all." She gathered her shawl closer. "It seems that for so long I've thought I was the only one who could see things clearly, but lo and behold, I've been as blind as a bat."

Mrs. Lindsey stood up and brushed her hands across the back of her skirt. "I don't agree. I think we all have blind spots while other things are in sharp focus. Don't be so hard on yourself, Susan, or on anybody else, for that matter. We all—no matter what color our skin—we all have common afflictions. We all make mistakes, and we all need to be fussed over. Babes and old folks. Men and women. Saints and sinners. We all need somebody to love and be loved by."

Susan watched the slow progress of the river as it snaked across the land and thought of another river that had almost become her grave, if not for a man—a man she had loved since she was a girl, who had taught her how to love as a woman.

"We should learn from the Creeks and put all this behind us now, Mrs. Lindsey," she said as she shifted off the rock and to her feet. "Let's go home."

"Logan, may I speak to you privately?"

He'd known she'd been standing there for a full minute and had wondered if she was ever going to say something. He gave her his most laconic glance, then returned his attention to the type tray. "Nobody's here but you, me, and Clarabelle, and I can't very well ask her to leave."

"Did you know that Tom Manygoats was Mrs. Brewster's lover?"

He hadn't expected that tidbit of news, and he couldn't help but whip his head around and stare at her.

"Mrs. Lindsey told me. I went with her this morning to the Creek village. They held a ceremony to honor their dead, and I wanted to pay my respects."

That he paused to notice her bottle-green skirt and starched white blouse irritated him. It was the same outfit she'd been wearing that first day at Mrs. Ledbetter's, he recalled. Even when his heart was breaking, he took time to admire her figure and the way she held herself—so straight and proper. He found himself approving of her hairstyle, upswept and curling at the crown, and of the hint of pink color she'd applied to her full, perfectly shaped lips.

"I'll miss Tom Manygoats," she whispered, her voice ragged at the edges. "He was the first Indian I ever called a friend."

"And I killed him," Logan finished for her since she didn't have the guts to do it herself. "Go ahead and say it. Your eyes are shouting it at me. Every time you look at me, your black eyes call me a murderer."

"That's not true." Her lower lip trembled and those eyes—those dark, damning eyes—melted with tears.

"Don't let a little truth get in your way, Susan," he went on, telling himself not to cave in just because she was crying. "No matter that the whole town knows it was Zeke Calhoun who shot Manygoats—you just go right ahead and think it was me."

"I never—"

"You never?" he repeated, not letting her finish. "You're a liar. You accused me right here in this office."

"Yes, but I was wrong."

He planted one hand over his heart and staggered backward. "What? Saint Susan is admitting that she's wrong, that she's capable of human frailties just like the rest of us?"

"Oh, stop it." She stamped one foot, her shoe rapping on the hardwood floor. "You have a right to be sarcastic, but—"

"Damned right, I have a right!" He advanced, bumping his chest against her breasts, but to her credit, she didn't retreat one inch. "I took a bullet trying to help Manygoats and his people, and then my wife—my trusting wife—called me dishonorable.''

"And your wife is apologizing now. Will you accept my apology?''

"No.''

"No?''

"You heard me.'' He spun away and went back to the type table. Leaning over the inkstained letters, he picked out vowels while he screwed up enough courage to speak his mind. "You broke my heart, Susan, and that I can't forgive so quickly. That you'd think so lowly of me makes me sick inside.''

"What can I do? I've offered my sincere apology and I—''

"Just back off, that's what you can do.'' He shot her a glare that took the color from her face. "Leave me be and let me lick my wounds. Words can't fix what's hurting in me.'' He tipped his head back, fighting tears. "I thought you were different from your mama and papa. They looked at me and saw nothing but trouble. I always thought I measured up in your eyes.''

"You did . . . do.''

He swung his gaze around to her and mocked her with a smile. "Now why do I find that hard to believe?'' he drawled. "I mean, what can a man rely on; what he's told or what he's shown? You tell me that I married you just to get back at your papa and that I looked at this marriage as temporary and that I was part of a murdering bunch of cowards, and then you ask me to believe that you think highly of me. You'll pardon me if I confess to being confused.''

"Logan, be fair. You wrote an editorial against the Creeks, so why wouldn't I think that you might side with those men?''

"Siding with them in theory and killing innocent people are worlds apart, Susan.'' He sat on a high stool, propped his elbows on the edge of the slanted table, and drove all ten fingers through his hair. The skin around his stomach wound itched and tightened. "I don't see how you can continue living here with me, thinking the things you do.''

"The things I *did,*" she said, taking a step toward him. "Logan, I told you that I know now I was wrong."

"Because someone *told* you," he said, gritting his teeth against the pain she was stirring inside him. "Not because of anything *I* said," he explained, jerking a thumb at his own chest. "Not because of anything *I* did. Not because you believed the best of me, but because someone else told you to." He swallowed against the thickness in his throat and turned away from her. He pulled a hand down his face, distracted and distraught. After a minute he could face her again, but when he looked over his shoulder she was gone.

Chapter 28

Making amends didn't come easy, Susan thought as she wiped off the kitchen table, then covered it with a lacy cloth. Two days had passed since she'd come home from the Creek village, and nothing much had changed between her and Logan. The winter chill lingered inside and out. Absently, she fingered the cross that she hadn't removed since the day Logan gave it to her. Through all the recent trials, it had remained a symbol of her undying faith.

Touching it always sent her thoughts to Logan. The current issue of the newspaper had carried an editorial lambasting the townspeople for trying to drive out the Indians by violent means. He'd pointed out that there was no proof the Indians had set fire to Main Street and that many of the town leaders had taken the word of a regulator, a man who thrived on trouble and bloodshed. The editorial had urged the community to make honor the cornerstone of their town and tolerance their pledge of allegiance. Reading it had filled Susan with such pride, she'd wanted to throw her arms around Logan and kiss him. But he'd constructed an invisible wall around himself, and he let in only Etta and Jacob, sometimes Coonie, never her.

She felt alone and helpless. The people she'd depended on—the adults, anyway—weren't there anymore. Logan, Coonie, Mrs. Brewster, Tom Manygoats.

Seized by a need to reach out before it was too late, she arranged leftovers on a long platter. Coonie had stopped taking meals with them, except on Sundays when he made

377

an appearance for the children's sake. They missed him. So did Susan.

After dropping a checked cloth over the platter, she carried it out the back door and across the yard to Coonie's house. He must have seen her coming, because the front door swung open as she made her way between the bare branches of towering rose of sharon bushes lining the path. Come summer, they'd be bursting with white and purple blooms.

"Hello, Coonie. I've brought you dinner."

"You didn't have to do that."

"I know." She didn't extend the platter, but held it back from him. "May I come in?"

"Uh, the place is messy."

"That won't bother me."

He moved back to let her inside. The front room wasn't too untidy for a bachelor. A few articles of clothing were strewn about, and used coffee cups took the place of knickknacks, but other than that, it was respectable. Susan went into the small dining area and set the platter on the pot-ringed table, then turned slowly to confront Connie's hangdog expression.

"I believe, and always will, that what you did to those Creeks was wrong, Coonie," she said, getting his attention. His head swung up and his eyes bugged a little. "But I don't get a mad on with every soul I disagree with. If I did, I'd have precious few friends, if any." She smiled, urging one from him. "I think of you as family, Coonie French, and family should forgive family." That said, she marched past him to the front door. Standing on the threshold, she looked out at the hens pecking for kernels and pebbles in the yellow grass, but she directed her words to Coonie. "I'd like to see you at my table for meals again, but it's up to you. Whether you break bread with us or not, I expect you and me to like each other again." Then she resumed her exit.

"Susan?"

Breaking stride, she looked over her shoulder at him. Sunlight hit his face. His eyes watered. He wiped at his bulbous nose with the back of his hand.

"There's been only two women I ever loved," he said, then sniffed loudly. His mouth trembled and jerked at one corner. "My mother—and you. See you at breakfast."

He closed the door, saving her from a response that would surely be inadequate. Emotion blocked her throat. She tugged a handkerchief from one cuff and dabbed her eyes. A fat hen ambled up to her and pecked at her shoe.

"Stop that, you silly hen," she scolded, kicking sideways and sending the bird fluttering. "If you don't start laying more eggs, you're going to be Sunday dinner."

Before she went back inside, she paused to admire the property. Even in winter when the yard was void of color, she loved looking at it, the mother-in-law's house, the outhouse, and the other outbuildings. She remembered the first stroll she'd taken here with Logan and how he'd pointed out the black-eyed Susans growing lush and tall. He'd called them a sign of good luck. Well, their luck had been spotty, she concluded, but she had no major complaints. She and Logan had shared the good and the bad. They'd suffered through lean times, scary times, had even shared the distinction of being shot. But those times had been sweetened by family life, laughter, and love.

Now that she had made friends with Coonie again, she had only one mission left: Logan. Gathering her skirt, she lifted the hem high to avoid the random patches of snow holding out against the sun. She went through the house to the front office where she knew she'd find him. He was seated at his desk, a yellow square of parchment in one hand, his new reading glasses—which had arrived only last week all the way from Chicago—in the other.

A lock of sandy hair curled on his forehead. Although he'd shaved that morning, his jawline and upper lip were already shadowed by his emerging whiskers. He sat on the wooden chair, one booted foot propped on the corner of the desk, the posture pulling tight the front of his wheat-colored trousers and loosing Susan's memories of pleasure and passion. His shirt was the same shade as his eyes, and his suspenders were the color of hers. The Logan tingle stirred in Susan's belly, where a new life blossomed.

"I can't live like this much longer, Logan."

His head jerked back, and his propped boot joined the other on the floor. "Wh-what?"

"You heard me." She moved close enough to see that he was holding a telegram. "Who's that from?"

He blinked owlishly, as if emerging from a trance, then put down the telegram long enough to carefully don the wire-framed eyeglasses. "You won't believe it." He picked up the missive by one corner. "It's from the territorial governor."

"What's it say?"

"He's congratulating me on the newspaper's stand against violence toward the Creeks."

"Good. You deserve a pat on the back."

"And he asks if I'd serve on the town's incorporation committee," he added, then his gaze lifted to hers. "Because the Creeks trust me, he says."

"He's right," she agreed. "Will you serve?"

"It might be construed as a conflict of interest . . . but yes. It's too important not to serve." He sent the telegram sailing to the back of the desk, then swiveled to face her. "What can I do for you?"

"Well, for one thing, you can take a few minutes to talk to me." She pulled up a stool and perched on it. "I just spoke with Coonie. He'll be eating with us again."

"And I'm next on your list, is that it?"

"Are you happy with the way we act around each other?" she asked, refusing to be baited into an angry confrontation. "Do you enjoy treating your wife as if she were a mere acquaintance?"

"Why should I waste my time on you?" He straightened from his slouch. "After all, as you have noted, this marriage is *temporary*. I married you as a *convenience* and for *social convention*. I certainly don't *care* about you, so why should either of us go out of our way pretending otherwise?" He picked up a ruler and tapped it impatiently. "By the way, when are you planning on leaving?"

She took a deep breath and looked off to one side as she fought the sting of tears behind her eyes. "I'm not leaving. I know that I threatened it, but I'm not leaving. I—I love Jacob and Etta as if I'd bore them. I couldn't possibly turn my back on them—or you."

"So you're staying for the children."

"And you," she added since he wouldn't.

"Why do you want to stay in a temporary marriage?"

"Logan, please quit throwing that at me."

"You're the one who said it."

"Well? What was I to think? You asked me to marry you after people in town started talking badly about us. You said it would be better for the children—better all around."

"Yes, I know, but things changed pretty quickly, didn't they? We became a real family."

She nodded. "But I never knew how you actually felt about me. You never said you loved me or that you wanted me with you for the rest of your life."

He chuckled humorlessly. Propping an elbow on the desk, he leaned his temple against two fingertips. "What do you think I was saying night after night in bed with you and every morning when I woke you with kisses?"

"You never said you loved me."

"Oh, Christ!" He closed his eyes and laughed again under his breath. "I said it, you just didn't hear me. Every time I spilled my seed into you, I said it. Do you think I'd do that if I didn't want a future with you? Did you think for yourself at all, or did you let everyone else do your thinking for you about me and my motives?"

Flinching, she averted her gaze from his flashing eyes and snarling mouth. "If I remember correctly, I practically had to beg you to stay inside me. That, more than anything, made me think you didn't want to be tied to me."

"I explained that."

"I wasn't convinced."

"And that's my fault?" he challenged.

She clasped her hands in her lap and directed her gaze to the windows. A buggy jiggled past, then three horsemen, saddlebags bulging. Two scraggly dogs sniffed each other in the middle of the street, oblivious to the horses and wheels passing within inches of them.

"I suppose men and women will always be stuck in the same ruts," Logan murmured, mostly to himself. He'd followed her gaze and watched as the dogs continued their superficial courtship. "Women will be waiting for their men to talk pretty and bold. Men will get all gummed up with the words and not be able to get them past their confounded Adam's apples, so they'll do the next best thing—better to their way of thinking—and they'll take their women in their arms and talk to them with their hands and eyes and tongues. They'll speak an eloquent language and then feel like damned fools because their women are still waiting to hear those magic words that are so hard for men to say."

"Why are they hard?"

"Because they strip you bare and bring you to your knees." Logan smiled, still watching the persistent male hound and the teasing bitch. "I guess every species has its peculiar mating habits, but damned if humans don't take first prize." His green-eyed gaze swung back to her. "How can you stay with a man you believed to be a cold-blooded murderer of women and children?"

She grimaced, then stiffened with affront. "That's what I asked myself over and over again, and that's what frightened me. Even while I still thought you were part of that raiding party, I loved you. I found myself dreaming up excuses for you."

"That you'd *think* such a thing of me!"

"That editorial you wrote—"

"Oh, hell!" He flapped a hand. "All I was asking for in that editorial was a solution. I even suggested that the Creeks govern themselves more strictly and not let a handful of young outlaw braves run riot. But I never said anything about murder or violence. I merely said that if they couldn't control their own, there was trouble ahead."

"But you went to those meetings, and I thought you—"

"You were wrong." He jutted out his chin. "So was I. Maybe we should both think the best of each other, instead of the worst."

She shrugged, knowing he was right. "It was all so

scary, Logan. I was afraid to realize that I loved you so desperately I was willing to forgive you anything. I loved you so much that I turned my back on my family. I loved you so shamelessly that I would stay here even after you'd told me to go." Chancing a glance at him, she found his intensity disturbing. "I think I've lost myself in you."

"Maybe that's good."

"How can that be?"

"Maybe loving somebody means you don't know where you end and the other begins. I've known couples who seemed bound that tightly. Usually it's after many years of marriage, but it happens. I had hoped it would come to pass for me and Catherine, but we drifted apart instead of together."

"Are you still mad at me?" she asked in a tiny voice that made him sigh with exasperation.

"I was never truly mad. I was—hurt. Deeply, profoundly hurt." He rested a hand just under his heart. "This wound was nothing. Your judgment of me was devastating. It still is."

"Logan," she said, sliding off the stool to stand before him. "Are you going to punish me forever?"

He screwed up one eye thoughtfully. "I . . . don't . . . know . . ."

"It's unfair." She looked at his hand resting on the chair arm and crooked two fingers under his pinky and ring finger. "We've both made mistakes aplenty. Maybe we were never sure of each other because of how I came to you. You thought I showed up in St. Louis to sweet-talk your children away from you, but, Logan, I came to St. Louis for you. It was perfect, don't you see? I'd get to live in a big city and I'd have you to watch out for me. And . . ." She directed her gaze to the toes of her shoes, suddenly too shy to look at him. "Well, I'd had my eye on you for a spell. It broke my heart when you took up with Catherine, and I told myself after a while that I'd gotten over it, but I never did."

"You were too young to know your own mind back then." His fingers curled over hers.

"But I knew my own heart," she said, choking a little.

"Papa knew, too. That's why he sent me. He knew I fancied you and that maybe you fancied me and would let me take the children away."

"I did fancy you. I do."

No sweeter words were ever spoken, Susan thought, then spun away as a giddiness set her in motion. "In honor of that telegram and your accepting the challenge to serve on the committee, I have something for you. Wait right here," she instructed, then flew to the kitchen where she grabbed the coffee tin. Spilling the beans onto the table, she clutched the cloth-covered watch she'd purchased for Logan's Christmas present and slipped it into her skirt pocket.

He had obeyed, having not moved from the desk chair. She pulled the watch out by its link chain and let it swing like a pendulum before his eyes.

"It's your Christmas present," she said. "I didn't wrap it because—well, Christmas was ruined for me and you."

He caught the watch, and she let it go. "For all of us," he corrected her. "It was ruined for all of us." Turning the watch over in his palm, he admired the polished surface, then pressed the latch. The lid sprang open. He read the inscription, swallowed hard, then slowly met her expectant gaze. His eyes shimmered, full of emotion.

"Well, do you like it?"

"Words again," he said, sighing. "She has to hear the words. She can't see the evidence in my face. No, she's blind to that." He fashioned a grim countenance. "Yes, Susan, I like it. Thank you. Will that do, or shall I expound some more?"

"You're a writer, so why are words so hard?" she asked, smiling at his discomfort.

"Susan, sometimes the words unspoken are the truest words of all." Clearing his throat, he looked for a distraction and found it by running a hand down his shirt-front. "I'm going to have to start wearing vests to show off this watch." He read the inscription to himself, then aloud. " 'The pen is mightier than the sword.' I believe that. I believed it before I met you, but I admit I lost sight of it. You made me hold to it, Susan. A man like me needs a calm, logical voice in his life." He smiled to himself, one corner of his mouth lifting briefly. "Like most, I find the temptation to follow strong, and I need someone who expects me to blaze my own trail and who firmly believes I can do it."

Susan held her breath, realizing he was revealing himself to her, removing the wall he'd built, brick by brick.

He ran the pad of his thumb over the inscription again. "This is why I became a newspaperman. I wanted to make a difference, to make people think, to change society for the better, and words were the best way." Standing, he pointed a commanding finger at her. "You stay put now and close your eyes."

When he was sure she wasn't peeking, he rummaged under the printer table until he located a ball of rags. From it he withdrew the linen handkerchiefs, which he arranged artfully on the slanted table. Then he went to the filing cabinets and took down the hat he'd bought her from the top shelf. He put it beside the handkerchiefs.

"Open your eyes."

She sprang on the hat first, lifting it and positioning it over her glossy hair which hung in a braid down her back. She pirouetted before him and admired the flowers on the hat's crown, then gathered the wide ties under her chin coquettishly.

"What do you think? Is it the most beautiful hat in all of Tulsa—in all of Indian Territory? Oh, it must be!" Her gaze fell on the other gift. "And what's this? Linen handkerchiefs! Aren't they lovely. Irish linen. Oh, Logan, you spent too much . . ." Her voice faded as her eyes focused on the embroidered corners. Initials, but not just hers. Theirs. Entwined. Inseparable.

"Susan," he said, grabbing one of the corners and lifting it closer for her minute inspection, "does this look temporary to you? Is this a gift from a man who doesn't care if you go or stay, believe or don't believe, respect or disrespect him? Well, does it?"

"No," she managed, just barely.

"I love you, Susan." He sucked in a breath and shook his head firmly, warding off what she would have said in joyful response. "I have known I loved you since the day I pulled you out of that damned river, but I didn't want to rope you in with my feelings. I wanted you to stay with me because of the love *you* felt, not for the love *I* felt." He laid a finger against her lips to keep her silent. "If you stay with me—and I hope you will—I want you to stay because you love me and not because of the children or because of family honor or any other such excuse." He removed his finger.

"I wouldn't stay if not for love," she assured him. She went to the shaving mirror near the cot which one or the other had slept on during their turbulent courtship and marriage. Looking into the oval-shaped mirror, she admired her hat with its white flowers and crimson feathers. It was a grown lady's hat—a married lady's hat. She saw Logan approaching in the mirror. "I'm proud of you, Logan Vance. When I read the editorial in this week's issue, I wanted to hug your neck, but I knew you wouldn't let me."

"I might let you now," he said, giving her one of his heart-squeezing grins.

She turned, her body brushing against his, and eased her arms around his neck. Rising up on tiptoe, she tightened her arms about him and gloried in the way he cleaved to her. His hands moved up her back, to her neck and higher. With careful hands, he took the hat off her head and tossed it atop one of the rolls of newsprint. He let his gaze roam over her with open appreciation. Leaning back in his arms, she allowed herself the luxury of filling her senses with him. He had so many good features, it was hard to pick her favorite.

"It's sad that my mama and papa looked at you and saw only the bad."

"What do *you* see?"

She placed her hands at the sides of his head and stroked her thumbs over his naturally arched brows. "I saw then and see now an enormous heart overflowing with laughter and love."

He chuckled and turned his head to kiss her right palm, then her left one. His eyes, heavy-lidded and beginning to smolder, flirted outrageously. Moving with purpose, he backed her into the cot and kept bumping her until her knees buckled and she landed amid the rumpled sheets and quilts. His hands moved to his fly. The first button shot free, then the second. Susan reached for the hooks of her dress and worked them loose, one by one.

"Papa? Aunt Susan?"

Logan curled his upper lip comically, rebuttoned his fly, and stepped around the rolls of newsprint that hid the cot from others.

"Yes, what is it, Jacob?" He combed his hair with his hands and told himself not to be impatient since Jacob was innocent to his father's throbbing condition. "Where's your sister . . . oh, there she is. I thought y'all were playing with the blacksmith's children."

"We were," Jacob said. "But they had to go inside for their baths. What are you doing?"

"Nothing now."

From behind the concealing rolls of newsprint, Susan pasted a hand to her mouth to keep from giggling aloud.

"Why don't you go upstairs and play?"

"Naw," Jacob said, kicking at imaginary stones. "There's nothing to do up there."

"Why don't you . . . Coonie!" By the way Coonie retreated, Logan knew he sounded oddly overjoyed to see his partner. He checked the reaction. "Hey, pal. How does ice cream sound to y'all?"

"Yeah," Jacob said, eyes lighting with interest.

"Yummy. Come on, Papa," Etta urged, grabbing Logan's index finger and giving a yank that popped his joints. "Take us to the ice cream parlor!"

Logan's eyes pleaded with Coonie. "I bet Uncle Coonie could use a lick of ice cream. What do you say, Coonie?" Logan looked behind him, then to Coonie. He wiggled his brows suggestively before Coonie got the message.

"Oh, yeah." Coonie grinned and stroked his stubbled chin. "Did Susan find you earlier? I think she was looking for you."

Logan nodded and glanced at the hat perched on the

paper roll near him. Coonie spotted it and snickered. "She found me, and I'm glad to be found."

Susan drew her knees up onto the cot and shook with suppressed laughter.

"Where is Aunt Susan?" Jacob asked.

"Oh, she's around here somewhere." Logan fished a silver piece from his pocket and flipped it to Coonie, who caught it in mid-air. "My treat, pal."

Coonie lowered one eyelid. "You said it. Come on, young'uns." He placed a hand on each head and ushered Etta and Jacob outside. "I'll lock the door after us." The bell tinkled, and Coonie's key rattled in the lock.

Whipping around the makeshift partition, Logan grinned at Susan. She had both hands against her mouth, but she let them fall away and rolled back and forth with laughter.

"Poor Coonie," she said, between gulping breaths. "We shouldn't—"

"He doesn't mind. He's tickled we're back together." Logan slid one knee onto the bed and reached out a hand to wrap his fingers around Susan's long braid.

"We are back together," she said, parting her lips in an invitation. "Say it again, Logan. Say those words you think I don't need to hear."

With his lips tickling hers, he said them. "I love you, Susan." Then his mouth engulfed hers in moist warmth, and his tongue thrust deep and lustfully. He bowed her back until she was lying on the cot and he was lying beside her, half on her and half off. The narrow cot guaranteed intimacy.

She ran her hands along his shoulders to his strong neck and, using her thumbs, angled his head so that their mouths separated. Susan dragged in a breath, then let it whisper out of her.

"Logan, I'm staying here because I love you. Believe me?"

"Yes." He started to kiss her again, but she stiffened away from him. "What's wrong?"

"Nothing. I just want to make sure you understand why I'm not leaving. I love you, Logan."

"Okay," he said, his brows dipping to form a vee.

"We love each other. Now let's make love." He looked down at the length of their bodies. "I think this is the perfect place to renew ourselves since it started here for us. But if you want to go to our bedroom—"

"Logan, you must know something before . . ." She swallowed, then laughed at herself. "Now I know how hard it was for you to find the right words to speak to me. I'm suddenly at a loss. Tongue-tied."

He grasped her hands. "What is it, Susan? Come on, you're scaring me."

"No, it's not scary." She pulled her lower lip between her teeth in a moment's anxiety. "At least, it isn't to me."

His eyes probed hers in a most unsettling way. If ever someone had read her thoughts, Logan did in those shattering ticks of time. Suddenly his eyes flooded with tears and his lower lip trembled.

"Susan, are you carrying my child?" he asked, his voice raspy, raw-edged.

She could only nod and then wait for the outcome.

He shut his eyes, and the tears rolled onto his cheeks and slipped into the corners of his wide, wonderful mouth.

"It's what I want, Logan," Susan said, catching a tear with the stroke of her thumb. "And I pray it's what you want, too."

When she thought he would embrace her, he swung his legs over the side of the cot and dropped his head in his hands. Tentatively, Susan touched his shoulder. He flung back his head and laughed softly.

"You know, when Catherine told me she was with child, I was the one who felt trapped," he said, his voice still raspy, the tracks of tears shining on his cheeks. "Lately, I've been hoping I could get you pregnant so I could trap you." He laughed, a breathy, choppy sound. "I thought, if only she were pregnant, then she'd have to stay. She wouldn't leave me. I guess what goes around comes around, huh?" He turned his head to look at her, eyes brimming like hers. "But, Susan—my beautiful black-eyed Susan—I'm glad this baby isn't a trap for you or me. This baby"—he flattened one hand across her stomach—"is our blessing, our miracle, our future."

She drew him to her, and soon their soft sobs became sounds of joy, of pleasure, of passion, of satisfaction. Their coupling was more than physical; it was an act of love in every sense of the word, binding them, entwining them, making them as inseparable as initials embroidered on Irish linen.

Postscript

Tulsa was incorporated as a city in Indian Territory on January 18, 1898. Oklahoma and Indian Territories became the state of Oklahoma on November 16, 1907.

On August 24, 1898, a girl was born to Susan and Logan Vance. She was named Sadie Catherine, and she had hair the color of sunshine and eyes as black as night.